THE WHISPER KIN

LUCIENNE DIVER

THE WHISPER KIN

Don't depend too much on anyone in this world because even your own shadow leaves you when you are in darkness.

—TAQÎ AD-DÎN AḤMAD IBN TAYMIYYAH

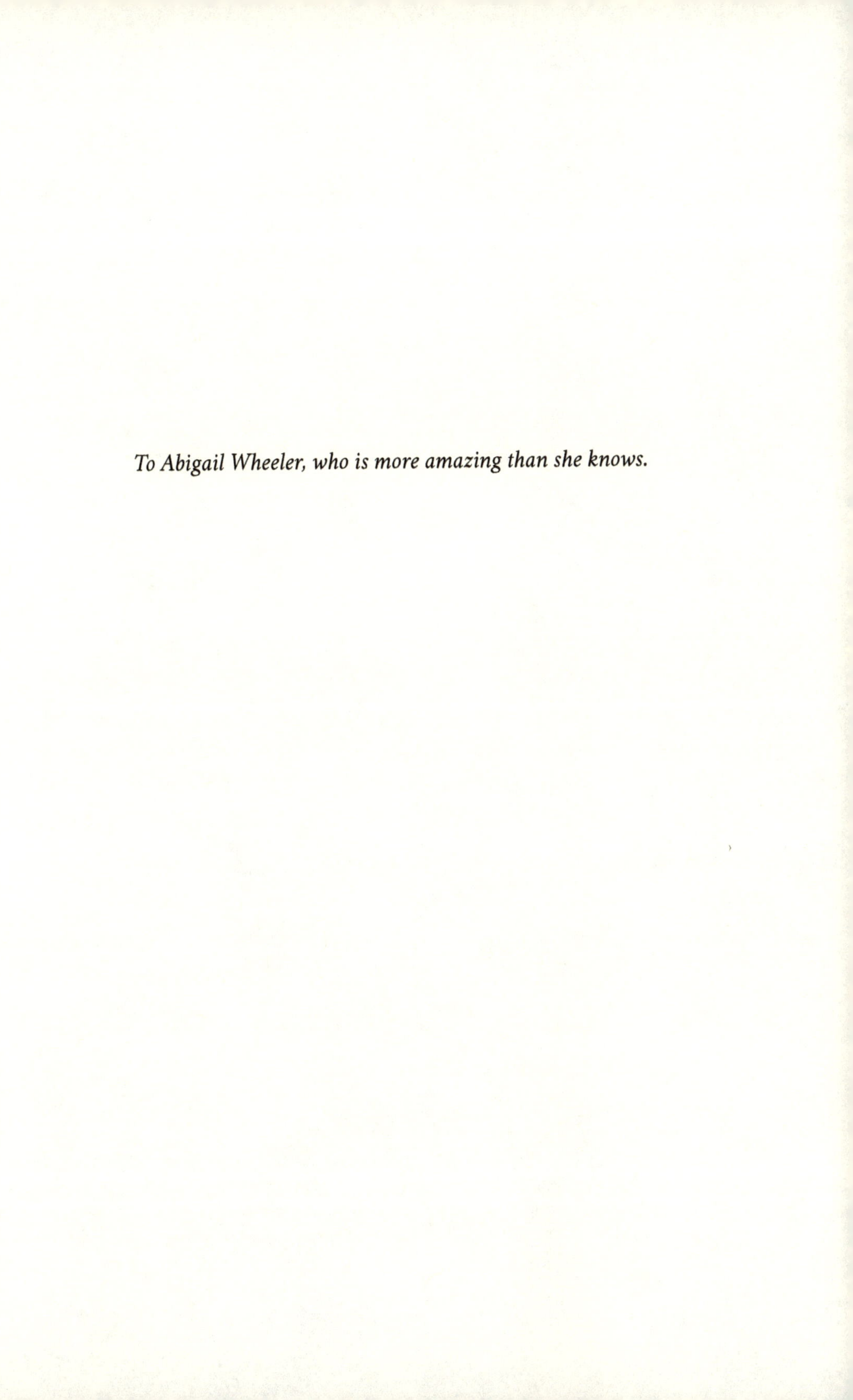

To Abigail Wheeler, who is more amazing than she knows.

CHAPTER ONE

Ludvin

Darkness was falling, and it grew difficult to tell the blood from the shadows. The Blood Princess and her forces had fled the battlefield in the wake of her collapse, but Ludvin didn't trust the retreat. Bloody Bess could not afford to let them live. Not with the knowledge that the anima of her shadow girls could be drained from her and returned to the land. Bloody Bess had thought herself invincible with their stolen life forces to power her.

She hadn't counted on Roha. No one had. Ludvin *commanded* nim and still hadn't been prepared.

Although it was becoming increasingly clear that *no one* truly commanded Roha.

The first to his lieutenant's fallen form, Ludvin lifted nim, bearing Roha's weight when he rose. Cia made a strangled sound, as though she wanted to be the one to care for Roha, but she was barely holding herself up in the wake of the battle.

Hedric stepped forward, throwing Roha a dark look before focusing on Ludvin. "Our archers gave the Crown forces a proper send-off, but we must move quickly. We can't trust that they won't double back."

"Deliver the orders—scattershot, like when we arrived. Set traps as you go. If they hunt us, they'll have to divide their forces and watch their steps. You know the place," Ludvin said. "We'll meet you there."

"*We?*" Hedric's gaze shot beyond Ludvin and Cia to the others who had aided them: the princess's former spymaster, Ruggerio, and his cousin, Ulan, whose ghost daughter had been part of Ruggerio's spy network. "There is no *we*. They are Crown. You brought these people into our midst, and Bloody Bess used them against us." Others were standing with Hedric now. Shoulder to shoulder. So many. "Who's to say she won't do so again? They can't be trusted."

Ludvin had driven the Restoration. It was *his* vision, *his* ideals Hedric threw back at him. Now he was telling Ludvin what would and would not stand?

He'd been too old to fight for Jucar when the Blood War was declared. Not so his sons. His eldest had never returned. The youngest had been bitten by a Monstrate, one of the terrible lizards conjured by the mageri. Its toxins left nerve damage, and Anson had never been the same. Ludvin would never believe in the magic-men or their constructs. He'd take any aid in fighting them. Their allies had proven to be different from their enemies, but Hedric's own biases kept him from seeing it.

"The princess *tried* to use them. In the end, they fought off her control. They fought for us," he said, meeting Hedric's gaze, willing him to see things the way Ludvin saw them. He wished he had Vizi here to speak for him. There was a reason Ludvin led by the hand but counted on others to lead by the heart. He was not a great orator. He didn't have the power to change men's minds. He believed. He planned. He organized and arranged and delegated.

"How many did they strike down first?" Hedric asked, eying Cia and the others. He had enough for an army standing with him. Hardly anyone stood to Ludvin's side, and he couldn't be certain that anyone there wasn't merely angling for a better view of the brewing rift.

"You can't be for them *and* for us," another man said from beside

Hedric. "You allowed sorcery into our ranks. If this keeps up, there will be nothing separating us from them." He looked pointedly at Roha as ni lolled in Ludvin's arms.

Ludvin looked down as well, at the currently comatose figure in his arms who had given everything for them. "But Roha isn't mageri. Ni is *Nim*. Ni doesn't take power from the anima all about or from any living thing. Roha harms none but nimself if ni goes too far, which is what you see here. Ni risked nimself for all of us. To return life to the valley. Just a start, but if we can spread this throughout Jucar—"

Hedric snarled. "You've said it yourself. *Roha has gone too far.* Power is power. It can be abused, whatever the source."

⸺⸺

Cia

Cia stepped forward before Ludvin could respond, her eyes alight as though she could blazon the night back into day. Her mouth was open to speak before she even knew what she intended. She'd had enough of silence. It had never kept her safe. Perhaps speaking up wouldn't change things now, but Roha wasn't awake to speak for nimself.

"*Us* and *them*," she spat. "So easily you partition the people who matter from the people you can turn against. Roha fought for you by drawing from nes own reserves, and you want to leave nim behind because you've decided *you won't have it?* If only you could return your very survival, tainted as it is by nes sacrifice. To the All with your principles! What do you think grants the Nim their power? What exactly do you believe you're turning your backs on?"

The words burst out in a raging fire that began to burn away the self-loathing over all the words Cia had held inside during her years of captivity to Garif.

The Restoration man started to respond, but Cia wasn't finished. "My mageri husband took over my body. He used it without my permission and against my will. I fought him off, yet you declare I am *not to be trusted.* I slayed him. With Roha's help. We all made sacrifices. One of the spirits Roha fed back to the anima was Ulan's little daughter, so attached to her mother she clung to her even after death. It was her spirit, and that of Bloody Bess's shadow girls, and the lives taken by Ceramor, the ankari, that restored these fields.

"We all bled and suffered and sacrificed, and you are alive because of it. *We* have been tested and tried. If anyone is certain to be true, it is us. But that is nothing to you and your *principles.*" She spat the last word, eyes blazing, waiting for the blow she was sure would come. It was what backtalk had always brought her.

Ludvin lowered Roha's feet to the ground and braced nim against his chest to free a hand for fighting if it came to that. Hostill and Ulan, clutching her wounded arm, stepped up beside Ludvin and Cia, followed after a moment's hesitation by Ruggerio, hand on his sword.

The six of them faced off with the swelling group of Restoration rebels Ludvin had once led. Maybe still did, depending on what happened in the next few moments.

"This woman has had the mageri, the *abomination* in her head, taken him into her body," Hedric said, loud enough for his voice to carry. Cia wanted to burn him to cinders. "We have only her word that he isn't there still. Or that he hasn't left anything behind. These people can't be trusted. However, you decide," he added to Ludvin, "whether you're with us or not, the boy is certainly ours. We can't allow them to poison the future king."

There was a gasp, and Cia grabbed protectively for Hostill, where she expected him to be, where she'd last seen him, but he'd launched himself forward. His entire body was stiff, like a longbow primed to fire. One hand was clenched in a fist so tight Cia was sure that his jagged nails must be biting into his palms. The other…the other was pressed against his thigh so that in the darkness the opposing side might not notice the knife he always carried. He was prepared for a new battle. For anything.

"*The boy* has a name," he said, enunciating each word as though he'd been brought up in the palace rather than in a ramshackle hut abutting a graveyard. "It's Hostill. And whether or not I'm to be your future king, I am my own being."

He raised the hand with the blade. It was dramatic and drew everyone's gaze. "I am not a game piece. If anyone tries to grab me, I will take myself off the board." He made a quick slash at his own throat, and everyone gasped.

CHAPTER TWO

Hostill

When the knife slid away, there were gasps of released breath as it became clear no actual blood had been drawn. Not yet, anyway. He desperately hoped it wouldn't come to that.

Hostill glared into Hedric's eyes, pretending he wasn't scared to death and unsure what to do, but his go-to when faced with anything bigger and badder had always been to wave a knife around and bluff it out. It had worked well enough when Cia had first stumbled upon him, hiding in his home that had been condemned as a plague house. He was more badly outnumbered now, but he also had people at his back.

He didn't know how to do it but to do it. If he was supposed to be king someday–which was ridiculous, because who put a boy from the streets on the throne?–he ought to start testing his power and diplom…er…diplomercy. Something like that, though he'd never known those in power to show mercy of any kind.

"How about this?" he said. *No, wrong to ask. I should be* telling *them.* "If you won't have Roha and the others with you, then I'm going with them. You don't like it, send Ludvin with us. You know him. You trust him. He can keep an eye on me and on the rest, and we'll figure out a way to get messages across. We'll find a way forward." He risked looking over his shoulder toward Cia. She was the first of the others he'd met, and while he wasn't so sure about her on one level, on a deeper level it seemed he was, and that one won out. She nodded.

He looked back just in time to flash his knife when two shadowy rebels on either side of Hedric lunged forward to grab him. His blade slashed one in the hand, and a spurt of blood glittered in the night. He didn't know what it said about the amount of death he'd seen that he noted that without remorse. *Huh, blood's a little shiny in the moonlight. Interesting. Shouldn't'a gotten grabby.*

The man hissed and stepped back, and Hedric barked something that sounded more like he was cursing the man for the failure than for the attempted kidnapping–kingnapping?

Then the lieutenant half-turned away and there was a buzz of hurried and irritated discussion. When he turned back around, he bristled with unhappiness. If he'd had quills, they'd have been standing on end, ready to fire off in all directions. "Ludvin's judgment has become suspect. We can't trust him alone."

"Fine, send others. But not Grabby-hands," Hostill said, cutting off Ruggerio as he started to respond, as if it was time for an adult to take over.

Hedric's gaze shot to the side where the man with the blood was wrapping a strip of fabric around his slashed hand. "Viktor, then."

A mountain of a man stepped forward, blotting out the moon and stars. Behind him, Hostill heard a gasp and Ulan cry out, "No!"

The deeper chill had fallen as fast as the sun, but the horror in her voice turned the blood in Hostill's veins to sheer ice.

"No," he said again. "Not Viktor." He must have been one of the men who had captured Cia and Ulan for the Restoration when they'd been treated as hostiles. Probably been rougher than he needed to be.

"Myrka," Hostill said instead.

He meant it as a command, but even he heard his voice rise at the end, making it into a question.

Myrka must have survived the battle. She'd recovered from the

Rot, though with burns over the left side of her face from being set too close to the fire to purge the plague, and with a nasty scar on her chest where an ember had leapt from the hearth. She'd survived on the streets when, like him, her whole family had been taken by the plague. She was a few years older and a whole lot handier with a blade. And very, very useful to the Restoration. But she was a known factor, and a child of the streets, and so they had an unspoken understanding of each other.

She stepped forward, shouldering in front of Viktor. She held a knife, as did Hostill, only her hold was casual, the blade an extension of her very self. Seeing that all eyes were on her, she flipped it and caught it again, winking at Hostill in the between time. Not exactly conspiratorially, but more to say *See what I can do? Mark it.*

"Fine," Hedric said with bad grace. "You go. And report." Then he looked at Ludvin so intensely it was as though he wanted to imprint his next words right onto his soul. "To put the boy on the throne, you'll need allies. *You'll need us.* Remember who fought this battle. If you had time to play with magic, it was only because we kept the blades at bay."

Hostill bit his tongue on that. He would not forget. He'd been part of the Restoration. They'd been his family after his own had died. Distant family, but family nonetheless. They'd given him purpose, jobs, and enough coin to keep going. But family could just as easily be a trap, and he was not going to fall into it. The rebels had fought, yes. For their cause, but also for their lives. Because they'd been captured and would have been sacrificed by Bloody Bess to restore the anima of the land. Not because the princess cared for the land itself, but so that she could proclaim herself the great savior of the people. And then plunder the power anew when she had need of it.

The Restoration had never been anything but direct about their motives–save the land by killing all those who would plunder it through magic, which had seemed noble to Hostill until he'd met Roha and Cia, and even Ceramor, a mageri gone feral with the anima he'd stolen from the former king's hunting hounds to save his wife, who hadn't lived long enough for it to work. The introduction of another's essence could twist and bend a person out of true. But the core of Ceramor had remained, and Hostill knew now that not everyone with power was evil. There were gray areas.

Still, Hedric was right about one thing. They had to stop Bloody Bess, and for that they needed allies. People ready to fight. If he was to be king, which still sounded as likely as cows birthing kittens, he would need alliances. Not all decisions would be as easy as berry or mud pies.

"We won't forget," Ludvin answered, while Hostill was still lost in his thoughts. "But without their 'playing with magic,' many more would be dead. Maybe all. Remember that. I'm *not* defending stealing power from the land. I'm saying there's another way. Roha found it. We must as well. It's our only chance to combat them and live."

"We're not afraid to die."

Ludvin hung his head. "Dying in itself accomplishes nothing if we don't *win*."

It was clear that talking to them was useless, and they had already stayed too long. Bloody Bess's army could double back at any time.

Hedric stepped forward, and Hostill tensed, ready for another grab or a knife slid between Ludvin's ribs, but Hedric only clasped his old leader's forearm. Ludvin clasped his in return. They gazed briefly into each other's eyes, gave a nod of acknowledgement, and parted.

As he turned away, Ludvin heaved a great sigh, his shoulders rising and falling with his expulsion of air. He said to no one in particular, "Let's go."

Hostill glanced around at the others and asked, "Where?"

"Frizenze," Cia said. So many undercurrents there, he was like to get sucked in. "I have people there. No one will be more motivated to put you on the throne than Jucar's greatest enemy."

The night made harsh shadows of Ruggerio's face, which appeared carved by a hatchet, leaving it all angles. His scowl at this turned him into a bosewight, a soul so wicked it rejected peace to stick around sucking the life from those nearest and dearest. "Let's get somewhere safe, and we'll talk. I know a way."

Hostill looked around for horses, but the princess's army and the Restoration, which had disappeared into the night, had taken all but the most skittish, some of which could be heard stomping or nickering to each other nervously in the dark.

Eventually, a few came to gentle calling, willing to be wooed. Four horses for seven people. Four. Including the bay Cia had stolen from the fallen soldier, who'd decided that he was hers now and would have no other. He was without the saddle Cia had cut away, upending the cavalryman bearing down on her, but they looted another from a downed horse that had to be put out of its misery. He had to look away. The bodies were bad enough, but to add one to the count... This war had gone on more than half his lifetime; Bloody Bess's reign was already too long. They had to end it. In that, he was glad to play a part.

CHAPTER THREE

Queen Bessory V'Alban woke again from a dream of her head exploding into a mass of seething tentacles, venting all the deathly shadows that beat themselves against her brain–the result of every life she'd stolen away to fuel her power. In place of suckers, each tentacle was awash in pustules, bubbling and bursting with corrosion, and those tentacles ensnared a three-headed hound of nightmarish proportions. If only it *was* a dream rather than a memory of her battle with the feral mageri Ceramor. Unwisely, he'd defected from the Crown to the Restoration rebels who would just as soon see him dead for his powers. She'd granted their wish.

Bess had declared herself Queen and her side victorious, the land restored by the Crown. She'd sent messengers ahead to prepare for her coronation. But her troops knew the truth. They'd seen her collapse, watched her being carried from the field. They feared her… for now. But how long would it last? She had to rebuild her well of power. Enough to exert her will over an entire army. Control their memories and the narrative before the wrong sort of stories could spread. There had been rumors before, and those had been bad enough, but there'd never been proof of her misdeeds and no alternate heir to the throne on whom to hang her country's hopes should she be overthrown. Until now.

She lay in the darkened tent on the quickly arranged pallet and tried to gather herself. She'd lived so long with her shadow girls—with the company of their cries, the agony of them trying to batter their way out of her head—that she felt empty without them. Bereft. Not just hollowed out but a sucking void. She needed to pull others in, and soon, not just for their anima, but so she wouldn't disappear into the nothingness herself.

"Maid!" she shouted.

She had a vague notion that one had been sent with her. Even to war, even going into battle. She no longer bothered to learn their names, but that didn't mean they didn't exist.

Her voice was like a clapper, and her head a poorly made bell. The sound echoed painfully inside the empty chamber. When her head was overstuffed with her shadow girls, their pain and pressure brought exquisite clarity. Those moments when she'd beaten them back after they'd ravaged and raged and threatened to tear her apart were everything. When she knew she had just so much time to accomplish a thing before she went back to the war within herself.

A face appeared before her now, its outlines wavering into place and finally steadying into a shining sphere that could have been the sun the way it stung her eyes. The woman's hair was locked down behind a veil, her eyes crinkled in concern Bess wanted to swat away.

"Yes, your highness."

"My *Queen*," Bess corrected. She'd waited long enough to hear it. She wanted it on every tongue.

"My Queen," the woman said with a bob. She popped up with less concern and more uncertainty—more fear—in her brown eyes. *Better.*

"I need to be clothed. I need to walk among my men."

"Yes, my…Queen."

Bess considered whether to strike her down for the hesitation. She was so hungry. She could start now, with this woman. Slide the tips of her sharpened nails into the soft flesh of her neck or hands. She could tap straight into her blood and through that into her essence, suck the girl's anima into herself. All her peoples' lives were pledged to the Crown, to *her*; she was just determining the way they would be used. Much more meaningful for this girl's energy to be spent directly in service to her sovereign than as a drudge until she died by some man's hand or popping out his progeny.

But the flashes of her stolen girls' lives played in her mind, their light not vanished with their shadows.

Being swung around in a field by her love, one of Bess's own guardsmen, waiting for the kiss she knew would come.

Running giggling down a deserted passage holding another girl's hand in hers so tightly it was as if they'd never let go, wondering if it meant what she hoped it meant.

A baby's cry, the fuss of need, untying her shift to let the babe nuzzle into her breast for a feeding, kissing her perfect head and inhaling her scent.

Cheek to cheek with a magnificent horse, who pulled back to look the girl in the eye, breathing into her face to claim her.

Bess let the maid live, not due to sentimentality, but because she wasn't sure there was another among the troops. And because there would be questions. At her full strength, at the palace, she had the power and the means to dispose of the bodies with none the wiser. Yes, she'd stabbed one of her guards and stolen his lifeforce on the battlefield, but none close enough had lived to tell the tale. And even if so, that had been done in the heat of battle. The act could be forgiven if it was credited at all. But take too many lives, and her people might turn on her.

She knew where she could more readily find blood and sacrifice.

The maid pulled a gown over her. She held herself together as the fabric crinkled around her. With no shouting in her head, no cries and cacophony, everything external was overly loud—the sounds of the camp stirring, orders carrying in the sharp winter air, cold enough to cut even within the protection of her tent, the whinnies and wickers of the horses. Her maid's breath was like a bellows and smelled as though she'd been eating onions. Bess snapped at the maid with her teeth when she came too close, nearly catching her ear, and the girl stumbled back, tripped on a hem, and knocked into the dressing screen, sending it rattling.

It was only a hand to the other side of it and a voice that said, "My Queen," that stilled them both.

"Yes?" Bess lashed out, this time with her voice.

Her maid stayed out of reach, unsure how to proceed.

Bess ignored her for now, startled by her own actions. She would not think of Ceramor. He had stolen the lifeforce from her brother's hunting hounds and had gone feral. The same would not happen to her. She'd drawn her power from her girls. Yes, it was forbidden, and it was said that mageri who held power for themselves rather than spend it on their creations went *ankari*…mad…but that was only a cautionary tale. Something to keep weak people in their place. She was anything but weak.

"You called for me?" asked the voice accompanying the steadying hand. It was Bowstan, her general. There was no mistaking the voice. It practically vibrated the dressing screen. "Grygof is here with me as well."

Bess gestured her maid forward impatiently, and the girl's hands shook as she hastily cinched the gown at her back. It was too tight in some places, loose in others, but she declared it good enough. She rocked as the girl yanked on the laces to tie it off, her vision fading out momentarily. She grabbed for the screen, the rattle like bones, like teeth, like the stick-fingers of winter-bare trees breaking in the breeze, like death and despair. The world came back in too-painful prickles of clarity, and she stepped out quickly from behind the screen to give herself something else to focus on, homing in on the men before her.

"Talk as we walk," she ordered, reaching out a hand to demand Bowstan's arm in escort.

"Yes, my Queen." No hesitation there, she noted, as she twisted to get a glimpse of him. And yet, his lips pressed so tightly together at the end of the honorific that they were bloodless.

"And so? Report," she demanded.

"You have not yet told me where we're to walk," he said, working at neutrality.

Bowstan was a man entirely built for war–neither short nor tall, but fortified, a solid block of a man. His lower jaw was in permanent want of a fight, jutting out and daring anyone to take a swing. His hair had ceded the field to his berserker brows, which refused to fall into formation. She'd seen them used to good effect when quirked to question a colleague's competency or lowered in menace.

That his brows were twitching in the attempt to hold position was telling and irritating enough that she wanted to go beyond holding his arm. She wanted to sink her sharpened nails directly into his flesh, tap into his blood, draw out his essence, and substitute her will. She wanted to begin the takeover of her forces from the top down. As with a horse, steer the head and the body would follow. But Bowstan was not a man to be trifled with, and if he felt the bite of her nails and fought back–if in her weakened state she was not strong enough to hold him, especially in the presence of witnesses...

No, now was not the time or the place. But soon.

"Ah, yes. I want to walk among my men, to see to the wounded. I want them to take heart, knowing that they will rise again, as I have. Restored, like the Dobrens Valley. That their sacrifices have been in the cause of victory and the Restoration rebels are on the run. That *is* what you have to report, is it not?"

She gave his arm a squeeze. She could feel that lovely blood, that vitality, just below the surface, as she had with the trees and the land and carried on the very wind when she was a child. As her mother had seen and shunned when she was only five summers old.

They began walking. Grygof, her new spymaster, took position on her other side, several paces back. In contrast to Bowstan, he was eminently forgettable. Grygof's stealth lay in looking like everyone's uncle or merchant or wine-seller. Everyone knew a Grygof. If pressed, the best anyone could say was that he reminded them of *someone*. He was of middling age and height with sparse hair that was losing its color but hadn't done so entirely yet. He had a beard either in need of a trim or still being grown out. His eyes were dark but indeterminate, and not merry enough to encourage anyone to determine them. Rather, they were darkened with troubles which suggested that if you asked, you'd be in danger of hearing about them at length.

Ruggerio had thought highly of him. Bess had bled him, and in doing so was able to read his racing thoughts. She knew that Grygof was in disbelief that Ruggerio, her former spymaster, would be so foolish as to give up the position to which he'd risen. That he would be more than happy to step into the role. And that *he* would not be so foolish as to betray her.

"We've gone through the dead. The boy is not among them," Bowstan reported. "We've sent out scouts, but it won't be easy. The rebels disappeared as they came, splitting off into small groups."

Bess hissed, though she'd felt in her bones that the boy was still out there. That this wasn't over. Maybe her father and brothers had trained her to expect the worst.

"Is there any way our mageri can track them?"

It would go against their victory to rip away the anima they'd just returned to the Dobrens Valley for such a mission, but if the boy escaped and was able to rally support, that would be far worse. The urchin could not be allowed to threaten her throne.

Bowstan started to glance over his shoulder, and she tightened her grip, enough that he could feel her displeasure.

He turned back to her rather than exchange glances with Grygof, which is what she was certain he'd intended. Men conferring with men when she was their Queen.

"Whatever the rebel faction did, they didn't simply restore the anima of the valley; they seem to have warded it," he said without further delay. "The mageri have no way to access power until we get beyond the ward."

"As soon as your scouts report back, *as soon* as you have a direction on the boy, on Cia and the others who escaped us, send a team after them. Mageri and your best men. Small, silent, deadly. You hear me? I want it swift and fatal. And I want proof." She released his arm.

"And you," she asked, turning on Grygof as Bowstan strode off to issue orders. "Tell me you have something better for me." She eyed him, considering how she'd describe him if he ever did betray her as Ruggerio had done. If she ever had to put *his* likeness on a poster. But there wasn't a single feature that stood out. No scar or one eyebrow higher than the other. No dimple of the chin.

"I've been through everything confiscated from the Restoration rebels," Grygof said. "I thought you'd want to see this. It was taken from the one who cast the spell when no magic should have been possible, the one who collapsed on the field."

He brought out a book from inside a fold of his tunic and presented it as though his hand was a velvet pillow, and it was a priceless artefact or diadem.

"I've glanced at it only briefly, but it proports to be written by Lehren Gelerte."

Bess took the book in both of her hands, expecting to feel something, but it was a dead thing. As reverently as Grygof had held it, there was no power in the book itself. But there must be something special about it or they wouldn't bother carrying it. Lehren Gelerte was the Churchman who'd been instrumental in defeating the last monarch to boast mageri blood. *Mad King Calestri*, they called him. But only because he'd failed. If he'd succeeded, her line would now control both Church and Crown. She would not be fighting the Restoration. Nor would mageri blood have been bred out of the line of succession. She could work completely in the open. Unquestioned and unchallenged.

This book could contain the key to it all. Show how Lehren Gelerte had been able to face off with a mageri king and how she could keep the Church from winning again.

"Speak of this to no one," she ordered.

Grygof bowed and touched a hand to his head, raising it an awkward moment later, causing her to realize she hadn't given him leave either by word or gesture. She was so used to having Regent Strego beside her as an erstwhile guardian, inviting and dismissing, playing at having her power. She couldn't let her attention flag now, no matter how *hungry* she was. She'd declared herself their monarch, their Queen, and she couldn't let them forget or doubt, even for a moment.

She dismissed the man who sussed out secrets for a living, and hid the book in her squared-off sleeve, which was meant for tucking away a kerchief or book of verse, but not a volume of this size. Thus, she had to be careful of her movements, especially as fragile as she was feeling, lest the additional weight send her listing or the swing of her arm do one of her men unintended harm. They were at the medical tent now, and she entered the flap with only her guards around her. The scent of blood greeted her like an old friend. She closed her eyes to breathe it in, only to snap them open again when the other scents struck her–voided bowels and stomachs, wounds beginning to go wrong. Surely it was too soon for the smell of it in the air. She was no Ceramor with his stolen senses, his feral instincts, his humanity no longer with the upper hand. Maybe it was the poultices and unguents, like those used to treat the sword thrust from which her brother Jannik had never recovered, that made her think of wounds gone septic.

She shook away the memory of Jannik thrashing, eyes hazed with pain, one gone red from a broken blood vessel as his temperature and temper spiked, the poison from the wound flooding his system. He made the medics suffer nearly as he did while he played death's gallows game.

Her appearance in the medic tent caused a stir. Instantly, voices cried out, moans grew louder, arms were thrown over eyes to blot out the sudden sunlight she'd let in. A woman straightened from one of the pallets and rose to greet her.

"I've come to comfort my men," Queen Bessory said, raising her voice for all to hear, as though she were on her balcony of the palace addressing a gathered crowd. The canvas of the tent seemed to grasp the words and hold them close.

The woman before her was plain. Things spattered her graying overdress that Bess didn't want to consider. The stitcher-woman hadn't prostrated herself or given way, but instead stayed planted in Bess's path, gnawing her lip as though chewing on her words.

Bess bristled, raised a hand to sweep the woman aside and begin her advance. Perhaps it would be more of a swipe, and in knocking her aside, Bess would draw blood, pulling in a bit of the woman's essence, some of her strength and resistance. If she would not learn her lesson, at least it would be some time before she was in any condition to repeat her mistake.

As she would have, the woman sputtered out, "Shall I call the medic?"

Bess was so stunned, she froze. It would only take a flick of the hand. She itched for it. The *Queen* demanded entrée, and this stitcher-woman worried whether she needed authority to grant it? If she had been her father or brothers or even her Regent, Strego, the woman would never have dared stand in her way. And if so, they'd have knocked her aside, leaving the woman in need of a medic herself. But then another thought crowded in, that the woman might be as afraid of the medic as she was of anyone entering. Or more. She might have been told to see that he was undisturbed, thus her positioning by the tent flap. Otherwise, it would have made sense to keep her close to hand to help him in surgery.

She wouldn't have expected to be confronted with her Queen.

She trembled even as she held her ground, her eyes downcast.

"*Show me to him*," Bess growled. She would find the medic with the most dire cases. That was where she would find her victim.

"Y-yes, my Queen."

The woman led the way, and as Bess followed her, she reached out, taking an outstretched hand here and there along with some lovely power, offered, if unknowingly, with the soldier's fealty.

There was only a further flap separating the medic's surgery area from the rest of the tent. As they approached it, Bess heard a great crack and hideous scream that cut off into nothing, as though the pain had ended the man who made it...or only his temporary consciousness.

The stitcher-woman turned to Bess. "Maybe you'd better be the one to interrupt him?"

But it was unnecessary. In the pallets closest to the medic's area were the worst off, on one side awaiting his attentions, on the other recovering from them. She spotted the man she wanted, and she had no delusions as to why. He reminded her of her brother Jannik, who, along with her eldest brother Cyril, had been her main tormentor growing up. Oh, not so alike in appearance, but in the way the soldier writhed on his pallet, his entire left leg swollen and bleeding through his bandages. He moaned, lashed out, as though still battling opponents or his own personal demons. But he was clearly a fighter, not yet ready to go. Which meant he'd hang on until the bitter end. His would be a slow, horrible, wasting death like Jannik's.

Killing him now would be a mercy. One her brother had never deserved.

CHAPTER FOUR

Ruggerio

Ludvin rode up beside Ruggerio, irritating the spit out of him. Ruggerio was used to working alone and in the shadows. When he'd commanded his own spy network, he'd had others for the less delicate or more group-oriented missions. Given his preferences, he'd take the speed and flexibility of his own horse. However, given the choice here between trusting Ludvin to watch their rear or saddling him with the boy-who-would-be-king, he'd chosen the former. Ludvin had just shown he couldn't be trusted with even that much.

No, he'd ridden past Cia and Ulan, neither with more mass than a starveling, all their substance bled away from them by Bloody Bess's machinations. Past Myrka, made entirely of ropey muscle and sinew that stood out so sharply it might snap like a bowstring. She'd bound Roha to her by nes cloak, so that the unconscious acolyte could keep nes seat. Ludvin had ridden shamelessly straight up to Hostill and Ruggerio as though it was a social outing.

"You're supposed to be at the back keeping watch," Ruggerio growled as soon as Ludvin pulled alongside them.

"We'll hear company well before I can see it. I wanted to talk to you without the others listening in."

It was true that they could barely hear themselves think above the clomp of hooves and the howling winds, but sound was a funny thing in the mountains. What might not be heard in one place would carry to another, especially in the crystalline winter air.

But it would be quicker to hear Ludvin out, if he could, than to argue. It was Ruggerio's job to get them over the Frizenzian border and out of Bloody Bess's reach before trouble could come calling, and he intended to do it.

"So then?" he said.

Ludvin flashed a glance at Hostill. In apology, it seemed to Ruggerio.

"I wouldn't trust Myrka," Ludvin said, only as loud as he thought he needed to be. "Not that she's a bad sort. Just...so very quick with a blade. The Restoration has become her family, and her loyalties will lie with them."

"Isn't that to be expected?"

Ludvin nodded and chewed his lips before wincing and spitting them back out, bloodied and broken. Chapped as they were, they hadn't held up to the abuse. "Hostill, I know that you chose her. I want to be sure you don't harbor any...illusions."

Hostill, seated in front of Ruggerio, knocked an elbow into Ruggerio's stomach as he whipped around in the saddle.

"You mean a tendré?" he asked, voice rising alarmingly.

Ludvin shrugged, itched his scalp, and looked away.

Hostill's face screwed up so that all his features fought their way toward center, his brows meeting in the middle, "I'm not...she's... *No.* Look, Viktor upset Cia and Ulan. Myrka is at least the bosewight I know, right? And maybe a little less threatening than a man who can blot out the moon. We want her by our side. Not necessarily guarding our back, I get that, but you all need to stop treating me like I'm stupid."

"You're not stupid, just young. The young think they know everything, but you don't have the benefit of experience," Ludvin said, glancing back.

"I grew up early. You know I've been caring for myself for a year now. I was fine with information being need-to-know when I was a runner for the Restoration. But now I'm in the middle of things. You can't treat me like a kid and tell me I'm a king. You want me in your plans, you include me. Not just because I'm riding with Ruggerio and I can't help but overhear, but because I matter."

Ruggerio chuckled, and Hostill glared up at him with such force that his heart would have swelled had it not been tempered steel. There was really no doubt the boy was Jannik's son. Those iceberg eyes alone! But this was Jannik if he'd been forged in the fires of necessity rather than entitlement. No, more than that, if Jannik hadn't lacked something fundamental, like the belief that nothing in the world was more important than his own interests.

"Yes, my...Lord." It came slowly. Awkwardly. And Ruggerio, who'd read people and situations for a living, could tell that it tasted off for Ludvin.

Hostill made a face again. "Sounds silly, doesn't it? If I ever get to the throne, *then* we'll worry about titles. Until then, I'm just me. When we set watch tonight, I'll take one of them."

Ruggerio met Ludvin's gaze over the boy's head, trying to signal that *No, the spirits, he would not.*

Hostill was all of eleven? Twelve? It was difficult to tell. He'd been malnourished and might be small for his age. But either way, he was a growing boy. Ruggerio's understanding was that they generally needed a great deal of sleep, but Ludvin wouldn't meet his gaze. He supposed he understood. Ludvin had just agreed to what in his mind was his first promise to his future liege. It was not something that Ruggerio could wrap his head around.

Yes, he'd been the first to suspect who the boy might be, but he was still a boy. To be groomed for leadership. Instructed on statecraft, manners, customs of various countries, on what was truly important to a well-run kingdom. He had seen what a V'Alban could do when left to their own devices. It was time to see what one could do when left to *Ruggerio's.*

No, the boy was not someone from whom to take commands. Not yet, certainly. But it was quite useful for Ludvin to believe differently, and he would have to tread carefully on the matter himself.

There was a sharp cry and a curse from behind them, then a terrified squeal from a horse, as scree skittered out from beneath its hooves when it tried to maneuver too quickly on the rocky pass they negotiated.

Ruggerio's horse hip-checked Ludvin's as he turned in time to see Myrka with her dagger raised over Roha, who'd begun to slip in nes bindings. Their horse, terrified at the over-balancing, threw its haunches the other way, trying to recover its footing. Myrka's dagger fell, a blur in the night. Ruggerio spurred his horse forward, even knowing he wouldn't be in time.

Closer still, Cia slid off the big bay she rode with Ulan. Ruggerio yelled that she should clear out of his way before he rode her down, but she darted forward and caught Roha as ni dropped, both of them crashing to the rocky mountain path. Cia rolled away with Roha, and Ruggerio's breath stopped, fearing they would go over the edge.

The blanket that had bound Roha to Myrka flapped like washing in a storm, ripped apart by Myrka's blade. He realized it wasn't entirely the blanket fluttering–Roha was awake and terrified, trying to fight nimself free of the fabric. Nes topknot was no more, hair spiraling down before nes face, eyes when they appeared between the strands shone sheer white around their central obsidian. Ni didn't know what had happened, only that ni'd fallen and was grappling with someone.

Roha's elbow caught Cia under the chin. Her head jerked back, her arms fell away. Their roll stopped in a small avalanche of ice, stone, and plumes of heated breath.

Myrka had fallen as well but against the mountainside. She was instantly on her feet, blood spilling down her face, daggers in both hands. One was pointed toward Roha, and the other at the rest of them who were closing in.

"Stop right there!" Myrka said, voice raised to carry over the winds.

"What the seven spirits happened?" Hostill asked, double Myrka's volume. "I trusted you."

"Seven spirits?" Ulan asked.

"Shht," said Cia softly, trying not to spook Roha further while gently testing her jaw.

"Trusted me?" Myrka asked. "Roha's the one who came to in a fury. Bloodied my nose with nes skull. Would have given me a head-knocking if I hadn't moved myself in time. Could have sent us both plunging down the mountain if I hadn't cut nim loose, and you want to blame me?"

Ulan made a rude noise.

Roha lowered nes hands, breath growing less erratic. Ni slowly sank onto one hip. "I thought I'd been captured. I thought…I don't like being confined."

They'd all been captured at one point, but Roha's response was on another level. Something had clearly happened to nim. But now, with Bloody Bess's people in pursuit, was not the time to pursue it, even if Roha had been inclined to share nes secrets.

But ni hadn't disputed Myrka's version of events. Did Roha nimself know the truth of what had happened when ni'd only just come to? And Myrka—what would she have done with that dagger if the others hadn't been alerted to the scuffle? Best to separate them for certainty.

When no one else spoke, Ruggerio put his head on the chopping block, "Should we redistribute the weight?"

His cousin flashed him a *look,* which he ignored. He'd hardly been subtle, though he was fully capable when necessary. Let them refocus their anger and attention on him. He could bear it, especially if it got them all moving again.

"There's no need," Myrka said with poor grace.

She glared daggers, but now at him and him alone, and she sheathed her actual weaponry to free the slashed blanket from around her body and sop the blood from her nose.

Roha gave Myrka a moment of study before agreeing that they could continue as they had been, less the binding. They'd both worked with the Restoration. Perhaps they could work together for a little longer.

Ni started to rise, and Cia offered her hand to help Roha, though she came only to the acolyte's shoulder. Roha was nearly as shaky as a newborn calf testing out its legs for the first time, but ni seemed to steady–if freezing could be called such–when ni saw the swelling already forming along Cia's jawbone.

Gently, Roha took Cia's chin in nes hand to angle it for a better look, and Cia averted her gaze.

"Did I do that?" Roha asked.

"It's nothing. I caught you as you fell, and you caught me. I hardly feel it."

Roha gave Cia's cheek one stroke with nes thumb, as though ni could brush away the pain. "I'm not Garif," Roha said, meaningfully. "I'm sorry."

"I know," Cia said, keeping her gaze averted. "I'm just glad you're okay. I was worried when you collapsed on the battlefield."

She moved away then, and so did Roha, but not without a glance back, as though ni felt Cia's pain.

"Come now, mount up. It's not much further," Ruggerio said, impatient to be out of the cold. Perhaps tempers would improve with their circumstances.

"What's not much further?" Hostill said peevishly. "You haven't told us a thing."

Roha and Myrka eyed each other distrustfully as they remounted their horse. Roha still rode ahead of Myrka, but now ni could sit upright, and Myrka had to hold either to nim or to the back of the saddle. She chose the saddle, but that wouldn't last long, as it was sure to be more uncomfortable even than the tension between the two.

"Abandoned cabin," Ruggerio said as they began moving again. "The recluse who lived there died, and it's too remote for anyone else to want it."

Except for a royal spymaster, who had used it as a rare waystation–rarer still once the war had devastated the surrounding land. The assault hadn't reached the cabin, though the stretch between the border and where they were now had become a dead zone.

Soon they turned off the barren, wind-whipped trail. The foothills led to a forest and a narrow path of trees ten times the height of men. They seemed to lean against each other like drunken revelers, forming an arch in the canopy, a shrine of nature. With the forgiveness of night and the moonlight filigreeing the snow and ice, it was impossible to tell that the trees were dead from the Blood War and not just winter-bare. It was the cold silence of the forest that gave that away. No owls hooting or creatures scurrying to escape them.

There was no making up any time now. Beneath the coating of snow that had sifted through the sticklike branches, old pinecones and fallen twigs rolled. Ruggerio was aware that some of the snapping beneath the horses' hooves might even be bones. When the mageri swept the anima from the land, anything touching it was taken as well, man and beast. Anything could be underfoot. Danger came from above as well, as brittle branches threatened to snap from the weight of the snow, ready to bring the heavens down on their heads.

Relief came when sound returned to the woods—beasts scurrying, chittering, skittering. He never knew how much he missed the signs of life until they returned. He didn't dwell; he wasn't particularly sentimental. But it was a sign they were nearly there, and that was something for which he could be thankful.

Ruggerio breathed a sigh that sent a great plume of vapor into the air when he saw that indeed the hovel remained untouched. He'd seen what drawing all the anima out of an area could do—crops dead, beams so desiccated they cracked and caved, fabric rotted away, mortar crumbled to dust, dead rodents decaying in the walls or birds in rafters adding a charnel house stench to the air so that every breath was redolent of death.

He had not counted on the winter-swollen door being completely jammed in place. The shutters were no better, frozen and thawed so many times over the years that repeated expansion and contraction had torn them out of true, twisting their hinges until they barely held on, clutching each other in place. They would have to break something to enter, and that would allow the elements in. The door seemed more likely to break *them*, but the few windows were too high and small for entry. And the horses... It was too cold to expect them to survive the night unsheltered. They would have to come inside. It would take all of the space.

The door then.

"Stand back," Cia said, as she let Ulan down, his cousin hissing as the dismount jostled her bad arm. Cia followed her to the ground.

The other horses danced to the side nervously, as though Cia was giving off an *energy,* and they were giving her space. He didn't know what to make of Cia. He'd mostly known her as a woman possessed by her mageri husband after she'd caused his untimely death. Roha had supposedly laid his ghost to rest along with all the others on the battlefield, but still...

Cia pointed her horse at the door, stepped back, and gave a command. The big bay looked at her as though to be certain, then whinnied, and rose to his hind legs, front hooves flashing at the door, pummeling it once, twice, with great cracks each time. At a final crack, the door gave, and the stallion fell back to all four hooves, shaking out his black mane and blowing steaming breaths as though proud of his work.

Cia stepped forward to put her head on the horse's neck, telling him how very well he'd done, and the horse leaned in, reveling in the praise, as though he hadn't been a full-on war horse a moment ago. As though he couldn't become a killing machine again in an instant. As Cia stroked the horse's neck and shoulder, Ruggerio realized it was more than that. At this point, she wasn't just appreciating the horse, he was also holding her up. Ruggerio felt the same exhaustion deadening his own limbs, pulling him down as though the earth was quicksand, and he might not rise again.

He'd faced off with a Caturnine–a monstrous cat with poisoned, barbed vines for tails. He'd been stung by those barbs, paralyzed by their toxins, and almost died. His rescue had come at the expense of a Restoration insurgent who'd lost his own arm and nearly his life in that fight. Ruggerio didn't even know whether Morley had survived the big battle with Bloody Bess's forces, though he feared not. Otherwise, surely Morley would have raised a voice in their defense against Hedric. His support might even have encouraged others to speak up; it might have turned the tide.

No matter how it had seemed on the battlefield, the rebels couldn't all be of one mind. They held a common belief, yet the Restoration was made up of individuals. Ruggerio had never met any five people who could agree on anything. Not when it came down to details.

If he meant to take Hostill under his wing, he couldn't forget that. Once you forgot that people were *people*, you could do anything to them. Like Bloody Bess did. Because *you* were the one with the vision and the power to achieve it, and *they* were just in your way. *They. Them. The others. Those who weren't you.*

Thus, when Ludvin also took note of Cia's weakness and offered that he and Myrka would walk the horses to cool them down, Ruggerio did one of the hardest things he'd ever done. He trusted, at least that far. He handed the reins of his horse over after dismounting with Hostill and let the two Restoration agents take first watch.

Cia gestured that Myrka was welcome to her stallion but took Roha in trade, slipping her shoulder under one arm while Ulan took the other on her good side. The three swayed where they stood, but much like hovel's shutters, held themselves in place, each supporting the other. They had to walk through the threshold sideways, but they made it, collapsing onto the sleeping shelf together and rolling into a huddle for warmth. They didn't wait for a fire to be lit or for any food that might be found, but fell into an exhausted sleep as soon as their bodies were prone.

At least one began to snore.

CHAPTER FIVE

Roha

Roha was caught in a nightmare of bruise-darkness. Flashes of red-glowing veins forked like lightning, the strikes flashing at nim, aimed with intent. Roha raced to stay ahead of them, dodging behind the spindly, spikey, spidery legs of the beast that crouched over nim. Roha yelled and struck at the legs to draw the monster's attention while Cia ran across the mindscape with Roha's sword to vanquish her demon, Garif. Always Garif. Cia had killed him once, yet it wasn't enough. It took the two of them to rip out the phantom that had slipped into Cia's soul.

Cia thrust the point of the sword into the beast. Roha woke with a start at its inhuman *scree* of pain.

Ni couldn't escape the dream memory. They almost hadn't made it out. Roha had special access to the anima, but ni was untrained except for the Church-taught wards and nulls. Ni'd barely dipped more than a toe into nes powers. Ni'd certainly never taken things so far.

Cia's warmth at nes back came as a huge relief. She was alive, safe, *here*. Ni didn't want to face her just yet. Roha'd always envisioned the anima as a well ni could draw from, but it currently swelled like a rain-swollen spring with an underground pathway that reached toward Cia. Maybe it was an ephemeral branch and would dry up in time, but it felt intimate. And undoubtedly unwelcome on Cia's end, after what she'd been through.

The last thing Cia would want was someone else having a link directly into her soul, and Roha had no idea how to shut it down. On top of that, ni had lashed out and hurt Cia, striking her chin. Ni only hoped it didn't bring flashbacks of her former abuse.

Roha lay there, trying to breathe shallowly, pretending to sleep, and processing what had happened. Remembering. The battle. Ceramor, in his bestial form, locked in a struggle with Bloody Bess. Not enough of him left after Roha returned all the unquiet spirits to the anima, including those he'd consumed. How many others hadn't survived the battle? Roha had been unconscious when they'd taken nim from the field.

Had they thought to rescue the book Roha carried?

Ni shot up in bed but was stopped abruptly by the tattered blanket ni'd once worn as a cloak, which the others on the pallet had rolled onto. Ni searched the room frantically from nes vantage, ignoring the screaming of nes body from its various abuses. They were in a one-room shack, Ruggerio and Hostill curled closely on the nearer side of the fireplace, horses huddled together on the other, taking up all the remaining room in the hut, but for the single table and chair in the corner. Myrka occupied the former, and Ludvin the latter, glaring at each other as though it was a staring contest, and the cost of losing was a life.

But both swung their gazes toward Roha at nes frantic movement. Ni tried to shimmy out from between Cia and Ulan without waking them, gently easing one end of the cloak from beneath Cia's dead weight.

"The book?" ni hissed, hoping not to wake anyone else.

"What?" Myrka asked.

Roha blew out a frustrated sigh, and nes hair puffed with it. Nes topknot had been destroyed, and nes hair hung in a ropey mess.

Without nes oil and a proper brush, it would be impossible to get back under control. In Jucar, it had been all about being in control. Ni was different enough without letting people see *more* differences. The Church was all that gave nim any protection. It had been fit in there or perhaps flee to nes mother's native Markens, where *'children like nim'* had a chance, if what ni'd overheard of nes parents' fight could be credited.

Ludvin shook his head. "The Crown forces took everything when they retreated. No chance to recover anything."

Roha's heart bashed itself against nes ribcage, as though it could beat its way out and warn all of those in need. "Then they know. Or will."

"*Know what?*" Myrka asked, glancing back and forth between them, scowling at their secrecy.

"The contents of a book I liberated from the Church," Roha said. "The Church and Crown are already at odds. They don't need more fuel for those flames."

"What aren't you saying?" Myrka's face was like a storm cloud.

Roha wanted to curse. Why couldn't Hostill have saddled them with a less perceptive member of the Restoration?

"It was written by Lehren Gelerte," Ludvin said.

"*The* Lehren Gelerte?"

As though there was more than one. At least Myrka could only know what everyone knew. There was no way she could be aware of Gelerte's greatest secret.

Myrka was a strong soldier for the Restoration, a zealot, ready to strike any blow against magic or mageri. Now that she knew about Roha, Myrka might be just as quick to use those knives on nim. Could Roha say for a certainty that wasn't what had happened on the trail? Or been about to happen?

Clearly Ludvin was concerned, or he wouldn't be staring Myrka down across the table rather than getting rest during her shift.

"Yes," he answered Myrka, ignoring Roha's side-eye.

"Did the book say anything useful for defeating Bloody Bess?" Myrka asked. "Or anything hurtful for our side?"

"We'd barely had the chance to open it, but we can't risk what she may glean from it. The book isn't safe in her hands," Roha said, trying to keep calm, but the more ni thought of Bloody Bess reading the gospel and the people it might expose...

Roha had to race back to Jucar. There was no time to waste.

"I'll go," Ruggerio said. His deep voice came from beside the fireplace, and there was no mistaking it. Only one voice was as cold as steel and yet begged you to test it.

"They've already got the book. They'll have time to learn its secrets. Even if you gain it back, it will be too late," Roha answered, as though ni hadn't been thinking the same thing. But ni couldn't stand the thought of anyone else with the book. Ni had liberated it. It should be kept with the Nim.

"Let us speak," he said, getting up from his place by Hostill as quietly as an assassin with his target acquired.

There was no place for privacy. Hardly any room to move around at all in the small cabin, but he motioned nim toward the horses, perhaps hoping their blowing and shifting would cover any conversation. One made to kick at him as he came close, but he caught the hoof and set it down, surprising the horse and making it redistribute its weight. Then they were in too close for kicks, though the horse's head came around to nip at Ruggerio instead.

"You have a way with them," Roha laughed quietly.

Ruggerio shot nim a disgruntled look, which only made nim more amused.

Roha valiantly set nimself between Ruggerio and his would-be attacker.

"I have no doubt that you could recover the book," ni murmured, "but there are people who might be revealed by Bloody Bess's reading of it. People I would need to get to safety."

"Or that you would endanger by leading the enemy to them. Better that I reclaim the book and deal with those who have it in the way I am best equipped to do," Ruggerio said.

Hostill made a noise in his sleep before wriggling closer to the fire, and instantly Ruggerio lunged across the small room to keep him from rolling into it. The boy grumbled in indignation. By that point, Cia and Ulan were stirring and wiping sleep out of their eyes as well.

All eyes had turned to them. Their privacy was at an end. Roha strode over to retrieve nes cloak, still wrapped around Ulan, and whipped it around nes shoulders to head off the shivers trying to shake the teeth loose from nes skull. It was still warm from their bodies. In fact, between the fire and all the bodies forced into the small space, it should have been quite cozy. There was no reason for nim to be so cold, unless it was the deprivation from the last several days.

"I'm going back to Jucar with you," Ulan said after the yawn that split her face allowed her jaw to rehinge.

There was no way she should have heard them, even if she hadn't been asleep as ni'd thought. But perhaps years of straining for the faintest whisper of Dazia, her little ghost girl, had sharpened her hearing.

Ruggerio began to object, but Ulan ran right over him. "I don't need your permission. I'm no good in Frizenze. I don't speak the language. I'm a liability in a fight. I could heal if I had any of my herbs or tinctures, but I don't. My Dazia..." her voice broke. "My Dazia is at peace and can no longer carry messages back and forth. If we need messages sent, I'll have to do it myself or find some spirit in the royal city. You need backup, whether you'll admit it or not, and I'm the only one who can be spared."

"Only if you'll let me set that arm. You can't keep on as you are," Ruggerio said, nodding at the arm Ulan was even now cradling to herself.

"What's going on?" Cia asked.

Hostill hissed as he tried to rise from sleep and nearly put his hand into the fire. He jerked it back, blowing on it, as though that would help, and then examining it for blistering. Ludvin rose from the chair to pull the boy back bodily by his collar. Two close calls had been enough for him.

"Hey!" Hostill said, fighting his way out of Ludvin's grip.

Safety assured, Ludvin fixed Ruggerio with a gaze that could pierce armor.

"Yes, Ruggerio. No more secrets. Tell everyone what's going on," he said, voice as commanding as Roha had ever heard it.

Ruggerio glared at the rebel, then looked to Roha, sketching nim a bow as though to say that it wasn't his story to tell, as ni had so succinctly informed him.

Roha flashed Ludvin a side-eye of betrayal before filling them in with as much as ni dared about the book that Bloody Bess now possessed: that it was The Gospel of Gelerte ni had liberated from the Church, that ni hoped it held some secret regarding the lehren's defeat of Mad King Calestri, and that it must be retrieved.

Ulan rose, a pang crossing her face. "Roha, I say this with no bias toward my cousin, I assure you, but he will fare better in the royal city than you will. He no longer has his spy network, but if I know him, he still has assets and bolt holes hidden away. The more power Bloody Bess takes for herself, the more she will alienate her people, creating discontent with her leadership and more potential allies for us. We need someone who knows the players."

"You would go back in?" Cia shuddered, and without thinking, Roha dared go and put an arm around her shoulder, offering to reshare nes blanket. Not so different than the previous night when Roha had needed Cia and Ulan's support simply to stand, but Roha could feel the weight of Ruggerio's gaze on nim, weighing the potential for weakness he feared developing there. Because, of course, he would see any tenderness as a vulnerability. It made Roha distinctly uncomfortable. Ni hoped Cia didn't notice and move away.

Roha refused to breathe easier when Ruggerio transferred the weight of his stare to Ulan. "You have a devious mind, cousin."

"Do I? I suppose I've learned it from you."

"But you're not wrong," he said, then looked to Ludvin. "I'll do you more good within the city than without. I've taken you this far. From here, you continue down the foothills into Frizenze. Look for fires, well-worn paths. Once you find habitation, Cia can let people know who she is and why she's come. You will be safe from there."

"Will we really?" Myrka asked dryly.

"To the extent that any of us ever are."

Myrka's only answer was to begin cleaning her nails with her knives, clearly for show, because it could not be good for blades or fingers.

Ruggerio looked to Ulan's arm, which he did not think was broken, but just strained by hanging from Bloody Bess's toppling watchtower. Roha's cloak underwent further indignities from Ruggerio's knife, as he cut off a ragged end to create a sling.

CHAPTER SIX

Ulan

Ulan was still as weak as a newborn kitten from being repeatedly drained to the edge of death by Bloody Bessory's mageri women, and with her arm in a sling, she couldn't very well hold the reins. That didn't mean she felt comfortable being locked in by Ruggerio's arms while he handled their horse. Her cousin was significantly stouter than Cia, but also significantly less gentle, and he couldn't stay rigidly encircling her for any length of time. They were both exhausted, and so, when he collapsed his arms against her sides, he jostled her arm, and she bit back a scream. She could feel a tremor in Ruggerio she wouldn't dare call attention to. Likely, it was a remnant of his encounter with the Catamount and its poison barbs.

She was focused on that–her concern for Ruggerio, the nip and bite of the cold and how quickly it would burn through their reserves of energy–so she didn't at first notice the mist was more than their breath in the cold mountain air. They weren't far from the cabin, not yet to the part where the trees went from winter-bare to dead, when suddenly all sound shut off. Everything but Ruggerio's breathing in her ear.

That was when she realized the mist wasn't mist. It was the anima being called up and out of the earth and everything touching it.

Their horse stumbled, then whipped his head back and forth, whites showing all around his eyes as he searched frantically for something in pursuit. Finding nothing, he flattened his neck, ready to run full out, nearly wrenching the reins out of Ruggerio's hands.

Ruggerio yanked back to regain control.

Ulan cried, "Don't!" her voice sharp and stinging as though it wanted to freeze in her throat. "Let go. The horse knows."

"Knows what?" he asked. But he let the reins slack, and the horse took off, picking his way as fast as possible through the magic.

The horse trembled in his haste, like a colt just squeezed out of its mother. He was connected to the ground, and the swirling, gathering eddy lifting from the earth like a fog was getting thicker. Ulan had witnessed it before when she'd attended the armies. She could see the anima, see the magics. Maybe that was why she'd been able to perceive Dazia after she'd passed on, or refused to, and other spirits when they'd done the same. Her only power was the ability to see the anima when it was summoned. Her greatest weakness the inability to do anything about it.

Except run.

Except insist Ruggerio give the horse his head.

"It knows someone is drawing power for a spell. The only way we'll make it is to race through and get out the other end."

But it was already too late. The horse was in trouble. With each hoof-fall, his own anima was being siphoned for the spell, sucked out like marrow from a bone. One leg wouldn't hold, and he veered to the side, driving them into a tree. Ruggerio, arms encircling her, took the brunt of it. He cried out as his breeches were sheered away, some of his flesh along with them. The horse rebounded from the impact but swayed like a drunkard. Ruggerio yanked at the reins, trying to right him, kicking at the horse with his heels to spur him on. Turning terror to speed.

"It's no good. The horse will never make it."

Ruggerio handed her the reins, and Ulan grabbed them instinctively. She didn't understand until she felt his weight shift, and then she panicked. The mist was so thick now, yet Ruggerio was sliding to the ground where he would be vulnerable. She knew he couldn't see the mist as she could, but he could feel the effects. He believed, which meant he knew the horse would never make it carrying both their weight. But while she'd always thought of him as pragmatic, this was sheer idiocy. Jucar needed him far more than it needed her.

Ruggerio's knees buckled as he hit the ground, as the pull of the spell affected him directly. The magic connected him intimately with the earth and the swelling anima, pulling strength from him as well. With him holding the horse and her atop it, they became momentarily one, along with the winter-bare woods, the wind, and the prickle of precipitation in the air that might turn into something or might not because it was being whipped away with all the other potential of the land. It was wonderful and terrible.

She was especially aware of Ruggerio's essence being wicked away, the dead matter of his boots affording him little protection now that he was on the ground. The tears in her eyes froze in place, never even making it to her cheeks. She felt Ruggerio's struggle to hold himself steady as though it was her own. Her muscles quivered with his, as though hers were the ones working or the spell was drawing everything out of her as well, through him, through her mount. Ruggerio pulled the reins from her numb hands and tugged the stallion onward. She fell forward over the horse's crest, let her arms dangle over his neck. His skin twitched, his muscles shook; his entire body swayed. She could feel his heartbeat as though it was her own—too hard and too slow. His haunches began to sink to the ground, and Ruggerio cinched up his hold until the reins were straight under the horse's chin, holding him upright through sheer force of will.

He dragged himself along, dragged the horse—the pull between them possibly all that kept them on their feet. The horse staggered, and Ruggerio with him. Knocking them into a tree. Ulan pulled her leg up before it could break against the trunk and slid it over the horse's side to dismount as well. If she stayed atop the stallion, she would be dead weight.

She left Ruggerio with the reins, walking backward in front of the horse instead, one hand out to his muzzle, close enough for him to feel her heat. Where Ruggerio muscled, she cajoled, walking blindly until they were out of the mist. One moment there, the next gone. They'd reached the deadlands, expanded now. The mageri Bloody Bess had sent after them had ripped all the moisture from the air and every shred of anima from each living thing in their path to form some monstrous construct, but had clearly sent whatever it was in the direction from which they'd come, which meant the others were in grave danger.

Ulan and Ruggerio collapsed, their poor horse falling to his knees and then onto his side. Foamy breath was icing up around his mouth, and his sides were crystalizing with frozen sweat. Ruggerio passed out half atop the horse. He'd been longer in contact with the ground than she had, and that had been more than enough. Her whole body was shaking, her teeth clattering together so hard they might break, but she knew that if she didn't get the horse rubbed down and warm, he wouldn't survive.

But first...

"Dazia!" She waited for her daughter to come, as she always had before when Ulan needed her, only to remember...her little girl was never coming to her again.

That was when it hit. Truly hit.

Not on the battlefield. Not that morning.

Now, when she was exhausted. When she realized that she'd been about to treat Dazia as Ruggerio always had, like a spy or messenger, and send her off on a mission. Worthy, yes. Warning their friends of danger so they could prepare and survive, but still...

Dazia was gone, and all she had to do to join her was lay down right here, right now. There was a very good chance she wouldn't get up again.

She was so cold. Brutally, mortally cold and tired.

The Church said that if she decided, if she died with a stain on her soul like bringing harm to herself or others, she'd poison the anima. She alone was insignificant, but there would be others who'd make the same choice and with enough of them, the collective spirit would turn dark and ugly, the world would be changed. Nothing born from darkness could be light. Nothing formed of chaos could be at peace.

So she wouldn't decide on the easy path to join her daughter and the All. As difficult as it was, she chose to continue despite the cold, despite exhaustion and aches and injuries.

She couldn't let the froth and sweat freeze on their poor horse or he'd surely die. He'd done his best for them, and she could do no less in return. She had to wipe him down and cover him. To keep Ruggerio warm as well. She would give them all their best chance at life, and if it wasn't enough, there was nothing more that could be done.

⸺⸺◆⸺◆⸺

Cia

Three horses remained for five people. Cia was shaky, bereft. For so long, she'd operated on fear and anger, terrified and tortured. She didn't know how to feel now that her husband was no more. Or even whether she truly believed it. He'd haunted her beyond death. He'd poisoned her from the inside out and nearly killed her. She'd caged him only with Roha's help.

She gravitated toward the acolyte, wanting to be sure they rode together. So that she could ask, *What became of Garif?* When they'd fought together in Cia's soul, Roha had grabbed something and removed it from Cia's central self. She was sure it was what had become of Garif's essence, much as the Stone of Gelerte was what King Calestri had done with the soul of Lehren Gelerte, the holy man who'd had the strength to stand against him. Well, one of the holy *Nim*, who like Roha embodied both the masculine and feminine and was said to be closest to the All. So close that they didn't have to draw from any but their own inner well of anima to access their powers. *Revered. Holy.* Why then had Lehren Gelerte felt the need to go under the guise of a man within the Church?

But that was a distant thought. The one that plagued Cia was that if the Stone of Gelerte still held power–and it did, the ability to tell truth from falsehood–what did that mean for Garif's soul? Was he still locked in there somewhere, his power distilled? If so, what would it be and how could they be rid of it? If, in fact, Garif's stone was a physical thing that existed outside of herself. Had it been left behind on the battlefield or did Roha still possess it? If the latter, did they dare destroy the stone and risk releasing him? It might return him to the anima, poisoning it in the process. Or he might refuse to move on and possess her once again. She might have destroyed her mental prison, but Garif still had her believing in the bars. She didn't know if she would ever breathe freely again. Or be confident that she was well and truly safe.

At least, not without Roha.

If that was what drew her to the acolyte, it was completely unfair. And so, she kept whatever she was starting to feel to herself. She didn't trust it. Didn't trust herself. Especially not so soon. Too many scars, and none of them healed.

Myrka stood before them all, hands on her hips, eying them as though to take charge. "Ludvin, as the largest of us, it makes sense for you to have your own horse now. Hostill and I can ride together. We're like siblings of the streets."

She looked to Hostill for backup, but Ludvin cut in before he could speak. "I think not. No one's trusting you with the heir."

"But you'll trust me with one of your remaining horses? Sure, makes sense."

Ludvin gave her a narrowed glance. "I doubt you're going anywhere without the prize."

Hostill waved his arms around. "Hello, right here. I have a name. You might remember it. We don't know for sure that I'm anything but a boy who resembles a prince. If that helps overthrow Bloody Bess, I'm all for it. But if you start treating me like a stick-ball, *I'll* steal the last horse and take off on my own. I've been alone before. Cia found me that way and almost got stuck for her troubles."

Cia smiled at the memory. She'd found him in a plague house–his own–hiding in the bedding. He'd come up fighting when she'd thought to hide there as well, knife out, much like Myrka on that mountainside.

"Fine," Ludvin said, voice not hard like Ruggerio's. More tough like worked leather. "How about Roha and Cia, me and Hostill, and Myrka rides free so that she can protect us all with her knives? Everyone's happy, yes?"

Myrka and Hostill grumbled.

Cia didn't say a word, her mouth suddenly dry. She ignored them all and went to the horse she now thought of as her own, going forehead to forehead with him and stroking his neck. She let him know that it was okay for the tall person to mount. That she was sorry they were going out into the cold again so soon, and that he'd once again be overburdened.

Roha waited for a moment before asking, "All clear?" as if ni understood.

When Cia agreed, Roha brushed a gloved hand down the side of the horse's sleek neck in thanks before mounting. The stallion's flesh rippled all the way to his haunches, as though resettling more comfortably. Then he nodded in Cia's hands, and she stepped back.

She accepted Roha's hand to swing herself up behind. With Roha being so much larger, it made sense for nim to ride in front and for Cia to hold on. But despite her calm with the horse, her nerves were on edge, and she didn't know why. Maybe because the previous times she'd sat the stallion she'd been in control. She'd had the reins and been able to see. She didn't like being relegated to the back.

She could hold onto Roha's waist, but it felt wrong. For so long, she'd scrutinized every look, every interaction for anything that might be misinterpreted and reported back to Garif. If she so much as acknowledged a man, she was accused of flirting. If she allowed a servant into the room, even to stoke the fire, she was having an affair. Errands he sent her on, which took an instant longer than he thought they should, proved that she was malingering, possibly plotting. And it was his job to school her. As the handmaiden to the foreign princess who'd married Bloody Bess's eldest brother and allegedly poisoned him, Garif had 'saved' her from being executed with her mistress when he'd married her.

Her life became his to do with as he pleased. It was his pleasure to be sure that she lived it the right way. *His* way. Only no matter how hard she tried, she failed. She was certain it was by design. He desired her punishment more than her perfection.

A wife he could punish and be praised for it was everything he'd wanted. A mageri was a hero of the realm already, but a mageri who took on disciplining a foreign provocateur… Oh, he was *so* good to see to the salvation of the unsalvageable. And if he had to beat the wickedness out of her, well, he was only doing what must be done.

Cia closed her eyes and let her face fall against Roha's broad back, but her forehead no sooner hit, Roha's warmth and solidity momentarily comforting, than she tensed up again. She couldn't do this, use someone else this way.

"Tell me about the seven spirits," Roha said, as though sensing Cia's need for a distraction.

"The seven spirits?" she asked.

"Something Hostill said a while ago, and you shushed him and Ulan. It's been going around in my head for some reason."

"I thought you were unconscious."

"Half-awake, I guess," Roha said with a shrug.

She held Roha as lightly as she could, remembering that ni didn't like to feel constricted, but even a warhorse was only so broad, and try as she might, there was only room to press against Roha's back, legs spooned together, toasty from the heat of the horse. There was no way for it to be anything but intimate. Yet it hadn't felt so riding with Ulan.

"It seems odd that Hostill and I would know the seven spirits, but not you, an acolyte of the Church," Cia said, trying and failing to make space between them. "Perhaps it is a Frizenzian thing and came from Hostill's mother?"

Roha coughed out a laugh. "I am of the Church no longer. They would no more have me back at this stage than I would have them. But yes, we should ask Hostill about his mother. If she was Frizenzian, even partially, that might ease our way with your people."

Cia chewed on that a moment. They would certainly welcome Hostill far more than they would welcome her. But that would come. For now, Roha had asked something she could answer.

"There's a prayer in our church for the seven spirits," she said.

Blessed are the truthful, they shine a pure light

Blessed are the peaceful, for the blanket of night
Blessed are the merry, they lighten the load
Blessed are the generous, who give without being owed
Blessed are the nurturers, encouraging fragile blooms
Blessed are the protectors, fighting when danger looms
Blessed are the healers, without them we are bent
Grant we be these spirits
To renew the power we're leant.

"It sounds better in the archaic."

"Oh, the virtues," Roha said. "We've learned the same thing. Just a bit differently."

"Shht!" Myrka said suddenly.

"But–" Cia started.

"Shht," Ludvin said as well.

Everyone hushed then. Ludvin, at the front of the party, held up a hand and closed it into a fist to show that he was stopping so the horses wouldn't plow into each other. He turned in his seat, scouring the path they'd traveled.

Even Cia, with no woodcraft at all, could sense it. Something was off. But it wasn't a tremor of the earth or cracking branches indicating pursuit. It was the opposite, the utter cessation of sound.

Into that silence, a great howling suddenly arose, along with the sound of tree limbs shaking, cracking, dumping their burdens of snow. It was impossible to pinpoint the source, as the canopy all around them was shuddering. The sound was eerie, unearthly. Like demented spirits come to drag them away.

As though Garif had been twisted into something even worse and more powerful. As though he wasn't dead and gone and Cia would have to fight him yet again. Terror rose in her throat, choking her as he'd always liked to do. Cia's vision started to darken, the world to shift.

"Gnashers!" Ludvin cried, pointing at something up in the canopy.

Cia realized she had her face crushed against Roha's back and was holding onto nim as though to a lifeline. As though she needed a tether or someone to fight for her. She tried to get her jagged breathing in hand, swallowing down the terror, gasping in new air, blinking away the darkness. She was *not* going to be a liability to Roha. She would *not* count on anyone to take her in hand as Garif had done.

She would never again cede control.

She forced herself to ease away from Roha, to look where Ludvin pointed, but all she could see was movement up in the canopy.

Until something dropped on Ludvin from above, limbs out with webbing between, obscuring the sky.

Cia screamed as a weight landed on her, spikes suddenly piercing into her shoulder. She clawed at the beast, craned her neck to see what had hit her. She came face to face with a creature of nightmare. The tiny eyes were all dark voids mashed together with the nose, nostrils flaring wide. The lower half of the face was given over to a hideous maw filled with needle-like teeth. Everything was terrifyingly disproportionate.

She tore her nails prying desperately at the beast, but its claws were as piercing as its teeth. It hung onto her in a grotesque parody of a babe clinging to its mother, kneading her back while it suckled her blood.

Roha pulled nes weapons to slash at the beast, but two more of the monsters were already leaping for nim, and ni slashed at them in the air. Cia's suckling shifted enough to snap her out of her terror and reach for a weapon of her own. She still had the dagger she'd stolen on the battlefield. Now to get to it before the beast made its way to her neck. The blood loss would kill her soon enough; if it tore out her throat–

Cia grasped the hilt of the dagger and dragged it loose from her makeshift belt. She plunged it into the beast before it could anticipate her. The blade went straight through the beast's back, grinding against bone that diverted it only slightly.

It was so stunned it opened those shockingly large jaws, all smeared with her blood and pieces of meat–pieces of *her*–stuck on its needle-teeth.

It fell away, and the roaring in her ears she hadn't realized was there dropped with it, but now she could hear the howling, the gnashing, the *feeding* going on around her.

Gnashers, Ludvin had called them.

A mageri construct. They had to be. Nothing like this existed in her native Frizenze.

Roha had fought one off and was at work on another, but Ludvin, Myrka, and Hostill had all been forced from their horses. Myrka raced to stand shoulder to shoulder with Ludvin, putting the boy behind them. But Hostill rushed out from their protection with his dagger, ready to fight his own battles.

Cia ran to help, leaving Roha to fend for nimself. She had seen the acolyte fight. More than likely, she would only get in Roha's way. Not that she'd do much for the others, but at least she could be one more barrier to the Gnashers on their way to Hostill. Maybe she could give the others time to get him to safety. The boy must be the intended target. Bess would want him slain to assure her succession. Hostill had saved Cia's life once. She had to return the favor.

A Gnasher leapt out of nowhere, landing on Hostill, claws digging deeply into his shoulders. He gave a pained yelp, and something inside Cia answered. She unleashed a battle cry as she flew at the creature, dagger out. The Gnasher's tail, made up of sharp quills and twitching like a tree-rat's, went suddenly dead still, as though it sensed her rushing in from behind, and then coiled in tightly. She froze as well, instincts telling her something very bad was about to happen. When the tail shot out again, she grabbed at her cape, whipping it around herself as though it were armor. The Gnasher's tail-pins shot out like needles, burying themselves in her cloak, piercing her hands where she'd failed to protect them. Hot spikes of agony shot through her, as though the quills were coated in fire.

She kept the cloak up over her face, only her eyes and burning hands free, and rushed the creature as the tail coiled again, desperate to get there before it could fire a second time. The Gnashers next to it were coiling as well. All she could do was throw herself at them. She barreled into the first before it could fire, burying her dagger in the back of the one on Hostill as her cloak slipped and another turned on her.

That Gnasher leapt before she could yank her dagger free, and she had to pull her arm back without it to block the creature before it could latch on. Too late, its claws sank into the fabric around her waist, tearing through into the flesh of her stomach, climbing her body so that it could finish her off.

Hostill gave a great cry and sliced his knife into the Gnasher's side. It howled, that same maddening howl they'd made in the trees, and lashed out with a claw before falling. It missed its target by a hair's breadth.

"Thank you," Cia said, breathless.

Ludvin suddenly choked and gurgled, and they both turned to him as a new howl arose. A Gnasher, red with his blood, looked them straight in the eyes as it finished its triumphant ululation, and leapt from Ludvin to Myrka, still fighting off her own Gnasher. Hostill dove straight in with knife blazing.

Cia spared a moment to search out Roha, shocked that ni hadn't joined them, only to see nes throw off the Gnasher ni'd been fighting, which howled as it fell back, but only to the neck of Roha's horse, where it caught itself and dug in with its needle-like nails. The horse was so terrified that it reared, flinging its neck around, wild to be rid of its baggage. Both Roha and the Gnasher were thrown.

Then Myrka screamed, and Cia's head snapped back, catching a Gnasher's quills full in the side of her face. The Gnasher fell under Myrka's knife, but Cia was falling as well, the pain from the quills dropping her to her knees.

Then abruptly, the Gnashers were fading to nothing, and they were surrounded by men with swords aimed to cut them down—except for Ludvin, who lay crumpled on the ground.

"Finish them here?" asked one man with his sword to Cia's throat, the tip already drawing blood in case it was his only chance.

Another man stepped up. She could hear it in the readjustment of those around, but she couldn't shift to look with a blade at her throat.

"The man, yes. He's half dead already, but take his head. The queen demands proof."

Queen?

"Kill the girl as well. But the boy pretender and the mageri-killer only if necessary. The queen might like to execute them publicly to quash any other conspiracies."

The blade at her throat swung away, and Cia cried out, but another voice carried over hers, calling, "Wait!"

A woman's voice. Yet the Crown didn't take women as soldiers. It must be one of Bloody Bess's newly made mageri, impressed into her service and trained speedily on pain of death.

"Not that one," she said, indicating Myrka.

Through eyes clenched in pain, Cia could see the man who was giving the orders. His face was carved of stone, the kind with flecks of different colors throughout. "If the girl's old enough to fight, she's old enough to die."

The woman glared, and Cia committed her to memory. The mageri woman's beautiful dark skin and steel-gray hair were woven with a wide streak of winter-white. Her face was younger than her hair suggested.

"If I was ever sentimental, this world burned it out of me," the mageri said. "I sense power, and the queen will want it. If you kill the girl, you'll have to answer for that. Your choice."

***

Hostill

Hostill's gaze shot to Myrka.

She had power? Myrka would happily kill anyone with even the suggestion of mageri magic. She had joined the Restoration to snuff it out. There was no chance she was mageri...unless somehow she didn't know of it. Or her zealotry was all an act. But he didn't believe anyone could act *that* well for that long. Unless she was some sort of spy.

He'd always thought that Myrka was a strange name. It didn't sound quite Jucari. But if she was a spy for somewhere else, wouldn't the first thing be to blend in? Choose as common a Jucari name as possible? The absolute venom of the glare she turned on the woman did nothing to convince him she wasn't a spy for Frizenze or Galitrüd or elsewhere. Markens or Arbilan or...

Then the rage burned away, and as it slipped, Myrka's true face came through. Something feral and afraid, like a wild beast cornered and refusing to be caged. She threw herself at the nearest sword. The swordman flinched it away, but not fast enough to avoid scoring damage on her. Blood shot from her throat, showering the swordsman in a red spray. The soldier behind Myrka quickly reversed the grip on his sword and thumped the pommel down on the back of her head. She fell on her face on the frozen ground, completely unconscious.

Surely only that.

Hostill fought to get to her, but other soldiers were grabbing him, yanking his arms behind his back and binding him again, as he'd been bound when Bloody Bess's army had captured them. When he and the other Restoration captives were marched to the battlefield for sacrifice. He was almost numb for himself, but then they pulled Cia to her feet and he saw the quills quivering in her face….

"At least help her," he said, appealing to the woman, though she hadn't sounded any less hard than the man.

She stepped forward and picked a quill from Cia's cheek with no warning, no soothing words. Then another. After the third, Cia no longer flinched. Her entire face locked in a rictus of pain. Another soldier yanked her arms behind her back, careless of the quills piercing her hands, and Cia gasped, collapsing with the pain. The soldier's grip was all that held her upright.

"Pluck them," the mageri woman ordered, throwing the quills she'd pulled to the ground, where they disappeared into the snow. The wounded side of Cia's face was red and raw, like butchered meat, and it was swelling over one eye. She bled so badly from her shoulder, the flesh torn and terrible, that he wondered whether she'd make it to Bloody Bess's public execution or whether blood loss or snow-death would take her first.

"If you don't do better than that, she'll die before Bess gets her," Hostill said, making it matter of fact. He addressed the man this time, since he seemed to be in charge. If Hostill appealed to the mageri woman, she'd still have to get his approval and having her on his side might be worse than not, because the soldier would see her interven-

tion as sentimentality rather than logic. He'd seen it in the Restoration–men rejecting good ideas just because they came from women
and approving the same ideas when they came from men, as though
they made sudden sense. As they sometimes didn't hear Hostill,
because he was 'a mere child'. The man turned from him.

"If she's determined to die, she'll certainly do so. We'll do our best
for her back at the camp, if she makes it that far."

He gave a nod to the swordsman standing over Ludvin, moaning
on the ground, and Hostill made himself watch as the blade fell. He
wouldn't spare himself the sight of Ludvin's sacrifice or the feeling of
rage building within him. He would take it, and he would use it.
Somehow.

But he left the contents of his stomach behind in the snow, the
soldiers' laughter ringing in his ears, and his vows to end them and
Bloody Bess's reign echoing in his heart.

CHAPTER SEVEN

Roha

Roha's horse screamed and bucked in pain. The reins ripped through nes left hand, taking skin with them as ni tried to hold on. Ni started sliding, thrashing for them with one hand while trying to keep hold of nes dagger with the other, but it was no use. Roha had swung too wide and lost nes balance. Ni braced to hit the ground, and the impact blasted nes vision away. Out and back and away again, as nes head bounced, nes ankle caught in the stirrups.

The stallion, free of his rider's restraining hand, took off in a frenzy, racing headlong into the trees, taking Roha with him. Ni cried out as ni was dragged along the ground, twigs and stones tearing at nes clothes, rucking them up until they could tear at skin as well as fabric. Roha's loose hair caught as well, ripping out of nes head and left behind on roots that refused to give way. Roha's tunic filled with enough filth and frost it was a wonder ni didn't halt the horse's wild run from the added weight. At least they left a large enough trail for the others to track.

Assuming they survived their own battle.

Roha twisted this way and that, but it was futile. Ni couldn't see, couldn't gather enough strength to bend in half to disentangle nimself. Nes wrist hit something hard, like a stone. Pain and numbness shot through nes hand and it spasmed open, dropping nes knife.

Vision was only flashes of light and dark seen through hanks of hair and spots of purple-hot pain. And when Roha thought the world had stopped, still it seemed to go on. Spinning. Roha stretched out nes fingers as though ni could hold it in place but couldn't feel them. Had no concept of whether ni was still tethered to the horse or had fallen away. Ni reached inside to center nimself and found only a void. Was this how it was now? Had Roha given too much on the battlefield? Was ni empty for the rest of time?

There was a sting on nes face, and Roha's eyes fluttered open. Light again, and shadows that wanted to form a face. But not one ni recognized. Not a friend. If it was one of Bess's people, they could very well wait.

Another slap, harder this time, meaning business. Roha let a sound escape.

"Good, you're awake," a man's voice. "Quickly now, what's happening and who's set on you. How many?"

Roha tried again. *Look deeply within. So deeply.* Think of the spring-fed stream feeding the well. It would refill. It always had. If ni could… *There.* It was only a trickle, the least little bit, but it was not nothing. Ni wanted to use it now to sharpen nes mind, nes vision, so ni wouldn't be at such a disadvantage, but Roha didn't dare empty nimself out completely lest ni fall unconscious again. Ni needed to nurture what ni had, not strip it like the mageri did the land.

Roha forced nes eyes open. "Water," ni said.

Because ni needed it, but also because of the time it would give nim. To recover. To study the man and anyone with him. It would tell Roha something–whether he provided or withheld the water. Ni still couldn't feel nes limbs. Would they obey nim? Had ni broken something irreparable in the tumble from the horse?

Roha ordered nes head to move, and was so relieved when it did, ni closed nes eyes again, only to flash them open when something cold was pressed to nes lips. A horn. With water cool enough to freeze nim from the inside out. But it was welcome all the same. At least with hydration, ni could take nes time in dying. Long enough to send help back for Cia and the others.

"There now, I asked a question?" he said, as though the kindness entitled him to an answer.

The man was now inches from Roha's face, which made it easier to focus, but only on one feature at a time. He was close enough that ni might bite off his nose if ni moved fast enough. An odd thought, but it was difficult to think of any Frizenzian as a friend since the Blood War, regardless of why they were here now. Ni's hand clenched for the dagger ni no longer held.

"Don't know how many," Roha said, trying for a civil tone. "But they're Bloody Bess's men and mageri."

The man's cold blue eyes bored into nim. He was hard, bitten, the lines on his face scoured into him like crags into rocks, through the weathering winds of time. "Why? Why are they after you? Why here, why now?"

Because of who we are. But it wasn't Roha's story to tell. And ni didn't know who ni was speaking with, highwayman or patrol guarding the now-disputed border. Either might run toward the battle with some chance of saving nes people. But the former would hold Hostill for ransom to Jucar if they discovered his identity. From the questions, Roha pinned nes hopes on the latter, and hoped nes wits were enough intact to know what ni was doing.

"Because they can. We must stop them now or they will be unstoppable."

The man didn't like that and chewed his lip, though they were bloodless beneath his onslaught. Ni could almost see him thinking that it might be best to let the Jucari finish the fight amongst themselves, let them take each other out and he could mop up what remained.

"The boy," Roha hazarded. *"The boy matters.* Save him."

"The boy?"

But ni'd said all ni would, and it wasn't an act for Roha to fall silent and let nes head drop to the side, eyes closing again. But ni listened intently—for discussion, orders, the rustling and jangling and restlessness that said he was taking off, following nes instruction.

Had Roha heard horses, others with him? Yes, wickering, blowing, shifting from foot to foot. And ni noticed ni was no longer attached to nes own horse, thank the spirits. They had at least cut nim free, likely so they could take the horse for themselves.

"Your orders?" came a younger voice. Not well trained, not in patience, anyway. Not Roha's problem.

No doubt Roha's interrogator wanted more information, but there wasn't time for thorough questioning. Either Bloody Bess's soldiers would come looking for the one who got away or these men would move out to catch her people before they could rejoin the bulk of her forces. Time was of the essence.

"Move out," the man called.

"And this one?"

"Leave him to the forest."

Roha's eyes fluttered open again. The cragged man had moved out of nes sight, leaving nim a vision of a younger man glancing quickly off into the wood before exchanging a look full of meaning ni couldn't plumb. The other made a sign before turning away, tapping a hand to his heart and his head, then kissing his fingers and releasing them to the sky—a spiritu anu, a prayer for nes spirit.

They expected Roha to die. But there was something more. At least one man felt Roha's soul would need help reaching the All. Because ni was an enemy combatant or because of something sinister in the woods?

And what would it mean to join with the spirits of Frizenze rather than nes home spirits? Were they all truly one? If so, what would the bad blood between the countries do to the All?

As though in answer, a chill swept through Roha's body, bowing nes up from the ground from toes to shoulders like a bolt of lightning arching through nim. Ni came down juttering, shivering, rocking with a cold so deep Roha thought ni would die, only to be swept up in the next instant by a heat so raging ni might burn to ash. Nes body leaked oily essence that slicked nes clothes, sweated so profusely the next chill racked nim that much harder.

Roha tried to call out, but nes teeth were clacking like castanets. Ni pried nes eyes open between shakes to beg the men for aid with looks if not words, but they were gone as though they'd never been. For how long? Or had they been hallucinations? Had Roha sent them to save nes people or had they been a delusion.

Roha rocked to the side, nes muscles contracted into a fetal position to protect some illusory core of warmth, of self. Hot and cold and sick rolled over nim. Ni wretched and wretched, muscles working painfully to turn Roha inside out, but perhaps it had already been accomplished. Ni was empty, and all the spasms did nothing more than send pain shooting through nim.

The earth quaked again. Or was it nim? Ni tried to quiet the shakes, to feel the land, to listen. Ni opened an eye but saw only shadows gathered about, the darkness of the winter wood or of consciousness drifting. But now ni felt as though there was something in the wood with nim.

Watching. Waiting.

Did ni hear something? Roha clamped down on nes chattering teeth, which only made them tremble all the harder, so ni let them go, gave them space from each other, tried, *tried* to even nes breathing. Maybe ni could slow it. Sleep until nes body healed itself or went peacefully to the All. Ni hoped peacefully. There had been enough turmoil. If Roha just managed to save the others, ni would at least consider nes life well spent.

A sound came from within the forest then and stopped Roha's breath entirely. Of something…being dragged along the forest floor? Or something very, very large slithering toward nim, the sound increasing as it came. Twigs breaking, leaves crunching, something large slapping against trunks, small debris being swiped from the path.

Roha braced nimself for what was to come.

Not peacefully, then.

CHAPTER EIGHT

Cia

Cia struggled to raise her head from her painful position flung over her captor's horse, his fingers digging into her backside to hold her in place. She searched as well as she could for Roha, wanting to see nim, assure herself that ni was well, and yet hoping that she wouldn't. If she found Roha, it would mean that ni too had been captured. But if she didn't… It could mean anything. Maybe Roha had ridden off after Ruggerio and Ulan to get help, though Cia couldn't imagine Roha would abandon them in the midst of a fight. Maybe a Gnasher had spooked their horse, and it had taken off with nim into the woods.

The possibilities crowded in on her as she failed to find Roha, each more dire than the last. The Gnashers had dragged Roha off to finish nim. Ni lay dead, ended like Ludvin by one of Bloody Bess's men…

Cia let her head fall back against the sweat-ripened blanket over the horse's heaving side. Hostill was loaded as she was. Myrka had been bandaged and was propped against the mageri who'd insisted on saving her life and had now become responsible for it. But Myrka was nearly devoid of color, as though she'd bled it all out, and Cia wasn't so certain she would make the journey back.

All for nothing. All of this, and they were being dragged back to Jucar.

Then there was a cry, and a shout, and suddenly steel on steel. The fingers that had been burrowing into her flesh released as the soldier reached for his blade.

They were under attack. Whether it was Roha, wildly outnumbered, or help from some other direction, Cia was not going to be caught powerless. While the soldier was busy controlling his horse with one hand, his blade in the other, Cia tried to throw her weight forward or back to launch herself off the horse, but it was no good. She was too well balanced. If her hands were loose...but they had bound them up. She wished desperately she had power she could use to snap her bonds and get free. That was the very danger of power, though, the temptation to throw it around simply because one had a need. Strip the land because it was convenient.

She could barely see anything with her head hung, hair streaming all around. To lift her head again would be to stick her neck out.

Then suddenly, the saddle shifted, the soldier going down and dragging so hard he was taking everything else with him, her included, and Cia was falling fast and uncontrolled to the ground. She cried out as she fell, watching the horse's hooves flashing. One caught her a glancing blow to the side of her head, kicking off to springboard his flight. Her sight went out and back. Images blurred, multiplied, trailed behind as she shook her head trying to right it. Watching other hooves flashing, feet stomping, and then... A body crashed, and she was staring into the cold, dead eyes of a Crownsman.

Her vision focused on those filmed eyes, as though the winter had breathed a haze over them that was there to stay. She had to force her gaze away to look down the length of his body, seeking something to aid her before she was trampled to death. His blade or a smaller piece. A knife. A dagger. Something she could back up against and cut herself free. Then, if she could grip a blade, she could join the fight. Maybe she could keep from becoming a captive again.

There, a blade. His hand still wrapped around it. For all the good it had done him. And yet, somehow it must avail her all. Well, she had come this far, hadn't she? Escaped her mageri husband. Thwarted a queen. Run off with a royal heir.

She only had to slither across the space like a serpent. Her Gnasher wounds lit up again in pain as she stretched and contracted, inching herself toward the blade, rucking up more dirt and damage on the way.

Die sooner or later, this was no time to be precious.

There it was, the blade. As soon as she reached it, she turned her back. She hadn't given a thought to how it would be to manipulate a full-sized blade between bound hands to cut them apart. She sliced one hand before her bonds, and the blood made everything worse. Slippery. Slower. Impossible. Until…wringing her hands trying to get them and the blade into position, she felt the rope slip the least bit. Maybe she'd bled just enough or the slickness had created some give, but instead of sawing at flesh as much as rope, she concentrated on slipping her hands through.

When it didn't seem it would be enough, she gave up trying to save her skin. Hands already throbbing from the damage left by the Gnasher's quills, she worked frantically, pulling and tearing until some of herself came off with her bonds. Finally, her hands broke through, and there she was on the ground. Snot and tears freezing to her face, but free once more.

Cia got quickly to a squat, low but on her feet, ready to dash away. A man fell to her right, almost on top of her, and she flinched aside before thinking to search him for a weapon, hoping her damaged hands would hold it, only to come face to face with the pointed end of a sword. She followed it up to the face of the man holding it and fell back in shock.

"Froeder?"

"Lady Cia?"

"But——"

"Stay down." And he was gone, whirling to swing that sword at one of Bloody Bess's men who was coming for him.

But she didn't stay down. She tore through the downed soldier's gear for a blade to defend herself or help Froeder, now that she knew who she was fighting for. Froeder had been one of her Uncle Frazier's men. Always and ever. How he came to be *here*, in the Ehdon Woods, she had no idea, but that was for later. If they survived.

The Crownsman's sword was too heavy with her hands torn up as they were, but she found two daggers, deadly and unornamented. They were agony to grip. It took every bit of strength she possessed to keep from flinching away from the pain, but she rose with a dagger in each hand as a Crown guard came in hot, catching her looting his comrade. She slid in cold, one dagger twisting into the pit of his arm as he raised his sword to plunge into her. She sidestepped his erupting blood and now-chaotic sword swing and rose to her full height, slashing the other dagger across his throat to be sure he wouldn't rise again.

When she whirled for more targets, she found the fight over. Or nearly so. Crown red and black littered the mountain path. She searched for Hostill and found him breathing heavily, a dagger in his hand. She tried to see whether it was bloodied but couldn't tell from her vantage. He caught her gaze and flipped her a salute with the dagger, going for a smile as well, but it pulled down almost instantly, tainted by the death all about them. Yes, they'd been Bloody Bess's men–or women, in the case of her mageri–but they'd been someone's lover, father, child, friend. They'd had lives. Until Bloody Bess had used them up.

Now Cia's hands did spasm open, the strength gone out of them, and the daggers dropped to the ground. She wished the pain had gone with them, but it throbbed and spiked, competing with the pain of the Gnasher's bites so that her entire body was on fire, burning away the cold numbness that had allowed her to keep going.

But it might be nothing to the fire in her Uncle Frazier's eyes. Or, more accurately, *Lord* Frazier, the man striding up to her, ignoring all others, including the bodies of the fallen he stepped over on his way.

"So, the traitor returns," he said, sour-mouthed, as though he smelled and tasted something most foul.

She felt it like a dagger to the heart. He'd hit her in the horror where she lived, but she refused to flinch away. Once she realized her marriage to Garif wouldn't allow her to plead for mercy on her queen's behalf, she'd called herself that and worse. *Traitor* because she hadn't been put to death with Queen Inaya when the Jucari had accused her of poisoning King Cyril. *Coward* because she'd allowed herself to be 'saved' by marrying an enemy mageri. Her lord and master and jailer and tormentor. She'd taken his abuse as fit punishment for deserting her queen. Until she couldn't anymore. Until it was her life or his.

Hostill hissed and tried to rush forward. "You have no idea what she went through–"

"Yes," Cia said, cutting him off, because only her pain would satisfy them. Him, anyway. Uncle Frazier had always been a hard man, and looking at him, she had no reason to believe that had changed.

His hair had gone bone white. His face was carved into the permanent scowl she remembered, eyes small and hard, more like the marbles her cousins played with than windows into any sort of soul.

"I will explain, but first, what are you doing out here?" Cia asked.

Lord Frazier's face flushed red. "Did you think they would keep us at court when they found you had married a mageri of the people who'd killed your queen? At least we were only banished to the farthest reaches. We retained our titles, if little else. Your parents–"

Cia's heart squeezed, that pain far outpacing all the rest. She hadn't heard from them since the war.

"What of them?" she asked, her fear seeping into her voice despite her attempt to keep it from him.

"You must know. We sent word," Uncle Frazier said, voice like the cutting wind.

"I don't. Garif…my husband…"

Frazier's lips became as thin as newly-formed ice at the word. Could he not hear the hatred wrapped up in the name? The disgust in the title?

"He kept everything from me," she finished. "I was never allowed to think of home."

Nothing about him softened. "My sister died of a broken heart." He said it as though he meant each word to be a dagger plunging into her heart, the last two words especially piercing.

"Mount up," he told his people. "We'll sort this out back at camp.

I've got her," he said to one of his men who stepped into view, and it took Cia a moment to reconcile that the man before her was her cousin Stansil, no longer reed-thin, unable to eat enough to keep up with his growing body. "You take the boy."

Hostill began to protest again, but no one listened.

"And the girl?"

Myrka was still hung over her horse, which another of Lord Frazier's men now held. Her head hadn't lifted during the whole exchange.

"Everyone comes until we learn who they are and why they were so important that Princess Bessory sent men to retrieve them."

Cia would explain. It was the plan, after all. But not here and not now. For now, her uncle got into position on his horse and she was made to mount in front of him, where he could trap her in. Her head hung down, and the rest wanted to follow, leaning as far away from him as she could get, though in truth, she was less heavy in body than in spirit. Her parents were dead. She'd known she would likely never see them again when she'd followed her then-princess to Jucar. But it was unbearable to be the cause of their downfall, to have contributed to their deaths. Cia had lived through so much; this one more weight to her soul might just break her.

Cia tried to turn her attention to the living, praying that Myrka still clung to life. She had once been strong in her faith, before coming to serve in a land that felt alien to her own. Still, she'd worked to live a good life, up until her princess had been put to death, and she'd harbored a secret wish that those who had a hand in it would meet fitting fates.

Then came Garif... She couldn't pray to the All for any of the things she harbored in her heart for him, so she cut herself off from the anima entirely. But still, she couldn't help reaching out to the spirits of her native land to pray for this girl. For Bloody Bess to fail and for Hostill to take her place and then rule wisely, as young as he was. Maybe succeeding in this mission would make up in some small way for the ones she had failed.

"Tell me," Uncle Frazier growled in Cia's ear, yanking her back toward him to make himself heard.

Now she knew why Frazier had demanded to take her himself—so he could interrogate her along the journey as she was propped uncomfortably against him with no escape. The fact that she'd already planned to reveal their purpose should make it easier, but the way he asked, all she wanted to do was resist.

"I'd prefer to tell it directly to King Avize."

"I'm certain you would, but no Jucari trash is getting anywhere near the monarch without telling me your purpose. Your friend said something about the boy—"

"My friend? What friend?"

Roha? Was Roha alive then? Did they have nim?

"One of your kind was dragged off into the woods by his horse. In very bad shape, and muttering about an attack and a boy who must be saved. We'd already seen animals fleeing and knew something was afoot. We were headed to investigate. That's why we were sent to the border, to guard against incursions. All but exiled because of you."

"But where is ni *now?*" Cia asked.

She tried to turn in the saddle so that she could see her uncle's face, watch for falsehoods, but her neck wouldn't crane so far.

"I will trade you the information," he bit off each word as though it tasted foul.

"Fine. You go first." He wouldn't respect her for giving in so easily, but there would be no way to win his respect, and it wasn't something she valued, certainly not with Roha's life in the balance.

"Still where we left him. We couldn't bring a wounded man with us into battle. If he's there on our way back through, and if you're cooperative, perhaps we can bring him along."

Cia's chest refused to expand for her next breath. Dragged by nes horse. Left for dead. It might be too late for Roha. But Cia refused to accept that. She would take her uncle's bargain. Though puffed up at his continued misidentification of Roha, she would not correct him. With Roha's white garments, he likely saw Roha as the acolyte ni had been and assumed ni was a Churchman. She didn't know how her uncle felt about the Nim personally, but she could guess. They were treated no better in Frizenze than Jucar.

But Roha had already told him something about Hostill, which meant that Cia would be giving away no secrets here.

"The boy you rescued is one of Prince Jannik's bastards, a contender for the Jucari throne," she said. "Bloody Bess wants him dead, and so we want him alive. We've come to Frizenze to bring him to King Avize. We want to put him on the throne to build peace between the two nations. Stop the war before it destroys both."

Lord Frazier fell back in his saddle, as though her words had dealt him a shock.

"And your friends?" he asked, the aggression draining from his voice, at least for now.

"The one you left in the woods defeated Bloody Bess on the battlefield, and the one who lies dying threw herself on a sword rather than be taken alive. We are not your enemies."

"Faster!" Frazier barked suddenly, making her cringe away. "Make for the one we left."

But when they arrived, there was no one there. No sign of Roha or the bay.

No sign of anyone or anything except a large swath of vegetation smashed down by something monstrous passing that way.

Frazier's men exchanged looks, but despite Cia and Hostill asking and asking, no one would tell them what it meant.

CHAPTER NINE

Bess

No, no, no, no. "For All's sake, NO!" Bloody Bess shouted.

The room went silent. Even Vedik, thrashing and throwing himself about as though he could tear himself straight out of her head since she'd taken his life, *even he* went still as her shout bounced around, reverberating in her brain through all the bruised, painful places. She hadn't drunk down another life since her return to the palace because Vedik was so out of control. He hurled himself against her mental walls as though his body was a solid battering ram, and it rocked her to her core. Her head quaked, and if she could have dropped him into an oubliette inside her head, she'd gladly have done so. But it was not so easy or safe to create a forgetting place inside one's own mind.

She could not give in. This was her domain. *Hers.* She would not cede any portion of it.

She opened her eyes to see everyone in the council room staring at her, except for Regent Strego, as he was behind her now in all ways. A Queen had no need to be kept. But he could still serve.

She met each gaze with all the fury Vedik built up in her. "No, I say, to your bickering and timidity. I do not *ask* whether we need the Church with us at this moment, I'm *telling* you that they have been against us from the start. The Church, like the Restoration, has said that anima is sacred. That all comes from and should be returned to the collective spirit and should not be tampered with. They have become more subtle in their teachings since their conflict with King Calestri." She would not say *Mad* King Calestri, as did so many. "More subversive. But they have not rooted out zealotry in their midst. They have, in fact, harbored rebels like Roha, one of the leaders of the Restoration. The Church will be with us because *we will become the Church.*"

The furor that broke out rivaled that in her head.

"The people will rebel!"

"Don't you remember what happened when Mad King Calestri–"

"She's just like him–"

It didn't matter that the angrier she got, the more she might prove their point. She couldn't accept their open defiance. Their discounting of her. Telling her what she could and could not do. She drew from the very depths of herself, pulled from the power she'd stolen from Vedik. *"Silence!"*

Wind swept through the room like a backhand, slamming all the men down against their seats so that they clung to avoid sliding to the floor. The remnants of the power beat against her face, and she drank it in, smiling with the wind in her teeth.

The councilmen looked up from their cowering places and knew fear. She was no longer hiding. She was their Queen and so much more, and they knew it now for a certainty. The question was what they would do about it. How soon before they tried to kill or imprison her and install one of their own?

Maybe she'd made a mistake in ordering the boy killed. Maybe she should have ordered him brought back. Before she'd declared herself Queen, they'd been pressuring her to marry, to birth heirs. As much as it disgusted her, maybe she should bring the boy back, do what she'd done with Strego all of these years, and draw a bit of blood, a bit of his essential essence and replace it with her will so that he became an extension of her the way a wife was supposed to be an extension of her husband. Then, when he was old enough, she could marry him, solidifying the V'Alban line and their hold on the Crown. Keeping it all within the family as had been done in the days before they'd been concerned with breeding out sorcery.

Queen Bessory flung a hand toward the page now plastered against the door. "Bring General Bowstan and let Grygof know that Strego and I desire his attendance presently." She gave a piercing look to each of the councilmen in the room and shot arrowed glances at the guards at the door, though they wouldn't acknowledge the hits by making eye contact. "I have noted all who attend me here. If word of these plans reaches beyond this room, if the Church is warned in any way, *I will know.* I will take my reparations from your hides. There will be no mercy for betrayal. Now, you are dismissed."

She flapped her hands at her councilmen as she would to shoo a flock of birds blocking her path.

There was a chorus of objections. Of "but surelys". *But surely you'll want our input. But surely there is much yet to determine.* But she let the pressure of her will mount again, the wind tousle their hair–in truth, all the power she could muster–and they instantly began to move for the doors.

The Queen sank into the seat at the head of the table and motioned Strego down beside her. His right hand rested on the table, and she reached for it, sliding her sharpened nails as easily as swords into their sheaths beneath his skin, sighing as she felt the vitality flowing through his veins. Less than it used to be, a stream rather than the raging river it was when she'd first tapped into him. She drew from that stream, meaning to take just a sip. Her eyes closed. It was so crisp, cool, pure. So unlike the raging, churning torrent of her own energy. Another sip. A hand fell over hers, and she realized it was Strego's other hand. She was shocked by how dry it was. How clawed and aged, almost like a talon.

Her eyes snapped open, and she gazed into his, blue bleached into ice. Once her father's friend, his contemporary, the only courtier to ever think to slip the young princess treats…or to think of her at all. And she stopped. Her nails withdrew. She couldn't tell from the look in his eyes, the look on his face, whether he knew what she did. But he must, mustn't he? Did he allow it for the love he once bore her father? Because she'd worked her will on him and he had no other choice? Did it matter?

And why did she let him live now that she no longer needed a Regent? Could she afford the sheer sentimentality?

"You may go too," she said, unsure of herself. Her voice was gruff, and she found she didn't mean the thought that had flitted through her mind. For whatever reason, she still wanted Strego around. Someone to see what she accomplished? Maybe she somehow still wanted her father's love and approval, and Strego was his stand-in. It was pathetic and sad. It was weak.

"But that means I may stay."

Her reaction was more relief than rage, which created its own anger.

She narrowed her eyes and would have blasted him if she could. "I suppose if you are here, you are one less person out there, plotting against me."

"Never, my Queen."

He sounded so sincere that it ratcheted up her anger another few notches. She had hurt him and was sure he would hurt her. Only the matter of when and under what conditions was in question. It was the way of the world. Certainly the way of the V'Albans. That he would pretend otherwise–

But then Bowstan was announced, and she had another thought. Perhaps he hadn't stayed out of loyalty, but to gain more information with which to betray her. *That* she could understand in the same way she understood keeping friends close and enemies closer. With that logic, she could justify keeping watch on him as well.

Kylia

Her husband was a fool.

Lady Kylia Ruland walked the ramparts, looking toward All Souls

Church as though she could see what was happening there. The sacrilege.

Bloody Bess had sent off Crownsmen within a turn of the glass from dismissing her council. Before anyone could possibly get word out, even if they weren't too cowardly to do so in the face of her threat. They should have seized the queen at that very moment. All those grown men against one small woman. Kylia'd heard what had happened on the battlefield, but it was beyond belief. There was no way the queen's head could have burst apart in such a manner and have come back together so prettily. The tale must have grown and grown in the telling. And still the Councilmen feared.

Enough to betray their faith.

Kylia hung her head toward the earth and said a spiritu anu, faced into the wind and said another, asked that the collective spirits carry her words where they needed to go.

But she couldn't trust to that. She had a brother in the Church back in her home province of Nerion, and it would only be a matter of time before Bloody Bess's orders reached that far. She had to send a warning. Bess had already threatened her men with what would happen if word got out. Kylia had no doubt that any messages leaving the palace would be read. But she had to do *something*. Perhaps she could get away to the village for shopping and send a message there, but what if it was intercepted along the way? Or she was caught sending it or…

Would she be a fearful fool like her husband?

She didn't yet know.

And so she walked the ramparts. And prayed to the All. And waited for an answer to whisper to her on the wind.

CHAPTER TEN

Roha

Roha hadn't been aware of the sounds of the forest until they fell silent. The whole wood seemed to hold its breath with nim.

Except for whatever was coming, too large to move silently. Roha could only gauge it by the sound of its body brushing the trees it didn't clear, the cracking of branches and twigs beneath its weight. It must have realized that it no longer had other sounds for cover, because it began to move faster, terrifyingly fast. Roha's heart pounded, but ni could do nothing but brace for what might come.

Roha's breath escaped in great gasps as it came into sight, towering over nim. Ni couldn't even take it in all at once, but nes eyes followed from head to coiled tail. The head, chest, and arms were those of a man, his body so dark he might be from Markens, like nes mother, or live outside, sun-darkened, but surely not this far into winter, and not in these woods. His hair fell like stacked slate, his eyes golden-green with a black slitted pupil like a serpent's, which matched the rest of him, as from his torso down, he was gray and black in a diamond pattern. A serpent-man. Ni had never even heard of such a creature.

No wonder the Frizenzians who had left Roha behind had warded themselves with a spiritu. Ni started one for nimself.

When he opened his mouth, Roha's spiritu became more fervent. He had fangs. Not especially long, but long enough to pierce, and if his serpent side was venomous, ni was in most desperate danger.

"Are you for the Sacrima?" he asked in accented Frizenzian, a slight sibilance to the last word, an emphasis that made it clear Roha's answer was important. Very possibly life and death.

"The Sacrima?" ni returned, hoping for some hint as to which response would keep nim alive.

He snarled, showing fangs, and Roha would have flinched back if ni could move.

"Do you want to go to the anima?" he asked. "If so, I will leave you to do so."

"No. No, please." Was ni that badly off? For certain, Roha was not yet ready to die. Not until ni'd seen Bloody Bess defeated. If the Sacrima could save nim, then there was only one answer to give.

The snake-man nodded and bent forward. Roha closed nes eyes, a primal fear screaming through nim, heightened by the behavior of the Frizenzians who'd run off. Or his fangs. Or just the unknown.

Ni was scooped up in his arms, every pain in nes body flaring to brutal, blazing life. Ni cried out, and the snake-man gentled his hold, cursing softly, as though he didn't know his own strength. Ni was cradled against a chest that was all muscle, but also surprisingly soft, as though the texture of the scales had somehow translated to skin. Roha couldn't hold nes head up without a tremendous effort, so ni let it fall to his shoulder, let nes eyes close, and tried not to think about what awaited at the Sacrima. The local men were afraid of him, of it, which probably meant there was something to fear, but ni was in no condition to fight, and so, ni allowed the snake-man's consideration to lull nim into unconsciousness.

Roha jolted with the whack delivered by Lehren Sefner. Years of practice had allowed him to aim his blow exactly where he had the last one, heightening the pain and thus, the punishment. Roha knew well enough to catch the gasp behind nes teeth rather than be struck again for weakness.

Roha wondered if nes robes were stuck to nes back with the drawn blood, sunken into nes flesh. If, rather than falling into nes pallet tonight, ni'd have to spend time carefully peeling away nes garments so ni wouldn't lose more skin, rinsing them out, despite the pain, careful to wash away every bit of blood and probably failing, being struck again tomorrow for soiled garments that were the Lehren's fault. He could have told nes that ni'd gotten it wrong. Loaded the null with too much or too little power, creating a dip or a surge that might cause unstable wards on the church grounds they were meant to protect. Ni would have worked to get it right. But he preferred to beat his lessons into the children, feeling that they took better that way.

And yet the Nim were supposed to be sacred to the Church. Closer to the anima. Perhaps in being one step closer to death at the Lehren's hands.

None of them had been given more than a cup of water and crust of bread to start the day, so at least Roha had no moisture to well in nes eyes at the pain. And ni would never risk speaking out.

Not then.

Not then, but I can speak now. Roha was still foggy, caught up in the dreamspace, but ni knew there was something important…that ni had to wake up.

But instead, ni drifted, and ni was back again in another place, another time.

"They know, Aja. We can't keep the babe any longer." The basso rumble of nes father's voice vibrated against Roha's breastbone. To him, ni was always 'the babe,' even though ni hadn't been so for some time.

"Then we'll go to Markens, to my people. Roha will be accepted there. Trained. Even revered. We've talked about this. We knew we couldn't keep the secret forever–"

"You've talked about it." This time when the timbre of his voice set up a vibration, it was at a different frequency. Even then ni could feel the anima

like a well or a stream. This disturbance was so strong it felt like a wave might rise to drag nim under. "My business, which supports us, is here. Our lives are here."

"Our lives? Is Roha not our life? If our child is not here, then my life is nothing."

"And what of me?" nes father asked in what ni thought of as the danger-voice.

"You're asking me to choose between you and Roha! You're saying that what I want is nothing. My people, my country, our child is nothing. Only your livelihood, your place in the world—that is your concern."

They had put Roha out—told nes to go and play hoop-stick or something, but ni hadn't gone anywhere. The children ni'd played with until recently now vanished as soon as they spotted nim. Ever since they'd all fallen into the fountain and Misra Jens had fished them out and everyone had stared when nes clothes had plastered against nim. They didn't stare at anyone else. Just Roha.

Ni was so embarrassed, ni ran home, doing nes best to cover nimself. It was only then nes mother explained why she'd always told Roha to cover up, not to talk about certain things with the other children. Only then, when ni wouldn't take 'We don't discuss such things' for an answer, did ni finally learn that ni was Nim and to think of nimself in those terms. Nes parents had always deflected, presenting nim as a girl, the easier to cover nim up and for 'her' to fit in.

Now, Roha had run round to the back of their house so that no one could wonder what ni was up to. Ni had an ear mashed against the garden door. Ma and Da were at the back of the house as well so that no one would hear their raised voices. But Roha heard them just fine. Tears didn't hurt Roha's hearing. They only blurred nes vision.

They wanted to send nim away? But why? What had ni done?

Well, Da wanted to be rid of nim. And they lived in his house, in his country, where people spoke his language and looked at nes mother as though they were good to treat her with the little respect they did. It was a small thing, but something Roha noticed, that people acted differently toward nes father than nes mother. Da they treated like everyone else—hailing, laughing, chatting. Her mother, darker, foreign, speaking their language with her

Markensian accent...her they watched, holding themselves back, never smiling with their teeth. Following dealings with her, they waited, as though for thanks that they had behaved like people ought. Once they realized that Roha was theirs, that Ma and Da were together, there was somewhat of a warming and the pointed attempt to pretend they'd been warm all along.

Now Roha felt as though ni'd failed them. Ni was supposed to bind them. Instead, ni was another reason for their village to reject Ma. Ni had become a liability. A shame. Just by existing.

Roha shuddered, and nes breath stuttered out of nim. Nes teeth cut into nes lower lip as ni struggled to keep nes tears silent.

"Roha will be revered here," he said. As if that was it. The last word. "The Church honors the Nim. They will make a place. What kind of life will the child have with us? Never a family, never finding acceptance. In the village there will be prejudice, bullying. Already people shy away. Roha needs a place to belong, to be useful."

"Yes, that's what every child needs. Not to be loved, but to be useful," her mother spat.

"It's the best thing for Roha." her father insisted.

Roha didn't hear what nes mother said next. There were footsteps moving away, and then ni heard nes mother bang out of the front door. She called Roha's name, but Roha didn't want to be found. Ni went to an overgrown part of the garden, curled into a ball, and tried to find that deep, quiet place within nimself.

Tears ran down Roha's face. From within the dream, ni called to nimself to wake. Ni never hugged nes father again. When ni was sent to the Church, ni clung to nes mother, who embraced nim back, their tears mingling until they were both sodden and salted, but in the end, nes mother gave Roha up as well. She elicited a promise from the Churchmen to take good care of her child and not try to make Roha other than ni was. That she would be able to visit. The Churchman agreed that she could after a year, but she had to understand that Roha was no longer hers. Ni belonged to the Church now.

Belonged. Like a possession. Something that could be given or received. Bartered or bought.

But the visit never came. Nes mother was dead inside of a year. Ni really did belong to the Church then, ni supposed.

Something ripped at nes hair. Roha thought at first it was in the dream, but it was too painful, pulling nes eyes open. Ni blinked, just the low light of the room suddenly too much, even filtered through the tears that had come in dreams. But when ni looked around, ni found…no one. Nothing. And then, a pluck at nes lashes. A twist of nes nose. An icy hand at nes throat.

Roha was confused to find nimself on a pallet of some sort in an otherwise empty room. The last thing ni remembered was nes horse dragging nim through the forest, and then… The memory of the snake-man crashed in. But where on earth had he brought Roha? Some haunted place full of bosewights? Was ni was meant as a sacrifice, a lodestone to draw the spirits?

The hand to Roha's throat started to close, and there was another weight on nes chest, as though something squatted there. Ni couldn't see or hear them—that was Ulan's power—but they were real enough, strong enough to kill. How had so many spirits come to be gathered in this place? Unruly, unsettled, and apart from the anima?

Now was not the time for such questions, and there wouldn't be time later if ni didn't act. There was no choice but to dip into nes power. Roha reached for it. The well hadn't yet refilled, so depleted was ni from the battle of the Dobrens Valley. But ni found more than before, a small rise in the level, along with the branch ni'd forged to Cia, still present and part of nim, despite running nearly dry. It made Roha feel less alone, though the knowledge pierced nim that Cia might not feel the same. Not after Garif. She wouldn't like the idea that Roha had a way into her mind.

But having and using were two different things. Roha's wild ride through the forest must have given nim some serious bumps on the head. Focus was a difficult thing, especially as the phantom hand tightened and the onslaught continued—of tugs and tweaks, blows and bites.

Roha closed nes eyes, the better to concentrate, and drew on that bit of anima at the center of nimself. Ni said the words of the spell ni'd unleashed on the battlefield to return the spirits to the anima, though these were darker and more dangerous. This area of land might be one people would avoid ever after.

Roha hit an instant barrier, and while the spirits stopped–stunned or blown momentarily apart–they didn't go to the land.

Ni couldn't reach the anima here. Wherever ni was, it was warded like Church land.

Ni didn't bother opening nes eyes again. Church land. To come all this way to be caught again…

Without the distraction of the spirits pinching and pulling, Roha became aware of voices in another room or perhaps a corridor, maybe the reason for the dream-memory of overhearing nes parents talking of sending nim away. But Roha couldn't make out these words. And nes power was so depleted that simply expanding nes chest to breathe sent fresh agony through nim.

Until the voices rose. "–what ni did drained the wards…must have felt it…can't afford."

There was a hushing then, a hissing, and Roha thought instantly of the creature who'd come for nim in the forest. Saved nim, most likely. But if they hadn't wanted nim dead before, they might now. What was it they couldn't afford? Why would anyone hide away in the woods, surrounding themselves with bosewights cut off from the anima, denying their land that replenishment? It seemed a punitive life and slow death. Was this some sort of prison then, and the snake-man one of the jailors, perhaps pursuing an escapee when he'd stumbled upon Roha? But then why bring nim back? And why, if Frizenze had such fierce creatures, had they never turned them on the Jucari?

But then, Roha realized that ni didn't know for certain that he was fierce at all, but was judging on his serpent half and what ni knew of the horrifying mageri creations called Sinuways, huge serpents the Frizenzian mageri combined with their poisons to create constructs that ravaged the Jucari forces. For all Roha knew, the snake-man had taken mercy on nim and brought nim back against orders, sparking the discussion ni overheard. Understandable, if this place was any sort of secret and they found out Roha was Jucari.

Ni might never leave here alive. Roha's Frizenzian would never pass a rudimentary conversation, and if they'd heard nim muttering the words of nes spell….

If Roha's door opened quietly, the footsteps that approached were almost silent, but at least they *were* footsteps. Roha slitted nes eyes open to watch, and they focused better this time. Well enough, anyway, to see a figure in a gray robe and cowl stop by a brazier lit low on the wall of a small cell. They twisted a key, and the brazier flared a bit brighter, illuminating a cheek wrinkled like parchment that had yet to be ironed smooth before the shadows of the hood swallowed the face once again. When the figure stopped by Roha's cot, they shifted so that the light fell fully on nes face while they remained backlit.

"Why are you here?" came the voice from within the cowl. "What did you do to our wards?"

There was no playing that ni was asleep then. Roha blinked nes eyes fully open and tried to sit, but the movement alerted the pain to flare to full life, and nausea blinded nim. It would be quite clear that Roha was completely at their mercy.

"I–I'm here because your…creature…brought me here. As for your wards, ask what your spirits have done to me!" It was out of nes mouth before ni could call it back. Ni'd remembered to speak the language of the land but was hardly fluent. Most of what ni'd learned had been for Church delegations, when there was still converse between their two lands. Ni hoped they would attribute the halting nature to nes recent unconsciousness and shock of being confronted immediately upon waking.

Perhaps if Roha had gone with dissembling, ni could have played into that, but instinct had put nim on the offensive, even though the Church had taught nim what came of demanding things, of not going along. The switch had fallen on Roha frequently at the sanctuary where Nim children were sent to learn duty, doctrine, and the *proper* uses of their powers. Nim were the stewards of the land. It was the entire point of their existence, Lehren Madrone said in that way that was like a switch striking; and the reason that they couldn't marry or bear children was so that they'd not be distracted from their true purpose.

"Our *creature*, as you call him, has a name. It is Reynal. He is a man, like any other, though twisted by the stolen spirit of the land mixed with venom from one of its beings. He was bitten by a Sinuway and somehow survived, though with unprecedented effect. That's all you need to know. You will treat him with respect. Should you survive, he will have saved your life."

"Then it's in question?"

"We are in a precarious place, and you've hurt us immeasurably. I'd like to think it was unintentional, but I don't have the luxury of like and dislike. If your answers to my inquiries are satisfactory, we'll see to your wounds. If not, you'll become one of the spirits you dread. As you've seen, there's no chance here of reaching the anima."

Ni tried to see into the shadows of the cowl, but it was no good, and the voice gave nothing away. It was neither angry nor threatening, raised nor ominously silent, yet had the sharpness of a dagger's edge to it, and Roha didn't doubt for an instant that the...acolyte?... would make good on the threats. Churchmen wore white robes rather than gray, but perhaps this was a splinter sect?

But why? lingered on nes tongue. Why would anyone sequester themselves with bosewights who would nip and tear and wear away at people the way Garif had done to Cia?

"I did nothing but try to settle the angry spirits, return them to the land. I had no idea there were wards until I encountered them. I wasn't trying to break your rules or cause trouble."

"You weren't sent to bring them down?"

"I–what?"

The figure stared hard. Roha couldn't see the eyes, but there was a quality to the unwavering silence that said ni was being evaluated. And then Roha thought ni felt something more. A flare or a tingle or a...something. But amidst the lightning strikes of pain still branching throughout nim, ni couldn't be sure.

It stopped when the cowled figure turned on their heel, leaving Roha to wonder whether ni'd sensed it at all. Finally, ni could lose nimself in the loop of shooting agony, throbbing pain, and more agony. Each new strike had Roha hissing and tensing, but that only caused other aches, and before long, nes body was too exhausted to do more than go limp and ride everything out.

It seemed forever until someone came and held something to Roha's lips. Roha fought it, spitting out the first few drops, unsure whether ni'd been found wanting and poison chosen as a good way to get rid of a troublesome guest. But eventually some of the potion slipped past nes efforts, and incrementally, nes body began to relax and nes mind to retreat.

CHAPTER ELEVEN

Cia

It was a long ride, and she must have passed out, exhausted, somewhere along it, because she jarred awake when they finally stopped. A stabbing pain shot through her temple, and a throbbing began behind her eyes. When Uncle Frazier lifted her from the horse, she swayed and the world tilted.

Her uncle pulled a knife from his belt, and she thought he was going to kill her right there, show his fealty by bringing back the traitor's head. It might even get him into good graces back at the palace, especially bringing with him Hostill, the contender to the Jucari throne, but he merely cut her bonds, which allowed her to hold onto the horse with her good hand until she felt her legs would support her. Eventually, the world stopped trying to throw her off, and while images grew sharper, the pain grew no duller.

He removed his supplies from the horse and wiped him down, and another man, as spare as a pauper's candle and just as sweet-smelling, came to take the horse, transferring Cia back to Uncle Frazier. The man walked away with the horse into a building that leaned significantly to the right, as though it could fall over at any instant. She supposed it must be the barn and hoped it would stand as long as they needed it to.

The cabin itself looked like it had been through a fire, especially along one side. It had been boarded over, but the work had either been shoddily done, or wood had been scarce, because the blackened areas still showed between the slats.

Once inside, Cia didn't have eyes for anything but Myrka, crumpled into a heap against a wall like refuse. Completely unmoving.

Cia went to her instantly, checked first to be sure she was even still breathing. "You have to see to her!" she said, turning on her uncle.

"I don't *have* to do anything," Frazier said, his voice thick with calculation. "But you tell me what's going on, hold nothing back, and I'll have my medic look to you both."

Whatever Myrka may or may not be, she'd cut herself rather than go with the queen's men and would have given her life protecting Hostill. Cia couldn't let her die if there was anything she could do about it. She knew all about making mistakes. Myrka should be allowed to live to regret them.

Because that was kinder? Cia couldn't honestly say that it was, but if she hadn't lived to regret her choices then she wouldn't be here to help Hostill and the others. To fight Bloody Bess, who so desperately needed fighting. She would hold onto that. She couldn't help choices she had made, but she could make up for them.

Cia nodded tightly.

"Rapha, see if the girl is savable," Frazier commanded, before Cia could change her mind.

Frazier strode to her and gripped her elbow, lifting her from her place by Myrka's side. Cia immediately flinched, but he tightened until he was bruising her, almost to the bone. Her flesh crawled, as though desperate to escape him. Her blood rose, and with it a red haze, the feeling of being trapped. Of wanting out by any means necessary.

She planted her feet, and when he shifted for a better grip, Cia ripped her way out of his reach and whirled to face him down, breathing hard. Fighting to regain herself.

Frazier stared back at her with that careful, pitying, superior look people used on those they deemed mad or simple.

"*What?* I want only to talk to you." He held his hands up to show that he had no weapons, and her reaction was completely unjustified. Beyond reason. He was the reasonable one here, his tone said. "If you'll just come with me."

Cia took a deep breath. Then another. It didn't work. She closed her eyes, opened them again immediately, unhappy with the darkness. Took a third breath and experimentally lowered her hands. "Then ask," she ground out. "If you want me somewhere, you ask."

He looked like he'd rather swallow bees, but he choked down his initial response and said through gritted teeth, "Will you walk with me?"

She nodded but gestured for him to precede her. Everyone was watching them. She could feel them. Judging, applying labels. The traitor. The madwoman. They would make decisions accordingly, without her input, because she couldn't be trusted. She'd lived with the enemy, allowed his touch. And yet she couldn't tolerate her uncle's hand on her arm. Never mind that it had been rough and unwelcome. That it was *because* of Garif, the reminder of him. Or that when she'd slept with the enemy, it was with one eye open, pain in her heart, aches everywhere, sometimes breaks and bruises, until she'd learned to wall away her reactions as best she could rather than incur more punishment. Never mind that she'd killed the bastard. Forget the battles she'd fought since. They'd only see what they believed to be there–the damage, the betrayal.

She couldn't even dispute them. She carried the scars of the first and knew herself guilty of the second. How could her family forgive the sins she held against herself?

"You said you would tell me everything about why you've come." Uncle Frazier said, his voice like a lash. The instinct to apologize, to step back was strong, but that had never saved her from Garif in one of his moods.

She faced him down instead. If she showed weakness, it would be exploited. *That* much she knew. "It certainly wasn't that I expected to be welcomed with open arms. Or even to be welcomed for myself.

There is much I could tell you, but let me begin with what you will hear. My friend told you that the boy is important, and I've explained that he's a claimant to the Jucari throne."

He sneered, his lip on one side going higher than the other. Now that she noticed it, there was a scar that prevented the full lift. Healed, but not old enough to be quite faded. Likely gained in the Blood War. "Friends among the Jucari. They falsely accused your princess. Killed her and her babe. And you *married* one. You lived in their castle. Ate their food. Served their princess. What do they call her? Ah, yes–Bloody Bess. She doesn't just invade and kill our people; we hear she kills even her own. Sucks their blood. Performs dark rites. And still you serve her."

The red fog that had been creeping over Cia's vision flashed over. She let out something between a screech and a battle cry, and the next thing she knew, her cousin Stansil was tearing her off her uncle. She'd laid hands on the hilt of Frazier's blade and had it half drawn from his sheath. She didn't know what she meant to do with it. Or maybe part of her did know. Rage raced through her body like an out-of-control horse, shucking the grasping groomsmen of will and reason. But it galloped past her, and she was left shaky and staring into the shocked gaze of her uncle as the haze subsided.

She shook off the hands grasping at her, but for the one set that wouldn't let go. She wanted to glare, but there was more fear than anger remaining. What might she have done if Stansil hadn't been quick enough to hold her back? He was the one who still dared hold her, giving her a carefully mild look, as though afraid to set off another bout of murderous madness. Was that what it had been? Would she really have run her uncle through? Surely her instinct was to do only what needed to be done, to show that she wouldn't be browbeaten again. That it was a dangerous proposition. It would only become deadly if he made it so, as Garif had.

Had it been only that? Maybe he reminded her too much of Garif. Enough to set her off.

Or maybe Garif had left something of himself behind. That was more truly terrifying than what she might do on her own. Whatever had happened, her uncle wasn't nearly as wise as his son.

"You viper!" Frazier raised a hand to her.

Cries rose up around the room, and Cia flinched away instinctively, her eyes shut tight. Stansil dropped his hold so that she could escape the path of his father's onrushing wrath. But it would be too late.

Uncle Frazier gave a startled cry, and she snapped her eyes open again to see Frazier's wrist caught by another huge hand, Froeder's, as the man slipped himself between them.

"We're all tired, and tempers are still hot," Froeder said, releasing Uncle Frazier's hand. "But I'd just as soon we not start fighting each other."

She couldn't see what look passed between Froeder and his lord. Meaningful perhaps. Promising retribution almost certainly. But after a moment storm-heavy with the possibility of violence, Frazier stepped back and turned away, seething visibly.

He took in deep breaths, possibly counting them to himself to keep calm, before he said, "Tomorrow we ride for the palace. I'll let the king decide what to do with you. I wash my hands."

He strode for the door of the cabin, yanked it open and stomped off, letting it close with a bang behind him, cutting off the wintery air that rushed in.

All the rage, all the pain and upset and fear, not for herself but for what she might have done, sent Cia to the floor with her back against the wall. The earthen floor was cold beneath her, but she didn't care.

Stansil came around her side and knelt, waiting for her to look up at him before asking, loudly enough that they could be overheard, "You didn't serve them, did you?"

Everyone was listening after the show they'd put on. There was that quality to the silence. No one so much as shifted if it could be helped. He asked so that all would hear her answer, and she realized that though he'd called her traitor in the woods, Stansil was not his father. He'd observed and maybe even understood something of what he saw.

"No, never. How could I? As your father said, they killed my princess," she said, the pain always fresh. "I hated them for what they did, and they never trusted me any more than you do. But no people are all good or all bad. Those I have with me are against Bloody Bess. We have information, and we have, perhaps, the means to challenge her. We have brought that with us to Frizenze. You can value it or you can abuse it, imprison it. That is the *Jucari* way. If you are no better than they, then we have chosen poorly. Jucar and Frizenze were allies once. We don't intend to give anyone a tool against the other. We want to *end* the war, not help you fight it."

"Well, we have you now, either way," he said meaningfully, glancing at the men around the cabin. "Father will learn your secrets."

It could have been a threat or a warning. She didn't know Stansil-the-man well enough to say, but she was hardly in a position to forget that they were essentially prisoners.

CHAPTER TWELVE

Ulan

Ulan groaned as someone shook her awake, rocking her body back and forth, calling her name. She grunted, and tried to burrow back into her bed, the outside air too cold to think of rising, but realized it stank of horse and sweat and worse… death.

Her head jolted up, bringing her torso with it, and she realized she'd been lying upon the cooling body of their horse. He hadn't made it. Too much of his anima had been drawn away, and he'd used up everything that remained in his flight.

Ruggerio caught her arms before she could collapse back down and began helping her to rise before she was ready. Before she'd even come to terms with what was.

"Ulan," he called again. "Ulan, look at me. Just at me."

She met his gaze, steadier than he was–she could feel the tremor through his hands–and held it.

"I thought we were dead," she whispered, cold air stealing her breath. "I thought it was over."

Saying it out loud like that, she felt robbed. She could have gone on to oblivion, joining the All that now held her Dazia. Instead, she'd risen to weakness and pain, pins seeming to prick her all over as feeling flooded too sharply back into her limbs.

"Not yet," Ruggerio said, "but we will be soon if we don't start moving. Come."

It was move or die, and Ruggerio wasn't giving her a choice.

"How are you so recovered?" Ulan asked.

He gave her a look of scorn, as though she should know better. Which she did. Really, she did, but she was angry that he'd not just let her slip away. Maybe at some point she'd be grateful, but now was not that time.

He got them moving, both of them shaking like leaves in a gale. They leaned on each other when it suited, dropped the support when it was more likely to bring the other to the ground, and made very slow going. But they'd come further in their flight than Ulan would have thought. In only half a day they were back in the Dobrens Valley, close enough to see the bodies left behind in the army's retreat. And the few motley-clad figures moving among them.

Scavengers.

Ulan hissed in a breath, but Ruggerio said quietly into her ear, "We can follow them back to a village."

"But–"

"Do you have another idea?" he asked, as out of patience as she'd been with him. They were both cold, weak, tired and hungry. Not in their best humors.

She only shook her head.

The looters avoided each other mostly, once scrabbling over a body two had descended on at once which must have had something worth fighting over. A weapon, a keepsake…

But as the sun lowered in the sky, they began to withdraw. Ruggerio and Ulan in their wake. They shadowed them to a small village. Not more than twenty or so houses, unless there were more spread further afield.

There was not even a public house where they could buy a hot meal with the money Ruggerio carried with him. But with night almost fully fallen, they chose a house a touch larger than its fellows with a gaggle of chickens running around the fenced yard and a small barn that from the scent housed other animals and trudged up the dirt path to knock at the door. The man of the house answered them with an oversized stick carved into a cudgel.

His eyes widened at the sight of strangers, then narrowed distrustfully.

"Yes?" he asked, filling the entire doorway with his frame, radiating menace.

"My cousin and I need a meal and a place to stay, transport on the morrow. We were hoping, good sir, that you might be willing to accommodate–" Ruggerio began.

The man stepped forward before he could finish, raising his cudgel. "Be off with ye. We've got nothing to spare and nothing to steal."

"We can pay," Ruggerio said hurriedly, hand going to his purse.

It was a risk. The man could knock them out and take the money with no one the wiser. Kill them or beat them and dump them elsewhere with no one to care, because they were strangers and, even if they were to be believed, had brought it upon themselves by coming up on the man uninvited. He could say, if anyone ever suspected him, that he'd been afraid for his life or what little he had, which if taken might mean the same thing.

But instead, some of the tension seeped out of the man, and he said gruffly, "Let me see it."

Ruggerio pulled the purse from a slit within his tunic where he wore it around his waist and took a coin from within rather than open the mouth of it and reveal how much he had. He showed the coin to the man, and he grunted.

"We've little enough to spare, but this will buy you a meal and a bed in our croft. You'll be gone on the morrow, though, yes? Even for coin, what we have can't stretch another day."

"I promise you, sir, we're as anxious to move on as you're to have us go."

The man called to his wife, only to find her behind him, shrinking back but listening to all that was going on.

"Not in the house, lest they kill us in our sleep," she insisted. She was a small-framed woman with circles around her eyes darker than her dirt-brown hair. "You can bring them a plate in the barn. I'll ready it," she said.

Ruggerio took another coin from his purse. "If you've got blankets or warmer clothing that might be spared as well…"

The glance she shared with her husband was full of such deep and sudden pain that Ulan knew what the woman would say before she said it. "I suppose that Verdis won't be needing…" the words cut off in a bitten-back sob, and the man put a hand on his wife's shoulder.

"I'll show you the croft and where you might wash-up. You smell of death. I won't ask where you've been or what's befallen you, but I also won't hesitate to use this–" he let the heavy end of the cudgel fall into his hand meaningfully, "–if you think to overstay your welcome or come on us in the night."

Ulan barely had the strength to make the climb into the croft. Ruggerio stayed below, waiting for their meal to arrive so that he could bear it up. He had to jostle her awake again to get her to eat and drink. She could hardly manage much of that either, but it was enough that when they awoke the next day to the enthusiastic crow of a rooster, she felt somewhat better. A moth-eaten blanket had been thrown over her and she might have fallen back to sleep had not the farmer himself called up to them that it was time for them to turn out.

There was a small caravan leaving for the royal city that morning, led by his cousin and joinable for a fee, if they were so inclined. If not or they were going in another direction, they were on their own.

***

Ulan's heart leapt in her chest at the sight of the smoke rising dark and dire above the walls of the royal city as the small caravan they walked beside approached the walls. The gates they headed for belched out a small grouping that moved too slowly to be fleeing the conflagration, but Ulan soon realized it was because they had no horses to speed the travel. Men strained to pull a wagon weighed down, it seemed, with all they owned. Beside it walked a woman and another man, and as their caravan rode up on the group, it was clear that the woman was not only with child, but had another swaddled against her chest, and that the boy at her side must be nearly full-grown, though still with the narrow shoulders of youth. Even Bloody Bess wouldn't be so heartless as to drag him into her war for another summer, maybe two.

"What news?" Kosk, their lead rider, called, his voice pitched to carry. "Is the city afire?"

The family had stopped at Kosk's approach, the men dropping the barrow, all hands going to weapons, prepared to defend it. Kosk held up his own hands to show that he meant no harm, the rest of their caravan followed his lead.

The men didn't stand down. The boy looked back toward the city, dividing his attention, unsure from which direction danger would come, but certain that it was coming.

"Parts of it are," one man allowed. "The queen is burning the plague houses. She's–"

The other man coughed hard, trying to shut him up. He continued undaunted. "If yer her men, I wouldn't keep her waiting."

"And if we aren't?" Kosk asked.

"Yer able-bodied, aren't ya? Ya still have your horses. Yer her men or soon will be. Ye've only to look to the parapets to see what happens elsewise."

He turned and picked up his side of the wagon again. When he straightened, Ulan realized that was more a figure of speech. His back was bent, and carrying the wagon would be agony for him before long. The boy moved to help the others lift the end of the barrow, only to have his hands slip straight through the handles. The older man never even noticed his attempt.

Ulan gasped. Ruggerio sent her a side-eyed warning.

"What is it?" he asked so quietly only she could hear.

But she shook her head. There was no point asking how many men he counted. She knew very well she was the only one who could see the boy. The fact that it was mid-day and that the boy was as clear as folk was terrifying. The bosewight shouldn't be any more than a suggestion. A flicker. He should need more power to appear so strongly, which meant that either the ghosts were getting stronger or she was. She'd always been able to see anima when it was worked. Then Dazia's death had brought the ghosts. Had Ulan come so close to merging with the anima herself when she was near death at Bloody Bess's hand that it was now as present to her as Ruggerio? As Kosk? As the woman and the life she carried?

If so, how would she ever know whether she was facing the living or the dead? She wanted to chase after the ghost, to ask him, but he wouldn't have any answers for her.

Hooves thundered from the gates. They'd been outside them long enough, and if they weren't coming inside, then those inside were coming for *them*.

Ulan clutched at Ruggerio's arm the way Sophie had once clutched at hers at the battle where Dazia's father had fallen, and she swore she could *feel* Ruggerio's entire body posture change. She'd seen it before, watched him shake himself out and become long and languid, like a cat stretching in the sun rather than his usual still, lizard-like self, looking as though he'd fit in nicely with stone and could very well have been carved from it. She'd seen him disappear when they'd met up in a marketplace, sometimes between one stride and the next, but she'd never before felt him collapse in on himself. He took the hand clutching at him and clutched it back, curving around it, his own chest going nearly concave. He shook his hair into his face like feathers and vultured his neck out, giving his back a curve and himself a frailty that he didn't possess.

"You there! Halt where you are in the name of the queen." A guard called, as though they weren't already frozen in their tracks.

None of them moved. In counterpoint to them, Kosk sat straighter in his saddle, as though to prove that he had no fear, nothing to hide, but his ragged breath gave him away. He saved it rather than call out a response.

Two horsemen rode up. Only two for a caravan of five, but there were others watching from the gate, including archers from the ramparts, and one man in mageri robes with a floor-length beard blowing in the breeze, the teeth of his enemies braided into it chattering as though they could still feel the chill. It was part of the mageris' intimidation that they kept something of their enemies with them so they could never go whole to the anima. Yet, the mageri never gave up anything of themselves—not so much as a hair on their heads.

The man fleeing the city had told them to look to the parapets, and her quick glimpse had shown her something impaled atop pikes. *Severed heads.* She flinched away from the sight, casting her gaze downward before the mageri took note of her. She'd once been trussed up on Bloody Bess's war tower; she could be easily recognized. If it was the palace mageri Erdain on the ramparts, there was no persona she and Ruggerio could adopt that he would not see through.

"State your business," the soldier said when he reached them. So far, he was focused on Kosk, the man in front, sitting his horse.

"We're here for trade," Kosk said.

"Come forward." The two horsemen circled behind, and it was clear that it wasn't a suggestion, but an order. They were being herded rather than escorted, and should they cut and run, they would be cut *down.*

Kosk gestured to them as though he was in command, and his brother, Lys, clicked to the horse pulling the wagon and twitched its reins. It jolted forward, jouncing his son's hands away from his weapons, where they could only cause trouble. Ruggerio and Ulan stepped forward as well. It would be futile to run, though Ulan's heart sped as though preparing her for it, rushing blood to all parts of her, overtaxing her system to the point she thought it might burst. In fact, her heart was knocking so hard, it beat against her ribs. She felt she might break one and the crack be heard over the clomp of horses' hooves and rattle of wagon wheels.

The horsemen stopped them just inside the gate, where they were faced by a half-circle of guardsmen, who insisted they would go no further without inspection. Two Crownsmen in V'Alban red and black supervised the city guards on the ground, and more watched from the ramparts above.

Guards stepped to either side of their two horses, Kosk's and the one harnessed to the wagon, to hold them in place.

"Where are you headed?" This from one of the two Crownsmen, the one with half-lidded eyes, as though they only opened entirely in surprise, but he'd seen too much in this world for that to be oft accomplished. His mouth was so cruel, even his black and gray whiskers curled back from it.

"To the Speckled Hound and then to market," Kosk said, slow to respond, obviously hearing the slyness of the question but unable to see where the trap might lie and having no ready answer but the truth.

"All of you?" he asked, his gaze sweeping Ruggerio and Ulan as well, noting their lack of horse or baggage, the much-mended cast-offs that were all anyone in Kosk's village had been willing to sell them.

Ruggerio clutched Ulan hard. Hard enough to elicit a gasp from her and to draw the Guardsmen's gazes to the hand that dented her flesh through layers of fabric rather than to their faces. "I went to fetch my wife home," he growled. "And we're headed there directly."

The Crownsman flicked a gaze up to her face then, as though to see whether she was worth it, as though possession was ever about anything more than power. He dismissed her almost instantly. Hardly worth fetching back, in his mind. However, the other seated soldier licked his lips, as though in anticipation of teaching Ulan the lesson she deserved. *That*, he must have felt, was worth braving a trip in the depths of winter.

But the attention didn't last before it was turned back on the wagon.

"What's in the wagon then? Go on, show us?" he insisted, voice carrying across the cold courtyard.

Ulan didn't look up again to the men on horseback, relieved when their notice passed her by. But the soldiers on the ground didn't wait for the Crownsman's command to take before circling behind the wagon and flipping back a thick blanket to begin the inspection.

Ruggerio's hold shifted but didn't lighten. He no longer held Ulan possessively, but with a hand to one upper arm, squeezing as though to tell her to be ready. She gave an imperceptible nod.

The wagon dipped as the soldier stepped onto it for a better vantage, throwing the blanket back further. He stiffened, hand going immediately for his sword, which sent all the other soldiers going for their weapons.

"Contraband!" he called. "Looters!"

Ruggerio's hand was instantly a claw again, and he pulled Ulan back. She turned as he did and sucked in a breath to keep from being impaled through the breast with a blade. Breathless already, she wasn't sure how long she could hold it, and was afraid to so much as shift backward for fear any movement on her part would inspire it on the soldier's.

"I'm not with them," Ruggerio insisted, his voice small, desperate. "I just hired them for escort. I had no idea. Please, sir…"

The soldier looked up to the ramparts, but everyone there was focused on the cart. Lys and his son, seated on the wagon, weren't in much of a position to fight, but Kosk was trying, flailing about with his blade, getting buffeted from this side and that, swaying in his saddle. Ulan cried out as a blow came from his left side while he was facing away, cleaving so far into his neck that his blood spurted like a fountain.

She cringed from the sight, and the soldier facing them watched with eagle-eyes. "Where is home?" he asked.

"Dockery Lane," Ruggerio answered quickly.

"Go, then. We'll find you if we have need."

"Thank you," Ruggerio said, while Ulan mumbled, "Spirits bless," thinking no such thing.

They went while everyone was caught up in the killing. Ulan wept silently. She'd seen men cut down on the battlefield, but never like this. Kosk and his family were just trying to earn enough to survive. Perhaps they'd looted the battlefield, but what harm had they done? Taken objects that would have been buried by time. Things versus lives—how did that balance? How did these soldiers sleep at night?

She thought again of Reynal, her lost love. A soldier as well. Would he have followed such orders? She couldn't believe it. Not as gentle as he'd been. The tears continued silently on, flowing harder now. For Reynal and Dazia. Kosk and…

"We didn't even know him," Ruggerio said, side-eying her tears.

They had put enough twists and turns between them and the Crownsmen that Ulan felt safe to stop in her tracks. To glare Ruggerio down, burning in her grief and anger.

"You don't have to *know* people to care. For their lives to matter. He died for nothing. Trinkets! He died getting us here. And what of Lys and his boy? If they survive, they'll go to some prison, maybe become Bloody Bess's next sacrifices, all because they came to market. If you don't understand that, if you don't get that people matter, what are you even doing here? It seems like you and Bloody Bess would make a merry murderous team."

"Should we have died to save them? What of our mission then? We would have been discovered and dead ourselves. Do you think Bloody Bess would risk letting us live a second time?

Ulan had no answer for that. Maybe they couldn't have saved them, but they should at least have tried. She grew larger and more livid with every inhale until she could contain no more. In the cold, she could see her breath, so hot she seemed to be steaming.

She breathed the chill air back in, half wishing it would penetrate to her heart. If it was encased in ice, she wouldn't hurt so badly.

Enough. Bloody Bess had declared herself queen. People like Kosk were being cut down in the streets. She would fight, and then... She would see what fate had in store for the 'and then.'

When she said nothing, Ruggerio said gently, "I do not see people the way you do. I won't lie and say otherwise. You know better. But I do care about this kingdom. I deserted Princess Bessory because I saw the path she was on and that she would bring about the downfall of Jucar. She must be stopped. Do you remember when we were children and would sometimes play sacchi?"

"And I stopped playing with you because you'd always win?" What did this have to do with anything?

"That was because you'd protect individual pieces. I was looking at the long game. I was willing to make sacrifices to win. You weren't."

Ulan wiped away her tears to blink at him. "Do you think that makes you better?"

"It makes us *different*; that is all. I think that maybe the world needs us both." He turned and started walking again. He'd had his say, and so the discussion was over.

Maybe it was. Ulan thought about it as they walked, sure that things were more complicated than that. Ruggerio was her cousin.

She loved him after a fashion, but she didn't necessarily like him. Not always. Did the world *really* need someone who killed on command, something she had no doubt he'd done for the Crown?

Then a part of her, a very small part that she'd never heard from before, whispered *But what if Bloody Bess was the target? What if someone could take out Bloody Bess right now, before any more harm is done? Wouldn't people's lives be better? Wouldn't the suffering stop?*

She almost stopped in her tracks again. She did stumble and catch herself and go on, but she feared that voice. Was this how Cia had felt having Garif in her head? Had Ulan somehow been possessed? *No!* she shouted internally, sick with herself. She wanted to scour her head like a pot; clean it like she did her pestle after grinding something poisonous.

The Church taught that everyone needed to live out their natural lives, have a chance of turning toward the light and bringing purity to the anima. Anyone could reform, be redeemed. Killing someone was cutting off their chance. Killing someone *evil* was adding that evil to the anima. It was *wrong*. Pure and simple.

And anyone who would set themselves up to decide who should live and who should die was themselves suspect. Putting themselves above the natural order.

No, if the world needed Ruggerio for the big picture, it needed Ulan to counter-balance him and make sure he didn't go too far. He might think he was the power player here, but if power was the poison, she had to be the antidote.

"Where are you leading us?" she asked, catching up to him.

"I have to check for messages. There may be some in the city still brave enough to oppose Bloody Bess. Maybe more so now that she's declared herself queen."

The smoke got worse as they went, the ash falling like snow, until the city was coated in it. Ulan brought her sleeve up over her face as the air itself started to thicken. Though fire was supposed to cleanse, she had the horrible feeling that she was breathing in the dust of the people, maybe the spores of the Rot itself.

She grabbed the edge of Ruggerio's sleeve as smoke became so thick in places she feared she would lose him. Her eyes watered so much she could practically have put the fire out with her tears. When she tried to brush the tears away, she accidentally rubbed new irritants into her eyes. They stung and watered even more fiercely to the point where she couldn't open them more than a slit. Closing them burned just as badly. She needed to wash away the pain, but had nothing for it. And so, she went on, following Ruggerio's lead until he stopped abruptly in front of her, and she crashed into his back.

Ruggerio's spine was ramrod straight. He didn't make a move or a single sound of admonishment. He was like prey frozen in its tracks, hoping not to draw the predator's attack. It was so absolutely unlike Ruggerio that Ulan was instantly on her guard. Slowly and silently, she blinked to clear her vision as best she could and moved to peer out from behind him.

He'd led them around to the front of All Souls, where it became clear why the streets and alleyways they'd traveled had been more and more deserted the closer they'd come. Ulan thought it was the smoke and fire that had driven people away from the area, but that was only part of it. The other was that everyone who hadn't fled was gathered here, where the uncollapsed section of All Souls Church was not yet engulfed by the flames but was playing out a special conflagration all its own.

Perhaps Bloody Bess had hoped the fire would keep onlookers away, or perhaps she didn't care. Her Crownsmen in their red and black that mimicked the flames faced down a crowd of increasingly angry townspeople demanding entrance to the church, demanding to know what was going on, though the most strident were at the back of the gathering rather than at the front with Crownsmen pointing steel at their chests.

Inside, visible through the partially collapsed wall, everything was bathed in a strange red glow, making the Churchmen's white robes look as though they'd been drenched in blood and glinting off the red-gold hair of the central female figure facing them like living flame. The casting of the red light felt premonitory, and Ulan fought down a chill. She didn't want a move to call attention in the face of Ruggerio's stillness.

Bess's hand rose, fell. The Crownsmen moved in on the Churchmen. Ulan had to stand on the tips of her toes to see what was going on, gripping Ruggerio to keep her balance as she watched one being cut from the rest. The Animist, the head of the Church. She'd watched him lead the services every week until Dazia had fallen ill and then simply…fallen. Then she'd stayed home. The bed where Dazia had died her altar, her home her temple, especially once her baby had returned.

The memory of Dazia died away in the face of the harsher scene playing out in the church. The Crownsman grabbing the Animist by his topknot, yanking hard so that his head pulled back, throat exposed so that Ulan imagined she could see his windpipe stand out in harsh relief, a blade held against it.

Bloody Bess said something, and Ulan strained to read her lips, but she was too far away. Whatever she wanted, it was clear the Animist denied her. Even with the blade at his throat, he shook his head clearly enough for all to see. The guard at his neck held his blade steady, but another sank his sword into the Animist's gut for his rebellion. At that, one of Church acolytes surged from the circle where they'd been herded, and a Crown guard leapt like a spark from a fire, catching and piercing him straight through the back. The tip of his sword slid straight out the front of his chest, blade and blood spurting forth. The crowd outside the church swelled forward. There were cries of sacrilege. Of rebellion.

It was a bloodbath.

Three Crownsmen plunged into the crowd, blades flashing recklessly about.

Some tried to overwhelm the Crownsmen with their numbers. Others cried out, turned to flee, ready to run down anyone in their way.

Ulan caught a cloaked figure who was thrown against her and would have fallen except that Ruggerio's solidity halted her downfall.

"Spirits bless," the woman mumbled from the depths of her cloak, and took off like the fire licked at her heels.

Ruggerio hissed at Ulan. "We have to go. Quickly."

As though she needed to be told. She wanted to rush the church herself. Here was Bloody Bess. *Right here.* Within reach. It wasn't enough that she'd declared herself queen. No, she must take down the Animist as well. Perhaps she thought to take his place as supreme spiritualist, or to dismantle the Church entirely. Declare that religion was dead, and hers was the only authority. Everything was only as she claimed it to be. No more and no less. Certainly no different. On pain of death.

But Ruggerio…

She'd already lost sight of him.

No! Was that? She caught a glimpse of him in the chaos of the sweeping smoke and the people running across her vision. She couldn't afford to get tangled in her thoughts and fears, or she might be truly lost. It was a good thing he was tall. Not so tall that he couldn't get lost in a crowd if he'd a mind to, but his movements seemed intentional, as though he was following the woman who'd fallen against her. She could just make out the edge of the cloak as the woman turned down a side street away from the church.

Ulan's breath hitched, and she swallowed smoke, maybe even ash. It went down chalky and wrong, scraping her throat raw as she tried to cough it out, but she stepped up her pace, chasing Ruggerio down, only one or two good turns away from being separated from him. They hadn't had time to come up with a plan to meet up again. She didn't know if he'd go back to any of his old haunts. None were safe. And the house where she'd made a home for Dazia, up against the church's walls… She couldn't bear to think of it up in smoke among the plague houses, and so she didn't. It would always be standing, frozen in time, as she meant to keep Dazia frozen, her little ghost girl with luminous moonlit eyes.

⸻ ◆ ⸻

Ruggerio

There had been no message for Ruggerio on the church's message board announcing prayers and masses, but the message Bloody Bess had sent, which she'd meant for all to see, was clear enough. The Church was no longer sacred or sovereign unto itself. The light that had bathed everything the color of blood must have been the Stone of Gelerte warning of betrayal, as though to make things crystal clear.

Ruggerio knew that the princess-now-queen would destroy Jucar. He just hadn't thought she would do it so quickly. Or so directly turn against her own subjects. Burning people out of their homes. Killing or imprisoning Churchmen and taking over holy places, not that he believed in the sacred versus profane, but the people did, and of such things were rebellions made. They already had a rebellion formed in Jucar, and this would drive up recruitment.

The problem with the Restoration was that they were limited by their imagination. They envisioned a world where they could win against Bloody Bess and her mageri with physical weapons alone, without tapping into the magical. Using only half the tools at their disposal doomed them before the fight even started.

There must be a better way. He and Ulan and the others only had to find it.

Lady Kylia might be their way in. Somehow. The fact that she was out here, hiding within her cloak and rushing away lest she be seen... it meant something, and Ruggerio intended to find out what.

She stopped in front of a storefront, and Ruggerio vanished into the shadows, turning to be sure that Ulan did the same. Sure enough, she hid as well, and he motioned for her to stay as he crept closer.

He *knew* this place. It was little more than a foyer and a counter with cubbies behind it, a place where the proprietress, Haelin, could take a message to be sent off or deliver one that had come in, far faster than could generally be counted on. If not messages, then parcels or posts. Not all were from far and wide. Some might be clandestine or, possibly, proscribed, but Haelin was useful to too many important people for her service ever to be shut down. There were things that even the powerful didn't want to entrust to anyone in service who might be bribed.

But the reason Kylia had stopped was that the foyer wasn't open. Instead, Haelin had cracked open the shutters on a window on the floor above and was telling the small crowd pounding on the door below that she was shutting down, her voice pitched just enough to carry over the noisy throng. Ruggerio was lucky he had sharp hearing.

"The queen, in her wisdom, has confiscated all of the city's horses for her war, and so there is no way to send your messages across the kingdom, even if–" Haelin cut off, and Ruggerio was sure she was about to say, 'even if it was safe to do so'. "May the *All* keep you safe in such precarious times. Please, be cautious in your words and deeds and in your person." Her gaze slid to the side, as though someone was speaking to her, and abruptly, the window shutters closed and didn't reopen.

"Go around to the back," Ruggerio ordered. "Hold her for me."

"Hold who?" Ulan answered.

He flashed her a look and was off. He had no time for what was evident, and he had to catch Lady Kylia before she could get away.

It wasn't difficult. His strides made up two of hers, and he caught her quickly. His hands snapped around her arms like irons. She tensed and bit down on a scream, angling her neck around to see who'd caught her, untensing only a fraction when she realized it wasn't the queen's guard.

"Ruggerio, what?" and then she began to shake. Not so relieved after all.

"Come with me." As though she had a choice. He dragged her off the street, down an alleyway, and into another after that. Then he let go of one arm, adjusted his grip on the other, and turned her so that she would face him. He also brushed the hood off her hair and tucked away a lock that had fallen free so that he might see her face unimpeded. Her dove-gray eyes were wide, terrified. Her nostrils flared.

"What are you doing here?" she hissed. "The queen will kill you. I half thought she had done so already."

"So then, you mourned me?" He didn't know why he asked. They'd been lovers, yes, but more in the way of slaking thirsts than an abiding need. Yet he'd felt a surprising lift on seeing that she survived Bloody Bess's court.

"No more than you thought of me when you left," she said with a twist to her lips. "Let me go. I'll be missed if I'm not back."

"You haven't answered my question, and I still thrive on information. One only comes to Haelin to send or receive messages. I saw you at All Souls. I know what you witnessed there, and I believe you have a brother in the Church, yes? So perhaps you're here to send a message? Should I search you?"

Kylia glared at him as though she could set him aflame like the plague houses, burn out the wickedness that he clearly possessed. But she didn't respond.

He started to move a hand, very slowly.

"Don't," she said, like a plea.

He stopped, and they stared at each other, until the smoke and ash in the air made them both blink. Her whole body lost its rigidity, and she sagged in his arms. They collapsed further into the shadows.

"One of my ladies told me there was someone in the city who could get messages in and out, and sometimes even very special parcels. I thought for a while that was where the missing girls had gone, that they'd been abused or had a lover elsewhere and had needed smuggling. I realize how naïve that was. So, yes, I wanted to get a message to my brother, to tell him he needed to get away, but as you've heard, Haelin is closing shop. And it's possibly too late anyway. I was foolish to hope that a city messenger could communicate faster than the queen herself, regardless of the rumors. The queen's orders are no doubt already speeding their way to the farthest reaches of Jucar."

Ruggerio chewed on that. He knew of Haelin's haste. He'd made use of her services a time or two himself. But he'd never considered how she did it. He simply assumed she was good at what she did, just as he was at his spycraft. She had her ways and would no more give up those secrets than he would his own. But now he wondered. He'd asked Ulan to hold onto Haelin so that he could question her about the sorts of messages going in and out. He didn't expect her to name names; it was the information he was interested in. He could no longer threaten her with the weight of his position, but he could be sufficiently intimidating in his own right.

"Help me, and I'll see what I can do for you," he said.

She stiffened again. "There's nothing I can do for you. You've been named a traitor. Simply being seen with you might get me killed."

He put her aside to emerge from the shadows, "Should I start calling for the city guards then? The Crownsmen?"

"You're a madman!" She yanked him back, pressing his body against the building with her own. Her breathing was so jagged it could cut.

"Bloody Bess will make all of Jucar her asylum and herself our keeper if we don't stop her." He held Kylia's hands. She'd forgotten to put mitts on before leaving the castle, and they were as cold as an iced-over fountain. "I don't want to threaten you for your help, but I will. I will do whatever it takes. She can kill us one at a time or all at once. But with the former, we have a chance. We can gather against her. Join us."

She tried to pull away again, but he held her firm. The white showed all around her eyes, which rolled toward the alleyway, desperate for her body to follow, but he would have none of it. When she looked back at him, there were tears in her eyes. "Please, I'm not like you. I'm not bold. I'm not brave. I just want–"

"Guards!" he cried, dropping her hands and striding out into the alley. No threats this time, just deeds. "Guards!" he called again, more loudly.

The alley, as anticipated, was deserted. All were at the church or running from it. No one would hear him above the melee there.

She gripped him by the upper arm and spun him around. "All right, *yes*. You have me. Anything, anything, but be silent. Let me go. Tell me what you want and how to reach you, but quickly, and let me be gone."

She held her own hands now, one fisted around the other and both bone-white.

"It's very likely that Bess will be watching her people closely. You may not be able to slip away again. Is Girda still your maid?"

She nodded.

"When you have a message for me, send Girda with instructions for Suni, the chemist. Use the cypher I taught you. She will think that perhaps you are having another affair and, I hope, not be too curious."

"No, I don't think she will be, particularly as Lord Ruland is not so interested himself." Her breathing had evened out. Maybe she felt that he was not asking her to risk herself so much as her maid, but that cypher would only put off those who didn't know where to look, not anyone already suspicious of Lady Kylia. She was right that she had to get back before anyone could suspect her.

"Go then, but if I don't hear from you, I will have to spy for myself, and we are both safer if word reaches me on the outside than if I have to come searching on the inside."

She stood up on her tiptoes and kissed him once, quickly, much like a door might crash into a frame before bouncing back, then she took off into the gray, ashy afternoon, running as though the plague fumes might overtake her.

Kissed him, as though he had not just threatened her and embroiled her in espionage. He would never understand women.

Or people.

Only power. And he'd meant what he said. Standing by meant that you decided that your death would be part of the wholesale killing when it came. It wouldn't save you in the end. Not unless you, too, were willing to commit atrocities to prove your loyalty. At least standing in the way of the advancing evil or dealing it a devastating blow gave purpose to death.

It came for everyone sooner or later. Best not to wait for the assassin's blade.

There was no way he could look back on the past and know whether he'd cut short any paths to Jucar's redemption. He could only look to the future.

❦

Ulan

Ulan raced as quickly as her wavering vision would allow up the narrow alley, down an even narrower cut-through, and up a parallel lane trying to head off the messenger, but it was impossible to determine the way back to her shop. Most buildings had only storerooms or workplaces to the back, and if there were doors, no placards existed for reference. Some had shuttered windows, which in better weather might have opened to provide air and light, if they weren't blocked by inventory.

There actually *was* a door to the place that housed Haelin's messenger shop, and, for a wonder, Ulan found it, but it remained stubbornly closed to her surveillance. Maybe it had taken her too long to get there, and Haelin had left already. Maybe...

There was a *pop* above her. Quiet. Almost imperceptible, except that she'd developed excellent hearing from straining for years to hear the voice of her little ghost girl and before that to assure herself that Dazia still lived and breathed. And before that...a mother's hearing.

But this was the sound of something busting free from its casing and the abrupt change of air pressure. A shutter had opened. Ulan craned her neck up, but her lids spasmed shut against the fine ash sifting from the sky. She wouldn't be able to see a thing. She backed quickly away, in case Haelin was about to dump her chamber pot. The alley didn't reek of it, but perhaps that was how Haelin dealt with loiterers, and she'd been caught out.

But no shouts or splashes rained down on her. Instead, there was a *th-wick*, which she couldn't identify, and then... Ulan forced her eyes open, protected them as best she could with her hand as a brim, and marveled at what she saw. Haelin—if it *was* Haelin—was now dressed in men's woolens. The *th-wick* had been the tension giving way as Haelin had cut one of the ropes strung from balcony to balcony across the back alleys for clothing to hang to dry. As she watched, Haelin took up the rope, crouched in her window and leapt out, swinging through the smoke onto a neighboring balcony. She caught, climbed over, and then proceeded to scale the building.

Ulan stared, her mouth hanging open, before she came to herself, spitting ash.

Ruggerio was going to kill her.

She ran to the building where Haelin had disappeared, feeling for likely foot and hand holds. There weren't any. She had no idea how Haelin had escaped like that. But that wasn't going to do for her cousin.

Racing back to her original place, she took a running leap for the balcony across the way, but her fingertips didn't even brush the bottom of it. Still not recovered from being drained for the mageri spell, she fell hard to the ground. Another attempt would be just as futile.

When Ruggerio rushed into view, Ulan shook her head, looking to the still-opened window in answer, hoping he could intuit the rest.

"She escaped out the window?" he asked, his voice so carefully neutral she couldn't tell what he was thinking.

Ulan simply nodded.

"Well then, she harbors secrets that necessitate a daring escape."

How could he be so calm? She didn't know what good it did Ruggerio to know Haelin had secrets if he couldn't access them.

CHAPTER THIRTEEN

Cia

Frazier and his men ignored numerous branchings in the road, except to scout out others traveling their way. The first night, they camped roughly, always two men on guard. Cia and the others were unbound during the day for the ease of riding and voiding bowels, but bound at night in an excess of caution, particularly in the case of Myrka. She stayed in whatever position she was placed, face ashen, sunken in on herself. Her eyelids shifted beneath her closed lids, and her lips twitched, as though she was in deep conversation with herself.

No, conversation implied a level of civility. Myrka was in an all-out war, cursing herself and flinching from blows.

Hostill, on the other hand, looked ready to launch into a fight he couldn't win. Cia shook her head each time he glanced her way. He scowled and nodded, *knowing* that he couldn't do anything, not outnumbered in a foreign land. He wasn't a fool, but that didn't mean he liked the reality.

On the third day, Frazier brought them to a town, but Cia had no idea what it might be. She was confused by their path. They hadn't veered toward the coast and Miránge Castle. The wind should have grown stronger and carried the salt spray of the ocean. Instead, they were keeping to a more westerly route, and while it was a relief when the wind all but died, the cold had settled into her bones.

She was exhausted, hardly caring that they drew sidelong glances from the people whose heads were down, rushing about their business to get out of the cold. Finally, they reached an inn. Frazier and one of his men went in to negotiate terms, while the rest waited in the courtyard in stark silence with the single groom who'd come out to hold their horses. From the way the groom's eyes flicked back and forth among the others, he seemed torn between counting up his earnings and balking at all the work, undecided between the hope that they'd stay and the prayer they'd move along. The inn couldn't see much business in winter. Likely, they had a skeleton staff.

Frazier reappeared in the doorway, gave a whistle, and his other men started dismounting. Cia watched the groom, who momentarily sank, and then steadied himself.

"Halt!" the boy said, his voice breaking, then catching. "Orderly, my lords, if you please. Wouldn't want any harm to come to the horses."

Those who'd already dismounted held their horses muttering rude comments. Her cousin Stansil, burdened with her, hadn't moved, but he spoke quietly to one of the men now. "Take her and the others. Stash them in a room with a blaze going. The fewer eyes on them, the better."

There was a part of Cia that suspected Stansil had sensed her shivers and fatigue and was veering toward kindness by sending her, Myrka, and Hostill inside, but she no longer trusted that part of herself. It was true that some in Frizenze might remember the Poison Princess's handmaid, but unlikely they'd recognize her after so long and in her current state.

That was when she realized how far she'd fallen. How much the Jucari had infected her. Princess Inaya, who'd become queen when she'd married King Cyril, was not *the Poison Princess*, as the Jucari had dubbed her. She was Cia's beloved majesty. The beautiful, amusing, sometimes imperious soul Cia had served from the time she was thirteen summers old. She no more knew how to acquire poison than she did how to cook her own meals. She had *not* murdered her husband. Cia was sure that his death had been dealt a lot closer to home, whether it had been his younger brother, Prince Jannik, who'd assumed the throne next, or Bloody Bess, the youngest V'Alban child who sat on it now.

Following orders, Stansil's man handed his reins off, grabbed another to help him, and martialed the three captives inside, where the man conferred with Frazier. Her uncle looked at them like dung he'd scraped off his shoes, but he handed the man a key and sent them off. Cia was manhandled up the stairs by one soldier. Myrka was half-carried up by another, with Hostill free to walk between them with the understanding that the women would be victims of his bad behavior. As ever and always.

Probably nothing would happen out in the open. Not with witnesses. What Cia worried about was what would take place behind closed doors. Her mind kept spinning on the possibilities.

By the time they reached the room, she was so tense that given her frozen state, one knock might shatter her like an icicle falling from the eaves. But when they arrived at the door, the men only shoved them inside and locked them in, as ordered. If anyone stayed outside the door, she couldn't hear it through the rushing in her ears.

She had only time to take in that it was a small room—one bed, one stool, small fire—before Myrka threw herself at the hearth.

Myrka thrust her hands into the fire, casting her face aside, as though the heat was too much, but then turned it back. As through the pain was a penance. Cia was so stunned she merely cried out, but Hostill didn't share her paralysis. He ran at Myrka with everything he had, knocking her aside, out of the fire. They both went crashing to the floor, sparks jumping away from them as they rolled. The scent of burned flesh trailed them.

Cia shook herself and grabbed the woven blanket off the bed, throwing it over the two and patting them down before they both caught fire.

"Enough! Enough!" Hostill cried. He must have been on top, and perhaps she'd been more vigorous than she'd intended.

But the blanket hadn't started smoking, and that was a good thing.

She peeled the blanket away, and Hostill rolled off.

Myrka was slower to sit up, blinking in the light. She didn't glance at either of them but held her hands before her face. They were red and blistered, but they would heal. *She* would heal.

"What in the good and All?" Hostill asked.

"I don't have to explain myself to you," Myrka said.

"Do you have a death wish?" he challenged her. "I thought you had a mission, that the Restoration's aims were everything to you. Tell me what's changed."

Myrka just blinked at him, her face a terrifying blank. Cia thought Garif's rages had been a frightening thing. Somehow, this emptiness was worse. There was nothing to appeal to, fight against, maneuver around. There was, well, *nothing*. "I would die for my cause. Wouldn't you?"

"Yes, but not *run* toward death. You're not supposed to give your life uselessly," Hostill protested.

Her eyes bored into him, until Cia was almost afraid that the emptiness was *more* than nothing. It was not benign. Not an absence, but a void, a violent sucking hunger, and if Hostill wasn't careful, he might get swallowed up in it.

"Myrka," Cia said, drawing her gaze, freeing Hostill, "*what* is going on?"

The door to the room burst open, slamming against the wall, and Frazier strode in, his face a mask not of comedy or tragedy, but of rage, the kind that brought consequences. *"You left them alone?"* he said to someone over his shoulder.

"What were they going to do? Where were they going to go?" his man was right outside the door.

Frazier turned toward them, that rage not a whit diminished by the response. His gaze landed instantly on Myrka, no longer slumped as though half-dead. He reached for his blade, drawing it as though he would strike her down right there.

Cia and Hostill moved without thought, without communication, throwing themselves between her and the blade. Frazier raised it anyway.

Behind them came Myrka's cry from deep within her very soul, "No!"

Myrka tackled them. Damaged as she was, she was all strength and the kind of power that came from desperation. As they crashed to the floor, heat blasted over them such that Cia felt her hair spark. The fire had blown out of the hearth, headed straight toward Frazier, who cried out himself. The flames caught him and didn't let go, the scent of burnt hair, burning flesh overwhelmed them, shoving up into their noses, into their minds to imprint there along with his screams. Frazier's clothes went up like a torch. His men shouted and grabbed for him, dragging him from the room and beating at him, desperate to put him out before he burned to ash, before the building caught fire with him.

Two more men nearly trampled over his smoldering, yelping body to face off with them, but there was no facing off. The hearth had burnt itself out now and was cold and cracked. Myrka lay shaking on top of them, her tears putting out the sparks in Cia's hair.

Myrka rolled away and distanced herself from Hostill and Cia, landing on her knees, arms splayed, head to the floor. "Kill me now, only spare them."

Cia lay stunned on the ground.

Myrka was a mageri. She had knocked Cia and Hostill over and wielded her power to stop Frazier from going through them to get to her.

No, she couldn't conceive of it. *Myrka*, who hated the very idea of magic, of stealing from the anima to power a man–or woman's–whims.

Myrka was a mageri.

And for that she felt she deserved death. She didn't exempt herself from the sentence she believed in. Perhaps she'd even joined the resistance to eradicate that which she hated within herself. Made the horrible decision to give her life purpose by ending that of others. It was when Bloody Bess's mageri had sensed something within her and threatened to drag her back for Bess's use that she'd thrown herself upon the sword.

Cia didn't know how to feel. She didn't want the death of all mageri, but at the same time… At the same time, what? She hadn't formed a thought beyond that. Couldn't. Not with the scent of her uncle's burning flesh still seared into her brain.

But Myrka didn't deserve death. That much she knew.

"No," Hostill said, quietly, pleading. "Please, no. Myrka, you can take your fire away again, yes? Quench Frazier?"

She hesitated, and the man who'd stepped forward gestured with his blade, as though he'd bring it down in the next instant if she didn't comply. "Won't," she said. "I won't use my power again. It was instinctive just now, like the one other time I used it. I swore off. I can't be trusted, so I must be killed."

She hung her head, ready for it to be sliced off, but not to see the blow coming.

"He's out," came a call from the hallway.

No one in the room moved. It was cold now. As cold as the outdoors, as though Myrka hadn't just stolen from the hearth, but had drawn the heat from the entire inn. Frozen as they were, they might have been caught in an ice storm, preserved until the spring thaw. Cia and Hostill gripped each other tightly, waiting on the commotion in the hallway to resolve into orders.

Feet shuffled. There were grunts, cries of anger and moans of pain. Pain was good. It meant Frazier was still alive, and perhaps a life wouldn't be demanded for a life. But if Myrka was allowed to live, it would only be because Frizenze wanted her power. Yet Myrka would rather die than offer it.

Cia strained to see into the hallway, and as a man moved, she got a glimpse of Frazier, his face turned toward them, eyes unseeing. His face…some of his flesh had bubbled, the rest reddened, blackened. Charred. His flesh hadn't melted down to muscle or bone, but he had to be in excruciating pain. He had no brow on the one side and only a partial brow on the other. His hair had been singed back and was black and brittle elsewhere. His pupils were only pinpricks, but the dark brown of his eyes was surrounded by angry red irritation, as though the embers of the fires were still with him. They flared as he smoldered at Myrka.

Stansil had to step over him to issue orders, and as he glared down at them, there was nothing of the cousin she'd thought for a moment might have given them some consideration. She couldn't blame him.

"Aivig will provide something to sedate her," he ordered, his voice as hard as flint. "Or knock her out if she so much as moves. King Avize will have final say over her fate, but we will not be lax again. If either of these–" *these* being her and Hostill, who were no longer people, as she was no longer kin, "protests, act as you must. I am done here."

The man with the blade and another–*not* the one who'd left them alone from the start–stayed with them, one to either side of the door, which was closed and locked behind Stansil.

The guards' eyes bored into the three, but particularly Myrka. No one tried to bind her while they waited for the sedative to take effect. Frizenze was famous for its potions and tinctures. It wouldn't take long, and it would be potent. They had only until it arrived to talk.

Hostill was ahead of her, and she was thankful for it. He and Myrka had a prior relationship, and Myrka would never trust Cia. "Myrka, what happened?"

For a moment, she didn't move, and Cia thought she might never again, but after a few heartbeats she uncurled minutely. Myrka glanced at the door, then at the guards' blades as though considering whether she could dash for them and run herself through before she could be stopped. But she must have decided it was impossible and finally looked to Hostill.

"I'm tainted," she said.

That was all. She tucked her head then, as though she was done.

"You're not," Hostill said. "You can't be tainted by ability, by something you've no say in. What you've been granted is not wrong. It's how you use it that matters. Think of it. That man there," he inclined his head toward the door, "is probably a natural with weapons. Maybe he's got a good eye or great aim. If he uses it to kill his neighbors and steal their land, he's a villain. If he uses it to defend and protect, he's a hero."

Her head snapped up. "That's not Restoration, that's rhetoric. They want to put *you* on the throne? You're as bad as the rest, a traitor to the cause."

There was fire back in her eyes. She'd momentarily forgotten she was resigned to death.

"I'm me, and I can think for myself. I've seen people using their powers for good. Not drawing from the land but drawing from themselves. Roha can do it. Maybe ni can teach you," Hostill said.

"Roha is Nim." Myrka's lips twisted as though she'd said a word that tasted filthy on her tongue. Cia was struggling to keep up her sympathy.

"And you are mageri. Do you want me to judge you as harshly?" Hostill said with more patience.

"I do."

Myrka glared into Hostill's eyes, daring him to say anything more, wanting him to take her on. So Cia gave her a true enemy.

"Why? Tell us about the first time you used your powers."

Myrka smiled, and it was the sort of smile one gave on seeing their opponent drink the poison for which there was no antidote.

"Oh, I'll tell you. I've been trying my whole life to outrun it. To make up for it, but I see now. I see…"

For a moment, she did see…far off into some past where they didn't exist. Nothing existed but her past pain and horror and self-hatred. It seemed a loop she'd revisited time and again and flagellated herself for ever since. The thing that had thrown her into the blade and the fire and probably numerous dangerous situations in between.

"My ma died of the Rot." She didn't look at Hostill. Didn't look at Cia. She was mired in that long-ago place, staring into the dead hearth, as chill as the memory. "Not a new story. So many died. We lived on a farm, and my da had to keep working it. He did as we were told, put everyone suffering the plague as close to the fire as possible–my ma, me, my sister–let us sweat out the impurities. Then he went off to the fields with my brother who still appeared well. My brother dropped before the sun. He'd been hiding how bad off he was, so my da wouldn't have to work the fields alone. Da came back to find he'd lost Ma too. Had only my younger sister and me left. Two girls, no boy left to work the farm. No wife to bear him more.

"Wasn't long before we had a stepmother. Nice enough to us at first, especially where m'da could see. He was okay with girls. Awkward once we were too old to sit his knee, but figured we could marry, maybe combine farms, something like that. Didn't have too much time or head for planning once he came in from the fields. But *she* wanted rid of us. She had a boy of her own from an earlier marriage. Not sure what happened to *that* husband, though I can imagine. She grew more and more abusive.

"By that time, I knew I could do things. My power started to want out, but I never let it. We went to church. I knew it was wrong, and I was untrained. Couldn't be trained anyway as a girl. But one time I came back from the well and Freyda was beating my sister for something she said she did. Shorted the market money or something. She made things up all the time for an excuse. And I just...lost it. I didn't even know what I was doing. I just saw red."

Myrka swallowed, and Cia swallowed with her, caught up in the tale and her own memories. She'd seen red when Garif had come for her that last time, knowing she would die. That time she'd run him through with his own staff. Cia suspected what was coming next, and she braced for it. She looked at the door and knew the guards were straining to hear, but they could strain all they wanted. Myrka's voice had dropped to a whisper, and unless they were going to step closer...

"I didn't think," Myrka continued. "I didn't plan. I didn't even mean to. I pulled up that power I'd been feeling all around me. All that rage and injustice and hurt and betrayal...it swelled up, and I let it go, straight at my stepmother. It was like a bolt aimed at her chest. Her eyes opened wide, her arms flung out, and that power pierced right through her heart. My sister escaped and started to run to me, but whatever she saw in my face scared her.

"*I scared her*. And she ran out to the fields to our da. My stepmother only had time to curse me before collapsing to the floor, *dead*, with her babe–because they'd had another babe by then, a boy, like they'd wanted–wailing in the background. I realized then what I'd done and collapsed to the floor myself. The boards that caught me were cracked and dry, as if I'd stolen what life they had left. Then Da ran in with Freyda's older boy on his heels and they clustered around the dead and ignored the living, except to shoot me fearful, hateful glances, and I knew. I was an abomination. I'd done what I was never supposed to do. I'd drawn from the anima to take a life. I'd killed my stepmother to save my sister. But even she wouldn't look at me. And so, *I* was the monster. Not my stepmother. *Me*."

Cia made a move as though to hug her, but Myrka flung out a hand and Cia stopped. Not afraid but respecting her wishes, particularly as there was no telling what Myrka might do to enforce them.

"Oh, Myrka," Hostill said. "It was instinct. You didn't know what you were doing. You weren't trained. You didn't mean to kill her."

She stared hard at him, driving home her next words. "And yet, she's dead." Then she turned away again, going so quiet she might have been talking to herself. "That's not even the worst part. I thought I was saving us, but I drew the power from our land. My father knew it. That was why he came running. He saw the crops wither–the stalks drying, decaying, crumbling before him, the ground cracking. The destruction had spread from the house, and so he knew... When I killed my stepmother, I killed our farm, our livelihood, my *family*. I sentenced them all to a death of poverty and starvation.

"That was why I was on the street. That was why I was on my own. I'd already doomed them; I didn't wait for them to turn me out. I left. No one to care for meant no one to kill for, and I would *never* use my power again. But I've done it, which means that it wasn't a fluke. I am death."

This time, Cia did lean in, heedless of the consequences. Myrka allowed it. Not, Cia thought, because she took any comfort from it, but because she no longer cared enough to protest. She allowed Hostill to add his support from the other side.

Hostill whispered, "You were untrained and pushed to the limit. You didn't mean it."

Myrka shook her head in denial but was done speaking. Her entire body sagged in defeat.

"I killed my husband," Cia said, trying to let the words slip out without acknowledging their pain. "He was an abuser and... He was an abuser. He was horrible, and I did it in self-defense. I realized that he'd married me specifically because he sensed that I had power. He drained me secretly when he was home and kept me isolated and starved for even basic necessities when he was absent. Then he haunted me beyond death. He did things through my body..."

Cia's eyes snapped shut, and a quake went through her, as though trying to shake it all off, as though she was a mountain and could cause an avalanche, sloughing off a forever-frost layer of pain. It didn't work, but when the tremor was gone, she opened her eyes again. She could see, but her body was fluctuating between hot and cold, running a fever as though to fight off an infection. If only it wasn't her own memories, and the battle lost before it was even engaged.

"The point is, there's no telling what I'd have gone on to do if I'd accessed my power. We each do what we have to in the moment. You saved your sister. You may have saved others. Maybe your father when Freyda decided her son was old enough to work the farm on his own. Maybe the next husband down the line. *You are not death.* Whatever you think. Whatever *they* thought in a single moment, you are not death. No one and nothing is so simple. Your father and sister may have come to regret letting you go. They may have gone looking for you. You cannot know. I only know that if you've decided one thing about yourself and never question it, you can never be anything else."

Myrka jerked her head up and stared hard at Cia, challengingly. She opened her mouth to fight back, but the door to the room opened again, and it was a new man with a potion for Myrka to drink.

Myrka dropped her jaw for the potion, and neither Cia nor Hostill fought it. It might be best for Myrka to sleep for a while. It would at the least keep her from racing to her death, and maybe in her dreams she could work on what Cia had said.

The only problem was that Cia was working on it as well. She didn't know why it was a problem, except that in absolving Myrka of her stepmother's death, she had implied absolution for herself over Garif's, and...it didn't feel right. She had *killed her husband.* Even though he'd been coming at her, even though it had been her life or his, she couldn't rid herself of the feel of that staff plunging straight through him and her hand guiding it.

But it was different for Myrka. It had to be, because she'd been but a girl. She had no idea the consequences of her actions. She hadn't even thought, just lashed out to save her sister. And when Myrka had acted this time, it was because she saw Hostill threatened. She'd been tasked with protecting him, and her power must have flared up at the thought that he was in danger.

Myrka wasn't a killer. Or didn't mean to be. She was a protector. If she'd been trained, not as Bloody Bess intended with her female mageri, but as…as what? What was a girl like Myrka to do with power like hers but suppress it? And what if that didn't work? The Restoration and the Church both taught that it was wrong to steal the anima of the land, and Cia didn't disagree, but they offered no training for what to do with these instincts, this power. Nothing except sublimation. There had to be something…

Myrka slumped to the floor. Cia collapsed beside her in relief, and so was unprepared when the guards grabbed her as well and bound her before she even thought to resist. Not that it would have done any good. Either alone would have been enough to overpower her. Together with reinforcements at their beck and call, it was no use.

She was glad that Myrka was out so that she couldn't see that the heat she'd stolen from the inn had put them back into their bonds and doomed them to a frigid imprisonment. At least the power she'd drawn had come only from the air, the heated hearths. If she'd drawn the power from the inn itself, she'd have split its beams and brought it down, killing them all. Myrka would see only her failure, not the restraint she'd exercised. The control it must have taken.

It was impossible to tell how long they remained in that room. It felt like forever. Days at the least. Cia thought that perhaps they would move on without Frazier, leaving him behind to heal, since his wounds wouldn't bear travel, but perhaps a messenger had been sent ahead to King Avize, and they awaited a response, because here they remained, long enough that Cia feared they would be left to die, to hunger and thirst and marinate in their own filth. Myrka's bowels gave out first, as regularly applied potions kept her unconscious. The smell was terrible. Cia held things as long as she could. Long enough that her body, desperate for any moisture, must have taken it back in, but eventually, even she gave out.

She tried breathing through her mouth for a while to lessen the smell, but her throat was so dry it quickly became untenable. When they were finally brought water, it was in bowls to lap up like dogs—except for Myrka, who was kept sedated. Cia worried that she would dry up entirely, the cracking of her lips just the start. She did the best she could to lap up some of the water, hold it in, and dribble it into Myrka's mouth, afraid that without it, the rebel would soon crumble to dust.

But several days in, something changed. There were loud voices in the hallway. Hale voices, a call and response. Hostill caught her eye. As weak and tired as he was, he tried to squirm against a wall, to get into a less prone position. To meet whatever was coming head-on. She emulated him, rolling against the cracked hearth. It was the lowest and roughest surface she could find, and she reached blindly for it with the hands bound behind her back but was not fast enough to discover what she sought before the door opened, and two purple and silver-clad soldiers strode into the room.

No, not soldiers. They couldn't be. One was a woman in a purple underdress and pantaloons, overshadowed by a full-on black tabard embossed with a silver spirit tree, widespread roots recurving to form intricate knots. The branches bloomed not into leaves, but the sugges-tion of plants and animals and human forms, of mountain ranges and waterfalls and storms. It was gorgeously done. The silver thread alone must have cost a king's ransom, not to mention the needlework. Cia's fingers itched to trace the design, to learn some of the technique. She hadn't thought of her needlework once since the night she'd run Garif through, but now she missed the artistry of the design and losing herself in the execution. She realized her mind was drifting and focused on what was important here. This was a royal emissary, which meant that their true fate would be decided here and now.

The emissary stopped just inside the room, her face contorting so strongly her nose would have retreated into her face if at all possible, and her brows into her hairline. "*This* is how you treat guests of his majesty?" she asked over her shoulder, but there was an air of theatricality about it that Cia didn't trust. Or perhaps emissaries so regularly spoke at full volume that they forgot to modulate their voices in closer quarters.

The emissary glanced back at Hostill, catching him with a gaze the color of good red-brown clay, before lowering herself into a curtesy and addressing herself to the floor, but without the hand to her heart, since Hostill wasn't *her* liege. "I am Zega, my Lord. King Avize sends his greetings. My apologies for your treatment. I will rectify this post haste. I look forward to meeting you under more advantageous conditions shortly."

She rose without catching his gaze again, flipped her dark, unadorned braid over her shoulder, and swept out of the room. The man in purple and black followed her, leaving Cia and Hostill stunned.

Cia finally pulled herself up on the hearth but had to hold herself in place. She was too weak to stay upright on her own.

Hostill looked poleaxed. "What was *that* all about?"

"Well, you *are* a possible heir to the Jucari throne."

"I don't trust it."

"No," she answered, "and you shouldn't." Though these were her people and this was why they'd come. Or they'd once been her people. It didn't seem that she belonged anywhere anymore, but that pain would have to compete with all her others, and she didn't have the energy for it now, so she pushed it down and down.

<hr>

Hours later, Cia was in another room in another area of the inn. From the personal appointments, she assumed that the family had abandoned their living quarters in favor of their guests when Myrka had blasted Frazier with her power. Or possibly the whole place had been abandoned after Myrka had stolen power from all the hearths in the inn and they alone had been left behind to reap what they'd sown.

Now, she'd been given a semi-warm hip-bath and left to clean off her own filth, but she was glad enough for that. And she'd been provided a simple overdress and woolens in undyed ivory with a deep brown at the cuffs and for the belt. Purple and black were expensive and reserved for royalty and those they wanted to demarcate as bearing their authority or favor. It was clear that Cia had neither. She was excessively glad for the belt, because the woolens wanted to slide right off of her, and the dress to swallow her whole. The belt did its best to hold the former in place and keep drafts from blowing straight up and down the latter.

She had everything cinched just in time for a perfunctory double knock at the door before it opened. The emissary, Zega, stepped through with a boy and an older girl, who she suspected to be members of the family they were displacing, in her wake. They proceeded directly to the hip bath and began to drain it, one bucket at a time, just as it had been filled.

Zega's nose tried to crawl into her face once again, but she forced it back into position and faced off with Cia once the door closed behind the siblings.

Cia had stepped out of the way of their efforts but otherwise didn't so much as shift under Zega's scrutiny.

"So, you are Lady Cia," Zega said.

Cia inclined her head. Here began the courtly games. She'd been an outcast in the court of Jucar, always suspect, and thus ostracized. Sought out only for her embroidery skills, if she was sought at all. Which suited her, as she had no urge to make friends among those who had killed her queen. She certainly hadn't missed the courtly intrigue. She'd been young when she left, but not so young that she hadn't learned there were those who could kill you with kindness, love you with lies, or even protect you with indifference. The only way to survive was to be on guard at all times with strict attention not only to what one said, but also to how one said it and how people appeared at the time. Did their face match their body language? Did their liege or lady react to what they said or didn't say? And who did they say it to? Were you asked to keep it in confidence, and if so, was that with a wink and a nudge? It was exhausting, and she was exhausted already.

But at least she'd eaten something. Only a heel of bread and some cheese which had been left on a stool beside the bath, but more than nothing. More than recent memory. Her head was a bit clearer anyway. She longed to sit on the stool, now free of bread and cheese, but she wouldn't yield Zega the advantage.

"How did you come by the boy?" she asked.

Like he was a commodity she'd picked up in the market.

Cia bit back her first response–*I met him at knifepoint*. She was where she wanted to be, she reminded herself. This was what she planned. She had to choke down her anger. Her resentment. She had to swallow her pride. She'd done it for so many years. For so long with Garif. Yet now that she'd risen up, she couldn't lie down again. She couldn't...

She could. For his sake.

She could. But it cost her. She hated it. She gritted her teeth. "I met him after I'd killed my mageri husband. When I was on the run from the Jucari Crown guard. He had survived the death of his family from the Rot, the plague that had run through Jucar; perhaps here as well? His mother worked at the palace. We're pretty certain that King Jannik is his father."

"But you don't know?"

"You have only to look at him. The timing is right. And Bloody Bess certainly seems to believe it. She wants him dead. Bessory's former spymaster is the one who smuggled him out of the palace when Hostill was captured; he believes it too. And he's laid the foundation for the boy's ascendancy. He's spread rumors and the boy's likeness about."

Did she tell Zega that one of the lives Bloody Bess had taken to build her power had been Hostill's mother? That she'd been one of the shadow girls living in her head until Roha had drawn them out and put their spirits to rest on that battlefield? It hardly counted as proof. No, better to keep it simple. Keep to what they knew, what they could prove.

"Where is this spymaster?" Zega's tone was sharp, and she looked about as though Cia might be hiding him in the shadows.

"He went back to Jucar. He knew that no one in Frizenze would trust him, and he could do more good there. He's seen firsthand how destructive Bloody Bess is to her own people. He wants her deposed as much as you do, but not to put a Frizenzian on the throne. He'll work with Frizenze if it's to end the war, if it's to put Hostill on the throne. He'll go that far and no further."

"So that he can then control the boy and the throne?"

"I'm sure he'll be part of the court, but Ruggerio is not meant for statecraft. He'd be happiest to return to the shadows, working with secrets and spies."

"What if he plans to play puppet master?"

"We would never let that happen."

"We?" Zega's gaze bored into Cia, and for the first time, she wondered if she was more than an emissary. Had King Avize sent a woman because he felt that Cia might be more willing to confide in her? That she might identify and commiserate? If so, he'd chosen poorly, because Zega so far hadn't taken the path of empathy. But maybe that was just it. If she had, Cia might have seen it as a ploy and closed up. This way, Cia was on her guard, but maybe not for the right things. This was more of an interrogation than an ambassadorial sort of meeting.

"We. Us. Those of us who have been working against Bloody Bess." That was all she was going to say. Zega could trust her or not.

"This woman, Myrka, who nearly brought down the inn, is one of these people?"

It irritated Cia that Zega asked questions to which she knew the answer. Maybe it accustomed people to answering her positively. Maybe it was a technique. Ruggerio could tell her if he was here.

"Yes," she said, biting off the word.

"You said that she threw herself on the sword before because she refused to be brought back to serve Princess Bessory V'Alban with her power?"

"I'm sure she must be queen now," Cia said rather than 'yes' again.

Zega ignored that. "And the girl asked to die again here? I presume through your actions and the young prince's that she is important to you?"

"Yes. To him especially." She saw the trap now. Too late; the words were already out of her mouth, and anyway, they were true. There was nothing else she could have said. Nothing else that would have mattered, because Frazier's men would have seen with their own eyes. "But I'm sure she will attempt to end her life again, especially if you try to use her in any way. Unless, perhaps, you will provide her with a null so that she can't possibly access her powers."

Zega smiled, and it was like a Gnasher before he clamped down. "In fact, we would insist on it."

CHAPTER FOURTEEN

Roha

Here it was dark, as though a canopy of trees shaded a mountain stream, water cascading over a jut of stone, the breeze soft and flowing. Roha dove into the stream buoyed by the energy within, the smooth, peaceful, replenishment of it. For once, demanding nothing, taking nothing–not like the Church or the Restoration or simply those around nim.

It had refilled so quickly. Ni feared…but it was a distant thing. The branch to the stream-that-was-not-a-stream called to Roha. The current surged, and ni had an instant of knowing that ni could continue along nes peaceful, personal path or veer in another direction. But ni let it pass without a decision, telling nimself it was the current that decided, and so. And so. It was not nes fault when ni drifted down the branch of the stream that led to Cia. Roha had thought it was ephemeral and would fade away over time, but now suspected they were inextricably linked. Roha could no more resist following it than ni could force nimself to wake.

Ni had to be sure Cia was all right, and that she and the others hadn't been captured. Cia would need to know Roha was alive as well, and as much as Roha could tell her of where ni was. Ni was only afraid the method of contact would be intrusive and unwelcome. The last thing Cia needed after Garif was another person who could get inside her mind.

If only there were another choice. Apparently, conscious-Roha wasn't in charge here. Ni was driven by the relentless current toward a feeling ahead like the first gasp of air after it was denied–fresh and cool and clean. As though Roha burst out of the stream and into an entire eddy of purpose and power. Not latent, though. Something had Cia whipped up, agitated, and she had no idea of her own strength.

"Cia?" Roha called mentally.

Ni'd done this only once before, when Cia was locked inside herself, being beaten down by her mageri husband who'd possessed her body and taken over her mind. Now, though, Cia was in control of herself. Or was trying desperately to maintain control. Whatever had her worked up was on the outside, and Roha was almost afraid to call again and distract her. What if she was in a critical state? Roha might not want to steal her focus.

As Roha drew closer, it was as though ni couldn't see the true Cia through an impression of teeth–small, dainty, the kind that would devour you one bite at a time and tap at the lips afterward to remove any trace, smiling sunnily to fool the world into thinking no such thing had ever happened. The very eeriest of smiles. Cia's society armor? She never paraded about in society, so perhaps she was building that which she'd have to adopt now that she'd be reentering it?

Roha felt the moment Cia became aware of nim, when her churning, swirling center went as still as glass. The teeth disappeared, along with the stream. When Roha tried to move, to extend nes hands out toward Cia, ni found the environment no longer fluid but hard and crystalline. Ni panicked, trying to beat against it, feeling the confinement, fearing ni wouldn't be able to break away, return to nimself.

But ni couldn't beat at anything. Ni could only remain and pray silently to be heard, because ni couldn't draw even a breath. Knew ni didn't need to breathe. Not here. It didn't help the panic or the certainty ni would die without air.

It couldn't have been long before Cia came to nim, but it felt like an eternity. Then, it was only her voice, but so loud that if the glass that held Roha weren't thick with betrayal it might have shattered. "What are you doing in my head?"

Cia! By the All, let me go. You're killing me, Roha thought hard. *I'm sorry. I never meant for the bond I forged to remain, but since it did, I had to make sure you were alive. I thought you'd want to know I lived as well.*

There was a pause.

"Now I know." The volume was less, but the *pain*... Roha wasn't sure whether ni could hear it or feel it emanating throughout Cia's anima, but it was as tangible as the glass pool holding nim captive. "Where are you?"

I've no idea. Someone found me. Half man, half beast, and brought me... somewhere. A place haunted with bosewights. Cut off from the world, Roha answered.

"We're on our way to court. We will find you. But not this way. Never again. My mind is my own. You understand?"

Roha tried to nod and realized that ni couldn't. *Yes. Cia, I–*

But ni didn't get a chance to finish before the glass shattered, and ni shattered with it, blasted back along the stream, battered and beaten, edges eaten away by gritting against the current, only possessed enough to fear that ni'd never fit back together again. Roha spilled back out into near nothingness. Nimself as a quagmire, the stream of nes anima not refilling, leaving only muck that wanted to swallow up the shards.

Ni drifted, stunned and stung by Cia's forceful ejection. There was nowhere. Not Jucar. Not Frizenze. Not the Church nor the Restoration. Not even the erstwhile band of others likewise cast aside. Nothing but pain, potions, and bosewights–and a snake-man who believed ni belonged among them if only ni would die and make it so.

But ni had been confounding people all nes life and intended to go on doing so. Most especially if the alternative meant being cut off from the anima of which ni'd always felt so much a part. Distinct yet connected. *That* was nes true sense of belonging.

Roha became aware of the sense of something *other*. Something watchful, waiting. Not nimself. Ni would have said ni was still, but now ni went rigid, an active rather than passive *don't-see-me* that probably gave nim away. A poor instinct, but then, ni wasn't used to being hunted.

That's how it felt. As though ni was prey.

Roha tried to open nes eyes incrementally, but they wouldn't obey, gunked together with grit the wind whipped into them. It took contorting nes face, giving away that ni was awake, but suddenly ni was panicked. Could no more keep nes eyes shut in the presence of whatever awaited than ni could stay down.

Ni got nes eyes open, but they shot wide, and the eyes staring back made nim flinch in a way that had pain flaring all up and down nes body as it prepared for flight ni had no room for, crowded as ni was against the bed by the snake-man who loomed over nim. A translucent membrane gave his eyes a milky look, something like the dead eyes of a corpse. It made nim think of seeing Ceramor on the battlefield. And those fangs…

At the sound that escaped Roha, the snake-man coiled back on himself, looking nearly as startled by nes wakefulness as ni was to see him poised over nim. His scales swished over the floor as he darted to the door, ducking to clear it. But why flee? He could have dispatched with Roha in seconds with no one the wiser if that had been the intent. So why stare at nim while ni slept as though ni was the curiosity?

As Roha tried to puzzle it, a gray-robed figure stepped into the room. Taller than the person from yesterday. "Don't mind Reynal. You remind him of his homeland." The voice was mellow, even warm, and aged like fine spirits.

Roha wrestled with all the things that surged to mind. When Reynal had picked nim up in the forest, Roha had noticed his Frizenzian was accented, but it was difficult to determine the origin around the sibilance caused by his fangs. Ni'd assumed that it was a regional dialect or that he was perhaps a creation. Ni'd never guessed–

"Then he's originally from Jucar?"

And Roha realized something else–the gray-garbed figure, ni was almost certain they were Nim as well. Something about the voice or the…Roha wasn't even certain, but ni had the sense, somehow. When the figure pushed back nes hood, Roha did nes best not to stare. Nes dark hair was close-cropped rather than worn up in a topknot, as with acolytes of the Church in Jucar, but then, the acolytes there also wore white as opposed to this gray, so it was possible ni had to dispense with comparisons and expectations. Nes nose was quite present and proud, as though a landmark for all the other features to radiate from, like some cities built outward from a central monument. But it was nes eyes that were most arresting–one green and one blue, both piercing, especially with the dark lashes to highlight them.

Roha said the first words out of nes mouth, and really, ni couldn't know, except that ni sensed it deep within. "You're Nim."

"Actually, I'm Arresta." ni said with a smile, and Roha recognized that yes, ni had lips as well, noticeable when they quirked in amusement.

Roha flushed. Had ni really blurted that as people had done to nim? "I'm so sorry. I didn't mean to assume. I just meant–"

"That I'm like you. And now I'm the one making assumptions. But yes, we all are here. We don't draw on the anima but protect it. That was why Tehardy was so upset when you damaged the Sacrima. We're the defenders, and we're the last in the line."

"How–?"

"Not yet. I'm sure I've said too much already. You may be like us, but you're not one of us."

Roha heard additional words that went unsaid, *Not yet, anyway*. Ni hoped they were only in nes imagination. It was clear they intended to let nim live, so why hold back from telling nim potentially too much unless leaving wasn't beyond the scope of possibility.

CHAPTER FIFTEEN

Ulan

An explosion rocked the building behind them, sending Ulan to her knees and Ruggerio into a ready position, weapons drawn. Ulan felt a stinging at her temple and drew a hand away wet with blood where something had grazed her. Ruggerio hissed and pulled a thick splinter of wood from one of the wooden shutters out of his wrist, exposed as he held an arm up to shield his eyes, searching out the escaped messenger. Thick smoke rolled from the building, fire roaring and hot, deliberately set; there was no question. The timing was too perfect.

"The messenger had secrets, no doubt," Ruggerio muttered. "We have to go. If there's any guard not containing the riot, they will come to the explosion. If Haelin has a way to escape the city, we can't stop her. Too much wall to cover. But if she's Restoration, she may be going underground. I can go to them alone. Convince them that I've left you and your magicking ways behind."

Ulan's eyes flashed, she was sure. She no more had magicking ways than he did, and he knew it. She could see spirits, sometimes talk with them, but she couldn't control the where and when. She had no sway over them. She couldn't work the anima, draw from it. Nor would she. But the Restoration made no distinction over those who had contact and those who had control.

But she and Ruggerio were here for a purpose. It was possible she could put her 'power' to good use. If Ruggerio was along, he would only try to stop her, tell her it was too dangerous. Alone...well, one perceived madwoman might be an easy target, but she might as easily be discounted, avoided for fear of whatever it was people feared from those who talked to themselves. That it was catching, perhaps.

"But how will we find each other after," she asked, a token protest.

"Be at the Hind's End an hour past sunset." He took a few coins from a hidden pocket and pressed them into her hands. "And again on the morrow. If I fail to appear for two nights, then I am lost and you must go on without me. If I'm alive after, I will find you."

She gave him a *look*. It was inconceivable that Ulan would survive in a situation that would see Ruggerio overwhelmed. It wouldn't happen. Even while her heart quailed at his words, there was another part of her that held rock steady, and that was what came through in her eyes. It told him not to be ridiculous and to get on with things already. Of course, she'd felt the same about the possibility that she could lose her precious daughter to the Rot when she was sure she could save her by sheer force of will.

Death was never conceivable even while it was happening. Sometimes even afterward. And the coping...sometimes the coping never came.

Ruggerio made a move toward her, and she was so startled that she jerked back, barely feeling his lips on her forehead before he was gone. He had kissed her goodbye, something he'd never done before, as though they truly might not see each other again.

She would not think on it.

Ulan rose, her knees protesting. Dropping to them in the hard dirt hadn't done her any favors. She coughed as she rose. All the dark, rolling smoke had curled into her lungs, taking up residence like houseguests that spread their filth everywhere, setting up a rumble of discontent in their host and overstaying their welcome. Her back was hunched and her muscles ached from the cough by the time she was back near All Souls, but it was the perfect excuse to hide her face in her hands as she coughed into them. Much of the fighting had moved on, and she slipped through the pockets of the rest, flinching in body and soul with what she saw around her but trying to move like a ghost herself.

There were still Crownsmen guarding the actual entrance to the church and others backing them up. They hadn't moved, though the injured Animist and the acolytes inside had been taken away, along with the body of the man who'd been run through. Bloody Bess and her Guard were gone. There was no way Ulan could get into the nave.

Her house, where she'd once lived with Dazia, had been burned down, so she couldn't go there or get onto church grounds through any of the torched plague houses where the walls of the cemetery had begun crumbling, bringing bodies and decay straight through. All she could do was get as close as possible to the sections of the churchyard still standing, hope she wouldn't succumb to the smoke, and pray–though it was the oddest sort of prayer–that she'd be able to spot the spirit of the acolyte who died, since he'd been killed *in* the church, and the wards meant that the anima was inaccessible there as protection against mageri interference. The ultimate irony was that the Church that preached union with the anima kept those who died within its walls from connecting to it. Their souls had to fly outside the walls to reach the All.

The smoke hazed her eyes until they filmed over, until she couldn't see for the tears and the ashen darkness that turned day to night. It was already cold, especially when the hacking coughs made her sweat, and the wind dried that sweat, and the process repeated itself. But suddenly, the breeze stopped entirely; it was then that she felt the chill straight to her bones. The chill said *something more* was coming. It laid like a pall over her–not like the gentle, childlike hand of her Dazia. Nothing so sweet and welcome. But like a blanket stifling a hard-won flame.

She straightened, fought a cough to a standstill, wrecking her body by holding it inside, waiting. She blinked back tears, tried to wipe them away with soot-blacked mitts, making her eyes water more. She could make out a shape coming through the cemetery wall. There were tunnels that she knew of through the Restoration. But this was not one of these. This was not an opening in the wall. It was not over or around, but *through*.

Ulan didn't need to wonder whether this was a spirit. Whether anyone else could see the man. She knew they could not, if there was anyone around to see at all. The first thing she noticed was all the blood. The ash itself fell right through the man, who was mostly washed out in a lighter gray, but the blood…the blood was still shining, wet, a dark, desperate stain. It obliterated the front of him. He was not the Churchman she had prayed for; not in acolyte white, but in riding gear. When she looked into his eyes, she fell back a step in shock.

No, it wasn't the Churchman, but someone much closer. It was Ludvin.

Ludvin. Dead.

He fell into her arms and then through them.

<hr>

Ulan was shaken. She'd found a public fountain glassed over with ice and punched through it, numb to the pain. She found a bare haze of water at the bottom, like the sweat at the brow of the stone, and used it to wipe her face and hands as clean as possible from the soot coating them. Then she found The Hind's End, ordered their darkest brew, and took a hearty swig.

And coughed it up, turning to face the wall to avoid hacking it into the lap of the man next to her with the braying laugh. He wasn't laughing now. She hazarded a quick glance to see him side-eying her with fear and using his bulk to shove everyone down the bench of the communal table, away from her and the Rot she might be carrying. It was still too soon. Would *always* be too soon. It was the smoke. She wasn't the only one in the place coughing. But she was the only one bringing anything up with it. Others were able to hide their faces in sleeves and maybe miss the cringing away of their compatriots.

Ulan muttered an apology to those around her, but now they'd all shifted and turned away as best they could, some with hands to their faces, shielding themselves from her. No one would meet her eyes, except one man farther down the table shooting fiery arrows at her with his glance, as though he could do enough damage to drive her away. She focused on her ale, and taking smaller, careful sips she could choke down more easily.

Before, she'd been searching the tavern for any sign of Ludvin's ghost returning. Or for Ruggerio. Now she kept an eye out for the innkeeper or his help advancing on her with purpose. She'd have to dodge them, and she didn't see how she could. The place was not that large, and her cough would give her away anywhere she went. But she could not get turned out for fear of contagion, and she could not long lurk outside the inn to watch for her cousin. The temperatures had fallen with the night, and she'd freeze in her tracks.

A man slid into the space left behind when her cough had cleared the room, his cloak so cold and clustered with snow that she felt it even through her own. The man on his other side gave him a glare and lurched up from the table, taking his ale elsewhere, and she risked a glance at the man who'd made it all possible, suspecting she already knew the answer.

And she was right. Ruggerio glanced back at her, looking as though an entire eave of snow had fallen upon him. He gave her a drunkard's wink and a bleary smile before shaking off the snow as a dog might, and a bit more space was made. Enough that in the noisy tavern, no one could possibly overhear them.

Ruggerio waved a hand aloft, making sure to show the coin in it, and it wasn't long before he had an ale of his own and had ordered a meal, staking one for "the lady," explaining why she might be willing to put up with him staying so close in the corner. As though anyone cared, which it was very clear they did not. As long as neither got any closer to *them.*

Ruggerio swigged some ale of his own before he said, "We have an issue." Another swig. "Whatever secrets Haelin has are her own. She's not of the Restoration. I did find the rebels...what's left of them."

"What's left of them?" Ulan felt as though she'd been dealt a blow. She didn't agree with the Restoration, but she'd counted on them. They'd been against Bloody Bess, the only group that she knew of working against her, at least within Jucar. If Bess had managed to break them...

"We know Bloody Bess has men on the gates to the city. They must be effective. Many of the Restoration never made it back from the battle. Maybe they're organizing against her elsewhere, but there's been no way to get messages in and out. There's a scattering of those left behind, but...well, it's not as though they would tell me numbers anyway, and the Restoration has always been organized in cells. However, it's clear their army is much diminished. Most able-bodied members left the city to fight with us in the Dobrens Valley."

"But with Bloody Bess burning the plague houses, taking the horses, killing the acolyte at All Souls, and imprisoning the Animist surely their recruitment will go up!" Ulan said.

"Maybe, but when Bess declared herself queen, she also claimed to be restoring the land, putting an end to famine and plague. She declared herself the savior of Jucar. Some are swayed by that, others by terror. The rumors from the battlefield–of her dark magic and monstrous form–have people afraid to cross her."

Ulan forgot about earlier and took a huge sip of her ale, draining her glass and still looking for more. She sat it down too hard on the long table. "What then? Where do we go from here?"

"There is only one thing to do. One way," Ruggerio said grimly. "The queen must die. I have to kill her."

CHAPTER SIXTEEN

Hostill

Hostill was pressed into the center of the carriage seat, squeezed between Zega and the other emissary, Grazi. All the other purple-and-silver liveried men, the soldiers, rode on horseback around them. Protecting them, he supposed. Or preventing their escape. He knew he wasn't supposed to be thinking that way. But he'd never stop being twitchy around Crownsmen. And these were *Frizenzians* at that.

Frizenzian Crownsmen.

Was there a difference between them and Bloody Bess's forces? Power was power. And soon that power was supposed to be him.

He shook his head, and Cia glanced at him from across the aisle. He didn't look back. He couldn't imagine it. The weight was too much. Like to crush him. Just to think–*him* making high and mighty proclamations. Policy. No one would listen. They'd assassinate him in a second. Put one of *themselves* in power. One of the useless, silk-clad, smooth-handed nobles who only knew how to eat the food others grew and wear the clothes others pricked their fingers for.

Myrka grunted as she shifted on her seat next to Cia and rubbed at her chest where the null had burned its way in like a permanent pendant. Back at the inn, Zega's healer had tried to put a special bandage over her, one imbued with a portable sort of magic, but the second Myrka felt it working, she thrashed and screamed, tearing it off and doing herself more damage.

Hostill came running at that, making it to her room in time to see the soldiers hold her down and Zega strike with the null. Myrka went boneless in relief. As though cool water had been poured over a burn. Yet it burrowed its way in. Became one with her.

Now Myrka rubbed her eyes and opened them, meeting Hostill's almost immediately and coming upright, bringing her head off Cia's shoulder. She rubbed at her null again, tracing it with her fingers, and Hostill watched her face. There was almost a wonder to it.

The carriage swayed Hostill into Grazi, who was made of stone as far as he could tell, and Cia lifted the heavy flap over her window a twitch to look out without letting the weather in more than necessary. It still let a chill creep through.

"We're not turning toward Miránge Palace," Cia stated, her voice measured, but shouting as clearly as anything *Something is wrong here.*

Hostill tensed, but they'd taken his daggers. He had nothing but his speed and his street smarts. Not that they'd do him much good in the wilds of Frizenze. And with Cia and Myrka to think about.

"No, the Palace was damaged in a siege with your queen. We have moved somewhere safer."

Cia nodded, and Hostill tried to relax. It made sense. Things got damaged in war. People got damaged. Look at Myrka. She was still healing. She was gray and drawn, but better for the care she'd been given. And the sleep. And possibly for knowing that no one could use her again, not with the null now part of her being.

Maybe that most of all.

There were a few more lurches and a few more looks, and Hostill took his cues from Cia, who grew more tense as they approached. He would think she'd be the most excited. He'd heard what her own family had hurled at her and knew family could cut cruelest of all. But he thought King Avize might give her a second chance. Zega had treated them with respect. They were riding unbound. In a carriage and not thrown over a horse. Headed for royalty. Certainly dressed for meeting them.

Then the carriage swung wide, like to capsized itself, and suddenly stopped, taking a moment to settle back down on its wheels. For a breath, nobody moved. There was a full jerk of the carriage as the coachman jumped down, and a thump as the same block that was set on the ground for them to mount was placed again. The door swung open, and the wind blew in, hitting them with a blast of winter chill. Only here, it wasn't quite so bad, a bit tamer than in Jucar. The night was quiet; the hooting of owls and the calls of other birds could be heard. His maam-who-was-not-his-maam would have known what bird call was which, but he just knew them as 'birds'.

"Well then," Zega said, glancing around. "I'll go first, shall I, and make sure everything is prepared?"

She didn't wait for a response. Her questions were more to give the illusion that others had a say in matters than to change any actual outcome. She ducked past Hostill and Grazi, who stayed as though to guard the door, though there were bound to be real soldiers outside. Or…was that how he was meant to see things? *Real* soldiers, as though Grazi was to be discounted when he shouldn't be? As large as he was, Zega did all the talking, all the drawing of attention. Grazi followed orders, faded into the background, waited, and watched. Something like a bodyguard.

But who, exactly, was he protecting?

When the door opened again, Zega's head and hand appeared, the latter reaching out to help him down. So, he was to be first. He wouldn't have said it meant anything to him until he stepped down onto the block and saw the people in purple and black arrayed on the front approach of what looked to be a grand stone hunting lodge. There weren't a large number of people. No nobles. Only the house staff, given enough time off to impress the bastard boy with a claim on the rival throne. Well, he was impressed.

He tried not to be. He looked back for Cia, but realized Zega hadn't relinquished his hand, so when she pulled him forward by it, he had to go or fall on his face. The house staff stood at attention, dipping or curtseying as he approached, eyes downcast as though he was now somehow above them. A sickness started to swell, and he had an idea there was more beneath the surface. This was just the start. He dug in, stopped, Zega's hand suddenly a claw, a clamp, an iron.

He couldn't breathe.

There was a push from behind, a body crowding him. Overlarge hands like shovels at his shoulder blades. They could scoop him forward. Propel him up those stairs. If his feet didn't move with the momentum, he might even be lifted up like a child.

He forced his feet to move. One, then the other. It would seem churlish to these people forced to come out for him, a commoner like them, raised up only because his mother had caught the eye of a prince or a king, to bolt from his destiny. Something some might dream of. He nodded as he passed, tried to catch an eye here, a look there. He failed each time, but for a girl perhaps Myrka's age, who glanced up quickly through her long lashes and down again before he could catch the expression in her eyes.

Then he was inside a grand foyer with stairways to the left and to the right and gilt-framed paintings of someone's forebearers climbing like ivy up the walls. To the right was a doorway leading to a red room decorated with enough weaponry for each liveried man and woman to help themselves, clearly not the intention. And from what he could see, various trophies hung on the walls. He would bet himself there was also an antler candelabra or sconce. One at least. Probably more.

To the left the doors were shut, and there was no telling what might be behind them. He'd never been in such a place.

Zega finally let go of his hand when a young man met him at the foot of the steps. "Ryall will take you to your room," she said to him. "The king will want to meet with you, but first you'll be taken care of."

Made presentable, he'd guess. Which was fine, because he'd had about enough of royalty with Bloody Bess.

"And the ladies," she said, turning to Cia and Myrka, who looked about dead on their feet. Myrka, in particular, still had a *long* way to go before it was in any way certain that she'd survive all of her traumas. "Will follow Joia."

One of the women from the entrance curtsied before them, joints popping as she rose again. Then they were off, Hostill and Ryall up the right staircase, Cia, Myrka, and Joia up the left. It would certainly be difficult for them to plot if it became necessary. He hoped that Cia was right to bring them here. The serpent swimming in the pit of his stomach wasn't so certain.

It was two days before the king would meet with them. Maybe that was his first lesson in royal time. The longer you kept someone waiting, the more important you were and the more you felt they could be crapped on. Like he didn't know that already.

Maybe that was how long it took for him to be 'taken care of.' To be cleaned and groomed and made half-presentable for a king. To be spun through etiquette–how low he had to bow and how he couldn't get any closer than the entrance he was granted, as though he wanted to get within grabbing distance of a king and get blamed for anything that might befall him afterward, as Cia said her princess had been. A street-rat contender for a rival throne would make a good scapegoat for about anything. Silver gone missing. Sudden seizures from some kind of poison. Hostill would be ripe for it. And then there was all the other stuff, what to say and not say. How to say or not say it. How to hold his head, present himself. Everyone at court had a lifetime to learn it, and he had it all crammed in at once until his head spun.

Maybe *that* was the whole plan. Keep him too busy to wonder about Cia and Myrka. Or worry that something was wrong when he didn't see them or hear from them. He wasn't answered when he asked about them, except by canes slammed to the floor to call his attention back to the lesson. They never touched him, but the sharp sound when they hit said that they *could*, and it would be something he would absolutely regret. Who would stop these people from hurting him? They were at war, and right now, he was nothing.

But who would he be then? Clay, once it was shaped and glazed and fired was no longer malleable. It was set in the form someone chose for it, and broke if heated or cooled too quickly. If used other than for its intended purpose. Good for nothing but for what it was made.

So he cooled his heels for days, during which Bloody Bess could be doing anything at all back home. He missed Jucar, and even his sad hovel of a home, with the force of a thousand suns. Every Frizenzian word he was forced to learn felt like a betrayal, despite the fact that he was doing it all for them. His people. Not *his* people. Or maybe…

The first knock at the door coincided with a fall of the cane, and Hostill almost didn't register the second knock. He heard the falling cane now in his sleep, the sound changed to the thwack of striking flesh in his nightmares. But Ryall crossed to the door before another knock could fall, and Hostill didn't miss him go rigid upon answering, nor the fear in his eyes when he nodded to Hostill's tutor and said, "It is time."

Ryall was trying very hard to freeze his face. Every tendon was pulled so taut with the attempt to clamp down on any expression whatsoever that the result resembled a mask. When he looked from the tutor to Hostill, he'd banished the fear, but Hostill had seen it. There was no mistaking.

"Come now," Ryall said. "The king is ready for you, and he's not to be kept waiting."

He strode forward and pulled at Hostill's tunic, which was a very fine honey color with deep walnut embroidery at the neck and wrists. The richest thing he'd ever worn. He brushed at Hostill's closely shorn hair as though there was enough of it to have gotten disheveled, and as he did, he was close enough for Hostill to whisper, "Why are you afraid?"

Ryall—he couldn't be sure, but he didn't think Ryall had been meant as a groom, not of men anyway. Maybe they'd pulled him in from the stables or somewhere else where he'd lost at cards with his comrades on a regular basis, because his face showed absolutely everything. Now he averted his gaze, as though Hostill had said nothing. Grazi waited in the hallway with two guardsmen to take Hostill to his audience, and his tutor closed in behind him, ushering him toward the door, as had been done upon his arrival at this place. These Frizenzians were good with closing in ahead and behind, cutting off pathways of escape, but only because he was not, so far, truly determined.

He wanted to meet the king. And maybe Zega was on the way with Cia and Myrka. He needed to see them again for himself, since no one would talk in this All-forsaken place.

He was half right. When Grazi stopped in front of a vaulted, hand-carved wooden door, Zega awaited with Cia, who cried out and ran forward to meet Hostill, holding her arms out to him as if he were her own child. Hostill, forgetting that he was supposed to be some kind of prince, stepped out from behind the guards to run to her and Grazi moved to block him. The halls weren't so narrow or Grazi so big that Hostill couldn't dodge him, and he was in Cia's arms for a quick hug, then standing back to assure himself that it was really her and not some sort of mageri conjuring.

After what they'd been through together, he had little faith. Her eyes were dark, shaded, haunted. If it wasn't Cia, they'd gotten even that much right.

"Myrka?" he asked her.

"Healing," she said. "Better."

Then he was being pulled away. "Prince," Grazi growled. He did have a voice then, not that he was much allowed to use it. "Remember your place."

Hostill cocked him a look, eyebrows full of askance. He opened his mouth to shoot back a response, but the sound of the cane falling closed it again, and he bit his lip. He had to behave like a prince or be treated like an urchin.

He turned away from Cia and toward the king's door. "I remember," he said.

He felt the glance Cia shot him, but he didn't return it. This was what she'd intended. He hoped he was doing her proud. That he'd have the chance later to find out. Act the prince well enough now, and maybe soon he could start demanding things and expect to be given them. Like access to his friends.

A guard stepped forward to rap at the door, and a moment later it was opened, first narrowly and then pulled wide. The person on the other side was bowed so low, he could do nothing but review their footwear as they passed.

The guards progressed to a point in the room that must have been drilled into them, because Hostill didn't see them confer visually with each other before fanning out to either side. Hostill had been told that he was to step up to stand between them and then bow deeply to the king. Cia must have known her place as well, because he could feel her at his back, though she didn't step up beside him. She must have been forced by her title or the loss of it to remain behind him as she dropped to the ground in a curtsey while he performed his bow. They stayed there until a hoarse voice from the bed gave them leave to rise.

It was only *then* that he allowed himself to look upon the king.

———◆———◆———

Cia

Cia had been prepared for King Avize to be older than she remembered, but not for him to be smaller. Perhaps it was a matter of being dwarfed by the large canopy above him. It could be that the same canopy that cast the dark shadows made him seem parchment-pale and sickly, almost sunken as he lay back, propped against the pillows all around him. But the impression could also have been fostered by the gray-robed figure beside his bed, hood pulled entirely over their face as they bent praying over their clutched hands. Or, she assumed they were clutched, as they were hidden under the voluminous bed coverings.

She didn't remember the king as a religious man, but then, she didn't remember Churchmen wearing gray robes rather than white, so perhaps this was a lay-brother of the Church. Something had certainly changed, because while she'd been young when she was sent away to Jucar with Princess Inaya, King Avize, then prince, had ever been in motion. Sword fighting through the halls, leading tutors on a merry chase, leaping atop furniture not to be leapt on, and swinging from whatever would support his weight...and some that would not. Until he settled down and then led charges and hunts and eventually, she was certain, battles. Maybe that was the difference. He'd been wounded and was recovering, hating every moment of his convalescence.

His eyes were still full of life. They caught her gaze, traveled up and down her until she shivered. Then he turned his gaze on Hostill.

"You are the claimant to the Jucari throne." The king's voice was as dry as a winter-scoured field.

"I am," Hostill said, and she was proud of the strength in those two simple words.

"Approach," he said. "Two steps. No further."

Hostill took two boy-sized steps, and King Avize cracked a smile, but it faded instantly as he leaned forward, shutting his eyes in what looked like concentration. It brought him a little closer to the light, and Cia forced herself not to gasp. The king's color was…not good. Had he been poisoned? Was there plague trouble here as there had been in Jucar? As far as she knew, King Avize had produced no heir, and with his sister having been killed by the Jucari and no other immediate family, if he died, it would create a power void. In the middle of a war, it would be chaos. If it came to an internal battle, they could be easily overtaken by their enemies.

Could Bloody Bess have arranged such a thing? Or Ruggerio when he'd been her spymaster?

Cia wanted to believe that this was a passing weakness. It had taken three days for the king to see them, so maybe he was stronger now than he'd been when they'd arrived and would grow stronger still.

"You'll do," he said, studying Hostill, his eyes, at least, sparking the way Cia remembered them.

"My Lord?" Hostill said, not daring to take a step back, but shifting his weight at least.

"You've Jannik's eyes and chin, certainly. Enough of him that anyone would note the resemblance. Your mother worked at the palace?"

Hostill gave a nod, but it wasn't quick enough.

"Here, boy, did she or didn't she?"

"He's only just learned that his mother isn't who he thought she was," Cia stepped in. "Give him a moment."

"He won't have one," the king snapped. "He'll have to answer, and he won't be able to hesitate. He'll have to name her quickly and clearly. Decisively."

King Avize seemed to deflate back against his pillows as he sighed out the breath he'd taken in, as though this sudden outburst had taken everything he had. "Take him away," he said, waving the hand not buried in his bedding. "More training. All the training. He must be ready."

He closed his eyes and didn't open them again.

Cia was left with an unsettled feeling.

Hostill caught her gaze but wasn't allowed to hold it.

Grazi placed himself between them, a wall of man and muscle. As soon as the door to the king's chamber was shut behind them, Hostill asked, "May I speak–"

Grazi said, "No," before he was even finished. "You heard his majesty. You need more training."

He shuffled Hostill quickly off to his wing of the manor, ignoring Hostill's protests and Cia's own.

Cia turned to Zega and asked, "I hope the king is in good health?"

She knew very well that he wasn't, but also that it was unacceptable to inquire more directly.

"He will recover."

It was all Zega would say. But of course. Not only wasn't Cia a close confidant of the royal family, she was considered a traitor. She would be told nothing that might get back to Jucar. Amazing that she'd been allowed to see the king at all. A fear began to take root that what little she'd been exposed to meant she would never be allowed to return to Jucar. But she'd helped set things in motion; she must be allowed to see them through. Overthrowing the V'Alvans was all that would give purpose to her abuse and the horrors that had befallen Queen Inaya. If it all came to nothing, she didn't know how she would survive in this country that hated her for the very abuses she'd suffered.

Back in her own chambers, she tried again with Joia. She might know something about King Avize's illness, but be far enough from the throne that Cia's pursuit of the information wouldn't make it back to the king's ear. Unless she had been placed there to spy.

"I was surprised to see the king so much changed," Cia said as she settled with her embroidery beside her arrow-slit of a window.

She and Myrka had been quartered together in small adjoining rooms probably meant for minor nobility. Myrka's bed came with a trundle on which Joia slept, blocking the connecting door, though the trundle was currently tucked away, and the connecting door open. The outer doors were locked each night–for their own safety, they were told, because there was no telling who might wish them ill, both Cia and Myrka coming from the enemy nation. So, Cia's small window was her one unobstructed view onto the world, and one too small for her to escape through, as she had after she'd killed Garif in self-defense. Perhaps word had traveled from Jucar. Never in all of her time cursing the Jucari had she ever thought V'Alban Castle might symbolize a time of freedom.

But also of burns and bruises. Fear and invectives.

"He is recovering from the siege at Miránge Castle. All will be well," Joia answered.

Cia nearly pricked herself with her needle. Her next question burned at the tip of her tongue. "Miránge Castle has fallen?"

"I know not. Only that the king is here and recovering."

Cia slumped down on her stool, embroidery near-forgotten in her lap. "From what? What wound?" It was unthinkable that she should ask. Unthinkable that she should not. If Bloody Bess had overtaken Miránge Castle… If the Frizenzian court had fallen back this far, the war could be over come spring and Bloody Bess…

"That is not for us to know. He will recover." Joia said it with the fervor of one who had to believe. She bowed her head and performed a spiritu, muttering a prayer before breathing a kiss into her cupped hands and releasing it to the All.

CHAPTER SEVENTEEN

Roha

Roha tried not to let nes fear show.

"May I work on your wound?" Arresta asked. "We haven't wanted to do too much too quickly and shock your system, and certainly not without your consent. Just enough to assure that you'd live, since you'd made clear you weren't ready to die."

Roha chose the green eye to gaze into. "Yes, but please, don't strain yourself."

Arresta smiled, "I have learned my limits. We can teach you while you're with us as well."

Roha didn't say anything to that. Ni laid back but didn't close nes eyes again. Ni watched as Arresta approached, gently laid one hand on the point where nes neck and shoulder met. It was cool, soothingly so. Roha hadn't realized that nes skin was flushed with heat—not quite feverish or ni would have flinched away from Arresta's touch but perhaps headed that way.

Arresta's hand only stayed cool for a moment, before it began to warm. Roha's eyes rolled back, and ni squeezed nes eyelids closed with the effort not to tense the rest of nes body. The healing that flowed from Arresta was like grappa. It started with a tingle, then with a bite, and ended with a warmth that spread throughout the body.

"Relax," Arresta said.

"Trying," Ni whispered.

Ni could *feel* muscles activating, regrowing, perhaps knitting together. It was wildly uncomfortable. Intrusive. Ni wondered if this was the way Cia felt when ni was in her head. Roha sensed it when Arresta withdrew as well, the loss of warmth. It left nes cold, shivering.

"It happens like that," Arresta said. "It will pass. Do you need a blanket?"

Roha tried to rise as ni had when faced with the snake-man–Reynal–and found ni could. Ni was weak yet, and the wound was sensitive, movement pulling in painful ways that reminded nim that ni was healing but not *healed*. Still it was an amazing transformation.

"Thank you, no," ni said, "but more clothing? If it's permitted, I'd like to walk. You say I've been here for days. I'd like to see the Sacrima. Learn more."

"You should rest. After a healing of this sort–"

"I've had enough rest, and I'll no doubt have more shortly. Please give me this. If I lay abed any longer, I fear I will go mad."

Something flickered in Arresta's eyes, but Roha couldn't tell just what. "I'll return," ni said. It felt like a promise, though it was a statement only.

Then the light was flickering. Or not the light, but things sliding and shifting in the room in a way that hurt nes head to follow. Voices half-heard, words unintelligible. Ni strained to make out their whispered secrets, the answers to life or death, closing nes eyes to blot out other distractions, but it was no good. And there was the rifling, the cold caresses–a mother, a lover–comforting, then corrosive, and ni understood it to be the spirits again.

Roha *oofed* when something landed on nim, solid and real. Nes eyes flew open in shock, and all other sensations hastily retreated. A robe lay across nes stomach, gray like Arresta's. Was ni making Roha one of them. Already?

"What?"

"If you want to walk the halls, you'll wear it. There are protections woven in."

"I need protections?"

"You do."

Arresta didn't elaborate, and after what Roha had just experienced, perhaps ni didn't need elaboration. Roha had asked to walk; it was up to nim to do what was required to make it happen. Maybe the tour would provide more information about what was happening here. What the Sacrima was. *Why* it was.

Ni rose slowly, cautiously, creakily, and Arresta turned nes back but didn't leave the room. Roha made several unintentional noises along the way but would not ask for help until nes arms refused to rise entirely above nes head, at which point modesty gave way to necessity. Arresta aided Roha into the robe with as much care and dispassion as though ni was an expensive doll. Then ni lifted Roha's hair, which had to be a rat's nest after being dragged through the woods.

"Sit," ni ordered.

When Roha obeyed, Arresta tried to finger-comb it into some semblance of order, but quickly became entangled in the knots while twigs and leaves fell to the floor.

"Good enough for now," Arresta declared it, raising the hood of Roha's robe up over the mess. Ni was instantly overcome with a sense of quiet, as though the whole world had become half as loud and demanding, and ni could simply *be* again. The relief was so great it was nearly ridiculous. As though there was no war, no Bloody Bess, no separation from nes friends and isolation in this semi-terrifying place...

"Do you feel better?" Arresta asked, knowingly.

Roha nodded, afraid of what Arresta might hear in nes voice. Afraid of what ni nimself might hear and have to examine.

"Then let's begin," Arresta said, leading the way to the door.

Roha followed, and would have to continue doing so, because the hallways were narrow. The Sacrima was built entirely out of stone. There were wooden doors to either side of the tight corridor, evenly spaced, indicating similarly sized rooms to the one ni'd recovered in.

Nothing more than cells really, about the size of nes room back in the royal city or slightly smaller, because that had featured its own hearth.

The only light came from arrow slits at intervals in the walls, and braziers that gave off an oily, smoky light, but as they approached, the one flared and snuffed out. Roha jerked, but Arresta continued on as though nothing had happened. There were no tapestries on the walls to keep in the heat, but ni supposed that if the bosewights wreaked havoc with the braziers, they didn't dare hang tapestries and risk them being lit on fire.

How did they live like this?

Arresta took a set of stairs that wound upward, and Roha followed nim, through another hallway much like the first, though somehow there was a sense of this floor being deserted. Ni couldn't explain it. It just felt…empty. Lifeless. And finally, there was a large room with an oversized hearth–currently unlit–and weapons in racks, upon the walls, the longer ones stored in barrels. It looked like a room prepped for siege. There were also pegs with heavy cloaks, some fur-lined. Boots or leg-wrappings. Anything needed to withstand the cold. Arresta gestured to those now.

"We're going out?" Roha asked, rather stupidly.

"I thought you might like to see where you are."

If ni never felt cold again, it would be too soon, though Roha did want to see where ni was. Not that ni had any faith that it would help. Ni was in Frizenze. Ni didn't know the country. All a jaunt outside might tell nim, given sufficient sun, would be which way was north.

Roha chose the warmest cloak ni could find–fur-lined, along with furred boots and leg wrappings to cover nes thighs. Ni still hadn't recovered enough warmth from nes illness. Or from the spirit hands which had roamed before Arresta provided Roha with protection. Ni could not allow the reach of winter to steal what warmth remained. Arresta garbed nimself similarly, but when ni opened the door, Roha feared that all of their preparations had still not been enough. The blast of winter wind knocked them back, Roha's intake of breath freezing in nes lungs nearly caused them to seize.

But Roha wrapped nes hands in nes cloak and brought them to nes mouth, breathed through the cloak, warming the air before it got inside. Doing nes best to unfreeze what had been frozen. Then ni stepped out into the crisp, moisture-laden air.

They were at the top of a three-tiered tower. The wind wailed through the crenels that allowed archers to fire their weapons and was stopped by the man-height merlons they could duck behind to reload their bows. Everything about the Sacrima said that they expected attack. And yet, they appeared to be a religious order.

"What is this place?" Roha asked. "The Sacrima, yes, but tell me about it."

The wind whipped Arresta's hood back, but the protections didn't seem necessary up here. Roha didn't think the spirits would have the strength to manifest against the force of the elements.

Ni turned those anima-filled eyes on Roha. One the color of the sky, and the other the fields. "This is not a well-known part of our history, and if you ever leave us, you must promise to keep it, and our location, to yourself. At one time, the Church would rather have forgotten about us, and now it is best that they do so."

"Best why?" Roha asked.

Arresta had said, 'if you ever leave us,' which meant that ni *could*. Roha was not to be kept prisoner. Unless Arresta said one thing and meant another. Ni would not be the first.

Arresta sighed, nes breath pluming up into the air, like a stream of animist. "I suppose if you're a vanguard of worse to come, you know already. And if you mean us harm, well then, we know how to protect ourselves."

Arresta's pause swelled with possibilities, dark against the winter-bright light.

"Tehardy tells it best, but centuries ago, an aspirant named Evreh led a rebellion from a Church training facility and broke away with other Nim, after seeing one of nes fellows nearly broken for exploring nes power. It was all to be preserved for the Church, all for creating nulls, setting wards on Church land. Anything else was anathema. Selfish. Tainted. As were any of our urges, including that of loving and being loved. All the other aspirant, Tres, had done was use a tiny bit from *the well of nes own strength* to escape for time to nimself with another ni had come to love. But the Church was jealous of even that.

All love, *all* devotion was to be given to the Church. Tres was to be made an example of, beaten publicly and left without food or water to fast and pray on what ni'd done. In other words, to live or die as the spirits saw fit."

Roha gasped. "What happened?"

"Evreh happened. No more would Nim be told they were venerated, close to the spirits, then treated as though they were nothing. As though they needed abuse to hone their abilities. Evreh didn't plan for fear that someone would report back. That night, Evreh slipped away, broke doctrine by using some of nes strength to fool the guards who walked the halls, and woke Tres's lover, Radeem. Together, they hid in the shadows of the churchyard, where Evreh used nes powers to break the lock on the stocks, where Tres had been put after being beaten and starved. Tres fell into Radeem's arms, and tried to use nes power for healing, but ni wasn't trained. The Church had *never trained* its people for even something so noble as that, so it did about as much good as the water they poured down Tres's throat. But it was enough that they could stumble off into the night."

"And the Sacrima?"

"So impatient! Are you unmoved by Tres's story?"

"Not at all. But if it is a long one, I wonder whether we might move inside for it."

Arresta barked a laugh. "Well, there is that. I begin, and I am lost, thinking how that must have been. Unlike some of the others who have found their way here, I have never been subjected to the Church's...*love.*"

Ni led the way back to the door, and Roha followed Arresta inside to the marginally warmer top floor. As Roha leaned against the door to seat it firmly in its frame, the cold cut a significant amount, but neither was ready to remove their outer garments. Arresta moved toward the hearth to add wood and tinder from the stacks beside it. Ni blew on nes fingers to warm them enough to fiddle with the flint and striker to get a spark and set the kindling ablaze. It would take time for the room to warm, but in the meantime, Arresta whirled to Roha. "Now, where was I?"

Roha was getting the sense that once begun, Arresta was single-minded when it came to nes tale. "They escaped together…"

"Ah, yes. Well, I'm sure you must have it in your own country, that the Nim don't always go to the Church. Sometimes, they're kept because a family has no other to work their fields, because they can pass and they keep themselves hidden or their family does, because they're useful to a village. Or sometimes they escape from the Church after being put into their care. Evreh knew there was evil in the world, had seen it firsthand, so ni found a place far out in a forest, almost at the border with Jucar. This place was mostly a ruin then. It had been abandoned, forgotten. Tres and Radeem and those Evreh gathered along the way rebuilt the tower stone by stone, and they created a safe place to learn, to teach, a sanctuary for those who needed it."

Arresta stared into the fire, as though ni was lost in a past ni'd never been a part of.

"Despite what the Church had done, Evreh had faith. When ni built the sanctuary, ni warded it so that its anima could never be drawn, so that we could always be safe in our own space. The anima would remain secure, sacred, and could never be used against us. Thus, when one of us dies, we must be brought outside the walls so that we can join with the All."

Roha joined Arresta by the fire, leaning in for warmth. "I understand how it started, but how then did it continue, if it was a secret sanctuary?"

"Well, yes, we have protections to keep people who aren't meant to from finding their way. But there's always been a way for people seeking sanctuary to discover us. It was always part of Evreh's plan. Also, while we do our best to be self-sufficient with our gardens and with Reynal to hunt for us, we aren't entirely. There are those from whom we buy supplies; they may not know exactly where we come from, but they know that we exist. A woman found us some years ago, when I first came to the Sacrima, begging us to take in her nightmare of a husband. She knew of our sanctuary, that our land was warded from the anima. She said that her husband's spirit would poison the All as surely as the aklusian spider that had bitten him was poisoning him. It was a horrible way to go. Already, he was sweating and thrashing. There was dried sickness on his chest and lingering in his beard. His hose had been cut away, and his calf was twice the size it should be. The bite was black at the center, and a diseased purple radiated out from it.

"There wasn't much time to decide.

"The man's sons brought him in on a pallet, and even while he was dying, he was swinging for them and hurling invectives. The Sacrimist at the time said that if the protections had let her find us, then it was a sign that we were meant to aid the family. Ni agreed that we would keep him, and people have been bringing us their tortured souls ever since. It is one way we have given back to the people we trade with for keeping our secrets."

"But at the cost of your sanctuary!" Roha said, horrified.

Arresta looked up from the fire. "Not all experience it as you did. We have learned to wear our protections, and it is not so much." *But it is not so little.* Roha heard the words ni didn't say.

"But you said that it's best that the Church not find out about you now in particular. If they have not hunted you all these years, why now?"

Arresta poked at the fire with an iron rod as though doing battle with it, though it was nicely ablaze, and the room was over-warm in their unshed outer garments. "We have not had new seekers in several seasons. I think something is happening to the Nim. Maybe it's just that they fear to travel right now. We've had Reynal ranging further than we'd like, listening for news, but we've heard nothing. You are the first new face we've seen in some time, and you almost destroyed us."

"Not intentionally."

"Even worse. You have shown how very weak we are when we need to be raising rather than lowering our guard."

"I can help," Roha said, gazing steadily on Arresta to show nes sincerity. If nothing else, Roha owed it to the Sacrima to undo the harm ni had done. Perhaps if ni showed nimself trustworthy. Repaid nes debt and a bit more, they would even be willing to point nim in the direction of the king's court with enough supplies to get there. How ni'd convince the king to let nim in, ni had no idea, but Roha had a feeling somewhere under nes breastbone that ni had to get to Cia. Ni didn't know what to call it. A queasiness. Was it at the forced separation when there was work to be done? At how they had left things? Or a sense through their connection that there was something wrong and ni was needed?

Roha didn't know. Ni'd never been through this before. If ni stayed long enough here, maybe they would train nim and ni could ask. Ni would not be beaten with a switch for exploring more of nes powers than the Church had given nim leave to do. That was, after all, why Evreh had left and founded nes own order.

As long as Arresta wasn't just spinning tales.

The sweat pooling under the fur-lined cloak suddenly seemed an ice-bath, and the room began to spinning. Roha's stomach lurched with it, and ni staggered to the wall to hold it in place, or let it hold nim.

"Are you all right?"

The question came from a long way away, as through a tunnel, some words longer than others, and hollow. Not right.

Ni had overdone it. Not ready.

Roha slid to the floor, and someone was pulling at nim. Roha let them, boneless as a doll, closing nes eyes against the spinning room. Hot-cool air hit as something was pulled away from nim. Ni breathed a sigh of relief, turned on nes side and tried to ignore nes rocking, roiling stomach and swimming head to spin away into sleep.

CHAPTER EIGHTEEN

Ruggerio

Ruggerio had ordered and committed numerous assassinations but always with intel. With himself or someone else already positioned on the inside, ready to strike or to gain him entrance. He had taken it for granted. Now... well, he had Lady Kylia, but she was a last resort. He wasn't certain how much he could trust her or what she could be pushed into.

The path he'd used to smuggle Hostill out of his captivity was closed to him. By now, the method of his escape was certain to have been discovered. He knew there was truth behind the rumored secret passage between the north wing and the royal quarters, but the only key was passed from ruler to ruler. Possibly Ruggerio could find the entrance and pick the lock, but if Bloody Bess was smart, and she was, she'd have placed furniture in front of one end of the passage or the other to prevent just such a thing, knowing that he was out there. He had to come at this from an entirely unexpected quarter.

He could strike at Bloody Bess while she was out of the palace, but that came with different challenges. Ruggerio couldn't know when she would leave, and when she was out, she was heavily guarded. He could plan for a ranged attack–arrows or poisoned darts–but again, that required planning, knowing where she would be so that he could set up sightlines and lie in wait. And still he ran risks, primarily with the unpredictability of people moving about and the whipping winter wind, which would suddenly kick up or abate, making whatever adjustments he'd planned for moot.

No, this couldn't wait. He'd have to kill the queen in her quarters. If that meant scaling the wall under the cover of night, he'd do it or die trying. Succeed or fail, he was likely to die. He didn't see a way to kill the queen and live. He trusted his ability to get in, but getting out after the deed was another matter. If he rid Jucar of the Blood Queen, it would be worth his sacrifice. All he wanted was to serve his kingdom to the best of his abilities.

"Ruggerio?" Ulan sounded halfway between irritated and concerned. She must have called him more than once. He'd forgotten she was there. Forgotten where he was, lost in his plans.

"Tomorrow," he said, continuing the conversation in his head. "I go tomorrow. If I succeed, you bring Hostill back, set him on the throne. You know what to do. If I fail, you carry on. You fight until you can't fight any more. Because she will kill Jucar. One way or another."

Ulan's big doe eyes shimmered even in the dark of the tavern. So like her daughter's. Ulan had lost so much mass over the course of everything, she was half-ghost herself. "If you fail? Ruggerio, you can't do this. You can't go alone. It's madness."

But she didn't say he was wrong to do what he intended. He'd thought she might. It wouldn't have worked, but he'd thought she would try to talk him out of it, argue that killing an unarmed woman was immoral. But Bloody Bess was hardly defenseless; she was a spreading poison, and he intended to cut her out of the kingdom like a medic would amputate a gangrenous limb for the sake of the rest of the body.

"Then I'm mad. And so are you, because you're going to help me."

"Help you how?"

All Souls was burning. Ruggerio thought it likely no one would see a man running into a burning, half-broken building under the cover of darkness, smoke, and ash, but he was not one to take chances. Bloody Bess's Crownsmen had battered down and chased away the rebellion that had risen in the streets. Now they formed a perimeter around the flaming church.

Bess must have anticipated *something*. Perhaps she thought the people might try to salvage the structure, cling to the dying husk as though it stood for all they held holy. There *were* those who had crept back and watched the fiery beams crackle and fall who might very well have rushed in if they could've found a way.

Ruggerio was happy to turn his enemy's weakness to his advantage. In sending a message, Bloody Bess had created an audience. He would provide them with a show. As long as everyone else played their parts.

But I can't, Ulan had hissed.

Think of everything you've done so far. How much stronger you've become. You can. *Think of Roha. Reach within yourself. Deeper than you ever have before. Find that strength, that power and* pull.

He hadn't read much of Roha's book, the Gospel of Gelerte, before it had been ripped from his hands, but he'd read something of it. It made sense that the Nim, composed of the aspects of both masculine and feminine, were closer to the anima and so able to access it within themselves without stealing it from the outside. They were in more perfect harmony. Balance. But weren't all people composed of both masculine and feminine? A combination of their mothers and fathers? Shouldn't everyone be able to reach the anima to a greater or lesser extent? He was numb to it himself, but Ulan...she had always been able to see it when worked. She'd been able to see the spirit of her daughter Dazia when she'd passed. Then other spirits. Her power had been growing.

Ruggerio was poised in the darkest area he could find, between guards who were spaced farther apart because their fellows had moved closer to share a flask to clear their throats of debris. He didn't pray, but he chanted under his breath, as though it might somehow lend Ulan power.

When he heard a murmur begin, and then sharper voices start to call out in the crowd, he allowed a grin to spread across his face, though not pull his lips away from his teeth. He didn't want their whites to show as he sprinted for the church.

Ulan

Always before, Ulan would close her eyes and exhale her anxiety, letting it fly away and dissipate, then breathe in the purity of the air, the anima. She'd let it fill her up and find her calm as best she could before reopening her eyes to face her patients so that they would take their cues from her. Cures worked better with belief.

Now there was no purity in this ash-laden air, and she didn't dare close her eyes. She had to be watchful. And yet, Ruggerio had told her to look inward. To dig deep inside and find her power. How was she to do any of that when each breath was ragged and hazardous?

Ulan gave herself only that short moment for self-pity. She had survived worse–Dazia's death, Bloody Bess's captivity, and having her life sucked from her to power the training of Bess's fledgling mageri. She'd even survived the battle of Dobren's Valley, and she would survive this.

Ulan closed her eyes after all and darkness fell. She pushed down on the panic. Focused on slowing her breathing. In, then out. Focused on calling…

No, not Dazia.

Ludvin. Call Ludvin.

She pictured him as she'd last seen him. The moment he'd walked through the wall, before falling into her arms. Ghost-white hair whipping around him, his eyes still somehow alive in shock and pain, the sword tip sprouting from his chest, blood a dark shadow glistening around it. Pain made her gasp and her eyes pop open to dispel the horrific image, only to find it standing before her.

Not *it*. Him. Ludvin.

Ludvin swayed before her. She was amazed and saddened all at once, the two emotions fighting like her stomach tussling with a meal that didn't want to stay down. She'd never called a spirit before. They'd always just come to her. But this wasn't the difficult part, and this wasn't just any spirit. This was her friend. He'd fought for them all, fought for Jucar. And he was dead because of them. Because of *her. Spirits-forsaken Bloody Bess. Queen of Putrefaction. Of the Void. Of true-death.*

Ludvin had returned on his own for a reason, and the first thing Ulan did was call on him with the intent to use him. It didn't make it any better that he would approve her motives.

"Ludvin," she said very softly, "I want to hear all you came to say, but right now, if I can lend you my strength, I need you to do something for me, for the cause. Walk out in front of the people and the Crownsmen. Make sure everyone sees you. I need rumors to spread that Bloody Bess's dead don't stay buried, that the spirits walk. I saw her men strike you down. Your head is one of those on a pike, isn't it?"

He dropped his head to his chest as though it held real weight. She thought she'd asked too much, that it wouldn't rise again, but when it did, he nodded. Perhaps he'd been able to return to Jucar because his head had come. Or maybe body and spirit no longer had any connection to each other. But it was nothing that she needed answered right here.

Right now.

She had to dig deeply, reach within, as Ruggerio had told her to do. She exhaled all of her air and almost coughed her insides out trying to take too much tainted air back in. She pulled her sleeve over her face, tried to breathe through it. Normally, calmly. Tried to control even her own muscle spasms to keep from choking on more smoke and ash, giving away her location. When she could do that, she silently prayed to the anima, searching within herself for her core of strength. Someplace that buzzed or hummed or shimmered with it, but there was so much pulling on her that she felt as though her whole body was a system. She couldn't isolate one place of power through all the noise. Maybe that was how it was for her.

Giving in to instinct and the pressures of time, Ulan ripped a jagged nail through the fleshy pad of her thumb and drew blood, tapping herself to transfer some of her energies to Ludvin's spirit. She pressed on the wound to make it bleed more and sprinkled some of the blood over Ludvin's shade. He grew brighter, and she grew weaker, but only a bit. Not enough. Not nearly enough.

Ulan reached out with her blooded hand and took his, not allowing her hand to fall through. He brightened more. Let go and he dimmed.

There was only one way. She would have to walk with him, continue feeding him power, at least until she was struck down. She took an extra moment to smear some of that precious blood over her face. Hopefully, all eyes would go to the shade, but if not, she would be a fearsome face in the night. The blood gave onlookers a focus other than her features.

"Go," she said, retaking his hand.

Ludvin's hand was frozen in hers, his chill seeping straight through her flesh as though the cold of the grave wanted to come for her as well. His eyes were luminous in the night, and fearful, but clearly not for himself. They held a question that he didn't spend his strength to ask.

He had to lead, and she would have to be very careful not to let his icy fingers slip away.

One step, two, and people were gasping, crying out, pointing and praying.

"This is the man Bloody Bess feared so much she sent men after him!" Ulan called. "This is–was–Ludvin, the head of the Restoration, the group that rebelled against her, which she would have you believe is impossible. She fears his truth. And mine. Your queen lies to you."

Men were running for her now. Men with swords. She had to hurry.

"She did not return the anima to the land. *We* did." She shouted it into the night. Into the frightful face of the Crownsman before her, sword raised to cleave her in two. She threw up her free arm as though it was a shield, as though the blade wouldn't cut right through it and swing back around for her neck. Her head the next to be added to a pike.

Something flew through the air beside her, and Ulan feared she was about to get an arrow in the back. She was shocked when a javelin pierced the upper chest of the soldier before her and quivered there as he bled around it. His arm dropped, and the sword with it, but another pushed him aside to take his place.

Another sword, another Crownsman with hatred and hunger in his eyes. He wanted her blood, and he meant to have it. Something leapt to her shoulder, startling her. Before she could react, it used her as a springboard to launch itself at the Crownsman. It landed, chittering, on his shoulder and bit into his neck, then was gone before he could lash out, but it was enough to destroy his aim. His blade turned, and he struck Ulan's arm with the flat of it, sending shockwaves from her upper arm on down, turning it numb.

Her hand fell from Ludvin's, and he faded away, as did their crowd, fearful as the Crownsmen began fighting them anew. The people had been beaten back once today by the Crownsmen. Bloody Bess had shown herself to be ruthless and a mageri in addition to a queen with command of all of the Jucar's forces. But the people here today had heard Ulan; they had seen Ludvin. She needed them alive to spread the word of Bess's falsehood. She only hoped they would spread the truth.

Ludvin's truth.

Someone grabbed her hand, and while she could see no one, she was almost pulled off her feet, yanked away from the frantic crowd.

She heard cries behind her, as though she'd vanished like Ludvin's ghost. As though she'd deprived the Crownsmen of their prey. But who? And how?

She couldn't see anyone. There was just herself and whoever pulled her along as though they were a force of nature. But that couldn't be so, because whoever it was had surely sent the javelin and the sleek creature to save her skin, and thus had to be at least partially mortal like her.

* * *

Ruggerio

He'd shunned a cloak or anything flowing that might catch fire, and ran only in a doubled tunic and leggings, thick boots, and a scarf that wrapped around his head and neck and across his face to protect his lungs against the fire raging at All Souls Church. Only his eyes were visible and unprotected, and they burned in the heat, so dry it felt as though they would crack as he dodged debris, headed straight into the flames. He ducked, rolled, searched for cornerstones, capstones or crossbeams where the null-wards would have been placed. The palace would be warded; he'd need nulls to infiltrate. The Restoration had taken their precious few into battle with Bloody Bess. This was the only place he knew to find more, but the smoke instantly infested his lungs, hazed over his sight.

He gasped in a breath and took in ash instead of air, spasmed over in a paroxysm of coughing. A crack barely registered over the razors of pain sawing his chest as his body betrayed him, trying to hack up his inner organs. The one wall still partially standing gave way. He dove to the ground but not quickly enough to avoid the beam that slammed into him, rolling him onto his back and skidding him across the floor until he was stopped by debris.

He choked and wheezed, gasped and forced his eyes open. At least the air was clearer here. Still superheated by the fire, but a touch cooler. He'd fallen with one arm trapped under him and forced himself not to use the other hand to wipe the gritty gumminess out of his eyes so that he could see better. He'd only make it worse, and he'd dried up any tears that might wash the sludge away. If he scratched his eyes now, there'd be no one to heal him. No rescue. No survival.

Ruggerio could see only as far as his other hand, stretched out in front of him. He shifted, rolling off his arm in time to watch the next fiery beam fall right across his middle. He was caught up against the debris. There was nowhere to go. He tried to let his body go slack rather than brace for impact and break anything, but it was no good. The only thing he managed to fight was the impulse to catch it, which would only burn and break his hands.

But his ribs....

He heard them crack, *felt* them crack like the beams swallowed by fire. But only one…maybe two. He feared they would pierce his lungs. That he would die here. In this church.

Become one of Ulan's ghosts.

Oh, bloody hell, no.

If he was already dead, then he couldn't do himself further harm trying to live. He pushed his pain as far from himself as possible. Doing what he'd taught his men to do. His spies. No longer his people, but *hers.* Bloody Bess's. It was up to him to do something about that.

Ruggerio ignored his pain, ignored what his body told him he could and couldn't do. Moved against reason and grating bone to get his hands into position, placing them against the burning beam, held in his equally burning need to cough until it burst out of him and used the force of that explosion to give him the power to thrust the beam off. It shifted but didn't lift. Not entirely, but enough for him to sit. For him to move. Perhaps, if he could manage to get his legs free, he could escape the burning church with or without the nulls. Looking at the beam, working at the problem, he realized the solution had, literally, fallen into his lap. One end of the beam wasn't burning. It was bespelled. Nulled. If he could hack it free…

He gave the beam another massive push, ignoring the agony in his hands, his lungs, his entire body aflame like the church. His chest a single moment away from a strong seizure that might push one of his punctured ribs through his lungs, ending him. But not until he got the null to Ulan. What she would do with it, he had no idea. He was the assassin. He was… Motes floated in his vision. Entire voids all their own. Voids, worlds. Possibilities of nothingness.

He suspected he was drifting. Maybe dying. There was a peace in it that he couldn't be allowed. Ruggerio and peace had never existed side by side, and he refused to accept it now. Pain would bring him back.

He heaved again, and it wrung a depthless cry from him, but the beam *moved.* Far enough that he could slide his legs out, get to his shaky feet, and draw his weapon. His hands were so burned they didn't want to work. So burned that the hilt buried itself in his flesh and he had to close one hand around it with the other, but he hacked at the flaking plaster that held the null medallion to the crossbeam until it fell to the floor. Then he sheathed his sword on his second try and picked up the palm-sized null to bury it in his garments so that he no longer had to hold anything in his hands. He need only hold himself upright as he escaped the flames. The church was no more.

Ruggerio himself was smoking as he stumbled out into the night. Had anyone been watching, they'd have sworn they'd seen two ghosts at All Souls that eve.

CHAPTER NINETEEN

Bess

Bess ignored the call of "My Queen" and the knocking at her door as she stood on her balcony and watched the heart of her city burn. From the ashes, she would build a new heart that would beat in time with hers. A new Church would rise, one that married mageri magic with the sacrifice of those who did nothing but draw on the nation's resources. The poor, the filthy, the diseased and damaged—

There were cries from below. Screams. The clashing of steel. Another upswell of rebellion, but her men had their orders. They would put down protests by force. Anyone not killed outright would be dragged into her dungeons for later disposal.

The knock at the door became a pounding, and the voices on the other side went from random guards to a voice she recognized more specifically.

Strego called, "My Queen? Certainly nothing we can't handle, but you wanted anything strange brought to your attention right away."

Had someone summoned him when she didn't respond? In a fury, she whirled from the window. She didn't like that they'd appeal to him for even a moment. It was her prerogative to keep her own counsel.

She had the door open and was snarling in their faces before she even knew she'd flown across the room. Strego flinched back, and the guard peering around his not insignificant form flicked spittle from his cheek.

He swallowed down his fear, lowered the hand he'd raised to knock again, and said, "My Queen, I thought you'd want to know. A spirit was spotted tonight outside of All Souls, identifiable to all because your people brought his head back on a pike. It was Ludvin, the former head of the Restoration. He was hand in hand with a figure who then disappeared. A woman, witnesses said, but it's impossible to say for certain because she was not caught, and all eyes were on the ghost."

Bess stared at him. Fury a torrent she couldn't unleash. Not without a proper target. And so it tore her up instead.

"Did he speak?" If he'd spoken…he could tell the people she hadn't returned the anima to the land as she'd said. But who would they believe? And with all the power she wielded, did it matter? Would they dare act on that disbelief? The clashing steel below said that the answer was *yes*, which meant that the greater question was whether she could crush that disbelief out of them and still have the power left over to defeat their enemies.

"He did not."

Not this time, perhaps. But the woman with him hadn't been caught, and that meant she might try again. Or the bosewight could reappear all on his own.

"I need to question the Animist," she said, stepping out into the hallway, glad that she hadn't allowed her maid in to help her disrobe.

"But my Queen, the interrogators have been with him, upon your orders," Strego reminded her as though she was daft. "It won't be a pleasant sight."

"I don't expect pleasant. I expect results, and they haven't brought me any. They've had their–" She'd almost said fun, and she had to rein herself in. When had she become her father? Her brothers? Thinking that other peoples' pain was the prize in a great game?

"They've had their time with him, and it hasn't been enough. It's my turn now."

She swept out into the hallway, leaving them to fall into position around her or risk touching her person and facing the consequences. They fell back. As Strego led the way through the corridors to the dungeons below, she recalled her last visit–to the mad mageri Ceramor in the oubliette. Flea-ridden, covered in his own filth, seeping wounds from scratching at the fleas and from trying and failing time and again to pull himself out of the hole. Ceramor had been her brother's top man before he'd stolen the anima from Jannik's hounds trying to store up enough power to save his wife from the Rot, only to find her dead on his return. Not that it would have mattered. The Rot, as they'd found, gave way to no magical means of healing. And Ceramor went not so quietly mad–feral–with all of those hounds baying in his head. The body was only meant to hold its own spark. Holding onto so much more without expending it burned out the system.

Which was why Bess used the power she stole. She hoarded some for when it was most needed, but she never kept it all. As for the voices in her head... She could contain them, wall them off. She'd almost managed it before Roha had wrested her shadow girls from her. They'd beaten and battered at her walls until her head felt it might burst apart, but it hadn't done so. Not until the battlefield, when she'd transformed...

She would not think of that. The tentacles sprouting from her neck and shoulders as though her skin had literally peeled away and the venom the voices spewed became poison pustules instead of suckers.

No, she would not think of that.

She'd lost time. They were at a large oaken door, and Strego was demanding entrance. She had missed their procession through the castle. Missed the turns they had taken should she need to find her way back. A chill overtook her that had nothing to do with the creeping dampness that she could now feel. *This was not her thought.* Bess would have no need to find her way back. She would have her personal guards. Strego. Other guards if something were to happen to these.

Maybe some part of her worried about whether she could trust them. Or maybe Vedik was bleeding through, a soldier checking for escape routes. Surely just his caution. Only that.

A pain in her right eye pulsed as though her heart were right behind it pounding with enough pressure to pop the orb right out. The oak door opened, and she flinched at the pain tearing through her head at the sound, biting back harshly on the wince that escaped.

No one asked whether she was all right. Her headaches had become so frequent that the only people allowed to ask were those ready with tonics. Anyone else risked her wrath, which could be anything from the worst duty assignments imaginable to having their heads nearly handed to them.

Now that was a thought. Rip one head off and assuredly it would never happen again. If only she could. She'd start with her own.

"Reg—Lord Strego and My Queen," said the man on the other side of the door, the captain, based on the full jacket he wore rather than the sleeveless vest of the others. He buckled to one knee, bowing his head. "Word was sent ahead, but I'm afraid that try as we might, there has been nothing new. The Animist says he had no knowledge of his acolyte Roha's rebellious leanings and that his Church has no ties to the Restoration. We have records of the other churches. Your men have already ridden to the closest outposts to them, upon your decree. I don't know that there's much else to be learned."

"Oh, I will learn it," Bess said, sweeping him aside.

He began to topple in the narrow passageway and had to catch himself on one hand. She didn't care. She continued on. Down the stone hallway unlined with tapestries to keep out the cold, past the rows of cells, all occupied. She ignored the stench of voided bowels and unwashed bodies; there had been no lavender-scented kerchief pressed into her hand this visit. She ignored the whimpers of those caged and continued past on her way to the torture chambers.

At the other end of the row of cells was another oaken door. She waited for the captain to catch up, amused herself by standing aside just enough that he had to blade his body to get by her without touching anything but the hem of her dress. Then he opened the door and led the way through. There were three more doors, all open, but only one with the shallow panting of pain emanating from within.

The captain led them there. Bess stepped inside to see the Animist stretched out naked on a huge wooden table. Or, he would have been naked, if someone, probably worried for Bess's delicate sensibilities, hadn't taken the remains of his white vestments and laid them like a blanket over his nether region. White vestments slowly turning dark yellow as the sword cut to his belly wept purulent fluids. He was tied at the wrists and ankles with thick ropes connected to wheels that when turned would pull those ropes tauter and tauter until eventually his joints would dislocate, his muscles tear, his stomach wound gape wide.

The Animist's eyes practically rolled in their sockets. Sweat covered every inch of him that she could see, matting his hair to his head, joining with tears on his face so that it was a sodden mess. The interrogator stood at the crank at the Animist's hands, as though he'd just recently turned it again, though already the Churchman was arched nearly off the table. Bess could count his ribs, see his sinews. Bards could probably have composed ballads to the creation of such steely tension from too-giving flesh.

The rack wasn't all they'd done to him, clearly. There were cuts as well, which had to be stinging from the sweat running into them and any filth along with it. And those cuts seeped, that blood calling, a way in for her, not that she couldn't find her own path.

"Everyone out!" she commanded. Her voice bounced off of the unadorned stone, echoing.

"Everyone?" Strego asked, softly, neutrally. Confirming, not questioning.

"See to it," she said with a regal nod. "Wait on the other side of this door."

"My Queen," he bowed his way out.

She didn't watch him leave. Or the others. She had eyes only for the Animist. When she heard the door shut, she knew they were gone. She could feel it in the desolation of the room. Pain strobed behind her eye again, but it was nothing, *nothing* to the pain she saw before her, and that meant she could ignore it.

She stepped closer to the table. "Animist."

He did not turn. Did not look. His eyes were no longer rolling but fixated on the ceiling as though he'd chosen a focus and was attempting something with it. Prayer or meditation, perhaps.

Bess hissed. "Most have the courtesy to respond when addressed by their Queen, but there is no need. I don't require your cooperation. Just your blood."

She drew a finger along the side of his face, through the slick of sweat and tears, almost a caress. Down his neck and along his collarbone, straight into one of the fresher cuts along his ribs. She drew her finger back and tasted his blood, sweat and tears on her tongue. The salt of it brought moisture flooding her mouth, then the tang, the spice of fear, but also fortitude. It was heady. It was–

She lowered her head, scented him like a lover, and then, with a sideways glance at the door she didn't want to acknowledge, she lowered her lips to the cut, darted her tongue inside, quick laps. Like a kitten given cream. The Animist's breathing changed, and she realized he was muttering a spiritu.

The pain in her head spread to the other eye, which throbbed in time. Her vision began to go unsteady, so she shut her eyes, blocked out the world and gave in to the pain. Her pain, his. She used the fingernail she kept sharpened to slice into his skin, a wound all her own, a fresh bleed, and lowered her mouth to it, going by instinct, and the call of all that lovely pulsing power, sucking in a rhythm that matched the beat of his heart. Until their heartbeats pulsed in time.

He tasted of smoke and anise. Lingering flavors, scents. Like braziers. Like churches or sickrooms. She felt the Animist convulse as she gulped him down, and pulled back to whisper her will into his veins.

You will *tell me what I need to know. You* will *acknowledge your Queen.*

She pushed with her power to send it along, then pulled back, blinking prisms of pain from her vision. The Animist collapsed onto the rack, his body still stretched taut, but unable to hold his rictus of pain, wrung out from hours of torture, the little bit of fight he had left in him stolen away. He turned his head toward her so slowly she growled and gripped it between her hands, wrenching it for him. His eyes made contact with hers, and they were full of fear. Recognition for exactly who she was and what she was capable of. Finally, someone who could see her and treat her with the proper respect…for as long as he lasted.

"Tell me," she said out loud.

His head twisted in her grip.

He shouldn't have been able to resist her.

She snapped out again with her will, like a lash. She would break him if she had to. He was no good to her if not for answers.

"Nothing to give," he said, eyes clenched shut against the new pain. "Didn't know…Roha."

"You lie!" She changed her grip to hold the sides of his head with her fingers so that she could pry his eyelids open with her thumbs, dig into the sockets as she did so, the threat clear enough. She could pop his very eyes out if necessary. It sounded horrible and messy, and she didn't relish it. Not when there were better ways. Primarily, she wanted him to look at her when he spoke. She wanted to gauge his honesty. He shouldn't be able to lie. Shouldn't be able to avoid her. But she'd had no teacher and no training. He'd had all the privileges of the Church behind him. Who knew what he had learned to withstand?

His eyes bulged as she held his lids open, reddened, pained. But he didn't glance away now. Couldn't. Her will held him. Her heartbeat called his, and right now it was pounding.

"I don't. If Roha's back, I don't know," he gasped. "I've no ties to… Restoration."

Bess stepped back but flicked a hand, using a touch of her stolen power to keep his eyes open, unable to blink or turn away. She flicked the other, and the wound she'd opened tore further, ripping straight across. The Animist found the strength to writhe as she peeled his skin back, then ripped off a section entirely. She pulled out the blood, sending droplets flying through the air. She turned the skin toward them so that it acted as a parchment and spattered the blood over it in the pattern she held in her mind, the face of the rebel whose head she had on her pike.

"And this man?" she asked, showing him the rebel's face drawn with his own flesh and blood. "Do you recognize him?"

The Animist was keening. His eyes open but glazed. She would not get much more sense out of him. She snapped him with her power, lashing him across the face like a slap.

"Animist, with me! Do you recognize this man?"

His features froze, and she realized he was trying to shake his head. "N-no," he said when that failed.

"Then you are useless!"

She dropped the power holding his eyes open, his head in place. She tapped into him through his wounds, grabbed onto that essence, and bled out his energies. That lovely spark that powered him. He wouldn't be needing it anymore, but it would do her a world of good.

CHAPTER TWENTY

Myrka

For the first time ever that Myrka could remember, the world was quiet.

Oh, there was that woman–Trusca? Veruska? something like that–breathing, waiting for her response to the question asked. But there wasn't the constant *thrum*, as though the whole world was a plucked string still quivering, agitating at the edges of her awareness. She'd spent her life aching to slap a hand over it. To stop it dead or pluck it again and again and again to make music until the song ended and there was no more. But the one time she'd done just that, it truly had been the end–for her stepmother, for her family's farm, likely for her entire family. She'd never been able to bring herself to go back and confirm what she knew in her heart.

When she'd done it again in Frizenze, she'd strummed, rather than plucked, and the result hadn't been quite as horrifying. The hearth fires had gone out, as had the initial blaze, but she had nearly burned a man alive and brought an inn down around everyone inside, including the boy she was there to protect. Still, the man had lived, hopefully been healed. The inn yet stood, though she had stolen all the warmth and cracked the hearth, at least in the room she'd occupied.

Now all of her power had been nullified. She was at last at peace.

For that alone, she would tell them anything.

If the Restoration could have done this for her and hadn't... Myrka's anger, her doubt burned. Maybe it wasn't fair. Nulls were precious and few. The Restoration had to keep them mobile, able to go where they were most needed. They couldn't afford to waste one on Myrka, to press one into her flesh.

Yet, Frizenze had done so on the king's orders.

But then, royalty had everything, didn't they? All the money, all the resources. All the mageri. One queen supposedly poisoned a king, and rather than accept her death as punishment enough, they had to start a war and throw commoners against each other, let them die to show who was right, if it was even about that rather than territory or pride or something she couldn't even imagine. People were killed, and the land withered from the anima stolen by the mageri for their battlefield constructs. The All suffered, which meant that more people suffered from crop blights, diseases, defects. It was what she was fighting against. It was the *reason* she'd joined the Restoration; they wanted to restore the creative energies. She couldn't lose sight of that.

But it was so, so hard, sitting with the first peace she'd ever known.

Trusca/Veruska coughed into half-gloved hands. They could have been to keep her warm in the chill, but Myrka thought they were also to hide her age. On the surface, they'd sent someone young, as though Myrka might be more likely to confide, but as they sat across from each other, she could see faint lines trailing off into the fall of Trusca's blue-green-black hair, like a raven's wing. Not that it mattered to Myrka. She didn't trust anyone of any age.

"You need our help putting your prince on the throne. We will need insight into fighting Bloody Bess," the woman said. "How were you able to defeat her on the battlefield and escape? A rumor has reached us, but it is hardly to be credited. Two beasts, one of them the queen herself..." Once again she trailed off, giving Myrka the opportunity to answer with the understanding that the conversation would not move on otherwise.

Myrka touched the bandage at her neck to signal that she couldn't speak, though the truth was that she could if she wanted to, very quietly and with a lot of pain. But it made for a good excuse to give as little as possible until she knew more. What was to stop Frizenze from taking all of their secrets, using them to defeat Jucar, and taking it over themselves? Why put a boy king on the throne when they could take it for themselves?

She signaled for a charcoal. Trusca—she decided to go with Trusca, because it was shorter and because she didn't care so very much—appeared surprised she could write, which made her care even less. She came back with a charcoal nearly as thin as a switch, and some paper. She didn't have to go far for it. They were in a small room, clearly meant for correspondence. No weaponry. No frills. This was no castle with places for interrogation and the like. They had to make do, as Myrka had to do the best she could, writing with the paper over her legs. The horrible handwriting would mean Trusca would see her as less literate than she already believed. It irritated Myrka even as she leaned into the perception.

One beest mageri who went feral. Ded now. Other queen, she wrote.

Trusca bit back a gasp, probably thinking there was no point in hiding her reactions around such a low creature as Myrka. "So, it's true. Bloody Bess truly is a mageri. Practicing blood magics."

Myrka nodded, tried to look relieved that there was no need to write more. Ludvin would be amused if he could see her now. But then she remembered. Ludvin...his beheading. The pain of his memory like a mule kick to the chest. She'd been out of it in the woods after running into the sword, but she had seen; she just hadn't been able to act.

He had been her mentor. The best way she could honor him was to stay true to his ideals. He used to say that she was as unsubtle as a knife, but there was no need to be subtle when people saw what they expected to see. It was only when someone acted contrary to a person's presumptions that they were seen and suspected.

"Then Bloody Bess will be going mad herself," Trusca said.

Myrka nodded again.

"You still didn't say how you defeated her."

Oh, bull bollocks! Of course, they would want to know. And she had no ready answer.

Yet, her charcoal was moving before she'd thought things out.

Thought she wuld sacrifice our people. Didn't count on uprising. Wen cast spell to return anima to land, pulled out sparks boosting her ohn power.

It was even true as far as it went, in case there was any way for Trusca to tell. If she was trained in spycraft or whatever. Bloody Bess *had* planned to sacrifice Myrka's people. And she never said *who* had cast the spell to return the anima. She didn't leave Roha out of it because of any love she bore nim, but she didn't know where Roha was and didn't want Frizenze searching nim out, trying to get their hands on Roha's power.

Oh, spirits! Myrka fought to get her breathing back to normal. She wiped the expression at the thought of Roha off her face, but she knew Trusca had seen it. She had to get to Cia. No doubt Frizenzian spy people or whoever were questioning her as well. They had to get their stories straight. They had to talk. They had to figure out what to say and what to hold back. Just until they knew who to trust and how far. Until they knew exactly what was going on. This had been their plan all along–get to Frizenze, enlist their help, get Hostill on the Jucari throne. Restore peace between the two kingdoms. The details, though, had never been clear.

And now that she no longer had to listen to the whole world, she could listen to her gut, which was telling her that something was seriously wrong here. She just didn't know what.

• • •

Cia

Cia lay on her side, knees to chest on the too-short bed in the wonderfully warm room. Any wider and she and Myrka might have been given the bed to share, but instead they'd been placed in small, side-by-side rooms. Their maid, Joia, who creaked and popped and bit back moans such that Cia felt too terrible to request anything not absolutely necessary to survival, slept on a trundle that wedged itself right up against their connecting door, which kept it from opening at night. Perhaps it was intentional to prevent them from plotting, since the corridor was also lost to them due to the guards patrolling their wing. Or perhaps they'd merely been given the last available rooms.

Whatever the case, she was alone, as she'd been in Jucar, but this time without any fear that Garif would return. Also, safe and warm, not hunted or fighting or freezing. It was enough to lull her. Her eyelids were so heavy, and a thick, sinuous weight wanted to roll her and pull her down. For once, she saw no reason to fight it.

But sleep was a trap that closed around her. Something beastly stalked her through a brutal snowstorm coming down so hard that it whipped into her face. She couldn't see it when she looked back, only hear its breath, its footfalls, sense its menace. When it picked up pace, so did she, snow sucking at her feet, threatening not to let her go, to pull her down and let the beast have her. There was an onrush, and instinct had her diving out of the way just in time to miss monstrous jaws, each tooth an icicle sharp as death. But now she was down.

She struggled to get back up, to run again, but wasn't fast enough. The beast's claws caught her clothing, pinned her down. The jaws came down around her, teeth catching the icy snow, and then she was inside the maw, a craggy, cavernous prison. The teeth closed around her, and the monster swallowed her up.

Cia fought as she slid down and down, thinking of Roha, for some reason. When Roha had come to her and she'd frozen nim out. Had there been something about ice? She could remember only the sheer emotion, an explosion of it. All the pain, betrayal, and fear she felt at being manipulated by another again.

The slide ended abruptly, and Cia was free-falling, her stomach left behind when her body was catapulted straight into a hot, bubbling pool. It shocked her system, knocked the air out of her, and for a moment, she was so stunned, all she could do was sink. Did she dare open her eyes? Was she in the belly of the beast? She knew on some level this was a dream. Told herself to wake, but she couldn't do it. Maybe she could at least control herself in this nightmare world.

Open your eyes. And she did, just for an instant, in case the water burned, but it was clear and pure, like a superheated mountain spring. She opened them again, looked around as she stroked for the surface. And stroked. And stroked. She panicked, thrashing around uselessly, using up her air faster. Maybe she'd lost sight of which way was up.

Maybe she did need someone. Roha? Ulan? Ruggerio? The panic was all-consuming. It drove every thought out of her head. Everything but *surface* and *breathe*. The one wasn't a possibility. The other–

She couldn't take it any longer. The breath she'd been holding exploded out of her, and in its place, she took a great gasp. Sucking in water. It would be the death of her, but that didn't matter. She couldn't do anything else. And yet… She didn't choke. Didn't start to die. Somehow, she breathed.

In the dream, she breathed in, breathed out, treating water like air. A calm swept over her like a wave. I can do this and not die. I can reach for Roha and not wither away. How those things got mixed up in her head…it didn't matter. She dove. Roha had come for her on a stream and she would find nim the same way. If the path between them worked both ways, if she could use it to pass messages, maybe she didn't have to fear it. For the good of the cause.

The spring ran deep, and her dive was as far as her fall. Farther. If she hadn't been able to breathe water, she'd have died a watery death. She called for Roha as she swam, as though her voice would actually carry, yet she was surprised when the response came.

Cia?

Roha? I don't know whether I'm here or in a dream. I'm sorry.

Something sent shivers along the pathway from the direction Cia had come, as though there had been a quake, and she froze, torn between going back to investigate and staying right here, but she could feel alarm radiating from Roha. Nes waves of worry almost cancelling the tremors on the other end. *Cia, wake up!* Roha cried through their connection. *Something's happening. Wake up!*

There was a spark, energy thrown through their link, and instantly, Cia was able to wake as she couldn't before.

Her eyes snapped open, and not an instant too soon to see the sword slashing down at her. She rolled aside, into the crevice between the bed and the wall. Her feet hit the ground, and she pushed at the bed, shoving it into the swordsman while screaming her head off against every instinct, because Garif had trained her out of making any noise, whatever he might do to her. But this was an assassination attempt, and Myrka–

She needed to raise the guards. The killer started to round the bed, and she pushed harder on the other side to cut off his path and make room for escape. She couldn't see her attacker's face, which was wrapped in a scarf, black like the rest of his clothing, and revealed only his eyes, voids in the scant moonlight through her arrow-slit window.

Without missing a beat, he leapt up onto the bed and struck again. She got past the end of the bed, but it only put her back to the windowed wall. There was nowhere for her to go in the small room. She ducked, but the sword rang off bone, catching the top of her head instead of taking it off. She felt the blow down to her toes, her head ringing like a bell. She wanted to hold it to make it stop vibrating. To get her vision back to single images.

He was slashing again, and there was only one thing she could think to do–rush in under his guard, within the arc of his swing. Risky, but he held all the cards, and the weapon. And she was losing blood and vision. Focus.

No time to think. She aimed for where she believed him to be and flew at him with all her might, knocking into him hard. Something much harder came down on the back of her head, the pommel of his sword. Pain exploded. Her vision blacked. But she had practice staying conscious under attack. She dropped, struggling to keep her death grip on him, determined to take him down with her, but he struggled and exploded free.

Her door burst in, and finally, *finally* there were guards. Two of them. Her assassin reached to grab her and hold her hostage. On her way up, Cia threw her head forward, right between his legs, straight to his most vulnerable bits. It must have hurt her nearly as much as it did him. The whole room spun, and her stomach lurched as she collapsed to her side.

But the assassin was making tortured noises, and that made it all worth it as her stomach turned itself inside out. She reveled in the pain she'd brought him. But it wasn't enough. She saw that in the instant before her eyes slammed shut against her own pain. She was going to die covered in her own sick. She waited for the blow she saw reflected in his eyes and in the backswing of his sword, but then she heard the rush of feet from her doorway and the ringing of swords. A stifled cry, and the assassin was toppling over.

She was alive, buried under the weight of her assassin.

✦

When she opened her eyes again countless hours later, the room was steadier than her stomach. A purple-clad torso came into view, but when she tried to turn her head, the pain flared so bright it blinded her, sending what little her stomach had left shooting up. She closed her eyes, bit back the pain, and swallowed down the acid and bile. Let the waves of hot and cold agony wash over her until they'd receded enough that she thought she'd live.

Then she tried opening her eyes again. Rolled them and only them up until she could see that the form belonged to Zega, who was looking down at her, concern written all over her face. Myrka was at her side, looking worried as well, which was something considering the way she felt about the woman who'd married a mageri.

"You have our humblest apologies," Zega said, seeing that Cia was awake. "Your assassin has been dispatched. A stronger guard has been set. It will not happen again."

Cia didn't want to face Zega lying down. Too big a disadvantage. And yet she couldn't rise. She closed her eyes again, breathed. Tried to think through what she wanted to say when her head was a nest of swimming pain and stinging bees. Stinging eels, in keeping with the swimming pain? It didn't matter. It was as though concentration was racing away from her like those eels that were only in her head. Thought eels shooting away before they could be captured.

"How did it happen? Why?" Cia asked. Let someone else grasp what she couldn't.

"Unfortunately, the man was killed, so he can't be questioned. He came from outside the castle, that much we're certain of. He wasn't anyone from within."

"You have no control here then? Hostill, is he safe?"

"We've doubled the guard on him as well, but yes, he's secure."

"Can I–" no, she wasn't going anywhere. "Can Myrka see him?"

"I can arrange that, but the attempt wasn't made on Hostill. Or on your friend, although we can't be certain the assassin wouldn't have tried for her next, if nothing else because those through the connecting door might have been struck down running to your rescue."

Myrka gave an exhalation that Cia couldn't interpret. "I *tried*," she said. "I heard you scream, but Joia sleeps like the dead, and I couldn't budge her. I had to run for the hall, and the guards, and– You know what happened from there."

"He was after *me*? Why?"

"We have no answers." Zega said.

"Speculations?"

Zega glanced away, which meant that she did. Or they did. The Crown.

Cia would have to be very careful with what she said next, and she didn't feel up to phrasing things properly. To look Zega in the eyes to see the truth, as though the emissary wouldn't be schooled in hiding it. "The king must have a plan to investigate this treachery? While the assassin may have come from outside, surely, he'd want to be certain he isn't harboring anyone who would conspire to hire or allow an assassin into his court."

With the king in residence, this hunting lodge must be the most heavily fortified place in Frizenze right now. Was the investigation over because the assassin was dead or because the king himself had ordered Cia's death, so that he would have sole influence over the Jucari heir? There were easier, quieter, ways to kill, but perhaps he'd wanted to make it appear someone held a grudge against her as a traitor to Frizenze. Though...if the king had wanted her dead, would his guards have foiled the assassination attempt?

If she could have caught her thoughts before they escaped, maybe she could have made some sense of them. Then again, there were so many secrets here. Inner workings she had yet to uncover. A pattern she had not yet pieced together.

"Of course, there will be an investigation," Zega said, "but that is for others to handle. Since you insist, it is not beyond belief that some might take it upon themselves to do what they feel the king cannot—rid him of the lady who allowed his sister to be accused and killed in a foreign land. Some in his court might take it badly that you live while she does not, and that you're close to the boy who would rule Jucar. King Avize has now ordered that you be heavily guarded when summoned about the castle, and that elsewise you will be locked in your quarters for your own safety."

"For my safety? I was locked in tonight and nearly killed. Am I truly to believe one of the king's people would attack me without his explicit instructions?" The words were out of Cia's mouth before she could think them through, realize that it was a dangerous thing to practically accuse the king of murder while dependent on his mercy and aid.

"Is there anything you would not do for your Hostill if you thought it was in his best interests?" Zega fixed her with a dark look.

"I have not yet encountered it," she said, too tired to see the trap.

"Then perhaps you need to consider your own family."

"My family?"

"Did your friend here not light your uncle on fire?"

Cia allowed her eyes to close. Could it be Uncle Frazier who'd ordered her assassination—either against the king's orders or believing he arranged what was left unspoken? Would Myrka have been next?

She heard boots shushing on the floor, as though the wearer tried and failed to go quietly. The door closed, and she realized she'd been falling back into sleep when a voice woke her.

"Cia, I'm sorry. I don't know that this was my fault, but if it was retaliation...I'm so sorry," Myrka whispered, for her ears only. "I don't know what to believe. What Zega says makes sense, and yet…something is wrong here, I can feel it."

Those were the last words Cia heard, and they resounded in her mind along with the pain, wrapping and redoubling. *Something is wrong here, I can feel it.* They gave her nightmares from which she couldn't wake.

CHAPTER TWENTY-ONE

Ulan

Ulan was pulled around a corner and down an alley. She'd just begun to recognize where she was when the phantom who'd saved her from the onrushing Crownsmen staggered into the side of a building. There was a gasp, then the figure fell to both knees, and Ulan's hand flew free. Ulan dropped too, and she fell hard, bruising her shins, exhausted and coughing. She clutched her stomach to remind herself to breathe shallowly rather than take great breaths of the smoke-filled air. They were in a back alley, a few buildings down from what had once been Haelin's messenger shop.

She turned her head to see that the person gasping beside her was none other than Haelin herself. She would have sworn the messenger would be long gone, but as she watched, Haelin slowly toppled from her knees over onto her rump. Only a splayed hand kept her from continuing her roll down to the ground.

Ulan felt as though she'd like to collapse as well, but might be needed to get them both up and running again at the first sign of Crown red and black.

"Why are you still here?" Ulan asked. "Why help me? And...how? I have to go back."

"You don't," Haelin said, the sound coming with a wheeze and a rattle. She waved a hand as though to ask Ulan to wait for her to gain more air before continuing. "My ferfal will lead him."

Him? She knew about Ruggerio?

"Ferfal?" *That* was the question that came out?

"My pet. The one...saved your life. Bandy. Smart." She breathed. "Will wait for him." Breath. "Come to me."

"How does it know him?" Ulan wasn't going to use Ruggerio's name, in case this was somehow a trap. She had a sense that Haelin and Ruggerio played some game she had only vaguely heard of and would never learn. Both too many steps ahead for her to catch up.

"Knows all my customers."

"Why?"

Haelin waved the question away. Breathed and didn't answer for several beats. Until she could rise to her feet once more. When she was eye to eye with Ulan, still wheezing, one hand held to the building as though to keep her upright, she said, "When Ruggerio comes. When we're seated and private. Don't like to repeat myself."

Two squeaks sounded, and Ulan looked around frantically for mice or rats that might have been driven their way by the fires. After the Rot, she was not going to take any chances. She would stomp them on sight, no matter how she'd once let the little beasties be. But Haelin put a hand to her arm, and when Ulan glanced at her to see whether they were about to disappear again, she had a tired smile on her face. "Be well. It's Bandy."

If it squeaked, it was a rodent, and...Ulan's heart quaked. She moved out of Haelin's hold and away. She didn't want to be anywhere near when Haelin's *pet* came close, even if it had saved her life. Had it known what it was doing or did it like to chomp necks? Maybe it wouldn't gnaw Haelin's customers or friends if she didn't signal it, but if she decided they were enemies? Ulan shuddered.

Then the thing bounded into sight, a long, low brown beastie with a purplish stripe down its back like fish oil, with Ruggerio fast on its heels. Ulan was so glad to see him, she forgot her terror of the beast, ready to throw herself at her cousin until he yelled, "Stop!"

He was about to fall down himself and smelled like burned flesh… Her touch might have sent him into shock. Or worse, snapped him out of it when the shock was all that kept him going.

"Follow me," Haelin commanded, leading them the dozen paces down the alley into the ruins of her shop. The back wall was no more. But miraculously, the explosion had done no harm to the wall it shared with its neighbor or to the front wall, which still stood. In the vee of the remaining walls, in a portion of the shop where Haelin had taken and received messages, packages and the like, lay a partially singed woolen carpet worn thin. Beneath that was a hinged door with a lock that opened with a key from around Haelin's neck. Haelin preceded them down a wooden ladder that bowed as though every step might break it. At the bottom, she lit candles that made Ulan flinch after all the fire they'd seen.

When the hatch had opened, Ulan expected nothing more than a root cellar, a room like she and Cia had been thrown into when the Restoration had first caught them. But what she saw was bigger than that. It had not only been dug out to good proportions, but had been covered in lime plaster to hold back the earth. There was shelving on every wall, but only a quarter full.

Ruggerio slid down the last few rungs, and Haelin and Ulan both caught him, though Haelin immediately sank to the ground, leaving Ulan to hold his weight. Her cries and his spun together as she felt her cousin's skin slough off under her hands, so burned it was a wonder he was still upright. And then he wasn't, instead on the floor of the cellar, the pain so unbearable his eyes rolled back in his head, and he went out like a candle snuffed.

"Ruggerio!" Ulan cried, afraid she really had lost him. She turned on Haelin. "Can't you do anything? Heal him?"

"I don't have much left in me. I'm weak already."

Ulan was glad they were past any pretentions that she didn't have the ability.

"Take from me then. You can do that, can't you? I give it willingly," Ulan said desperately.

Haelin's eyes were dark and intense as she stared up at Ulan from her half-reclining position on the floor, propped up on her elbows, even that seeming an effort. "That way lies a dark path I won't travel, and you don't have much left to give. Not after your display with the spirit in the courtyard."

"I will give anything I have. Please, you must. He's all I have left. He can't die on me too." The last broke out of her, along with tears she thought herself too dry to cry. She raised a hand to her face to catch them and found it coated with ash.

"I'll do what I can on one condition," Haelin said solemnly, and Ulan looked up, vision blurry through the debris in her eyes.

"Anything. Name it. Please, he's our hope."

She was sure she'd never thought any such thing about Ruggerio, and wasn't certain she believed it now. Yet it had come out of her mouth. Ruggerio had conviction and the willingness to act on it, which was more than most. She didn't know whether he was right about his methods, but she didn't know that he wasn't. Not in this instance. She only knew that *this* was wrong. Ruggerio dying right here, right now, when there was something they might do about it. When she'd already lost so much.

"If I help you, you help me."

"Yes. We owe you already. I do, certainly. You help Ruggerio, and we're both beholden to you."

Haelin nodded and reached for Ruggerio's closest hand. She closed her eyes, took two shaky breaths, and then opened them again.

"He has some kind of ward. I can't reach him."

Ulan jerked. He'd been successful then. But at what cost?

"A null," she said. "Taken from the Church. I can take it away…"

"No," Haelin answered. "It's not safe out there. I have something."

She went to one of the half-filled shelves and took from it a hinged metal box the size of a small bread loaf. She dumped out the contents, and Bandy squeaked, racing up Haelin as though she was a spiral staircase and leaping from her to the shelf. Haelin quickly grabbed up a handful of whatever was there, which looked something like congealed sawdust, and a chain dangled free before Haelin twisted her hand to catch and hide it. She then tucked it away into a fold of her tunic.

"Now, now," she said as Bandy began scarfing up the detritus left on the shelf, "not too much or you'll be punch-drunk like the last time!"

Bandy squeaked again, and Ulan imagined it sounded indignant, which was ridiculous. The rodent couldn't possibly understand.

"It's a waste, keeping his treats in an artefact box, but it's the only way he can't sniff them out." She sighed. "I suppose I'll have to find a new place to hide them in the future."

"An artefact box?" Ulan asked.

Haelin rifled Ruggerio's unconscious body and came up with a palm-sized amulet. "Ah ha!" Then to Ulan, "Yes, it keeps contained any magics shut within, including null effects."

She placed the amulet within the box and shut the lid, though she didn't replace it on the shelf where Bandy could get to it.

Instead, she knelt with it beside Ruggerio, and worked again on evening out her breath.

Ulan watched for the rise of anima from Haelin's working, suddenly fearing what it would do to the root cellar, wondering how Haelin would prevent the same spell that was supposed to save Ruggerio from draining him, her. But if Haelin feared the results, she would have said something, and Ulan couldn't force the word 'stop' past her lips. Instead, she stared at Ruggerio as though she might see him magically flesh out in front of her.

His breath hitched as Haelin's steadied. Ulan took a great gasp in and held it, praying to the All as she hadn't since Dazia lay dying of the Rot. Then bargaining. If Ruggerio lived, she would work harder to repair their relationship and to be his conscience. To get herself right, not with the Church, but with the All itself. When she had to breathe or collapse, her pent-up air burst out of her, and she gasped in more. At that moment, Haelin's hand went slack, falling open with Ruggerio's still inside. But she hadn't seen any rise of anima. Any cracking of their foundations. Had Haelin already been too spent even for a working?

Bandy squeaked in fear, racing up and nudging Haelin's cheek, and when that didn't yield results, putting its cold nose in her ear. Her head rocked minimally at that, away and back. It chuffed, hopping away as though in triumph, but not going far before it sprinted back to her, climbed and sniffed and then settled itself under Haelin's arm, head on her chest, which rose and fell with her breaths.

Ulan pulled the hatch shut behind them. There was nothing she could do about the rug if anyone came looking, but at least no one would see the light from their cellar. Then she finally allowed herself to sink to the floor as well. She watched over the others as long as she could, assuring herself of each breath, but eventually, sleep overtook her.

When she woke, it was to a cold nose on hers, and a pair of glowing eyes staring at her. She jumped and the creature squealed and practically levitated into the air, back bowed. Ulan crab-crawled backward, into one of the shelves, which she sent rocking. The ferfal disappeared beneath the one opposite, and reappeared in an instant, shaking its head fiercely from side to side with something in its jaws. Ulan screamed when she realized the *something* was still moving and trying to flap its way free. When it *got* free, she screamed again, but the ferfal leapt faster than she would have thought possible and batted it straight out of the air, down to the ground, and pounced before it could retake flight. The carapace cracked with a sound out of proportion to its size.

Ulan flinched aside rather than watch it devour its meal, but couldn't resist sneaking glances when it finished, fascinated by the way it fastidiously gnawed clean its tiny, nearly hand-shaped front paws. Then it curled into a ball to do the same with its middle and back sets of paws, finishing with a chirp and heading back toward her. She was already pressed against the wall and had nowhere else to retreat, but it stopped short of touching her this time and sat on its back and mid legs to regard her, front paws in the air, crossed together as though over the head of a cane. Its head was cocked, its whiskers twitching. It chirped again, inquisitively, she thought, before inching forward and chirping once more.

Ulan didn't move, and the ferfal butted its head against her knee as a cat might do when it wanted to mark a person. Maybe there was a musk in the air along with the scent of smoke and blood that clung to them, but she couldn't be certain. Tentatively, she moved her hands from where she discovered she sat on them and held one out for Bandy to sniff at, hoping he wouldn't take it as an invitation for a bite. He took a whiff and head butted the hand as well, and she scratched him behind his tiny ears, but he moved his head to rest his chin in her hand, and she ended up petting his neck while he closed his eyes in bliss.

"He likes you," a creaky voice said. Haelin moved around until she, too, was sitting up, supported against a shelf that rocked before steadying. "He's generally shy at first. Or mischievous. Surprised he didn't make a nest of your hair."

"He wouldn't have enjoyed the screaming."

Haelin gave a tired smile, "No, I suppose not."

"Is that how you met?"

"He was stealing my food. It was my mail he tried to make a nest of. I had to 'leave' things around for him to use instead, ribbons and bands from around my mail packets. Between that and the little bandit that he is, Bandy seemed appropriate. We now have an understanding. I give him tidbits; he keeps my place vermin-free."

Bandy squeaked, as though in agreement.

Haelin rose and immediately wavered. She steadied herself on a barrel, and Bandy squeaked again, racing with that odd leaping gait to her side as though he could provide support with his long, lithe body. But Haelin got her tremors under control and reached for a layer of linen on a shelf, then kept her hand on that shelf, supporting herself as she pried the top off a barrel with her other hand. She dipped the linen into the barrel, let it drip off the excess moisture, and replaced the top. She carried the sodden material to Ruggerio and unspooled it the little way it would go. There wasn't much. Cloth had been scarce since the Blood War had begun.

"It's just water, a rain barrel I keep for emergencies. If I hadn't collapsed with exhaustion, I'd have thought to bind his wounds last night," she said. "I hope it's not too late."

The candles had burned down but not gone out, and Ulan could see that Ruggerio was still unconscious. His wounds were not so horrible now, but they were far from healed. There was hardly enough new skin growth to cover them. It would be so easy for them to tear or for anything at all to get into them. For infection to set in.

Ulan stepped forward. "Let me."

She took the linen from Haelin and knelt beside Ruggerio, holding the linen off to the side to drip a bit more before laying it on him, but she was not careful enough, and a drop landed on him. He hissed and spasmed up in pain, the movement causing more agony, which created more involuntary reaction.

"Shh, shh," she soothed, as though that had ever done any good.

She'd have to lay the cloth down quickly to minimize the pain as best she could. She gauged her target and her timing and wrapped the worst of his burns across his chest and shoulders, up over his neck and the right side of his face in the cold, wet cloth. She could only hope that the healing Haelin had done already would help, along with this protective layer, and that they were keeping further irritants out rather than inviting anything in.

Ruggerio hissed in several breaths, taking them in through his teeth, awake enough to work with them rather than against. So strong in the face of tremendous pain. She hoped he would go out again, that he wouldn't have to stay awake for what had to be absolutely excruciating. But she also hoped that he wouldn't sleep, so that they could get answers. She knew how important it was for someone to *want* to hold on. And nothing would make Ruggerio fight like something to focus his mind on, apart from his pain.

After what felt like a lifetime, he opened his eyes, looking briefly at Haelin before slamming them shut again, the touch of air too much on his probably smoke-scoured eyes. For once, Ulan thought she could read his mind.

"Thank you for saving my cousin," Ulan breathed. "How can we repay you?"

"I need to escape the city. I have ways, as you've seen. But the queen has mageri along the walls, and I can no longer do this on my own. I know who you are. I know you can help. I was prepared to offer my help in return when I came upon you in need."

Ulan would have said that was convenient, but it had been far more convenient for them than Haelin.

"Kill…queen," Ruggerio said, without opening his eyes. His voice sounded like branches cracking in a windstorm or the popping of sap in a raging fire. "Nowhere to run while…lives."

"I have responsibilities to others. It's not up to me," Haelin answered, which was…interesting bordering on disturbing. What other players were there in this grand farce?

"Who is it up to then?" Ulan asked so that Ruggerio wouldn't have to strain himself again.

Haelin wouldn't meet her gaze, and Ulan sighed loudly. She'd told Haelin earlier that Ruggerio was their hope, but maybe not their *only* hope. Ulan had shown that she had more to give than she thought, and if she waited for Ruggerio to be well enough to take the lead… well, things were happening in the world with or without them. They wouldn't wait for him to heal. But she wouldn't give a thing until she knew who she was dealing with. Haelin putting them in her debt could have been a trap from the beginning.

"You saved our lives tonight," Ulan said. "We won't turn you in for anything you might say here. It must be clear to you that we are no friends to Bloody Bess. I would expect it is the same for you, since you went against her Crownsmen."

"It is not simply my secret to divulge. There are others who might be at risk." Haelin said, turning back and staring at Ulan as though willing her to understand.

Ulan stared back, holding strong.

"If you want us to risk ourselves and our cause to aid your escape, we have to know we're on the same side. You said you know who we are. We need to know who you are, who your people are, especially now that my cousin has opened his mouth about killing the queen. But he is right, as long as she is in power, there will be no safe place to run."

Haelin chewed a lip. Bandy chirped, stretched to make himself long against her, top paws rising as far as her knee. Then he latched on like she was a tree he intended to climb before doing that very thing. He ended up on her shoulders, claws kneading into her hair as though to offer comfort.

She bumped him with her head, and he bumped her back, and finally she said, "You will swear to absolute secrecy?"

Ulan considered her words. "I will swear to only share your secrets with those whose knowing will not endanger your life and will be for the good of Jucar as we see it and not as Bloody Bess reckons it." Ulan looked to Ruggerio, who shut his eyes against his pain and nodded his head fractionally.

She chewed her lip again. "Whose knowing will not endanger my life or the lives of others like me?"

Ulan felt a stirring, something she should have known from the moment Haelin had grabbed her in front of the church and brought her to safety, all without stealing the anima from the land. Nothing had cracked or died. And when she'd healed Ruggerio… Ulan should have known. Maybe she'd suspected on some level, because instinctively she'd trusted Haelin not to destroy them all with her power.

Ulan agreed.

"I am Nim," Haelin said, watching for her reaction, as still as a statue. Ulan nodded as the truth she'd already guessed settled over her. "My people are the Nimistry."

Beside her, Ruggerio was as still as a stone. She suspected that even with all of his spying this was news to him, an entire secret society that he knew little or nothing about. She wanted to tread carefully, but what came out of her mouth was, "The who?"

Haelin smiled wryly. "If you'd heard of us, we wouldn't be doing our job. All you need to know is that not all of the Nim go to the Church, and not all who go to the Church stay there. Regardless of what you hear, we are not venerated. The Church's way is not easy; it is not often kind. Some run away. Others are never sent to the Church, which looks less than fondly on babes who come without doweries or offerings to help cover their care. Some parents simply put their Nim children out to the elements and let the anima take them back. They don't kill them, you see. They only "offer them back". Other parents do try to raise them. Some successfully. Others less so.

"But quietly, secretly, there has been a group that finds out about these children, takes them in, teaches them. Such things come at a cost, so there are some, like me, who go out into the cities, who take on jobs, identities, and send monies back to the others. Most especially, we also keep watch and send messages and warnings about anything important to our wellbeing. Bloody Bess's attack on the Church is also an attack on the Nim. It's an attack against everyone with an inherent connection to the anima. And...there are some who know of us, else none would find us at all, nor we them."

Ulan gasped. She had no idea. None at all. And while Ruggerio might be filing away the information, she was thinking of the children. Those poor children, set out only because...because nothing. For no reason. They were blessed. Closer to the All than anyone. Than she was, than Ruggerio. Than Cia or Bloody, Blasted Bess and her evil death magics. She felt tears she was too dry to cry stinging her eyes.

"I have sent warning ahead, and we have all been called home. I have to get there before there's no home to return to."

"How do you get...receive messages so quickly?" Ruggerio asked, voice still horrible to hear.

"We have ways. That is all you need to know."

"Of course, we will help," Ulan said. "I don't know how yet, but we'll find a way."

CHAPTER TWENTY-TWO

Roha

Roha bolted upright yelling Cia's name, cracking nes head against Arresta's. Roha bounced back and glared at Arresta only to be confronted with wild eyes and an upraised hand. The way the side of nes face stung, ni'd been slapped at least once.

"Hurry, the wards are failing and the bosewights are attacking the Sacrima!" Arresta said. "You broke them; you have to unbreak them!"

Roha's heart was pounding. Now it threatened to gallop its way straight out of nes chest. Ni threw off nes bedding, and Arresta lowered nes striking hand to pull Roha up and along.

Roha took Arresta's hand long enough for the boost upward, but it was too awkward for running, and both released the hold to race full out. Roha could hear but not see others, a panic of raised voices along with a tolling bell, a deep, mournful sound striking straight against nes chest.

"To rouse the Sacristers, and warn the countryside," Arresta said, out of breath at the rush. "A night like this, the sound will carry!"

Roha picked up the pace until they were out of the keep, into the bailey. Others were spread out, circling the tower, so ni couldn't get a count of numbers, but they didn't appear thick. Neither was the magic. Tehardy was almost directly in front of them and had nes hands raised. Ni'd made the wards visible by nes will, streams of silver-purple like a web falling over the entire courtyard and tower, encompassing it all like a mist on a fine fall morning, but not one the sun would burn off. Not this mist. *This* one was being eaten alive by the deep purple damage ni'd done to it in nes panic. Roha could see it, right in the center of the tower, but leaching like red wine spilled on fabric and spreading along the threads.

Tehardy sensed nes presence without turning. "This is your doing. You've rested, replenished. You must join your power to ours to restore our wards. If they fail—"

A howl came from their backs, rising to a shriek that ate at nes sanity. Roha spun to see a sunken, spoiled face forming out of the dead, purple-dark space. It was rotted flesh that seethed with maggots before melting from a meat-and-sinews skull. The jaw dropped open, unhinging, releasing a cloud of mist so foul it smelled of putrescence, decayed flesh, rancid food, and voided bowels. Roha choked on it, tried to cough it out.

"Ignore it!" Arresta said. "It can't hurt you—" ni cut off, eyes going wide, as though they might pop out of nes face.

Arresta pulled at nes neck, grappling with something Roha could barely see. Ghostly hands, strangling nim, choking off nes words.

Roha reached to help but was knocked forward by a hard blow between nes shoulder blades. Ni fell headfirst onto the frozen earth of the courtyard. Blooming fever-fields of pain awoke behind Roha's eyes as nes forehead hit hard, then nes stomach threatened to erupt as ni was lifted from behind by one leg and pulled into the air. Terror had Roha clawing at the ground for a handhold, but the blow to the head made nim too slow. The ground was a distant memory, and ni was whirled once, twice, before being flung clear across the courtyard, straight into the web of magic Tehardy tried to hold. Ni struck it like it was a physical thing, slid down, and fell to the ground, feeling as though ni'd been crushed against a wall.

But more than that, the ward felt...alive. Like nothing ni'd ever felt before. If *this* was weak...

"Join us!" Tehardy shouted.

Bosewights pulled at Tehardy's hair, which flew about nim like dandelion fluff in the wind. Behind Tehardy, the snake-man who had brought Roha snapped with teeth and lashed with a whipcord tail and chased bosewights around the courtyard. They disintegrated before him, only to appear elsewhere. Other Nim circled the Sacrima, but the bosewights focused on Tehardy now that Roha was down, and Arresta… Arresta lay motionless.

Roha forced nimself to move. Everything hurt. Bone ground against bone, but ni got to nes knees and from there, wobbled to nes feet. Ni stood beside Tehardy, one hand to nes back, the other thrust out before nim toward the web.

"I don't know how!" ni shouted over the howling.

"Pool your power with ours."

"How?"

But Tehardy was focused too hard to answer. It was enough that ni'd taken Roha's question for agreement. Roha didn't see that there was any other choice. Ni had done this damage. Ni had to stop the bosewights from escaping if this was the kind of chaos they would unleash on their families should they escape.

The next Roha knew, ni felt a questing within nim, something alien and unfamiliar along nes lines of power. Then a tug, as someone picking up a rope, and a very definite *pull* of power being drawn out. Roha wavered, went so dizzy ni had to close nes eyes, set nes feet, lean on Tehardy, who leaned back so that they steadied each other.

Was this what Cia endured when Roha joined her? Something foreign and uninvited invading her? Dizzying and instinctively other that had to be chased out?

But ni couldn't spare the focus to follow this thought right now. The bosewights outside grew in pitch if not in volume, until Roha felt nes ears would bleed. Nes hair was grabbed, yanked, head pulled back until nes breathing was labored.

Ni heard something snap and whip at the bosewights, and realized it must be the snake-man, the sentinel, Arresta had called him. The pressure against nim let up, but then the bosewights gathered themselves and rushed in again, pinching, pulling, twisting, yanking, shrieking.

Roha started to shake but steadied nes knees and dug deeper. This was a problem ni had created. Ni didn't just want to lend power. Ni wanted to help. To learn. Roha found the core of nimself, watched the swirl of energies there, let them feed out and join the purple mist of magics coming from Tehardy. The moonlit magics were the energies from the others meeting up–gold and silver, blue and green, a faint verdigris, blush, carnelian, cardamom, and citrine, all woven into the webbing that wrapped around the Sacrima. Tehardy was the spider at the heart of the web, which was a horrible image after Garif.

Ni forced nes eyes open to examine that web, see if the void-purple patches were mended, and saw that they were, but that Tehardy was still working. The bosewights had stopped howling and pulling, stopped putting any energy into being fearsome and destructive. They were all making a run on one portion of the web, which ni could see because it was bowed. If they broke through, not only would they escape into Frizenze, but also, there was no telling what the backlash of the magic would do to the others.

Roha hadn't been trained, but if Tehardy was holding back on pulling everything out of nim, not knowing how deep Roha's well ran, they would lose. Ni dove back into nimself, into nes well, and threw everything ni had at Tehardy and the wards.

Empty and shaking, Roha opened nes eyes to see the web snap back into place and all go dead silent in the courtyard.

CHAPTER TWENTY-THREE

Bess

There was such unnatural silence in Bloody Bess's head that every time Erdain swung his head in disagreement, the click of the bone-beads woven through his beard echoed throughout the empty chambers. Made of the carved teeth or bone of enemies felled in battle, her mageri wore the adornments braided into their hair and beards. When the wind whipped up on the battlefield, the chattering set the enemy off-balance. Warned that when they were killed, they might not be so lucky as to meet the anima with all of their parts. The symbolism was satisfying.

But not the silence in Bess's head. She didn't trust Vedik's quiescence for an instant, though it aided her for the moment, as she spied on her own men–General Bowstan, her battle-mageri Erdain, and her former-regent, Strego–from behind the screen at the back of the Council room. She could clearly hear them over the missing voices in her head. But she would have to investigate. Things had been off, *she* had been off, ever since she'd killed the Animist. She could feel his stolen power, but not *him*, as though he had managed to do what she'd never fully been able to against any of her conquests, completely isolate his essence. It might have been a good thing, a happy thing, except that the others had gone quiet as well. Too quiet. Was it even possible that the people in her very own body and mind could plot against her?

Even if they could plot, there was nowhere to go with it. She controlled their power and not the other way around. It was the people in this room she had to worry about, and she was only getting distracted by the lack of distraction, which was just...

She was not going to use the word. Not think it. It was a word *others* used, walled people away with. But... she was missing things while she was caught up in her own head, and she needed to listen.

"–snowblind in the passes, then the Frizenzians don't have to defeat us. The terrain will do it for them." It was Bowstan, voice, as always, louder than it needed to be, as though having spent so much of his life shouting orders, he had no idea simply speaking was an option.

There was a pause, and Bess leaned forward, as though it would help her see better. Really, the secret room and its panel were too badly placed for more than a glimpse down the table. Or perhaps it was placed as it was to keep it hidden, but it provided her a mere impression of light and shadows. She knew there were three men only by their voices and their roles. She wanted to know what happened in that pause. Had someone shot a glance at the screen? Did they know she was here? If she could have perfected a spying spell without bankrupting her power...

"You will have all the Crown *and* Church resources at your disposal," Strego said into the silence. The corners of her lips quirked, and she breathed a silent sigh, pleased that her will had held. "And the Queen is pursuing their trainees as well. By the time we march, we should have *all possible* recruits at your disposal." Another pause. "I suppose that's truly more your bailiwick."

More clacking. Perhaps Erdain stroked his beard. Did the beads catch in his fingers? Did he worry them like the prayer beads her devout mother had given her before her father had insisted that she give up 'all that nonsense'?

"But do you not see the problem?" Erdain's voice rose to her.

"Emptying the Magery, I can understand, though I believe the youngest, greenest mageri should remain. They will gain us nothing, and risk us everything if we leave no one behind to learn, to teach, should we… Well, we won't fail, I know that," he quickly said as Strego cleared his throat.

"But will you be able to trust the Nim who come to us from the Churches? They will be extremely resistant after what the Queen did at All Souls, what she did with the Animist, after we take them by force. And I warn you, the Church mageri will refuse to be brought in alive."

"Church mageri?" Bowstan said it like a strike, followed by a string of curses. "The Church is against the use of mageri powers."

"Exactly," Erdain said. "It's antithetical. The *Desperata* are a self-flagellating sect of the Church."

Bess had never heard of the Desperata, and now she was on the edge of her seat. She wanted to learn more. Everything. If there was a source of fresh mageri to join her fight…

"They are zealots. They spend their lives in prayer and repentance, purging their urges by whipping themselves and offering their blood to the anima. They do penance by becoming stewards of the land rather than drawing from it, sometimes ministering to a small flock who have no church nearby, but more often hiding away in small enclaves, most unaware of their presence."

"Then how do you know of it?" Bowstan challenged Erdain.

"Let us just say that I bear the scars."

Bess breathed in. There was a stirring in her head, as though someone had thrown rocks at a hornets' nest. A buzzing, a bumping, a swaying of hive-shaped energy this way and that. Bess's hands rose to her head to hold it steady. She was surprised to find it so small and not swollen to twice its size. Still, she held on to contain it, tried to shush the stirring, closed her eyes against the shifting, strobing light, struggling with the shadows coming through the screen as though they were at war. Another of her headaches was not just coming on, it was here with all the sudden violence of an ambush. If she couldn't hold her ground, she would be hurled right to it, hanging onto the earth as it spun or vomiting parts of herself up onto it.

She struggled to focus, to make sense of Erdain's information. He had been a mageri as long as she'd been alive. At least as long as she could remember. Which meant he'd been part of the Desperata even earlier. How old would that make him? Had he been sent as a child by his parents, religious and mad for him to deny who he was, as her mother had been with her for entirely different reasons? Or had he been old enough to be horrified with himself, only to balk at the sect's methods and give in to his powers after all?

"They will fight or they will die," Bowstan said.

"I believe we've established that," Erdain responded, and the buzzing in Bess's head increased in volume. She would have to leave while she could. Make her way back to her quarters. She should have brought the Stone of Gelerte, but she hadn't wanted the glow to give away her presence behind the screen. She wasn't ready to have that exposed yet. It was too potentially useful. More useful than whatever the stone might tell her, which she was certain she could determine for herself by simply sitting and listening. But none of the men had plotted to overthrow her. Not openly, anyway.

It didn't mean she'd learned nothing. Bowstan and Erdain had suggested that there was only fight or die. But they'd grown up in positions of relative power, where they had the privilege of choices. Bess had grown up in the V'Alban line, yet never treated as one of them, destined to be married into another family with another name, all for political advantage. What she'd learned time and again at the side of her father and brothers was that choices were an illusion. People could be made to do what you wanted; it was only a matter of the price—in coin, pain, or pressure. This was where she was the greatest of them. It would cost her nothing at all to force the Desperata to use their powers against their will. Maybe they could hold out against torture or treasure, but Bess could shackle them to her actual desires. She could grip them as she had Strego and others before and since.

She only needed to bolster her own strength.

The bloody buzzing droned on and on, drowning out the voices in the room.

"What was that?" Bowstan asked, cutting through the noise.

Had she cried out? Or was the buzzing so loud now that they could hear it too? Maybe it was something outside herself. Something real that could be beaten back. She went so still she might have been a statue.

When nothing happened, nothing at all, she silently slid from her secret compartment and made her way back to the guards she'd bespelled to remain down the hallway and forget the journey altogether. She allowed them to escort her back to her rooms, where her maid waited anxiously.

"Megrim powder," she ordered to the top of her maid's head, as she curtseyed so low Bess could see the graying hairs in with the chestnut. "And stoke the fire."

Bess marched straight to her balcony and threw open the shutters, which had been closed and latched to keep out the cold and the smoke. There was still smoke in the air. Still ash falling, but she could no longer see All Souls burning in the distance. Maybe there were still embers, little fires burning themselves out. Smoldering like her fury. Roha had escaped her, not once, but twice.

Pain stabbed like an ice pick into her right eye.

It had to be Roha who had made the dead walk tonight. Ni was the one who had drained away Bess's shadow girls. But if it was Roha, wouldn't ni be more inclined to send them straight back to the anima? All that Church training and those Restoration ideals. It could have been Ulan, who seemed to have an affinity with the dead. Either way, one of her enemies had found a way back into the city, which meant her people had failed. It was even possible someone had aided the rebels. Her defenses couldn't be trusted.

Pain now stabbed into her left eye, pulsing with the...voices. There *were the voices.* Raised, cacophonous. The spirits in her head. Were they talking to each other? Plotting against her?

She strained to listen.

"My Queen?"

She struck out to stop the voice that kept her from making sense of the sounds, the back of her hand hitting hard bone. Her maid fell to the floor, goblet clattering, watered wine spilling across the floor, her tonic along with it. The maid's hand went to her cheek, tears pouring from her eyes, but she didn't make a sound, just gazed up with fear.

Bess shut her eyes against the sight, chasing the voices, trying, failing, following…they were never more than maddening murmurs. Sounds down corridors she couldn't access, behind walls without passageways through.

"My…my Queen?"

The voice came so softly. The terror had Bess opening her eyes again. The maid lay as she'd fallen, except that the hand that had gone to her cheek was now half raised, prepared to block any blow that might fall. Expecting it.

"Should I prepare another drought?" she asked, voice quivering.

"No," Bess said, her voice coming out too harshly. She couldn't sleep for fear the voices might take over somehow. "Call for choffee and for Strego. I will sit."

She turned her back on her maid so that she could loosen Bess's stays, but she twisted her head to keep watch.

The choffee arrived before Strego, as did the brindle boy with more fuel for the fire, his eyes downcast and back arched like a cat who'd been riled. Or a child expecting blows and protecting his center.

She watched him, half inclined not to disappoint. She needed blood, needed power. But she would have to be careful from whom she drew it. With the voices… Maybe she needed to walk her streets. Cloaked, anonymous. Find subjects who were nice and pliable. Who wouldn't be missed. Maybe… It was difficult to think over the buzzing, piercing, shooting pain.

There was a knock, finally, and Strego was announced.

He bowed deeply, and when he straightened, she took his hand, sliding her sharpened nail into his arm as always, tapping straight into his blood and spirit. He'd been a strong man when she'd started. Her father's age, but as strong as an ox. Built like an ale cask–a barrel chest that extended to his stomach, with stout arms and legs to match. But she'd been drawing on him for so long, little by little, that his vitality was seeping away. She hadn't realized it as she went along, until now, when the buzzing made it so that it would have taken a strong energy to break through the noise, and she had to feel for him.

Bess closed her eyes again, against her pain, against any external distractions, because there was enough going on in her own head. She couldn't drink from Strego, but she had to stay with him in case she needed to exert her will.

"Tell me about your meeting."

There was no hesitation, so whatever they talked about after she was gone was fine. Or he was a very good liar. When he finished, she said, "About the Desperata–if they'll die rather than come along, we can't move on them directly. We can't give them the chance to fall on their swords. We have to go quietly in the night. Spirit them away. Bring them to me."

It hurt her to talk. Her own words seem to echo. Have sharp edges, like teeth that ripped and tore apart.

"They may take time to find. Their retreats are not like the Churches, in the cities and towns."

"I have faith."

And the buzzing swelled until Bess could no longer concentrate. She pushed what she had into Strego and let go. If he didn't quite flee, it was a very close thing.

CHAPTER TWENTY-FOUR

Roha

As soon as the ward snapped back to full strength, Roha dropped to nes knees beside Arresta. Ni reached out a hand to nes neck, which lay at an angle that left no doubt as to Arresta's state, and yet, Roha couldn't accept it. Arresta was already cooling, and…there was no pulse. Ni put nes fingers to Arresta's lips to be certain and felt no breath. Ni was dead. Strangled, and nes neck snapped. Killed by a bosewight because Roha had weakened the wards, and the evil spirits had tried to escape.

All Roha's fault.

Roha let nes head fall to Arresta's chest, and lay there as though in prayer, subjugating nimself to a higher power. The thought made nim send up a spiritu anu, commending Arresta's spirit to the All before realizing it would never make it there. Not with the wards in place. That was the catch at the Sacrima. Even the good people would never go to their rest here. Arresta's essence would be locked in with the bosewights. Would ni be tormented for all eternity? Would the spirits wreak their vengeance on Arresta for their failed coup?

Roha sat back on nes heels, tried to feel for Arresta's spirit, tried to see, but that was Ulan's ability. Roha couldn't see spirits unless they made themselves known, and Arresta was newly dead, would still be in shock, essence scattered. Ni could only hope the bosewights weren't able to pull nim apart.

A hand landed on nes shoulder like a blow. Roha craned to find Tehardy's eyes blazing down at nim. "*We* will see to our dead. You and I have to talk."

A serpentine body checked Roha out of the way, as the sentinel–Reynal, ni remembered now, incongruously–moved to lift Arresta. He scooped nes body and cradled nim in his arms. Arresta's head lolled, as though ni might be merely resting. Nes legs dangled, swung as Reynal turned around, and Roha rose quickly to side-step out of his way. Ni had the sense he might plow nim down otherwise without compunction. He didn't glance at nim, focused entirely on the tower. His eyes were like coals, jaw set so hard it might be stuck in place.

"Dead?" Roha asked, turning to Tehardy. "How many?"

Tehardy didn't look around. Ni didn't seem to require it. Maybe Tehardy sensed it through nes magic. After all, ni'd woven the web. Ni must have known whose magic had dropped away.

"Too many." Tears glistened in nes eyes but didn't fall. "Come. Now."

Roha followed nim. Behind Reynal. Behind a tall acolyte who was helping another to walk–did they call them acolytes here? Into the sanctuary and a room where Tehardy shut the heavy wooden door firmly behind them. Ni stoked the embers of the fire until it caught again, all of it in silence. It should have been an intangible thing, but instead it seethed, breathing down Roha's neck like a hunting dog that had found nes warren in the woods.

Why that analogy had come to Roha, ni didn't know. Ni was hardly prey here. Or in hiding. Ni had brought this on. Ni had lashed out, nearly taken down their wards, in fear. And now Arresta was dead. Others were dead or wounded. Ni didn't know what Tehardy could say that was worse than what ni heaped on nimself. Inside, Roha was a great gaping void, literally as well as spiritually. Tehardy had drawn out everything ni possessed and more, but worse, Roha had come to the edge of nes beliefs and gazed out on a great emptiness.

Roha's work with the Restoration was based on the absolute knowledge that power was insidious, that any influencing of the natural order *disordered* the anima. Mageri stole the lifeforce of the land, used it up and left death and destruction in their paths. The earth was leached of life, plants shriveled and died, foundations cracked, animals fled or succumbed to the spell. Nothing could grow there afterward, and so nothing could survive off the land. In the mageris' wake were shortages, starvation... People would eat anything they had left or could scavenge–mealy fruit, rancid meat. And as bodies mounted, so too did disease, like the Rot that had left so many dead or scarred.

But what they did at the Sacrima, keeping sinful souls from poisoning the collective spirit–wasn't this what the Church always taught? That the purity of the anima must be preserved?

"Arresta said that you are not a spy. That you came fleeing Bloody Bess and oppression. Ni trusted you." Tehardy fired the words like arrows. Meant to strike.

And they did. Roha felt them pierce, each one straight through the heart.

"Ni was right. I came with others, though we were separated in your woods. In Jucar, I was with the Restoration. We fought against Bess and her mageri, their use of magic to destroy both our lands."

"Then we have a common enemy."

"Oh?"

Tehardy studied nim, coldly. In nes place by the fire, one side of nes face was in shadow, and the other flickered at the whim of the flames. "Arresta died for your mistake. You have seen how vulnerable we are. You have seen what we defend against. Will you take Arresta's place, vindicate nes faith in you? You are strong. Strong enough to have been our undoing, so either you are with us, or..."

"Or what?"

Tehardy spread nes hands, as though to say it was all up to Roha. Ni had to get back to Cia and Hostill. Had to finish the mission. Defeat Bloody Bess; get Hostill on the throne. But for now, it was clear there was only one answer if ni wanted to live. Tehardy was carefully not saying that. Maybe it was a bluff, but when it came to matters of survival, people would do things they might not otherwise, particularly if they could justify that they were protecting others and not merely themselves. And if one could order it done rather than get one's own hands dirty, so much the better.

"You said we have a common enemy?"

There might be only one response for now, but once Roha gave it, ni lost any leverage for getting nes own questions answered.

Tehardy blew out through nes nose. "We do not have time for this. We must mourn our dead."

"And I will mourn them with you. Once I have my answers. You want me to join you. Will you believe any loyalty given under duress? The dead will keep."

"You are a cold one."

"I believe you see your reflection in my eyes."

They faced off, and slowly a smile spread over Tehardy's face. It didn't transform it, only set it into a secondary mask. "Since the Blood War, we have had no new members. Before the war, other Nim would find their way to us or us to them, but since the battles began, they have been caught up in the king's war machine, used for the null spells to protect his troops. Willing or unwilling, we don't know. We've been unable to reach them. But that is not all. More recently, our Sacristers who have gone out to the towns for supplies have not returned. We've had to make do on rare offerings brought to us, on what we can grow and Reynal can forage, as we can clearly not send him into towns. I believe something or someone is swallowing up Nim."

"Our enemy is the war, then?"

"Just so," Tehardy said, turning away to poke further at the flames.

Roha studied nes back, evaluating. It seemed to nim that the answer then was to end their isolation and help stop the war. If the Sacrima didn't have enough to get through the winter, if the Nim were being chewed up by the war machine, then staying here was dying a slow death. But Tehardy had already made a choice. The Sacristy would remain as it had been founded. They had a sacred duty. Maybe by staying, Roha could find another way.

"I'll stay and help," Roha promised, but ni hadn't said for how long.

CHAPTER TWENTY-FIVE

Cia

It had been a week since she'd seen Hostill. A week Cia had spent occasionally being questioned about Jucar, drinking up those rare times when she was led through the corridors of the manor-palace to build a map in her mind should she need it, but more often pacing her room or peering through her narrow window onto the world at the snippet of scenery afforded her, woodland and naught else.

Sometimes the maid opened the connecting door, and Myrka was allowed entrance, nearly overcrowding the small room. They were permitted to talk, probably in the hope that there would be something to overhear. It should have been an end to the monotony, but was instead the most awkward part of it all. They had never been friends and weren't likely to become so in what Myrka would see as enemy territory. Cia tried to see it as her home, but she belonged here no more than Jucar now. She was a woman without a country.

To distract herself, Cia asked for embroidery supplies as the only way to keep her sanity. Myrka didn't know anything about stitching except what it took to sew a seam or a wound and wasn't inclined to learn until Cia showed her that she could stitch words into the fabric and tear them out again in the guise of teaching her to embroider. They didn't conduct full conversations following that, but they made themselves understood in a way that couldn't be overheard.

Seen H, Cia stitched the first day, which was followed by Myrka's terribly jagged *N,* which could have been sewn straight through her heart.

U safe, she stitched, tapping it with her needle for emphasis as she looked up into Myrka's face to let her see her sincerity, that she could come to Cia with anything. Absent other allies, Cia was all she had. And vice versa.

Y Myrka stitched back, and then, shockingly. *U*

Y. Did Cia add her unease, vague as it was? *But.*

Joia leaned in from her own seat, and Myrka stuck her needle into the fabric, began to go over Cia's stitches with her own, muddling the lettering. "I don't know how you do it," she said. "I start to stitch and instantly it looks more like a bird's nest than a bird. Perhaps we need to start more simply."

"A border, then," Cia said. "Follow my lead. We'll start with the very basic feather stitch."

Joia eased her joints back down into her seat. And so it went.

Cia lost track of the days before she was summoned to prepare for a small dinner, already accepted on her behalf, though she was told that Myrka would receive a tray in her room. Joia flew into a tizzy at the thought of one of her charges at a command appearance. Face flushed, hair flying out of her bun as though reacting to her stress, she rushed about.

"But you have nothing to wear. They didn't provide you with finery! They have set me up to fail!" Joia wailed.

"The messenger said a small dinner," Cia protested.

"Nothing at court is small," Joia said.

She knew that to be true. Joia's panic was starting to get to her as well. Who was this Duchess Lamerra? Was she someone to fear? Possibly one of Uncle Frazier's old allies? If so, and he had been behind the attempt on her life, she would have to beware of everything she ate or drank. But how? She couldn't refuse to partake or she would risk offending, and that was as close to death at court as the real thing.

But after the fear of Garif, this fright was a far-away thing, and she couldn't give it her energy. She would be wary, that was all she could do. And so, she stepped into the coral dress meant for another's coloring, certainly someone else's cast-off. She'd have done better in a deep blue to pick up the iridescence of her hair, the blue-black of a grackle's wing, but these days it might have emphasized the circles beneath her eyes that Garif had put there. Unless they had gone with him. It had been so long since she'd seen herself in a glass. How long had it been since she'd cared?

But when Joia made a noise after half a lifetime of ministration, she sounded pleased with herself. She grabbed the hand mirror Cia had face down on her small table, holding it straight up to Cia so that she couldn't help but look, and… She was transformed. Almost back to herself before she'd ever left Frizenze. Except she'd been almost a child then, and now she was a woman. Her face had thinned out, hollowed. Her cheekbones were prominent. Her eyes, golden before, had aged like whiskey in sherry casks, and swam with secrets. Her flesh hardly needed the powder Joia had applied to be white as snow. Garif had never let her see the light until she'd fled him.

She looked like someone who'd seen things now. Someone of interest. At court, that was currency. She took a deep breath–. Well, tried and was brought up short, almost choked. She let out the air in stuttering breaths and took it in again slowly. Two, three, four until she got back on track.

Just in time for the summons at the door. She thanked Joia for what she'd done and rose to meet her challenge.

Two guards waited on either side of the door to escort her. *Four guards.* They fell into place two before and two behind as she exited into the hallway, so that she was trapped between them. She wouldn't have minded the men at her back if she didn't have them to her front as well. If there was somewhere for her to go. But sandwiched between… She couldn't breathe, and it wasn't only her chest bindings.

She was so short of breath that spots began to form before her eyes. She made no note of the path by which she was led, barely able to see between the towering men. But at a crossway, they had to stop and step aside for two Crownsmen in purple and silver dragging a gray-robed figure between them, head lolling out of his cowl, feet scuffing a protest. That she could hardly fail to note, though she failed to make sense of it. Could he have stayed too long in prayer and fallen into so deep a slumber?

By the time the guards knocked on the door she was to enter, she was ready to be dragged herself. Cia reached out to steady herself on the guard before her, only to draw her hand back before making contact. She took control of herself, got her feet under her, and forced her breath to steady. She closed her eyes so she wouldn't be distracted by the voids threatening to swallow her. When the door opened, so did her eyes. She pasted on the smile she remembered from courts past and entered when she was invited. Into the anteroom, then into the receiving room, which had been set up with a small feast.

A woman came forward immediately to greet her, pulling her into the room when she wanted to drink it in, take inventory of who was there, size it up as she would Bloody Bess and her battlefield.

Commanding was the word that came to mind for Duchess Lamerra. She took Cia by the elbow in a grip that wasn't painful but could instantly become so if she tried to slip it. She was overly familiar with the type. The Duchess was built like a ship, where the prow came first and everything else after. She steered Cia toward her Duke, who didn't command but vibrated with something restrained that Cia couldn't identify. It wasn't fear or rage. Those she would have recognized. So perhaps it was conspiracy with whatever his wife plotted. Cia only knew that she would have to watch herself, her hosts, and probably guests alike. Then she felt a glance so strongly it was a wonder she'd felt anything else.

She turned to her right, following the feeling, and it led her straight to Hostill.

"Hostill!" she said on a long exhale.

"Our guest of honor," Duchess Lamerra said proudly. "But, of course, you know each other. The king asked us to arrange this. To help the lad learn his manners and how to speak with his betters." Her husband coughed into his hand, but the lady sounded not at all chastened as she said, "I'm sorry, his peers. And so, this dinner. You will sit, won't you?"

She guided Cia into place, and that was the cue. Servants appeared out of nowhere–or maybe Cia simply hadn't noticed them–and the rest of the assembly took their places. Miraculously, she was seated next to Hostill, who shot her a glance that said *save me*. She reached for his hand under the table to squeeze it for reassurance, but he quickly pulled away, either because he was a boy of the age where he could handle anything and didn't need mothering or because he thought someone would notice.

It was a small party, as the message had promised, only two other women besides the Duchess and two men besides the Duke. One was a woman of advanced age who wore it so well that Cia had to look further to determine what gave it away. Maybe she was just that arresting. Her spring-green eyes were–there was no other word for it, but *alive*–which all eyes were, of course, but hers were the most so Cia had ever seen. As though she was more aware than the average person, and what she saw entertained her wildly. Her crinkles were so fine it seemed they felt sheepish about gracing her face. Her husband, introduced as Lord Ojardian, made up for her in wrinkles and jowls, like a hound that it might be permissible to scratch behind the ears. The other couple were more formidable, gazing on Cia and Hostill like something they had wiped off their boots and would as soon have left behind them.

Cia was not certain why the pair had agreed to come unless it was for the novelty and the horrible stories they could tell afterward. Baron and Baroness Afgell were both tall and ascetically thin with aquiline noses and lips that disappeared when pressed together as they were now. They were so alike, in fact, that they very well might have kept the marriage within the family. Old lines often did. Their matching blue-black hair said they might have hailed from Cia's Grenalle region of Frizenze, but that possible kinship didn't win her any points, clearly.

Cia was able to ask one question of Hostill about how he was, and he to half-answer that his head was spinning from having etiquette and statecraft drilled into him at all hours and that this dinner was to be both practice and test of his skills before the others were on them.

Several courses were brought, but Cia and Hostill were the main. Or perhaps they were the entertainment. The others fired question after question at them, ignoring their own rules about speaking to this person or that person beside them—it wasn't a formal dinner, after all. The nobles wanted to know about Jucar, Bloody Bess, whether it was true their mageri wove teeth and bones into their beards and wasn't it barbaric? And then they turned on her. All those eyes, all that focus, zeroing in on her like prize falcons on their prey. And *her mageri*, that was what they called Garif, did he have the beads and bones? What was it like? How *horrible* for her, they said with a tone of wicked delight.

Cia's head spun. She gripped the edges of the table so hard, either she would drive her fingers into it and dent the table, or it would indent her flesh. She saw red, her vision zeroing out as though everyone was scoping away. She wanted to flip the table, send the solid wood and cutlery and food slopping and sliding and pinning everyone. Ask how *that* felt.

A small hand fumbled for her under the table, but her hands were clenched too tightly round the edge. Hostill then reached for her elbow, patted it, said her name, gently. He sent a full glare around the table and raised his voice, "How dare you."

Only it wasn't his voice. Or, it was—it commanded the attention that Hostill had always commanded. But now carried. It shut up everyone in the room.

He stood, his seat making an awful noise as it slid back with no servant to ease its way. "How dare you," he said again, this time aiming the glare and making sure that everyone felt it. "Cia is not here for your amusement. She could not have saved your princess, and she paid for her marriage to the mageri every day of her life. You have not earned that story. She joined the resistance. She is here now, and yet you mock her. What have you done to earn the loyalty of such a woman? It's as though you beg her to betray you. Is that what I should tell your king? That you mock us for your merriment? My understanding is that time is short and that there was a point to this dinner.

Was it to discover that King Avize's court is petty and cruel? All I have learned tonight is to fire back barbs under the cover of false civility. Was that my true lesson?"

Cia was so shocked, she found her hands sliding away from the table, and when Hostill offered her a hand this time, she took it. Hostill did not sit again. Instead, he pulled her to her feet, and together they turned.

"My King," Cia whispered.

Hostill took a deep breath and released the last of his seething on the exhale. Then he shot her a wink. "M'lady," he said.

There was consternation behind them, but Cia didn't listen to any of it. She walked with Hostill, head held high, toward the anteroom, hoping they were free to leave.

"Lady Cia, Lord Hostill," she heard a soft voice behind them, tentative, as though unsure of their titles. She wasn't sure herself. She didn't think she retained any in Frizenze, and Hostill was as yet just a boy, a bastard with a father who wouldn't have acknowledged him even had he lived. But a claimant to the Jucari throne nonetheless.

It was the very alive Lady Ojardian, and when they half-turned, the lady looked back over her shoulder, making sure she hadn't been followed. They hadn't made it as far as the guards, and so they were in the one spot least likely to be overheard.

"I told them I would see you to the door. I'm sorry," the lady said. "I would tell you to trust no one, but it seems you know that already."

Then she pressed a parchment into Cia's hands and was gone, back to the others to discuss them in their absence.

"What does it say?" Hostill asked.

Cia unfolded it and showed it to him, only thinking as she did that he might not be able to read it, but it seemed he had no trouble. It was a time and a place for a meeting, midday tomorrow in the hedge maze.

"I won't be able to get away," Hostill said. "They have all of my time scheduled. I'm never alone."

"I'm not so certain myself, but… You don't think it's a trap, do you? A few days ago, someone tried to have me killed. A maze with its walls would be a perfect place for an ambush."

"What? No one told me! Cia, you must–"

His voice must have raised just enough to bring a guard to see to the disturbance, because they had company in an instant.

"There is nothing I can do," Cia said, careful with their company. "The king is investigating."

"Be watchful," Hostill said.

"Be safe," she ordered him.

"Take me back," Hostill commanded, turning to the guard who was about to inquire, and that was it. They had no more time to talk.

Cia had no idea what was going on, but she didn't like it. Frizenze was no less fraught with secrets and plots than Jucar. A king battling back death with Churchmen wearing themselves out praying over him, courtiers running amok while he recovered, possibly ordering assassinations, or alienating allies without his consent. And what did this new note mean? If she could get away, she would find out on the morrow, but what if it was a trap? If not a setup for an assassination, perhaps she was supposed to be discovered in a compromising position, 'caught' plotting against the king. She didn't know enough about Lady Ojardian or the factions here. Nothing in fact. She was expected to make a decision based on no information with only her gut to go on. It hadn't been very reliable thus far.

Yet, she knew she would go, if she could find a way. She had to investigate on her own what was happening here, because something most assuredly was not right. It meant she'd have to get free of her locked room, lose her guards, only she hadn't the faintest idea how to go about it.

She had no special skills of her own. Whether the magic she'd accessed on the battlefield had been Garif's or her own, she didn't dare use it. She didn't have Roha's power or Ruggerio's speed and spycraft. What then? If she knocked out guards, they would eventually come to. Even if she had it in herself to kill them, their bodies would be discovered. There was no way she could conceive of in which she would not be caught.

Was there nothing? Truly nothing?

And then it came to her. It wouldn't help her on the morrow, she'd still have to think on that, but down the line…

That night, she thrashed and cried out in her 'sleep', enough to wake the dead, which Joia most certainly was once her aching joints allowed her to drop off. She escalated it until finally the door between her room and Myrka's opened, and Joia had to pull back lest she get swatted across the face 'waking' Cia.

"Mistress, you must wake else you raise the entire palace. It's naught but a nightmare. You are safe, truly. There's no one here but old Joia."

Cia pretended to startle awake, which was no great difficulty, as she could draw on all the times Garif had dropped a heavy hand over her mouth as she slept. Or slid a hand between her legs when she was deep in slumber, using her startlement as the reason she made him hurt her. *Made him.* As though she were the one with the power and he wasn't in control of himself, though if she'd said anything like that out loud, it might very well have gotten her killed.

Cia brought that terror into her eyes as she stared up into Joia's. "I–I'm so sorry. I have a terrible time falling asleep, and once I do, my time in Jucar haunts me. Or I remember the assassin's strike. I fear to fall back under. Please, isn't there anything that you can give me? A tonic. I remember my mother–"

"Shh, shh," Joia was saying before she could continue. She looked back over her shoulder, as though her own bed was calling her. "I have just the thing. A sleeping drought. It works for me, even with my old aches and pains. If you hadn't cried out so loudly, I wouldn't have waked 'til morning. I'll mix it up for you now, and every night before you go to bed. Then we will have no more of this."

Joia shuffled heavily back to Myrka's room, and the time dragged by until she returned, but she'd mixed the tonic into a cup for Cia and stayed to watch her drink it down. She had no choice but to do so. But now she knew that Joia kept a tonic in Myrka's room. She either had to get it or convince Joia to leave a stock with her. For now, her eyes were too heavy to stay open, and her brain was too muddled to think. It was no wonder that Joia hadn't heard the sounds of her would-be assassination until too late.

The next day it was as though someone had filled her eyes and head full of sand. She had to wipe the grit out of her eyes before she could even open them, then had to protect them from the weak light of morning.

"You've slept late, m'lady," Joia said with a certain smugness to her voice. "No more dreams?"

Cia was certain that what escaped her lips couldn't be mistaken for language.

"It's like that at first. Perhaps a half-drought the next time, you being so slight."

Cia mumbled something back, then realized that it might be very late. She hadn't known what she intended to do about the odd message that she'd received the day before until the fear struck that she may have missed the assignation. Her room was rarely bright, receiving only the arrow-slit of illumination, unless she lit candles to fight back the gloom, so it was difficult to tell the time by the shadows that fell upon the floor.

"Water?" she asked, voice cracking like a clay basin left too long in the fire. Joia grumbled but provided it, moving with all the swiftness or lack thereof her aches allowed.

Once Cia'd drunk and lowered the glass, she said, "No more dreams, bless you," and Joia's hard face softened as she took the cup back. "But I'm so foggy, as if I still have half a foot in dreamland. Perhaps some brisk air will wake me. A walk in the gardens?"

Joia's face stiffened, the softness gone to suspicion. "The gardens, my lady? It is winter. Even the trees that have kept their leaves and winter berries shiver in place."

"Then perhaps the hedge maze, where I'll be protected from the wind by the living walls."

"I—but there was just an attempt on your life. Surely you do not want to go out unprotected."

"I will have my guards. Even you, who is with me day by day, could not predict such an outrageous request. No one could anticipate it and be lying in wait. It should be safe enough for me to escape these walls and breathe fresh air however briefly I can stand to do so. I don't ask for much time."

Joia might have been asked to spy or simply hinder them, but she was certainly not seasoned in the art of deception, because her face went through contortions and calculations as she considered how much power she had to grant or deny Cia's request.

In the end, she said, "Briefly, my lady. And make no protest, I shall bundle you like a babe. You have been through a lot, and I don't intend for you to catch your death. I am too old for such outings, so I will count on your guards to keep watch. I am *not* too old to tan their hides if you come back as so much as a scratch. Do you understand me?"

Cia nodded, keeping amusement from twitching her lips.

"They will be under strict time constraints, because I have to clean you up and get you ready for this afternoon."

"What happens this afternoon?"

"Zega would like to speak with you again. You and Myrka both."

More interrogation. It was inevitable, but Cia would have thought they'd worn out all their topics of conversation…unless something else had happened. Some other dire news of home that had raised new questions.

Cia nodded. "I agree to all of your conditions, but I need to escape. Just for a while."

Joia's gaze sharpened on the word escape, but she helped Cia out of bed, gave her some hard bread and cheese to break her fast, and began to prepare her for her short trek outside as though she were a child and Joia her overbearing wetnurse. Before she was finished, sweat was molding her woolens to her legs, and she didn't see how they would keep her warm when they were already sodden. Over those were fur-lined boots. Then came a warm and serviceable dress, a long woolen scarf that was wound around her head and neck, a long cloak with a hood that pulled over her head, covering the scarf, and mitts that dwarfed her hands. She wouldn't be able to do anything for herself but nod, and if she did that too aggressively, she might over-balance and somersault like an acrobat for a noble's amusement.

Joia presented her to the guards with stern admonishments about what she would do to them if any harm came to her charge and threats involving switches and turning them over her knee. They exchanged amused glances, which Joia pretended not to see, before taking their places. If they thought Cia's outing was ridiculous, they didn't say. They stubbornly refused to be engaged in any sort of conversation, as though they'd been warned off. As though the ghost of Garif was still with her, and they might be on the bad side of mageri magic by treating her with a shred of human decency.

She would not let it get to her. Someone, Lady Ojardian, saw her as important enough to meet with in the hedge mage. Either to kill or to embroil in some scheme. At this point, she felt it hardly mattered, though she knew that was only her anger talking. If she *were* to die, she would at least make it count. She would fight tooth and nail, and take all of them with her to the anima, where she might finally have her peace.

So, she walked with the guards at the stately pace they set, only two this time, as though a state dinner merited more protection than the outside world. She kept her face impassive as they left the manor halls for the frozen, winter-flat gardens over which the hedge maze sat sentinel in the center. The entire sky was a glowering gray, lighter toward the bottom and more ominous toward the top. A storm-cloud sky. Based on the biting wind, snow might be in the offing. Not gentle, fluffy flakes, but the kind of snowfall that coated the earth, as though claiming it. Later, it would melt, provide much-needed moisture to crops, water back to streams. Part of the cycle of life. But for now, she worried that it was an omen and this was her funeral procession speeding her toward her doom.

They reached the hedge maze while she was measuring the sky's temperament. The lead guard stopped just inside the entrance, holding an arm up to signal the halt so that she wouldn't crash into him as he turned on her.

"*This* is what you wanted to see, my lady?" he asked, glancing dubiously at the evergreen walls, which rose perhaps seven feet high, a less-than-vivid green in the grayness of the day.

At last, he speaks!

"It is." She owed him no explanation as to why, but something more was needed. "It will hardly be an outing if you lead me in and then out again."

The guard exchanged a glance over her head with one behind, and she wondered if they knew whether she was about to die. Perhaps they were to be her executioners? Or perhaps it was a commentary on their belief in her abilities and concern that they'd be standing far too long in the elements before they'd have to find and rescue her, assuming *they* knew the way in and out. But then, these mazes were meant for the diversion of the nobility, not as true mental stimulation.

"I should like to find my own way," she said to be certain she was understood. "Perhaps you could follow at a reasonable distance?"

Silent signals continued to be passed over her head, and she cocked it listening, waiting. Would Lady Ojardian find her? The Lady must expect her to be accompanied, but Cia was near-certain she could lose her guards in the twists and turns if need be.

Finally, the guard before her nodded, stepped to her right, and gestured for her to proceed him to the left. Whether it was a clue or either direction would lead to the egress, she didn't know, but she took her cue and let her mitted hand brush the hedge wall until it was caught, at which point she stopped. At the first choice of a turn, she chose poorly and ended up at a dead end.

Cia turned to find her guards looming. She looked up at the two tall men, truly hedging her in, and her heart kicked like a wild horse not yet broken. Her hand went there, as she thought her chest might break wide open. Then they stepped away, letting her out, and it was with a jolt that she could breathe again. Her exhale came jagged, and she stepped shakily back into the main branch. It was then that she heard voices, cheery voices, as though the weather affected them not a whit.

"Oh, be a dear, won't you, and run back to fetch us some warmed cider? There's a girl!"

As expected, Lady Ojardian strode into view, resplendent in a rose-gold gown with deeper rose and garnet accents, strolling on her husband's arm. He was in nearly all black with the rose tones at his collar and cuffs, making Cia wonder whether they had all their clothing designed in matched sets.

"Why, Lady Cia," the lady said, as soon as she spotted her, "I didn't know you had the run of our gardens!" No doubt it was meant to throw off the guards, but she bristled all the same. "I've just called for mulled cider. Join us, won't you? Guards, I think perhaps one of you can see to a table and chairs? As for my husband and myself, we could just keep to our cups, but with Lady Cia here, we must have a bit of a visit. I promise, she will be quite safe with us!"

There were looks exchanged again, and a sigh aborted. Cia didn't know how they decided who would go and see to the table and chairs—seniority, perhaps, because they'd be temporarily warm inside, or youth, because they would have to fetch—but one man turned to go. Lady Ojardian then dismissed the other from further thought by turning back to Cia.

"Come, my dear, let's get somewhere a bit more sheltered. I didn't get to hear a thing about that attack on your life? Too terrible! You must tell me everything!"

Lady Ojardian slipped her arm out of her husband's and through Cia's instead, pulling her along, and leaving her husband to follow in their wake with the remaining guard. The Lord did not move with alacrity, which gave them the space they needed not to be overheard.

"You had hardly come to court before you were sent off with Princess Anaya," the Lady began, waving at the greenery around them, as though giving some sort of history of the gardens. "So you don't know me. You will have no reason to trust, unless what I say matches with your own instincts. I do not know how much time we will be granted for our tête-à-tête, and so I will get right to the point, and you will laugh and then we can discuss, yes?"

Cia pasted a smile on her face, as though Lady Ojardian was a most amusing companion. "Yes, of course!" she said. "Lovely!" in case it carried.

"The king has designs on your boy heir. You must take him and go. Get him away as soon as may be."

Cia's heavy gown wanted to trip her up, and her breath to freeze in her throat. It was all she could do to keep walking. Was that why her attempted assassination, so that Hostill would have no guardian but Frizenze? Could the king himself have ordered it, but at a remove, so that it could never be traced back to him should it fail or someone object? Or could his courtiers be plotting against him? Sowing discord? Lord and Lady Ojardian might even have ordered her assassination themselves, planning for it to fail so they might win her trust, or even to succeed so that they could control Hostill themselves somehow.

Lady Ojardian drew her ever forward. "You have doubts," she said. "Why should the king do such a thing, you wonder? He and those who issue his edicts hide how damaged he is, but the Nim who minister to him at his bedside, locking him into his dying body, are wearing out faster and faster. Soon, he will run through them entirely. And so he starts to look to the body of a boy who may rule all of Jucar and Frizenze if he plays things right."

Cia gasped, her head spinning. It couldn't be true. It was unthinkable. Unnatural. Against everything she'd thought or known or believed.

"Yes, yes, dear. Keep walking. We're saying nothing untoward here," Lady Ojardians murmured. "They struck your attacker down!" she said, more loudly. "Oh, what a relief he'll plague us no more!"

But it explained the gray-robes. Cia had never met Nim in Frizenze. Perhaps they wore the gray robes at the Church. But using them to keep the king's soul locked into his body so that he could continue to rule! He was as much a horror as Bloody Bess, stealing the anima of her shadow girls to fuel her power.

If Lady Ojardian was right, and King Avize now meant to take over Hostill's body as a way to control both lands, Cia had delivered him right into danger. It was as though all power begat was the hunger for more power.

Lady Ojardian prodded her with an elbow that felt like a dagger even through her layers of fabric, and Cia forced out a laugh she was certain sounded manic. She had to hope that to the guards, all noble banter rang hollow.

"But he can't… How…" Cia began.

"We're not privy to that. But he has a way."

A young girl came bustling up then—well, a courtier, no doubt a hanger-on of Lady Ojardian—her face flushed and pleased at her speed, a maid at her heels, bearing a cozy-wrapped pitcher of cider, another with biscuits, a guard behind with a table, and a squire with chairs. All conversation stopped as Lady Ojardian turned to say that she'd changed her mind. It was, after all, too cold for such a thing, and they'd better get inside before they all caught their deaths.

Cia was stunned. How could the Lady drop this information without giving her any idea of how much time she had or how she might escape with Hostill? She was more desperate now than ever to investigate after her disturbing conversation with Lady Ojardian. She hoped that night Joia would leave her with a packet of powder and instructions, but it was not to be. Joia brought the tonic already mixed and watched Cia while she drank it down.

She made a face at the taste and asked what was in it to make it so bitter, but Joia only told her to lie down before she fell down. The night after, Cia'd frightened herself at the thought that Joia herself could become an assassin and kill her by simply doubling the tonic. She might fall asleep and never wake. Joia might even do such a thing accidentally. A pinch more than intended, and Cia was no more. She took the tonic when Joia offered it, but laid it aside.

Joia eyed her like a disappointed mama and crossed her arms. "Shall I take it back?"

"Please don't," Cia said, letting instinct pull it out of her. "I appreciate it more than you know. I just…it makes me feel so heavy. I had a fear that if an assassin comes for me again, I might not wake. I couldn't scream or fight him off. I would be dead before anyone noticed."

Joia's body lost its tension. "Ah, I understand, dear. Would you like a softer potion?"

"I…" Cia had the bed sheets twisted between her hands and looked from them up to Joia's face, like a child pleading with a parent. "Would it be possible for you to show me? That way, I might mix just a bit on those nights I feel I need it and go without if I feel I can make do."

Joia froze, which seemed odd because she hadn't been moving, but it was a sense that everything but her mind ceased operations as she worked out whether this could be done. Whether she'd get in more trouble if her charge was murdered or given a harmless little sleeping draught. *Oh, please, let her find it harmless,* Cia prayed. She prayed as she hadn't since before Garif had come into her life.

"Fine," Joia said. "I'll give you a bit of the powder, and I'll show you how to use it. But you'll have to promise me just the one dose and no more. Two in a night and you might not wake the next day. And I'll still have the door locked between us, so don't think you can use it on me, missy."

Cia gasped. "I would never. Is that what you think?"

"One never knows, in this place." Joia said darkly and turned for her room.

It was a confirmation of everything that Cia feared. Frizenze was just like Jucar with its sins and secrets.

The difficulty was how to use it on her guards. They were unlikely to take food or drink from her, and the very attempt to provide it would seem suspicious, at least without a certain amount of lead-up. But she had so much experience having to outthink men with devious minds–well, one man terrifying enough for ten–that she'd become well-versed in manipulation. And so, she engaged them in conversation when she could.

When she couldn't, because they were hardly chatty, she would carry on the conversation herself, knowing that most men would accept that women were vapid and could speak of fripperies all day long. She was locked in most of the time, but when she was called out for social outings, she would always bring an embroidered ribbon or piece of lace she thought they might want for a sweetheart or daughter or wife, as though they had told her a thing about their home lives. They were so bemused that they would take the gifts and tuck them away.

The time it took gnawed at her, ate at her insides like a poison, cramping her stomach and making every smile she flashed more and more difficult. But she managed it because she had to for Hostill. Because long ago, the Cia who suffered was wedged back into a corner by the Cia who stood and took the brunt of the beatings. That Cia, somehow, knew how to smile convincingly, no matter the cost.

But even she was antsy. Something was wrong. She knew Myrka felt it as well.

She tried her best to catch a private moment with Hostill at one of the numerous dinner and supper parties they were invited to for others' amusement, that his keeper Grazi said were integral to Hostill's training, but it seemed someone was always running interference.

If the king was really going to take Hostill over, why all the training? Why not have done it already? Yet, Hostill had been granted several audiences with the king, something he'd let slip in a brief moment of privacy. He was immediately overheard by eagerly listening ears and raked over hot coals with questions.

Hostill was very careful in his responses, telling them what he knew the king would have them hear–that he was in good health, recovering well. Hale and hearty and certain to be among them any time. But it was clear that there was doubt among the courtiers, few of whom had seen the king since his injury, all of whom resented the low-born boy who had, pretender to a foreign throne or not, though some at least tried to hide it.

They all made the appropriate exclamations of joy or relief, but beneath was a simmering sense of unease. The king had been abed for too long. None believed he would rise again. Glances were exchanged. Cia sipped from her wineglass and pretended not to notice. At the end of the latest meal, she asked whether she could carry back some of the lovely fig tarts with her, since Myrka had missed out, and perhaps they could include Myrka next time? She might have wonderful stories of the Restoration, their rebel faction within Jucar, with which to regale them. Oh, there were gasps and a few hand claps from the ladies, some mumblings that might even have been sincere. And she made off with some lovely pastries that might tempt the guards at her door.

She met Myrka just within her rooms and started guiltily. They'd had no unattended time to talk since this had all begun. Myrka had been stolen away as frequently as she had for discussions with Zega, but here she was, as though she'd been searching Cia's rooms. And no Joia in sight.

"Joia?" Cia asked.

"Off on an errand. We haven't much time. Are those fig tarts?" Myrka eyed them like they were life.

She supposed that she could spare one. It might even be better that way. Supposing the guards had noted how many she'd come with, she could say that they hadn't agreed with Myrka and she'd refused the rest. Joia, she knew, couldn't stomach figs.

"You can have one. No more. The rest–"

"Are for the guards, perhaps with the addition of the sleeping potion you've been squirreling away?"

"You've searched my things?"

"I was bored," she said with no apology in her voice. "And also hopeful. There is something going on here. Zega and others keep asking me about Jucar, as if they have any hope of defeating us. I know that we came for their help placing Hostill on the throne, but I thought the plan was that we hide him here safely until our people, Ruggerio and Ulan, the Restoration, could take down Bloody Bess, then we'd coronate Hostill, he'd declare peace, and joy would fill the lands or some bollocks. But these questions…"

Cia went to her armoire, where she'd been hiding her powder, to set down the pastries. It was the only place she had to hide anything, so it was no wonder Myrka had found her out.

She turned and handed one pastry to Myrka, who held it to her nose and breathed it in.

"Ah, figs, I've missed you," she said, before taking a great bite of the small tart, a full quarter of it gone.

As she chewed, Cia said, "Since you've surmised enough to get me into trouble already, yes. I mean it for the guards. I don't have a good feeling about what's happening here either. A few days ago I was told that Hostill is in danger, and we need to be off with him as soon as possible, but I don't know if it's true or if we're being used. I mean to do some spying of my own. I'm no Ruggerio or Ulan or even you or Hostill, but I'm not helpless."

By the end of her short speech, Myrka was brushing crumbs off her hands and onto her skirts. She held up a finger to indicate that Cia should wait until she was finished chewing. Her eyes nearly rolled into the back of her head with pleasure. She even made appreciative noises as she chewed, Cia was amused to hear. It made her smile. If she'd known a figgy tart would be good for both their souls, she would have claimed one sooner.

When Myrka opened her eyes again, she said, blasting a stray crumb or two, "I'm coming with you."

Cia's smile fled. "What? But you can't. How will you get past Joia?"

"How will you get past various locks if I don't?"

Cia had just assumed she would work them until eventually things fell into place.

"I'm not saying that you're helpless without me," Myrka continued before Cia could protest, "but we're certainly stronger together. And it's always best to have a look-out."

Cia felt she should *want* to protest more. One person risking her life was more than enough. She didn't want to be responsible for another, but that was belittling Myrka. She could clearly be responsible for herself, and probably Cia as well, since Myrka was likely the more capable of them. But was she trustworthy? She was awfully happy Frizenze had given her that null, and she'd been spending a lot of time with Zega. What if she'd turned on them? But she could hardly say no. Myrka could just follow, and she'd be on her own with a spy on her tail.

"Thank you," she said instead, vowing to keep a close watch on Myrka.

"Thank *you*," Myrka said back. "I was going mad from boredom."

"Speaking of Ruggerio and Ulan, have you heard a thing from them? Or from any of the Restoration? I know it's a silly question—how would we have heard? And if you had, you wouldn't have kept it from me, right?"

"I wouldn't. It's terrifying to think of what might be going on back home," Myrka said, her hand going to the null on her chest as though it was a talisman.

They waited until nightfall when Joia was in with Myrka brushing out her long, wavy hair and braiding it up for bed, before Cia mixed her potion into a paste rather than a tonic and stirred it into the fig filling of the tarts with one of her hairpins. Cia made certain to finish it off in waves so that any disturbance in the paste appeared decorative and intentional before knocking at her door, where they had locked her into her own quarters.

Of course, they said it was for her safety, to keep her from wandering the halls in her sleep or otherwise, as though she didn't have two burly guards for that. They said it was for her own protection, but then, the assassin had managed to find his way to her in any case. He must have had a key and collusion.

The guards opened her door, and she was holding the figgy tarts out before her, hair already down, looking drowsy and guileless. "Will you take them?" she asked rather than *Would you like them?* which might be too direct. Too suspicious. "Joia can't stomach them, and Myrka and I have had our fill. I don't want them drawing beasties."

One guard raised a brow to the other, and Cia could read in it an entire commentary on the faintheartedness of womenfolk. The other nodded in agreement, a smirk crawling up one side of his face as he relieved her of the pastries. She smiled in thanks and watched him hand half of the spoils to his partner as she shut the door.

She had to allow Joia to ready her for bed, and to lie down in it. Every moment that passed after that was torture. Even with the tonic she took nightly, it took time for Joia's aching bones to settle themselves and for her gentle snores to begin. As soon as Cia heard them through the shared wall with Myrka's room, she readied herself as best she could, throwing on the easiest of her dresses to arrange by herself, wishing she had something even simpler. That she'd been able to steal one of Joia's gowns and head coverings. But even as bird-boned as Cia was, as sparse as she'd grown through Garif and Bloody Bess's mistreatment, she still wouldn't fit into Joia's gowns. Joia was at least half a head shorter, and spare in the way that some women were crab apples, nothing but center and skin, and barely a bite between.

Cia froze. That seemed like a Garif thought. Was he still inside her somewhere? Lurking, waiting, somewhere in that red haze she'd felt when Frazier had laid hands on her? Or was it all her? Was she rotten deep down in her core? Had Garif been right all along when he'd said that it was *all her fault* that she forced him to beat the badness out of her?

She closed her eyes, put her frozen hands on her neck hoping the shock of the chill would stun her back to herself. She breathed a deep breath in, filling up with clean, fresh air. With her slow breath out, she tried to send away all the bad. No room for it. Chase it away. For a moment, she felt almost mad. Like she might cackle crazily and never stop. It would feel so good to let go. To stop trying to be good, to be sane, to make a difference, to do anything but sit in a corner and rock and croon to herself. To throw herself out into the cold and dash herself onto the rocks. But no. This wasn't V'Alban Castle. There were no battlements and no crashing surf and killing rocks below.

Besides, they had defeated Garif. She *knew* they had. He was gone, except for the scars he had left behind. He wasn't right about her.

He was wrong and cruel and cutting and deadly.

But in the end, she had won, and she wouldn't let him destroy her now. Wouldn't destroy herself and give him what he'd always wanted.

Cia heard the rattling of the door, and it shocked her back to the present in a way that none of her cleansing breaths or cold hands had done. She stared at the door, terrified it was the guards and they'd discovered the tainted tarts. She faced it head-on. Ready for anything.

Relief swept her when it was Myrka who poked her head in furtively and waved her out. She had her hair wrapped up in a scarf, and Cia realized she should have done the same. But at least it was still in its bedtime braids, and at night, the iridescence shouldn't catch the light.

The two guards–only two, because Myrka's door was so close to hers that the king hadn't seen the need for more–lay like articulated wooden soldiers discarded at play. One snored and the other drooled. Neither stirred.

Myrka smiled her approval back at Cia, who felt vaguely triumphant, but also nervous. Anyone could discover them. And now that she and Myrka were out...

"Where do we start?" she asked.

"At the top," Myrka whispered back.

Cia's heart kicked hard in her chest, but she nodded. The king had been abed all this time, so there was no question of where to find him.

"I'll go first," Cia said. "If anyone gets caught, it's me, understand. I want you to get back. You're the one who can lock herself back in. I want you here for Hostill. Get him out and away, if you can. If not, do your best to protect him."

Myrka didn't protest that she wouldn't leave Cia behind. Well, of course she didn't.

Cia led the way. She had at least one useful skill; she knew where she was at all times. Knew entrances and exits. Escape routes. She remembered the path they'd taken to the king's quarters, and every other route she'd ever been down.

It was late, but not so late that no one was about. They doubled back several times to the splits of corridors, hoping the footsteps they heard further along weren't turning their way. Hair done up for bed, even covered in scarves, they couldn't pass for maids, and the manor-made-royal-residence was not so hugely attended that they could pass unrecognized.

Then Cia peeked her head out to scout for the safety of their next turn and caught sight of two lords walking together, one upstanding figure of a man looking ruminatively before him, the other with his head turtled toward his companion. She instantly knew the second man to be Lord Ojardian. *This* was a conversation she wanted to hear. It was her chance to learn more of Lord and Lady Ojardian and what they were scheming at, and something of this other lord as well…as long as they didn't get caught.

She ducked back quickly and hurried Myrka along the corridor to a set of armor they'd passed, a battle horse in plated armor with a mounted knight. They pressed themselves into the shadow of it. She felt certain deep in her bones that the lords would turn their way. She didn't know how she knew it, but the certainty was like the ache of an oncoming storm. She trembled with it and wished that she had the reins of Garif's power at her disposal to deepen the shadows. She reached for calm, reached for darkness, and tried to pull it about them like a cloak, tried to control her heartbeat and her breathing until they were nearly as still as death.

"But will you do it?" Cia couldn't see the speaker yet, but the voice was older, and she suspected this to be Lord Ojardian.

The footsteps neared and, as she knew they would, the men turned into their corridor, one heavy on his feet, one foot landing harder than the other. The other man almost whisper-quiet. Myrka's breath caught entirely, covered by the sound of the clomping boots.

The men stopped cold, as though they'd heard. "Not here," the younger said, a dangerous note to his voice.

Cia realized her breath had stopped as well. If this conversation went on for long, she would have to let it out, and for certain they would hear.

"There is no one about." Lord Ojardian again. "This is perhaps the safest place. We can see anyone who approaches from either direction."

There was an almost strangled sound of frustration. "You risk your head to discuss things in the open where anyone could happen along. Come."

He dragged Lord Ojardian down the hallway, not looking into the shadows where they hid as stock-still as the suit of armor that sheltered them, and into a room on the right. Myrka and Cia stared into each other's eyes.

"We have to hear," Cia whispered, as though it wasn't obvious.

They crept to the room and pressed their ears to the door, one going high and one low. They would be caught if anyone came along, but they couldn't risk trying for one of the adjoining rooms, and it was better to listen at doors, something Cia had learned during her mischievous youth. They were never as protective as people seemed to believe, especially when that illusion of safety kept people from lowering their voices sufficiently.

"The plan is insane, that's all I'm saying. His consciousness in that boy's body. He wouldn't be our king; he'd be a chimera." That was Lord Ojardian, she was certain. It might be rougher, older, but it was also quite bold now that he wasn't keeping to the quiet of the hallway.

If she had thought his wife the instigator, perhaps she had been wrong.

Cia shot a glance at Myrka, who was staring wide-eyed back at her. So it was true then?

"What you say is treason," said the other man she wished she could see. "The king's body is dying. There's nothing they can do. The mageri couldn't keep him alive without killing the land, and they're running through Nim faster than they can find them. They can't keep their own selves alive with the effort it takes for his. King Avize must do something drastic. If he takes over the boy, and the boy takes over Jucar, he can assure Jucar and Frizenze come to a peace through marriage or treaty. We all win."

"*If*. It all hinges on that *if*. His soul is barely being kept to his own body, and you believe it can be transferred and held to another? To my knowledge, such a thing has never been done," Lord Ojardian said, voice rising a bit before he remembered himself. "And do you not hear yourself? How much of Frizenze did we kill to save our king? Did Bloody Bess do as much to us? Now you're fine with conscripting Nim with no concern for killing them? By all means, kill people, but don't kill the crops."

"We all sacrifice what we must for the good of Frizenze," the other lord said stiffly.

"Where does it end? What if it were you being sacrificed? Or your son?" Lord Ojardian asked.

When there was no immediate response, Lord Ojardian exploded. "Bah! I see there is no talking with you."

Myrka jumped away from the door, and motioned frantically for Cia to do the same, but Cia shook her head and kept her ear pressed. She had to hear the rest. About the Nim being conscripted. She'd seen that gray-robed figure being dragged through the hallways but had misconstrued the entire thing. She felt sick to the depths of her soul. It could have been Roha. It *was* someone like nim. Like Princess Inaya, she'd let another person be tortured and killed and done nothing. She hadn't known, but it didn't make her feel better. Somehow, she should have realized. And she knew *now*. Which meant that something had to be done.

Cia waved her on. "Go," she mouthed to Myrka.

Myrka made more frantic gestures, urging Cia to flee with her, but when Cia didn't come, she turned and ran off, back toward their rooms.

But Cia stayed and listened.

"Explain it to me. Explain to me how this is bad for Frizenze, and I will listen."

"Even if the mageri or the Nim can lock the king's soul into the boy, it would take an immense power, and I think we have come to the end of our supply. And if they can do it, will it stay locked? Will he have to be attended to at all times? Though the soul would be our king, the seed would belong to the urchin. We won't have royal *Frizenzian* heirs. We will have street rats," Lord Ojardian said, just as Cia was starting to like him.

"As you know, we've found an untapped source of power, and we're preparing to march on it," the other lord said, and it sent a swarm of spiders over Cia's spine. "It is not for you to approve or disapprove. Simply to continue to support the king's orders. He will, after all, still be issuing them. No one needs to know they'll be coming from a different body. If word goes out that the king, as we knew him, has died, there will be a civil war for power that we can all agree will be bad for the country. As for the other, our king will be raising these rats to believe they are royalty. Or perhaps he'll be marrying into it on this side. I hear your own line has some small tie to the royal line?"

Cia's stomach was churning bile. She pulled away from the door, yanked up her skirts, and ran for her rooms. It was a good thing she didn't meet anyone else on the way, because she couldn't see or hear anything but disaster.

Hostill and Roha, both were in danger. She had to warn them. An untapped source of power, of Nim. It could only be the Sacrima.

But the guards waiting for her when she returned to her room—awake and alive—said that she would not have the opportunity to warn anyone.

CHAPTER TWENTY-SIX

Ulan

Ruggerio's body might have been quiescent while he healed, but not his mind. Never that. While he plotted, inventing and discarding a thousand scenarios for killing the queen–as Ulan knew from his occasional outbursts of *no, no, no, it'll never work!*–she practiced what Haelin taught her.

Haelin hadn't been willing to share anything at first. Not until Ruggerio confessed what he'd read of the Gospel of Gelerte and what he'd surmised. Not until they had a long, philosophical discussion and Haelin realized that she wouldn't be giving away any secrets. She was only confirming and providing greater context.

There existed people like Ruggerio, Nulls, who couldn't sense the anima at all, couldn't touch it, feel it, taste it. People like Ulan, Talents, had an affinity in one particular area, but one that must be nurtured. If they dug deep and practiced hard, they could make beautiful music. But their talents could only grow along their natural aptitude, the way a soprano might expand her range, but never sing bass. Nim were… Nim. They began with an intimate connection with the anima, an understanding on an instinctive level, though it took time and teaching to grow or fully come into their gifts as well. The Mageri could reach the anima, but they weren't truly attuned. They were like children who could pluck at strings, but what they created could not be called music. They could steal their magic from all around them, but only twist it into something *other*, leaving instruments so broken in their wake that no one could play them ever again.

Perhaps, Haelin said, no person was meant to hold more power than they could contain. Not enough to control the natural order of things or lord over others. But then, there had always been those who wanted more.

Oh, and they could continue to call her Haelin, continue with *she* and *her*. It was her identity in the royal city. Her name might change as she moved from place to place, but she was most comfortable taking on the feminine form when she had to blend.

Now Ulan practiced as Haelin had taught her. She shut out the world, took slow, thoughtful breaths that she followed inside herself, searching for the nexus of her strength. At first, she breathed herself out as quickly as she breathed the air in. Eventually, she stayed inside, sending everything *not-her* out with each exhale—the fears and frustrations, doubts and damage that she did to herself, wondering what she could have done to save Dazia, to stop Ceramor from sacrificing himself, whether there was more she should be doing besides waiting while the world quite literally burned. She winnowed herself past the recriminations, sinking deep into her core. Her body zipped around her, alive, frenetic, but she sought the calm she felt down low. Below her heart and her ribs. Low, low, low. Not a place, but a warmth, a strength...a power.

She'd known it must be there; she was able to see the anima where others could not. But to see it within herself was still a wonder. She was afraid to do more than feel for it, acknowledge it. She'd seen what Bloody Bess and her mageri women could do. Yes, she'd tried to reach for power of her own to help Ruggerio get the wards back at the Church. To strengthen Ludvin's ghost, but...that had been in the moment, necessary to the fate of the kingdom.

She still didn't truly believe in herself, and maybe that was for the best. If she did accept enough to work with that place of power, she was afraid that she wouldn't know the limits of her own strength, and that in reaching too far, she'd break not only herself, but also bring the rest of the shop down around Haelin and Ruggerio.

She quieted the doubts again, pushed them down. They were not living in safe times, best she learn where the lines were drawn while Haelin was there to stop her, shake her out of her daze if need be. And so she started with a call for Ludvin. This was her inherent ability; the spirits had come even without her call before she knew anything about Haelin's teachings. If she was successful, there would be more she could learn if she and Ruggerio helped Haelin. The Nimistry knew things. Important things. If only the world were ready for them.

Things it might be important for Ulan and Ruggerio to know to help Jucar.

Ludvin came. Not falling into her arms this time but appearing slowly, at first faint and flickering, as though he was light being thrown on a curtain blowing on a brisk day. But then he settled and stayed, and she breathed out an extra measure of what she thought of as her strength, willing it into him, and she could hear him mumbling to himself, "So many. So, so many."

"So many what?" she asked, flicking a glance at Haelin for a sense of whether she could see and hear Ludvin as well.

From Haelin's start at Ulan suddenly speaking after so long in silence, the answer was 'no.' Ulan worked on staying attuned to her center of power with her eyes open, ignoring distractions as she took the small blade Haelin offered. Ulan pierced a finger, then strode forward, holding her hand out to the spirit.

Ludvin looked up, as startled to see Ulan as Haelin had been to hear her. He met Ulan's gaze, his own haunted, which caused a hitch in her step. But he took her hand, brightening at the touch of her blood. She felt his fingers like frost.

"So many dead. Going to the anima. After you released me, I went out like a candle. I could have let myself go too. The All called to me, as it did before. Peaceful and promising. The harmonies, oh, the harmonies. Every song you ever wanted to join. Every beam of sunlight ever to touch your face. The first spring day after the melt and the first briskness of fall. Tart cider and crisp apples and sweet honeycombs. Every caress you leaned into. Then there were lights shooting past–so beautiful–and I could have followed them, only I realized that they were those sent on their way by the Crownsmen," Ludvin said, an unshed tear sparkling in his eye.

"So you didn't go?" Ulan asked.

"My work was unfinished. I was lost for a while, but then you called me, and I came to the churchyard. So that people could see me, see that Bloody Bess's dead would not be laid to rest, that we would rise up against her even beyond. That was the message, yes? But then, I was lost again…"

"I'm so sorry." Haelin spoke the words as Ulan thought them.

Ludvin's gaze shot to hers. "You…were there last night, yes? Who are you?"

It wasn't quite suspicion, though it might have been without the understanding that if Haelin was going to betray them, she'd already have done so.

"You led the rebels?" Haelin asked Ludvin.

"We're not rebels if we're the only ones looking to the good of Jucar. Say instead that Bloody Bess rebels against the interests of her people. Against all that is good and decent. Against–"

"Yes, yes, all of that," Haelin said with a wave of her hand as though clearing it like cobwebs from in front of their faces. "The group I am part of is a rebellion in its own way, and I saved Ulan and Ruggerio last night. I would join my cause to yours, at least as long as our interests ally."

"Oh?"

"Ludvin," Ulan said, grabbing back his attention, since she wasn't sure how long she could feed him her own strength. "Do you think you'd be able to reach the others all the way in Frizenze? We have to know if they've gotten Hostill to safety. If Ruggerio accomplishes his purpose, we need to be able to tell them it's time to return."

"I can try," he answered. Ludvin looked to Ruggerio, still clearly suffering, then to Haelin and back to Ulan. "Can I trust her alone with you?"

"If you can't trust Haelin, trust me to handle myself," Ulan said.

He gave a bob of the head and released her hand, vanishing as soon as they lost contact.

"You did it," Haelin said proudly.

Ulan was still watching the spot where Ludvin had disappeared, tears in her eyes. For Ludvin, for her little Dazia. Now she knew what her daughter had missed not going to the All for the many years she had stayed with Ulan. She'd never let her mother know of the pull she must have felt or the beauty of the universal anima she resisted. She hoped Dazia was at peace.

Her heart ached for Ludvin, killed by Bloody Bess's men, denying his well-earned rest to continue his fight. And there she was, behaving just like her cousin, mercilessly sending him off on missions out of necessity, and not even expressing her sorrow because time was fleeting, and it would do no good when what was done was done.

⊰ ━━━ ⊱

Ludvin

Ludvin spent time lost in the eddies of the anima, which pulled him along as though they wanted to slowly unfurl him and make him one with the All. He could feel the thrum of the earth like a heartbeat and wanted to lay his spiritual body down upon the breast of it, sink into eternal sleep. There was such peace, such languor, such a sense of rightness. *It was a struggle to keep himself together, sensing for the others back in the corporeal world. The anima itself was everywhere, flowing through the land, through every beast and flower, blowing about on the breeze and rising in the sap of every tree. So easy to be caught up, twisted, and turned around. Awareness ebbed and flowed into light and beauty. Whirlpools and eddies and snippets of sound and sonnets, music and conversations, scents...*

He forced himself to focus on Hostill and the others, listen for their particular voices, remember what they felt like, but he'd never experienced their individual energies and the distractions were so great.

In the end, it was all he could do even to return to Ulan mumbling, "Too far, too far."

Ulan felt like a monster when Ludvin came back to her. How cruel of her to keep him when the anima called so strongly.

On the other hand, he'd come to her to start with. She had never been the one to keep him from the All.

He was flickering even as he insisted on trying again, and Ulan had to convince him to regain his strength first. He couldn't go exhausted and rattled as he was. Since the collective anima was universal, everywhere, she didn't quite understand how distance mattered in getting to Hostill and the others, so she asked Ludvin a few questions while doing her best to hold his hand and feed him from her well of energies as Haelin had taught her. Maybe the problem was that he was focused on a group rather than just one person. He was trying to hold too many voices in his head, and if they had split up, then it would be nearly impossible. He should choose one person to whom he had the strongest connection.

Roha, his long-time lieutenant in the Restoration. He would know Roha's mind almost as he knew his own.

This time Ludvin was gone for hours, so long that Ulan began to despair that he would return at all. When he did, it was so faintly that she didn't see him until he had spoken in her ear, one word, "Gone."

She whipped her head around, hand to her chest, and fell back against the wall of the basement, rattling one of the near-empty shelves.

"Ludvin," she tried to get her breathing back under control, "you scared me. What do you mean gone?" she asked for the sake of the others. She broke open the cut she'd made earlier and let her blood flow so that her power might strengthen Ludvin again enough that he might appear to Haelin and Ruggerio.

"If Roha's still alive, ni's cut off from the anima. I can't find nim. Not anywhere," he answered.

"And the others?"

He shook his head. "I didn't have the strength to look for them and come back to you. I'd have been lost. A few days. I have to rest. My head…"

Though she tried to hold him, Ulan watched him fade to nothing. She wondered whether he would come back or whether the pull of the anima had been too much. She knew she should wish him his peace, but what she felt was terror at their only chance at reaching the others vanishing before her.

"Can ghosts feel pain?" Ruggerio asked.

"There are all kinds of pain," Ulan answered.

"We have to go to the Restoration," Ruggerio said, and it was such a shock coming out of his mouth that Ulan couldn't even process it at first.

"The people who turned their backs on us?" Ulan exchanged a glance with Haelin. She'd told her everything while Ruggerio was healing.

"We can't do this alone, as we've said all along. The assassination, yes," Ruggerio said, awake now, color regained. "I'll be the one to take that risk, but we want the queen and her people expecting the threat from other quarters. You gave things a start with Ludvin's ghost, with Bloody Bess's dead rising. But you've been timid and tentative with your power and what Haelin's had to teach you. It seems time for a practical application. We know the city has its share of those who haven't moved on. I would venture that the palace has the same. There must be angry spirits there, bosewights who would come to your call, know things that they are willing to share. And if you can lend them power—"

"Assuming she can call to them past the palace wards," Haelin cut in. "And she can't lend them enough power to act on the living. I didn't teach her the Nim way for her to become your assassin by proxy."

Ruggerio didn't flinch. He didn't consider 'assassin' an insult. "I never considered that the wards around the queen would allow for that," he said calmly. "Nor do I believe we'll be so fortunate as to have King Jannik's shade still around or that he'd materialize to acknowledge Hostill as his bastard son and heir if he was. However, if more of the spirits 'rose,' if they struck out against the Crownsmen, perhaps scared them off a parapet or gave them a small hand–"

"No," Haelin said again.

But Ruggerio ignored her as he continued. "Then the Restoration can say that Bloody Bess has so far upset the natural order of things that spirits are too angry to move on to the anima. The Restoration can sound our truth of what happened in that battle in the Dobrens Valley about who truly restored the land and how. They can tell everyone that it was Roha, one of your own people, who gave back to the land by settling the unquiet spirits and returning their strength to the magic-deadened earth."

"And what if they do say that?" Haelin snapped, and Ulan drew back from the unexpected lash of her words. "Do you think the queen won't retaliate? The Nim are already used and abused. We will be *cut down.*"

"Not if I succeed," Ruggerio said.

"And if you fail?" Haelin looked ready to commit murder herself, only from her glare, Ruggerio would be her first target.

"Then spirits save us all. We can throw everything we have at success or resign ourselves to a slow death," he answered, voice rising in what was, for Ruggerio, a surprising display of emotion.

Haelin let out a sound Ulan knew well. It was how she felt when Dazia had died. She went to Haelin and put her arms around her, but Haelin didn't turn into her embrace. Instead, she stiffened and then flinched away, whirling as far from the two of them as she could in the small space.

"You are insane, both of you. You will get us all killed," Haelin spat.

Ulan's arms dropped to her sides, useless. "Perhaps it is easy for me now, because I have no one else to lose."

There was a flicker, and then Ludvin was with them again, so faint that she knew she was the only one seeing him. "I will try," he mouthed.

She reached out a hand to him, and he reached back. Just as with Dazia, her little ghost girl when she'd put her arms around her or stroked her face, she couldn't feel him except for the chill, but she knew he was there, and when she focused, he brightened a bit, but just a bit. She was wrung out herself and not concentrating the way Haelin had taught her. She wasn't reaching inward, reaching anywhere, just lending him strength the way one person would offer it to another in the squeeze of a hand, though hers went right through his.

But when he didn't go, she looked to him, to see that he was chewing on a thought. When she caught his translucent gaze, Ludvin let it out, "Do you think we're no more than whispers to be sent along with messages for the living?" And it hurt, because she knew better. "I was never good with words, and so I left the rallying cries to others. Now I will find the words. But I'll need your strength."

"They despise me," Ulan said. "The people who share your philosophy cast me out."

"That was before Bloody Bess burned down the church and killed an acolyte in full view of the people, before so many of their number never returned, when they thought they could be precious about allies. They may feel differently now. Especially if you and Haelin explain."

Haelin couldn't hear Ludvin's side of the conversation, but something about the way Ulan glanced over at her must have tipped her off. "No," she said. "I will not tell them what we do so that they can understand. I will not expose the Nimistry. It is more than enough that I've shared things with you. Has he told you that the Restoration recruits from the Desperata? Was possibly even started by one of their number? Desperata *torture* themselves to keep from touching on their abilities. If they thought for even an instant that people like me might teach others to reach the anima inside themselves, they'd turn on us as well. It's not a risk that we can take."

Ulan turned back to Ludvin. "Is it true?"

She'd never heard of the Desperata, but then, she'd never heard of the Nimistry either until Haelin. Secret societies were meant to be secret, and she'd spent years focused on Dazia and preserving secrets of her own.

Ludvin's shade blinked back at her, which was answer enough.

"So it is," she said for him. "You're right, Ludvin. You are more than a messenger. You can still make choices and a difference. If you want to talk with the Restoration, I can't stop you. But please, don't expose Haelin's secrets or those of the Nimistry. It's not safe."

Ludvin gazed down at their linked hands, and then pulled his away, so easy when his were as insubstantial as animist. Then he floated away enough to bow, and winked out again. She hoped it wasn't a goodbye. There was no reason it should be when he was talking with the Restoration about tying their messaging into Bloody Bess and her unruly spirits, which Ulan would be raising. But the peace of the anima must call to him after all this turmoil, and she wouldn't blame him if he answered that call. Going against lifelong beliefs wasn't easy. But if Ludvin had ever taken the easy path, he would surely still be among the living.

CHAPTER TWENTY-SEVEN

Ruggerio

Ghosts, as it turned out, were no good to Ruggerio at all. Oh, being incorporeal, they could flit about wherever they liked and could come to Ulan at her call, were half-inclined to come to her anyway, as the only person in the city with the talent to speak to them. As Haelin explained it, talents or affinities came to people naturally. Others could work at them, but no one was inclined to practice speaking with the dead when they so rarely hung around to make it worthwhile. All known mageri were either in training or in service to the Crown, and there were much better things to do with their power, like create grand constructs to crush their enemies.

Ulan, being corporeal, couldn't carry herself into the palace with Ruggerio to lend her strength to any spirits there to do things like steal the secret-chamber key from the queen. Even if one could muster that much strength on their own, they couldn't carry keys to Ruggerio past the palace wards. They'd certainly never be able to move the furniture Bloody Bess would have placed in front of her end of the secret passage.

So he had to rely on someone on the inside. But only if he could get there. For now, he was entirely on his own, and while that was typically the way he liked it, he was up against the elements, and it was far from a fair fight.

He clung tightly to the limestone walls of the eastern tower, finding handholds and footholds wherever mortar had worn away or where the stone itself had been rougher cut. But the deep winter chill of the stone seeped into him, stealing what little heat the wailing wind had left him. It had already torn the hood back from his head and whipped much of his hair loose from its queue, slashing it across his eyes, making them water to where he could barely see. His fingertips were raw from the friction and the cold and from holding on, bleeding right through the holes he'd cut into his gloves. He had to hold tight, because he'd lost feeling, and it was the only way to trust that he was truly gripping at all. The muscles in his legs began to twitch. If they went into a spasm now, it would be the end for him. Each new handhold might be his last.

Only the null he'd stolen from the Church, negating the nearest wards laid upon the palace ages ago, allowed him to hold on at all. The wall should be unscalable. The castle was also impregnable to ranged weapons, and no magic could be used on the palace or the grounds, though small magics could still be used *within* the palace, in case the mageri were called on to defend it against invaders or heal someone inside.

He had no idea how the spells had been laid without the land being destroyed. Maybe the long-ago mageri had done what Bloody Bess was doing now, employed death magic, taking the power straight from the people. Maybe that was how they planned to defend the castle without destroying it in the event of a siege.

He only knew that the guards patrolling the grounds trusted too much in the passive defenses and didn't look up as they should, and that those on the ramparts didn't look down. Even if they had, they'd be at a poor angle to see him. Ruggerio himself was the only one who could mess up this part of his plan.

He had to force himself back from his death grip on the palace walls to get a perspective on where he was in relation to Lady Kylia's window. She had set a lantern burning in her window, shutters opened just enough for him to see it. The wind immediately shot between him and the stonework, trying to rip him away. An instant of vertigo spun the world around him. He yanked himself back in, hugging the cold of the stone, letting it shock him back to true, only it didn't. The world still spun. He closed his eyes, counted five breaths in, five out. He was already exhausted from the mageri spell that had killed the horse he and Ulan escaped on and nearly destroyed his cousin and himself. Then, from getting caught in the church fire from which he was barely healed.

This was deadly. Every second weakened him, but if he continued climbing with the world so unstable…

Maybe the vestiges of the castle magic were fighting the stolen null. Maybe it was a natural reaction. It didn't matter. He'd come too far. He'd seen enough in his brief glance. He adjusted his climb to the left, not much higher, and he kept going. He left his eyes closed a little longer. He was going by feel anyway. His eyes were useless until he got to Lady Kylia's window.

Two more handholds and his foot slipped, taking one of his hands with it. His heart plummeted with his body as he desperately held on by one hand and foot. His other side swung in the breeze, threatening to carry him off like a kite. He growled into it and opened his eyes defiantly, only to snap them shut again as they were near-frozen by the wind. His remaining arm was shaking. His fingers awoke only so that they could protest their pain. They were gripping, sliding, bloodied…

He might not have Ulan's power. Or Haelin's. But he had his own. He was himself, and he had never failed on a mission. He wasn't going to do it now. Not with this most important one of his life. Not by falling off the side of a tower when he'd scaled dozens of others before.

Ruggerio used the force of the wind. He swayed into it, just a little, terror gripping him as it seemed it might go too far, rip him away. Then he let the momentum swing him like a pendulum back the other way until he was within grabbing distance of the wall. He scrabbled for it. Trying, failing, flapping away again. He cursed himself, cursed the wind, Bloody Bess. But he did it again, swinging into the wind and back. This time he caught. And held.

For a moment, he clung there. Said a spiritu. Shocking the collective spirits as well as himself.

And then he climbed. He didn't stop again until his hands curled over Lady Kylia's windowsill, uncaring whether he knocked over the lamp, as long as he got in before his grip gave way.

Lady Kylia saw him and cried out. Quietly, though. As quietly as she had during their assignations.

She pushed back the shutters, removed the lantern to somewhere further within the room, and reached for his arms.

"I have this," he said, before she could help him to his death, well-meaning though she would be.

Then he was through the window and leaning against her wall, breathing hard to prove he was still alive. Fingers too raw to chafe feeling back into them. Face and legs too numb for the warmth of her fire to make an impression. But he was in.

Now for the hard part.

Lady Kylia took his hands gently in her own and drew him away from the wall. He wouldn't let her lure him into the chair by the fire or offer him a goblet of watered wine, though his throat was as dry as the wood crackling away in her hearth. She tisked and cocked her head at him.

"I risk everything for you, and you don't trust me?" she asked.

Truly, the moue of her lips, the sadness in her eyes were all perfectly primed. He could almost believe her wounded if he were the believing sort. But distrust never killed anyone.

"If all goes well, I will be the most trusting man in Jucar. But that's the very thing–I ask you to risk yourself. It occurs to me that it's much safer for you to drug me and roll me back out your window. Do away with me entirely and be done with the threat."

"What a terrible place your mind must be for you to even consider such a thing. Or what horrors you must think of me," she whirled away from him, toward the door, but he caught her by the wrist before she could move even a step away, not that it would be any help if she had guards waiting for him beyond the door. A raised voice would be enough to summon them.

She swung back to him, fury lighting her face now, but while some people were ugly in anger, Kylia was transcendent. She puffed up like a bird or, more apt, lit up like a phoenix, even her hair seeming to rise like flame, making herself a larger threat, ready to battle and burn the one who stood against her. He only wished he had the time to pull her into his arms and temper his steel in her heat before rushing off to do what had to be done.

"I'm working toward a time when I no longer need to look for betrayals and motives in every word and deed."

Ruggerio stroked her wrist with his thumb before letting it go. Feeling was returning to his fingers now. He had no excuse to delay. She hadn't called anyone down on him, and he'd been…

"I'm sorry," he said quietly, surprising himself. "I will make certain none of this comes back to you."

She let her gaze flicker up to his then, briefly, and there were tears in her eyes when she said, "Don't get killed."

She went back to the window, replaced and latched the shutters, and blew out the lantern. He looked back once as he listened at the door, to assure that no one had come as they'd talked, but she didn't look back. He pulled the door inward to peer out, and seeing no one, let himself out and closed it behind him. He was down the hallway and dodging into the shadows before anyone at all came along. It was a particular skillset. He could be as still as a statue when he meant to be, and as quiet. Already, his hair was as black as ink, and his skin dark as gloaming shadows. He wouldn't be seen or heard unless he intended to be…or in the unlikely event that someone was as good as he was.

He knew which rooms were likely to be locked or unlocked and unattended. Where the secret passages lay, the beginnings and endings. But none would get him into Bloody Bess's quarters. He had to do this the hard way, and no matter what, he would have to fight his way to her at the end.

He heard voices coming from the cross-corridor he approached and doubled back the way he'd come to the last unlocked door. If he wasn't mistaken, one of them was Marius, who he'd trained, and who just *might* notice an extra shadow behind the plinth with the bust of King Rudin's first wife–emphasis on the bust–in front of the grand threadbare tapestry of the Hunt of the White Hind.

When they were gone, he ventured out again. He'd chosen his ascent in the early twilight, as the sun was going down in the west so that he would be difficult to see scaling the castle, but also because it was likely that the queen would be in her chambers. From his time as her spymaster, he knew that she would gather herself to do formal dinners if she must, but due to her dreadful megrims, she would generally retire to her rooms after any meetings of the day to take her meals, to pour over maps or plans with Strego–who he supposed had been downgraded from regent now that she'd declared herself queen. But even better if she were not yet there, because then he could hide, the better to ambush her later, facing less opposition. Not because he feared opposition, but he wanted the greatest chance for success and to escape alive. He was prepared to die, as long as he achieved his mission, but he worried for Ulan. He worried about the others pulling off everything without him. Of them all, he was the only one with court experience to guide the boy once he achieved the throne. The only one who could think like *them.*

He had a few more close calls and then...none at all. The queen despised having anyone near her, and the servants used other corridors, so except for a couple of roaming guards, he encountered nothing until he was half a hall away from Bloody Bess's suite and could see her guards standing at attention.

This was it. His moment. He took in a deep breath, loosened his shoulders, reached for his sword...and felt the tip of a blade press deeply into the small of his back. Deeply enough to draw blood.

How had he missed someone coming up on him?

No time to worry about that now. He dropped and rolled, flicking his wrists as he came up facing his attackers so that daggers appeared in both hands. He slashed immediately at them before they could come in close, making them dance back and giving himself time to get to his feet. He faced two men with swords, himself only armed with daggers, and the sound of a door opening down the hall signaling reinforcements on the way.

He threw the dagger from his dominant hand into the soft spot exposed when the one attacker raised his sword for an attack aimed at cutting his head from his neck. The Crownsman staggered back, his sword clattering to the ground. The other swordsman was slicing down, and Ruggerio had only the guard of his right dagger to catch it on. But now his left hand was free to go for his sword, which he did, pulling it from its sheath as he threw his forehead into that of his attacker while pushing him away with the dagger's guard.

Then he whipped his own sword around, but the Crownsman caught it. Ruggerio didn't have time to play with him. No time for finesse. He brought his foot down on the guard's instep and thrust his dagger into the man's stomach. As he reeled back, Ruggerio swung the sword for him again, cutting in, but not so deeply that it would take time to pull his sword free.

More guards were rushing in, and he threw his remaining dagger for one, catching him in the neck. The man's eyes widened in surprise, and he swatted at it as though it were a large bee and he'd just been stung, but when he pulled it loose, blood came with it. The guard collapsed, and Ruggerio quickly evaluated whether he could get his dagger back in time to use again.

But there was no chance of that. The others were on him already, their swords flying, and he whirled, parried, swung, caught. He freed a dagger from another Crownsman's belt when he ducked under his guard, and used it on him, but there were two more behind him, and they were waiting for Ruggerio. One kicked his knees out from under him, crumpling him forward, right into the swords of two Crownsmen waiting before him. He was on the ground looking up with no way to rise without getting run through. He was out of moves and surrounded.

He nonetheless began to rise, only for the tip of a sword to press into the base of his neck, drawing blood.

"That's far enough. Throw down your weapons," the man said in a voice like the rumble of thunder. "All of them. Now. Orders are to bring you to the queen, but I'd just as soon run you through after what you've done to my men. Your choice."

As long as he lived, there was still a chance. From his time as spymaster, he knew Pell, the guard captain, and that he was always as good as his word. He would kill him here in the hall rather than risk harm coming to the queen if Ruggerio didn't do what he said. Or he'd justify it that way. Pell would take any punishment necessary for not bringing him to Bloody Bess alive.

He was too thorough for Ruggerio to get away with hiding the two daggers still in his boots, the knuckle-knife in his belt, or the null. But the poisoned pin was another matter. Pell would know to look for poison rings, perhaps even lockets, but Ruggerio had never used anything so traditional. He'd brought this very fast-acting and irreversible poison back from Frizenze and dipped in it the tip of a pin he usually wore on his cloak in case he ever needed to employ it. A weapon of last resort.

As soon as he'd divested himself of his weapons and they searched him to be certain, they bound his hands tightly behind him and began manhandling him down the hallway, right to where he wanted to be: the queen's quarters.

He was surprised to feel a modicum of fear. Without his null, he was vulnerable to magic. While he didn't fear Bloody Bess's mageri, the queen herself was another story. She could spill his secrets with his blood and drink down his anima. She could use his essence to power the dark schemes he was trying to thwart. What happened to him then? Did his spark die out entirely or did he live on within her, an observer to everything he despised? Roha's restoration of the anima to the Dobrens Valley suggested the latter.

Death didn't scare him, but becoming flotsam in the queen's shipwrecked mind, *that* was truly terrifying.

The Crownsmen knocked at the queen's suite and performed a call and response before her door was opened to them. Ruggerio closed his eyes, took deep, slow breaths, and did his best to center himself, the way he would when he was trying to listen at a door or wall that didn't want to give up sound.

His eyes flew open again as he was thrown forward onto his face, the entire world lurching. His nose and cheekbone cracked on the hard stone when he couldn't catch himself, and his blood flowed. They'd bound his hands, now loose to the point where one good twist might free them, as slick as they were with blood and sweat, but he couldn't let them see that. Not until the perfect moment to go for the pin and the queen in one movement because he wouldn't get a second chance.

Bloody Bess's gaze bored into his for an instant, then riveted on the blood. A smile fissured her face. Her lips were bloodless, as pale as the rest of her, her tongue shockingly red as it darted out to wet her lips, as though she could taste his blood from afar. Her dress was a shade off the Jucar scarlet and black. More the garnet of a Ridaldo red wine with black lace set in a ruff framing her neck, exposed by her high-gathered rose-gold hair. The same lace formed a modesty panel at her bust and trimmed her sleeves. Garnets sparkled like blood droplets through her hair.

"You may come to heel," the queen spoke, and she was very much *The Queen* in that moment. Cold, distant, untouchable, though perhaps a good lunge…

He used the strength he had left to get from his prone position to sitting back on his knees, no easy feat with his arms bound as they were. But he had no choice. His nose was swelling, and breathing was getting difficult. He needed to choke down the blood or spit it out. Wouldn't that go well for him? He also had to be in a better position for his chance at the queen.

One step closer.

"What am I to do with you?" Bloody Bess asked, savoring his pain, remorseless over the blood running down his face.

But then, he *had* come to kill her.

"Let me go with a warning, and I will promise never to do it again, realizing what a futile effort it would be?" Ruggerio said, choosing one of the roguish personas from his bag of tricks, knowing that she would never go for it. But the attempt must be made, if only because she would expect it.

He'd thought at one time that she had feelings for him but had discounted her then as a mere child. Now, he thought of her as something more–more dangerous, more devious. Someone who must be stopped at all costs.

Also, someone who'd become suddenly, horrifyingly, fascinating.

She snorted, and it would have been childish on anyone else, but she was no longer that. If only she hadn't put Jucar on a path of destruction, if only she weren't a royal and he a mere peon, oh, how they might rule. There would be no stopping them!

"You must think me a fool," she said.

"I think you're wonderful. And horrible," he said. Truth.

She did nothing but gaze at him for an instant before she said to one of the guards beside her, "Sword."

His fear came back, stronger than before, but he used it to bolster himself. There was nothing to lose now. There was no right moment. There was only *this one*.

She took the sword handed to her and tested its blade on her own finger, smiling at the sight of the blood drawn. As she sucked on the wound, taking her blood back, Ruggerio twisted his hands free of the bonds, pulled them loose, and whipped the pin from his doublet in the same motion. He sprung forward, pin out, aiming for Bloody Bess's leg, which was what he could reach.

There was a great cry, and the sword came bashing down, ringing his head as though it was a bell meant to be heard throughout the land. Another bit into him from the side, a sharp pain in the back, until he couldn't tell them apart.

He couldn't take in air, couldn't breathe, couldn't *feel*. He didn't know if his pin had hit home, only that it was on the ground and so was he. He could feel nothing, and the world came and went in bits of darkness like clouds obscuring the moon. That was more terrifying than all the pain in the world. If he were alive but unable to fight, Bloody Bess could still steal his essence away. And he would be powerless.

Another blow came, and he shattered.

CHAPTER TWENTY-EIGHT

Cia

As soon as Cia stepped into her room, past the guards still slumped outside, she knew she was caught. It wasn't the guards inside who slammed the door behind her to make sure she had nowhere to run–she didn't even register them at first–it was Joia glaring poisoned darts at her from just inside the connecting door. She held a dagger in each hand, making Cia wonder whether she'd been overplaying her infirmity all along.

Beyond her stood Myrka, her face entirely blank. Was that for the benefit of their audience or had she betrayed Cia? To save herself or because Frizenze had given her what she'd always wanted, to be cut off from the temptation of her powers? Was the null worth betraying even her own country?

A blow cracked across the backs of her knees, and they buckled. She fell forward uncontrolled, caught herself on her hands, only to have them ripped out from under her and her arms twisted behind her back with no consideration of the way arms might actually move. Cia screamed as one shoulder jolted out of place. Her vision blacked as the pain blasted from the joints all across her neck and back, up into her head, and then to throb, pulse, as the agony took on a life of its own.

She didn't know much after that, lost in the pain. The guards got her up and moving, but the walls and floor canted, and she weaved in what little slack her captors allowed. At some point, she vomited. Then she was thrown somewhere, landing on her shoulder, and the pain exploded like royal fireworks.

When she woke, it was to such complete and utter darkness that fear screamed up her throat. Her jaw unhinged, though she'd learned to be silent in her terror, and that was when the *real* fear hit. She met resistance. Like Garif's big hand over her mouth and nose, only different. She knew it was different, and yet the panic that struck was mindless, jibbering.

Her breathing went shallow, and what air she blew came back to her, heated, stifling. Hot and wet and insufficient. Her chest felt barely able to expand. The darkness was so absolute that light might be a myth.

She reached for her face, surprised to find her hands free, though only one was functioning. She lifted it to her face, shaking all the way, because she knew what she'd find. She knew, and then she *knew*. Her hands traced the metal straps wrapped around her head to hold the scold's bridle over her face–the iron rings around her eyes, the molded nose with pinholes for air and the rictus of a mouth with only a short, narrow, straight line like the one she'd been meant to walk as a guest of the king to allow for breath. It wasn't enough, but it could be worse.

At least they hadn't fitted her with the bit to depress the tongue and keep her from speaking, as they would have done if they'd set her up in the village square for the crime of gossip or bearing false witness or being a public nuisance. After what she'd heard, they very well might have. Unless, as the darkness indicated, they'd locked her so far away that no one would find her, and she'd have no one to whom she could spill her secrets.

Or she'd be dead too soon for concern.

She forced herself to calm. Now that she knew she could breathe, she wouldn't let fear take that away from her. It was the flashback to Garif. Panic setting in. She was stronger than that. Than *him.*

She practiced her breathing until the throb of her shoulder was worse than the suffocation of the mask. She still didn't feel as though she was getting enough air, but she'd experienced the same lack being high in the mountain passes with Bloody Bess, and she'd survived that. And she knew how to put her shoulder back into place, but it would be tricky to do in the dark. Cia reached for the closest wall. Her feet, as they shuffled, encountered no rug–not that she'd expected any. No luxuries for the prisoner–and she didn't shuffle more than two steps before she hit a cold stone barrier.

She felt along it for the dimensions, and met another wall in a few more steps, but she wasn't concerned with that now. Only that she'd have enough space to do what needed to be done. She backed up to where she'd been and took a deep breath, as though that would fortify her against the fresh influx of agony. Then she rotated the shoulder until it felt right-ish, gasped out the held breath, and fell against the wall to slam the joint back into place. It hurt like a fresh beating, and she let herself slide down the wall, leaning toward her good side as she sobbed.

Her shoulder throbbed, and she let herself wallow for a moment, knowing that it would take that long to marshal the focus for the more immediate concerns of mapping out her confines and thinking of a way to escape or somehow get the word out to others about what was happening. Hostill and Roha were in trouble, and no one else knew. No one but Myrka, and she couldn't be trusted.

Roha…could it be ni was both the problem and the answer? As far as anyone in Frizenze knew, Cia couldn't access the anima. The only time she'd ever had power was when Garif possessed and worked through her. There was no reason for the king to order nulls set on her or her prison. And this wasn't the castle. There wouldn't be a block of warded cells already arranged here. It was a hunting lodge, a manor, albeit a sprawling one, undoubtedly royal.

If Cia could tune out the pain of her shoulder, and the panic at the metal mask over her face, and the terror that they'd leave it there until she died of thirst or starvation… She was hyperventilating again and beginning to feel dizzy. Cia slowed herself down, tried to think calming thoughts so that she could search out the path she'd once found in a dream, the one that led to Roha.

She imagined herself back in her rooms in Jucar, not because they were soothing, but because she could envision herself there by the fire with a pattern in her head, a needle and thread in her hands, embroidering a beautiful woodland border. Here, a titmouse with a tiny seed held in his beak, head tilted just so, inquisitory, as though asking if you might like it instead. There, a dappled fawn frolicked while his mother looked on.

Somehow, in the midst of everything, it made her smile. She could see the fawn as clear as day, imagine the stitches she would use on the fluffy white underside of his tail. If she were to stay in this dark room, she would provide her own sights. Her breathing smoothed out. Her eyes were already closed.

She searched for that place within herself that must be closest to the collective spirit, for that spark that kept her going, kept her fighting after everything she'd been through. She was surprised to find it not in her heart or in her head, but like a fire in her belly. It was possibilities and promise and, yes, the sort of blaze that could obliterate everything to allow for new growth.

She remembered ice when she'd wanted to blast Roha, a chill rather than a fever to deny an intruder. But she wanted to find Roha now, and so she concentrated on searching out that warmth within her that felt like power, hope.

There, the connection thrummed, almost as music she'd hummed along to all her life. Knew it as the images that came to her for embroidery—the titmice and sparrows and doves, brambles and vines, streams and eddies and breezes that caught the falling autumn leaves just so to send them flying across the paths of foxes and kits...

The anima was right there, the connection to the All. It had been the backdrop of her life, and she'd never realized it, but it had never called to her, tempted her as it had Myrka. If it had, she might easily have done what Myrka had and turned it on Garif, taking everyone in the castle along with him.

That shocked her straight out of her body. She'd been so young when she came to Jucar with her princess. Perhaps she hadn't yet been aware of her power. Had *that* been what had drawn Garif to her from the beginning? Had he been siphoning off her strength for his own all along, every time he beat her and savagely drew blood?

Well then, he'd been playing with fire. And if he hadn't exactly been burned, he had slipped and fallen on the char stick.

She sat with that. And sat. But she couldn't wait for it to process. This was too monumental. All of it. Once she warned the others, then she could think about herself, wallow, cry, scream for all the good it would do in this cursed iron mask.

But for now... Cia closed her eyes, as though the dark was her own choice, and reached for that place. She found it quickly this time, but it wasn't the fire she wanted. Not *her* fire. She was looking for the quiet stream that was Roha. It would be nearby. No longer iced-over. She only hoped she hadn't burned it off, that she wouldn't find a dry streambed. She realized that she was putting words and images to things that had none, but she thought in patterns.

There was Roha's path, a quiet thread not so like a stream, but an energy that she could follow like a line unspooled in a labyrinth, back to the start. Only, when she gave it a tentative tug, she was instantly pulled in and along, as though Roha had been waiting for a sign. And yet when she arrived at the other end, there was a sense of surprise, alarm.

Roha was there, but nes attention had been elsewhere. The rush of Cia flowing along the path must have been surprising. Perhaps even aggressive. She had never done it before and didn't know what she was doing now, and when she reached the end, it was as though Cia had bumped into Roha, who had to catch her before their collision wrecked them both.

Cia? Is everything all right? They were thoughts more than words. Impressions, but somehow clear as they'd been in her dream.

No, nothing is right. You're in danger! Cia tried not to shout her message but knew she was unsuccessful.

She told Roha everything. Tried to pass it along exactly as she'd heard it in case Roha had any other interpretation. She finished, *I don't know when they're marching on the Sacrima, but I don't imagine it will be long, not with the king doing so poorly. You have to prepare.*

But what about you? Not that I want you otherwise, but why leave you alive? Roha asked.

I don't know. It wasn't the king's men who caught me. Not as such. It might have been too suspicious to kill me. They may still need to use me as a hostage for Hostill's cooperation. Not that they'll tell him he's to be taken over. You have to save him when they bring him to the Sacrima.

Cia's urgency was getting to her, and her breathing came in gasps, as though she wasn't getting enough air. She started to panic again, and felt herself slipping away and Roha reaching for her to keep their connection. She clasped on, and the rush between them was like nothing she'd ever experienced. Like warmth and energy and vitality and so the opposite of pain that she had no words for it. A lightness, a levity, a...peace. A happiness? She gravitated back, and in that moment... She couldn't. It was too much. A fullness. An abundance.

I–, she started to say, and she stopped.

Roha didn't say anything either.

For a moment, they just *were*.

Then Roha gasped out a breath in this place where they didn't breathe. A sound that expressed what neither could put into words.

You ask a lot, Roha said when the sound died out, and Cia was both disappointed and relieved that the words were not as momentous as the feeling that had preceded them.

That their thoughts hadn't been spoken, so they didn't have to be faced. She wasn't sure what the feeling meant and wasn't ready to examine it. She'd just survived Garif. She wasn't certain she would live out her captivity. She didn't need to be obligated to anyone else that she survive. Or for anyone to mourn her passing should she fail.

She was being ridiculous. One moment of connection, and she was making more of it than it was. Making it everything, because she was that starved for basic humanity.

Save the sanctuary. Save Hostill. Roha said. *Shall I save you while I'm at it, my Lady?*

There were tears in Cia's eyes. Her heart contracted in a way that was infinitely more than pain, but she would not let it show.

If you please, she answered lightly.

I will take it under advisement.

Before Cia could make any kind of fool of herself in response, she sensed something in her room, a creeping coldness, *someone watching her.* She didn't know how she knew, but she did.

I have to go, she told Roha, and she could feel the regret through their link as she hurried back to see what fresh torment awaited.

CHAPTER TWENTY-NINE

Bess mourned Ruggerio. She wasn't a monster. Not like her father and brothers.

He wasn't dead yet. But down in the oubliette, his wounds untreated and left to fester, he might as well be. He would be soon enough, she supposed.

She'd once thought him dangerously attractive and that she might dare to dally with him for a while. Perhaps even continue that dalliance after settling into an advantageous marriage of her choosing with a man she could control. Power or no, she was certain that would never be Ruggerio, which was also why she hadn't drained him and sucked out his soul. She had enough going on in her head. She already feared revolt. If she took Ruggerio in, he would certainly be the one to lead it.

It was a risk even to send him to the oubliette, the place of forgetting, though Ceramor, the mageri who'd gone mad with all the power he'd taken in and not spent from her brother's hounds, had never escaped. But better to imprison Ruggerio than risk him coming back as a bosewight to haunt her or to spill his secrets to whoever was raising the ghosts in the city.

Yet as he was dragged away unconscious and bleeding, all she could think was, *What a waste.* He could have stayed her spymaster. He could have become her paramour. Instead, he'd decided to throw in with rebels and tossed his life away.

There was a knock at her door, her guards' particular code, and the door was opened to reveal a messenger on her doorstep, out of breath but trying to recover himself.

"My Queen, your dead—"

"Are rising," she said with a snap, "yes, it's happened before. If we react, it is certain to happen again. A weak trick by my enemies who have no more arrows in their quiver. No doubt a distraction to call off my men for that assassination attempt. As you can see, there is no cause for alarm. Certainly no cause to come bursting in—"

"Those are not the dead he speaks of," came another voice, stronger. Strego? *Strego* would dare interrupt her? She should have drained him down the second she shed the pretense of playing princess. She'd thought he might be helpful managing the councilmen she had so little use for. They were still her lords. She still needed them alive and on board with her plans so that they could convince *their* barons in return. So she wouldn't have revolt within her own kingdom while she took down Frizenze and Galitrüd, but…

Her thoughts tangled and tripped over themselves. But what? They wouldn't dare. And if they would, she could simply bleed them and take them all over. Perhaps she shouldn't have thrown Ruggerio away so easily. She might have found a way to bring him back. Placate him. Or bleed and control him as she had Strego. She could have *insisted* he use his sly genius on her behalf. But again, she couldn't be sure, and that was her only true safety. And how good could he truly be if she had beaten him?

But Strego had spoken. He stepped over Ruggerio's spilled blood but misjudged his step and caught a heel in it. He made a face and tried to scuff it off.

"A woman's body has been raised from the waters outside the

North tower by the spirit of a fisherman who had his throat cut. Or if not by the spirit, then by whoever nearby was powering him."

"Leave us," Bess commanded the guards.

"All?" dared the one. "My Queen, you've just had an attempt on your life."

"And it will certainly be the last. The traitor has not gone on to the anima, but to live the rest of his miserable life in a hole, basking in his own stench. The wards hold. You will protect me as you have. From *outside* my quarters. And you will not question me again or you'll share the traitor's fate. Understood?"

Fear struck him dumb, but he bowed deeply and was gone with his compatriots, one missing his sword, which she still held. She wasn't leaving herself in striking range of Strego without a weapon. She'd trusted Ruggerio once. Not that she wasn't threat enough, but she would not waste her power needlessly. And drinking and disappearing Strego was certain to be noticed.

"Why do you say this was one of *my dead*?" she challenged him immediately.

"The fisherman said as much, his shade unencumbered by the slit in his throat. His likeness flickered into life at the docks some time before twilight–about the time, as you say, your would-be assassin began his infiltration. It garnered a great audience, as you can imagine, since many of the fishing boats go out at that time. It's one of the best times to catch–"

"Get to the point."

"Yes," he said gruffly. "Well, the fisherman moaned about a body and a great wrong. Some ignored him, but two women commissioned a boat to take them where he led–"

"Where are these women?"

"Vanished, my Queen. Lost in the crowd."

She growled. "Continue."

"Other boats followed, all the way around to the North tower, and the hidden dock there that no one is supposed to know about. When the spirit reached a certain point, he got anxious, agitated. He jumped over the side of the boat and came up again with a body floating before him. *A woman's bloated body.* He said that in life he reported it to the watch, who held him for the Crown. Then suddenly, it was as though the spirit became…possessed. He stilled, his neck stretched as though someone stretched it for him; his shoulders grew taut as if held. The crowd was treated to a reenactment of his death. The slash across his throat reopened, gushing phantom blood, and he vanished before everyone's eyes. Only the bloated body remained."

Bess cursed under her breath, something colorful she'd learned from her brothers. It was wholly unsatisfying.

"Quite the scene," was all she said aloud. "Where is the woman's body now?"

"We have it, my Queen. Down in the dungeon, surrounded by sage. It stinks to Markens and back."

"Then why–"

"The earth is frozen. There will be no new burials until the spring. We can–"

"Burn it," she said. "I will not have some decaying stench wafting through the palace because my enemies wanted to put on a pageant."

"My Queen, we will have to take it outside the palace walls to burn. Into the courtyard surrounding. There will be no way to cover it up. People will talk."

"Let them," she said, biting into the words as though they had meat. "If I cannot rule by love, I will rule by fear."

"My Queen–"

It hit like the pounding of a gavel. Like the slam of a mageri's staff into the earth. Like an awl piercing straight through her skull–the creatures in her head timed their attack, throwing themselves up against the walls of her mind in perfect unison. But while her shadow girls had attacked from all directions, threatening to blow her head wide open, these were targeted with painful precision. They should not be able to coordinate. They should not be able to turn against her.

She swayed hard to one side. Her whole body thrown off true.

Strego caught her arm. As soon as she could stand, she ripped it out of his hold, snarling and whirling to face him. She sounded like Ceramor. She…

Bess got hold of herself, straightened. Ruthlessly flattened her features.

"My Queen," Strego continued in his most careful voice, gaze slightly averted, but not looking entirely away from her, wisely keeping track of the threat, "it may not be advisable. This woman was dressed too finely to be a servant or someone else who might not have raised a cry. If you burn this woman publicly, someone will recognize her."

"Should they not?" she asked, mistaking his meaning, playing innocent, though her nursemaids had said it never wore well on her. "Do you not find it suspicious that no one ever missed this woman? The fisherman was the only one who ever gave a care for her passing, and he earned a dread death for his troubles. Tell Grygof I want her identity, who she communicated with while she was here and why, or he can very well burn alongside her."

The violation in her head was now reaching her stomach. Strego must have seen it on her face. She could not bear his look of sympathy, his witnessing her weakness.

"Go!" she all but shouted. "You have your orders."

Her voice went up as her desperation increased to get him gone before the world canted altogether and herself with it. But then it was too late, and she was reaching for Strego as a touchstone to centrality as the whole room curled and flipped as though to fling her off like dust from a rug, as though the shades in her head were–she didn't know what they were. Her shadow girls had fought and fractured her in all different directions, cracks forming as though she were porcelain. Maybe these three were whispering to each other through the cracks the shadow girls had created.

Strego's arm was as firm as a tree trunk beneath her grasp, and this time she allowed him to help her. The world was spinning, her stomach churning. She would lose what was in it if she didn't sit or lay down soon, holding to a bed or a chair that she could convince herself was anchored in place. Even that, she knew, was not certain to keep things down. She had to close her eyes and trust where Strego was leading her. She hated it with a venom equal to the bile burning its way up from her stomach.

Her maid? Would he send her maid with the compresses? Should she drink her down and heal herself? *Could* she? Or would that be another shade added to *their* side of the tally?

Strego settled the bedcovers over Bess, and she howled with the pain of it. Even the rustling of them, the weight and heat of them was too much.

She thought she heard Strego apologize, ask a question she was too lost to answer. But she no longer cared about him. She cared about the three she could hear whispering and conspiring. Their laughter hurt her head, and all she wanted to do was retreat from it. Hide in some tiny corner where it couldn't find her. But that was what they wanted. To lock her away so they would have free rein.

No, she had to weather this. And somehow, sometime, she had to follow it, find it, kill it dead.

CHAPTER THIRTY

Ulan

Ulan watched the pub entrance for Ruggerio over what was now her third mug of ale, though her second was only half finished. She'd nursed her first two until she must order another or risk the proprietress turning her out of her seat at the common table for a better-paying customer. Still, there was no sign of her cousin.

Her eyes were going blurry, and she didn't think it was entirely the strength of the ale. The more time that passed, the more certain she became that something had gone terribly wrong. It was a feeling in the pit of her stomach where Dazia had once nestled. Where she felt the place of her power. A growing, painful certainty that Ruggerio wouldn't be coming. Couldn't come. Killed or captured, it almost didn't matter. Almost. If he was alive, Bloody Bess's reasons for keeping him so would have nothing to do with mercy. She'd make certain he longed for death.

Haelin was dressed in masculine clothing, her jawline shaded, with a cap pulled low. She'd walked in with a completely altered stance to present the appearance of a man so they wouldn't seem to be two women traveling together and draw unwanted attention. She also kept up the better part of a conversation until it became too much, at which point she fell into a sullen silence better suited to Ulan's distraction.

That was, until the Crownsman entered the pub, hand to the hilt of his sword, gaze sharp and sweeping for prey.

Ulan stiffened immediately, and Haelin's hand went to her arm, tightening there. "Hold," she said, keeping her voice low and gravely.

But the Watchman wasn't content to leave at a casual glance around, particularly not with dark corners of the pub still unplumbed. He took a step forward, and Haelin's grasp became almost painful.

"Ruggerio said to meet him here. If we leave now, we'll miss him. Not to mention, be terribly conspicuous," Haelin said quietly, hiding her words behind her mug as she raised it to her lips.

"Ruggerio isn't coming." The words had settled on her as a certainty, and Ulan merely breathed them out, as quiet as a sigh. Yet, the Crownsman's gaze snapped toward their space in the tavern as though he was trained to home in on whispers. He couldn't quite pinpoint the source, but he began moving in their direction all the same.

Bandy shifted restlessly and popped his head out of Haelin's hood to lay his chin on her shoulder, causing a gasp from the man beside her. The Crownsman's gaze flew to Haelin, who cried, "Okay, now!"

Ulan felt the tingle of power that said Haelin was gathering herself. When she pulled Ulan to her feet, she knew it to be the same spell Haelin had cast at the church the night they'd met, when she'd made them both invisible to avoid the guards.

Ulan went along. She'd been the one to say it. Ruggerio wasn't coming. If he'd been successful, there'd have been such a hue and a cry from the palace there'd have been no mistaking his success.

Silence meant his failure. But more than that, there'd been a moment when they were on the run from the waterfront back to their bolt hole to change their appearances when she'd stumbled, because... because *something* had tripped her up. A feeling, a horror, an overwhelming sense of wrongness and failure and onrushing death. Then it was over. She got her feet back under her and convinced herself that it was nothing. But the delusion had died away with every moment he'd failed to show.

The way out took them too close to the Crownsman, and though he couldn't see anything, he could clearly feel it. Haelin, fleet of foot as she was, dodged him entirely, but Ulan, dragged along by one arm, didn't quite manage it. The Crownsman spun and grabbed out as she brushed against him, hauling up on Ulan's collar. She squeaked, and he shook her like a dog with a rat in its jaws. She came loose of Haelin's hand, suddenly appearing.

"Drop her or lose your ability to father children," Haelin's voice carried through the tavern as all conversation abruptly ceased. She must be holding a dagger to the Crownsman's privates. The Crowns-man, holding Ulan with his sword hand, was unable to retaliate.

Or so Ulan thought, until he swung her toward the sound of Haelin's voice, risking that he could take her out without losing his parts or his prey. He gasped, so he couldn't have come out unscathed, but Ulan hit something as well, and that was it. Her moment of stunned stillness was over, and she fought like a desert cat, struggling, twisting back on herself, trying to flip in his grip until he had to drop her. They both made for his sword at the same time.

He got there first, only a gash opened up across his hand as Haelin struck a blow to keep him from drawing it. He retracted his hand with a keen of pain, and Ulan swept in to yank his sword out of the scabbard and threaten him with it. It was heavier than she'd expected, badly balanced for her, but she held it out, tip pointed at his midsec-tion, and she put distance between them so that he couldn't just knock it away. If she wanted to escape, though, she was going to have to look behind herself toward the door.

Haelin took care of that, grabbing her again, this time by the back of her cloak so that it didn't restrict her movement. She had no idea whether she winked out of sight again, but the tugging allowed her to maneuver backward until they were out of the tavern, at which point she dropped the sword, Haelin popped back into view, and they *ran*.

The Crownsman must have been right on their heels, because they heard him howl behind him for others of the Watch. He would have reinforcements soon, and Ulan was fairly certain that she and Haelin were both at the limits of what their powers could accomplish. Now it was all up to them. Just them. With nothing else at their disposal. And seeing where that had gotten Ruggerio…

Haelin jogged down one road and another with Ulan racing as hard on her heels as she could. Haelin seemed to know the streets where Ulan had been born and raised better than Ulan did. Maybe because she'd never felt the need to know them. As hand-to-mouth as she'd survived, Ulan'd had no idea what it was also to live in fear until Bloody Bess decided that her ability to speak with spirits might be useful. And now Bess was burning the plague houses and going after the church buildings and the people at the heart of these ministries, not because she determined them not *useful*, but because she thought them hazardous. All that power she wielded and still so much fear.

There was a *thwack* behind Ulan as something smacked the ground, dropped from a window as she passed, and she jolted but refused to turn until she heard her name called in an unfamiliar voice, no louder than it needed to be for her to hear. It came from that same window, and something told her to turn, prickling up her spine. It would cost time, but she did it anyway, glaring up at the window to see a man leaning out, his face almost devoured by his dark beard and mustache, hair falling over his eyes.

"Ludvin sent me. Quickly!" he said.

The thing that had fallen was the weighted end of a rope ladder.

Haelin immediately put her foot to the bottom of it, holding it in place. "Climb!" she said, catching on while Ulan still stared dumbly.

"But–"

Haelin grabbed Ulan and pulled her toward the ladder.

Ulan started climbing, pursuit an effective motivator. She wondered how Haelin would follow, as difficult as it was for her to climb even with Haelin holding the bottom while the man at the top anchored the rope on his end. But then, she'd seen Haelin's dexterity when she fled her messenger shop before the explosion; perhaps she was wrong to worry.

As she hit the window ledge, the man reached over for Ulan's hand, and she gave it to him. He hauled her bodily through the window, which was just large enough for her, and then looked back down for Haelin. Bandy chirped and made the climb ahead of her, startling the man at the window. Ulan caught Bandy as he made the leap from the sill, and then watched for Haelin, but Ludvin caught her attention first, standing quietly and faintly in the corner, as though he'd worn out all his energies just catching the man's attention. Or maybe speaking with the Restoration folk, what few he could still find in the city.

"How?" she asked.

He only took a deep, relieved breath, hung his head, and vanished.

When she glanced back toward the window, Haelin was coming through it, and the big man was pulling the ladder in behind her.

"How?" she repeated for the man. "You said Ludvin sent you?"

He tucked the ladder away in a sack that he had laid up against the wall and turned toward Haelin and Ulan. It was dark in the room, since he hadn't lit anything that might silhouette him or otherwise call attention. Ulan caught only a glimpse of his face from the side as it was limned by a slice of moonlight through the open window and was struck for a moment by his rough beauty, his skin only a few shades lighter than his beard. Like Roha, he was probably at least part Markens.

"You can imagine our surprise," he said. "We'd heard about Bloody Bess's dead rising, and one of our people was there at All Souls when Ludvin walked, but she'd reported… Well, we'd thought…." He looked uncomfortable. "Here, let me start at introductions. I'm Amory."

He said it with a roll to his 'r' and the *y* sounding like 'eh' so that it struck her ear as melodic, but Ulan was too irritated to find it beautiful.

"And I'm Ulan," she said, before she could rein herself in, think it through. "You've saved us this time, but perhaps your people told you that they cast us out on the battlefield after Roha's power *saved* the day. Nes power did not draw on the anima, harmed none, and practically cost Roha nes own life. So, I will thank you for our rescue, but that is all, unless Ludvin has convinced you to overlook our differences or, better yet, see them as strengths, so that we can work together rather than apart."

Amory went wide-eyed, startled, and well he might be. She had sent Ludvin to convince the Restoration. But had the Restoration come around or did they merely want to imprison Ulan again to press for whatever information she might have about Hostill? However necessary it might be to their coming together, she couldn't bring herself to trust.

"I can only hope I have begun to repay our debt," Amory said. "It's not for me to judge."

"In return, we will be on our way quickly, before you taint yourself with any further exposure to our kind," Ulan said, since he had made no further overtures to peace.

"Wait!" Haelin and Amory said in unison, glancing at each other in surprise, and the former with no small bit of suspicion.

Bandy leapt to Haelin's shoulder, circled once, then settled atop them, chittering, as though to add his commentary for consideration.

Ulan huffed out a breath and crossed her arms, waiting as requested, unable to imagine what might come next.

Haelin must have had especially acute eyesight because she moved to the back of the room where the shadows were thickest and found a table and single chair that had been abandoned in the empty flat, the table probably built in the one-room rental, because it seemed unlikely to fit through the door. But instead of taking the chair, she merely leaned against the solid wooden table.

"I'm Haelin, and I'm Nim, like Roha, in case Ludvin didn't tell you," she said, staring Amory down. "I'm unclear about how Ludvin's told you anything, but if your next words are going to be 'we've reconsidered,' then by all means, continue. Otherwise, as Ulan said, we won't hold you up further."

Haelin swept out a hand, clearly indicating that Amory had the floor. Ulan thought she raised a brow as well, but it wasn't so easy to see in the dimness.

Amory drew a hand through his hair and moved to reshutter the window. To give himself time to think up a suitable lie? The longer he took to answer, the more Ulan worried that it would be a prevarication.

Once the shutters were latched, he asked, "Do you mind if I light a fire?"

Ulan was becoming so enflamed that she hardly felt the cold.

"If you think it will be a long conversation," Haelin allowed.

"I do."

Amory went to the hearth and struck it up. He seemed to have had it prepared, which begged many questions, not the least of which was how he'd known where to find them when they hadn't known themselves where they would run and when.

"I suppose you're wondering how I knew where to find you," he said, as though he'd read her mind. He didn't turn, but was squatting before the fire, poking it to be sure that it had fully engaged.

Haelin and Ulan exchanged a glance, and Amory settled onto his bum, letting his legs sprawl out before him, only then looking over his shoulder. "I didn't. Not really. Ludvin talked to us–some of us were gathered together, and he managed to summon enough of himself somehow. We couldn't see him or hear him. Not as you do, but he got himself a parchment and coal. He wrote out an impassioned–well, practically a treatise, though he started to lose control of himself at the end.

"The words petered out, but we had the sense by then. Verienne saw the coal moving and called to others, and we watched it play out, saw the struggle to set down those last words before the coal dropped entirely. There was no evil in it, and no external aid. We could see Ludvin's determination, his spirit, his soul. And there were those of us already talking–not about mageri powers. We will *never* agree to the ravaging of the anima, the assault on the earth and the collective energies. It kills the land and the people and–"

"Halt!" Haelin said. "We're in agreement there. We're not trying to talk you away from it or into anything else. We don't want the draining of the anima. There's another way, if only you will listen."

"Another way?" he asked.

"We are not to that point of trust. It has yet to be determined whether we will get there. You said that there are some of you talking..."

"Hedric is not everyone's brand of leader. He doesn't listen to advisors, doesn't solicit information. He makes decisions and expects everyone to fall in line with them. He sees things only in the light of his own biases. I'm not saying that he was not a strong soldier for the Restoration, but as a leader… He does not speak for all, and there are those of us who see shades of gray. You and Ludvin are some of those shades. *I* am one of those shades."

"You are?" Ulan asked.

He went back to poking the fire rather than look at them. "You wanted to know how I found you. I have always had an ability to find things. I never did anything to enhance it. I never knew there was anything I *could* do, but it was always there. If I really focused on something important, I could track it down. It wasn't anything I used often or much considered. I thought about it the way some people are lucky at cards or dice or others are naturally graceful. But now, I think it's like the way that you, Ulan, can speak with shades. It's what Ludvin called an affinity. It's nothing I can control or should be shunned for."

And finally, he did glance up, as though to gauge their reactions.

"But you did control it," Ulan said. "You called on it. You used it to find us, just as I've used my affinity to help Jucar. That's all right with the Restoration? At least, parts of it?"

Amory took a deep breath, let it out. He was backlit by the fire, so she couldn't read his face from his profile, but from his breathing, she thought that this was still difficult for him. "I only used my natural ability. Like flexing my muscles."

"That's all we've done," Haelin said. "Only, you can strengthen your ability, the way you can build your muscles. You can be taught to do it without drawing from the energies around you, but only up to a point. The mageri choose the easier way, the more destructive way, and act as though it's the only one."

No one spoke for a moment, as Haelin pushed herself off from the table and took to one knee to go eye to eye with Amory. Ulan, to one side, watched them both carefully, in case she had to intervene.

"We will not plead the mageris' case and say that they do not know better," Haelin continued. "But ask yourself, if the Nim, born from the anima with the balance of the masculine and feminine energies, are revered, why are they often killed at birth or beyond? Or given to the Church and treated as servants, worthy only to create nulls and wards and not to explore the abilities granted them by the All?"

"Because–" He stopped there, brows meeting in the middle as he realized he had no answer.

"Exactly," she snapped. "It's something you've always accepted. Never questioned. Either it's so clear that you just *know*, like that the sky is blue. Or it's not relevant to you, and so you never even think about it. I know that rebel groups are organized into cells, so perhaps you've never met Roha. But I want you to think now. Ni was an important part of the Restoration for years, and highly trusted until that one part of nes life was revealed. And why? Not because of anything ni did but help others. For that, Restoration soldiers would have lumped Roha in with the mageri and killed nim. People kill Nim children as well; the *Restoration*'s own doctrine would support it. *Children*. What could possibly justify the killing of a child?"

"I–I don't know."

"Well, I've had a lot of time to think on it. My whole life, in fact. Your people put far too much weight on the ability to bear or father children. My people remind them that there are other types of creation, of value. In your society, men and women can be born with no special abilities and yet have value, maybe in terms of wealth or dowry or carrying on the next generation. Part of the reason that men are always lording things over women is that they realize that *she* is the only one truly in control of conception and whose babe she carries. But men might carry mageri skills, and *they* are the only ones trained. Perhaps to even out the balance of power. And the only training they're given is to steal the energies from the anima around them."

Amory started as though to argue, but Haelin rode right over him. "But when a Nim child is born to you, you behave as though your value has dropped. You won't be able to pass the wealth or name through a family line that may end with us. Or maybe you're afraid of the disparity in power because of the Nim's special connection to the anima. Maybe in that secret place you don't admit even to yourself, you feel lesser than your own child, and thereby want to dispose of them. Those who've tried to speak about it, to write about it, have either been silenced or have had to do so in secret. If their work hasn't been destroyed, it has been hidden away. And so, some Nim escape from society, from the Church, form their own splinter groups, like mine."

Amory had been bursting to respond, and he did so now. "But if people know the Nim have a special connection to the anima, wouldn't killing them be an irredeemable act?"

There was no mistaking the horror dripping from his voice, as though he was stunned to realize this was part of the Restoration's beliefs, though it shouldn't be any surprise. Maybe it was the idea that some of the mageri they fought against, like those being trained at the Magery, weren't fully grown, as though killing innocent people with a few more years on them made murder more noble. But maybe outright killing went unspoken, simmered under the surface, revealed the deeper someone got into the inner circle of the organization. Surely, Roha wouldn't have been working with the Restoration otherwise, though it was clear from the way they'd treated Roha that they considered nim no better than anyone else who used magic.

"Most parents who choose this path lie to themselves. Those who expose their child to the elements, reason that the anima can 'take them back'. That is where we come in," Haelin said. Ulan had no idea how she was maintaining her calm through all of this, but she was a master at it. "The All cares for its own. It whispers to us, and we come for our children. In that way, the Nimistry has grown. Other Nim whose parents sent them to the Church, anonymously or with donations and dowries, have run away to join us.

"As for killing us being an irredeemable act?" Haelin shrugged. "It is not for me to say. The anima is the collective energy of all things. I would assume that all are needed, and that the reason you don't cut someone's path short is that they're not finished walking it. There is still time to be better, to *do* better. To become the person you should be rather than the person you are. But I am not a theologian. I am merely a foot soldier, and I need to rejoin my people.

"It is clear that we can no longer stay separate and safe. If your faction of the Restoration does not consider the Nim abominations, if you split off or take over, I believe we would welcome your help. But I would have to talk with my people before revealing them."

"And I would first have to convince mine," Amory said, brows still furrowed, face as shuttered as the single window in the room.

"But we've got you on our side?" Ulan asked.

"It's a lot to chew on," he said.

Yet she could feel it, the shift happening within him as it had for her when she'd met Cia. She knew that initial resistance to accepting that the world was different than she'd always believed. It was difficult to let it go, but once the dam broke, reality came flooding in, and things made a great deal more sense.

"But aye. Stay. You're safe here, I swear it. Ludvin spoke for you, and I'll not turn around and do you harm after lifting you from the grasp of the Crownsmen," Amory said. "I'll talk with the Restoration. At worst, we'll get you out, because no one should go to Bloody Bess. At best, maybe we can help each other."

CHAPTER THIRTY-ONE

Cia

Cia!" There was a pounding on her door that seemed to reverberate straight through the walls. As her head was resting against one, the waves traveled through the metal of her scold's bridle, rattling it against her head, her skull, her cheekbones.

"Cia!" the call repeated, hushed but urgent.

Myrka?

Cia got quickly to her feet, her every joint having cramped up in the cold, cracking as though it might break as she tried to move. She threw herself against the door, but the harness got in the way of pressing her ear against it.

"Here," she said, only with the constraints of the mask, it came out more "'Ere."

"Oh, thank the spirits," Myrka said, out of breath, "I didn't know what they'd done to you. This whole place is in an uproar. Cia, they're planning to move out! I got away in the confusion only because *everyone* has been enlisted to get them ready. Even Joia's being called to help provision and pack, but I don't know how long I can be away. Or even how long I'll be free. I might very well be beside you soon."

"What's going on?" Cia asked, or the closest thing to make it through her mask.

Myrka understood well enough, or she anticipated the question. "I think whatever 'resource' they found, they're marching on it now. Hostill…I don't know what that's going to mean for Hostill."

"Roha!" she gasped.

"Roha?"

Cia hadn't had the chance to talk to Myrka about what she'd heard after she'd left. Hadn't even been certain Myrka didn't turn on her to save herself or because, like others of the Restoration, she had no loyalty to anyone who'd dealt with the mageri, despite being mageri herself. Cia didn't believe that, not deep down, but was she willing to wager her life on that? Did she have any choice?

"You have to get me out of here. We have to stop this!" Cia said.

There was a pause while Myrka pieced together Cia's words, then, "How?"

"Your power. You can cut out the null–"

The door jolted against her as Myka slammed a hand into it, or maybe her entire body by the way it jumped. "No!" she said, and Cia quaked at the volume. "You know better. You know what the power did to me. What *I* did. I won't touch the anima again. There's another way or no way at all."

"But if you just draw power out of the door, enough to break it–"

"And if I take too much, I might crack the whole manor and bring it down around us. Isn't that what happened to the palace, what killed the king? I haven't come for you to whisper temptation to me. If that's your purpose, I will go and consider you're where you deserve to be."

The first flush of anger crackled like a fire in her ears. The thought that Myrka was putting herself and the horrors of her past over the needs of the country… She let it burn her up, sweat breaking out all over her face, superheating the mask until it was unbearable, branding her cheeks.

Shocking sense back into her, but also something more. Something she'd buried. Didn't want to think about it, and she was left with the cold, wet chill and the sound and feel of her own heartbeat pounding against her eardrums as though the pressure might rupture them.

She tried to take deep, calming breaths to no avail. What would her escape accomplish? Myrka might well be right; using her power could lead to greater loss. There was no way to know, and if Myrka couldn't be guided by foresight, then hindsight could be her only guide. That and her own scruples, which Cia was asking her to bend.

"I'm sorry," Cia said.

There was a gentle thud against the door, as though Myrka had let her head fall against it. "So quick to put my soul in danger, yet spare your own," Myrka said so quietly that Cia had to strain to hear her.

Cia was certain she must have heard wrongly. She couldn't parse the words. "I don't understand."

Myrka hissed at her, as though they were opponents. Cia was losing her only hope of aid, and she didn't even know why.

"Do you think Garif helped you out of the goodness of his heart?" Myrka struck out like a viper.

Cia jolted back from the door. Myrka's response was venomous enough that she no longer needed her ear pressed there for it to slither through to her.

"He helped *himself*. To my body. To my pain and torment," Cia hissed back. "*Do not say* he helped me. Go, if venom is all you have in your veins."

"Choose yourself then," Myrka said without pity. "It was not merely that you were vulnerable, and he could do what he wished with you. There were any number of women he could have chosen in such straits. He was *mageri*. He could do what he liked. He chose you because you are bright with power, else he would not have been drawn to you like a moth to a flame."

Cia couldn't catch her breath. It was as though Myrka had dealt a blow straight to her chest, compressing it against her heart, and it couldn't beat, her lungs couldn't expand. She'd considered the possibility, but hadn't really *believed*. She'd never cast a spell, never felt an instant of... But hadn't she? Hadn't there been a moment when Garif's spirit had first tried to invade her body and she'd fought him off, setting her fire to his ice? Those times she'd seen red...had those been a preamble to something more and potentially deadly? If so, was she the monster Garif had always proclaimed her to be? Had his drawing off of her energies been the only thing that kept her from hurting others? The only thing that kept people safe? Kept her from being like him?

But then, fires had never flared in her presence. She'd never done anything like what Myrka had described in her youth. Bloody Bess's mageri hadn't pointed her out when she'd told the soldiers who'd captured them about Myrka's power. Perhaps it was because Myrka was about to be put to death, but Cia dragged back to Jucar. Could that mageri have been trying to save a life, resist the Queen in her own small way?

But...what if Myrka was right, and Cia had power?

And what if Garif had trained her instead of taken from her?

But, of course, women weren't trained. They were too emotional. Too unpredictable, uncontrollable. Hence, Garif controlled her. Or tried and died for his sins.

She became the monster he'd made her. It rang over and over in her head.

And if she did have power, was there a way she could have escaped Garif sooner? Was she to blame for staying in captivity or was that Garif speaking again, saying that everything was her fault? All of it. He hurt her because she brought it on herself.

It didn't really matter. The guilt, the horror of it, crashed down as though the walls of her prison were falling in on her.

"Just go." She didn't have the energy for much volume, but she was certain she was heard.

She felt it with the instinct women were said to have. At least they were granted that much. Allowed instincts, but only about domestic things–children, when meat and milk turned or fruit was ripe. Nothing else was credited. And like *that* the switch flipped from stunned unacceptance to anger.

She had let Garif make her feel small. Less than she was. All this time, she'd had power, and he'd taken it from her. He'd had more opportunities, more training, more standing. She was raw, foreign, *female,* and handmaiden to the Poison Princess. She let all of this bow her. There was a small voice that wanted to remind her that through all of Jucar's abuses, she'd bowed but didn't break.

But she felt that voice retreat with the sound of Myrka's footsteps and didn't call her back.

If she was bright now with power, it must be a recent thing, replenished since Garif had left her body, stopped drawing on her resources. Perhaps she was refilling, like a rain barrel. And perhaps she could get her own spirits-forsaken self out of this place.

The monster he'd made her.

But then she thought about Myrka's story, about the king's story, and she sat down instead. She wasn't ready to try her power. Wasn't ready to become Garif. Not that using her power would make her into…anyone else. But there was one thing she could do. If the king was marching on the Sacrima and the Nim, she had to warn Roha that the attack was coming sooner rather than later.

Ludvin

It took effort for Ludvin to manifest, but none at all to allow himself to fade back into the anima. It was like falling asleep, though he remembered that even that took time and trouble some nights when worries weighed on him. This was more like closing his eyes or—better yet—breathing. Natural, effort-less. So easy to be pulled along. Troublesome to remember that there was a mission, a place and a purpose he must pursue, especially when he saw/felt/sensed pockets of blinding light that called him like a beacon.

Then there were the dark places, the voids, that repelled and sent energies spinning away. The All should be everything. The constant influx of energies mixing like tributaries feeding into glistening rivers, flowing seamlessly into one pristine, peaceful ocean, rebirthing and replenishing. And yet there were those mageri-touched places locked out of the cycle, so devoid of the anima that they were like dry, cracked streambeds, drained of life. Of no use at all.

The disparities themselves were dangers. He was still self-possessed enough that he wanted to do what he'd always done, direct change. Perhaps when his job was finished, he could find a way from inside the anima. Or enlist others like himself. Or...

He wanted to go, examine the voids now, on his journey to Frizenze, so that he could think on the problem as he traveled, but he dared not get distracted. He hadn't made it the first time he'd tried. Or the second. But he'd gotten further with each attempt. He didn't know how much time had passed on this attempt or what might be happening, and he already had one problem to solve, how to get Cia and Myrka to see or hear him once he arrived. He was still tired from the charcoal trick in Jucar and wasn't certain he could do it again, especially not after traveling through the anima.

Ludvin focused on Myrka, since he'd known her longer. She'd been one of the Restoration's foot soldiers since she'd come to the city and heard Vizzi talk about their cause. But...she was no longer bright. He could find her, but she no longer burned. Her spirit had been altered, her energies dampened, darker. She was still molten at her core, but there was something crusting it over. The analogy wasn't right, but there was none he could think of to fit. Her fires hadn't been banked; they'd been walled off somehow.

He pulled himself out of the anima stream into a new kingdom, the energies of Frizenze truly feeling no different than the energies of Jucar, because they were part of the collective spirit. If only the people could understand, maybe there wouldn't be war. If only... But they couldn't see the spirits, couldn't hear, and many who stayed behind did so because they were angry, had scores to settle. They were not there to speak for the land.

Myrka raced down a dim hallway and passed right through him, unseeing. He didn't gather himself to call out, but flew after her, chasing her to wherever she would stop, hoping to find there a piece of parchment and a quill. Or even a coal or charred stick from a fire and something, anything, that he could write on to get his message across. He was sure if he tried hard enough...

It was nothing for her to run, but nearly everything for him to pursue. If she didn't stop soon, he wouldn't be able to rally for a message. When she did stop, Ludvin blew past her, straight through her door, and into a small room barely able to fit a bed, an armoire, and a window-desk. From the scrapes on the floor, it looked like the bed was a trundle, which would take up the last remaining floor space when employed. But he wasn't concerned with that. He floated straight for the desk, small and tidy enough that he didn't have to rifle for parchment. There was none, but for a single note of invitation.

Ludvin hoped the room was hers and that she was merely listening at the door to determine that she had it to herself, but he wouldn't be able to pull himself together if he waited any longer to be sure. Whether she was coming to inhabit the room or search it, surely she'd notice a quill moving on its own.

He summoned all the power he could. He no longer had any inner well of his own because he had no body to safeguard it. He'd heard Haelin talk about that as she taught Ulan, and wished he was still alive to learn as well, that his mind had been open enough while he was. But he could feel the flow of her personal anima as Myrka had passed through him as he'd passed through her door. There were thoughts there, realizations he could almost grasp, like water from a stream. Try to cradle it, and it sieved through your fingers. And yet people always wanted to hold something, possess it. Change its form. Water cupped in a hand was a puddle at best, quickly running dry. Water left in a river continued as an elemental force, and if a man trailed his fingers in it, they would remain wet.

Applying the same thoughts, Ludvin didn't try to gather the anima to himself or draw it out of anywhere, especially when he had no place to hold it and believed fundamentally that it was wrong to steal it, even more so after seeing the voids left behind when he traveled the anima way. He simply let the anima wash over and around him, naturally buffeting him like a wave toward shore and using the power imparted to grasp the quill pen sitting on the desk and dip it in the ink. It took all the focus he could muster to remember what a hand felt like and how to hold a pen, how to shape characters.

He thought up the shortest message to convey the most information he could.

✦

Myrka

Myrka let herself back into her room, and not a moment too soon. She had just closed the door behind herself and turned to find the source of the scratching when she heard a knock at her door. It wasn't terribly forceful, not followed by a shout for her to open up or, worse, boots kicking her door down. Not that she'd done anything to be fearful of. She'd only gone to see Cia. She hadn't even entertained her request to set her free.

Had staying true to the Restoration been itself a betrayal of the people of Jucar? She could never use her powers again, but neither could she leave Cia rotting in that hole. She racked her brain trying to come up with a workable plan, one that would save Cia and leave them both free to rescue Hostill, but nothing came to her.

Another knock, this one more demanding.

She was no great lady, here or anywhere, who could ignore a summons.

She opened the door, shocked to see such a lady on the other side of it. Lady Ojardian, in fact, done up in garnet and obsidian, her blood-moon hair piled on top of her head with curls fetchingly left framing her face as though she'd sat for a portrait earlier in the day.

She sailed into the room as though she'd been invited. Sailed because she seemed the figurehead of a great ship, bust leading the way, her entire figure giving the sense of strength, daring the elements to take their best shot, and promising they would still be found wanting. Myrka's hands danced for her daggers, tightening on themselves when, of course, she found none.

But she didn't step back, leaving the lady to skirt around the obstacle in her midst, which she did as though it was nothing. In fact, as though it gave her a reason to be equally rude and to continue on into the small room past the point of politeness.

"My Lady," Myrka said, closing the door behind her now that she'd already let the danger in, "to what do I owe the honor? I would have thought that I would be a pariah with Lady Cia locked up for treason."

"I'm sure that's true, but King Avize has chosen your boy for some great honor, and so I thought I might get to know—"

She stopped in front of the desk and grabbed up the single piece of paper upon it, gripping it in one hand, and then crumpling it into a fist before she whirled on Myrka. Her heart flew into her throat, although she didn't know why. There was nothing there that could have caused such a reaction. No one here would have sent her a message, and she knew she had written none. She was not trusted with parchment and had no way of getting a message out in any case.

But there was *something*. That was absolutely certain from the hawkish look on Lady Ojardian's face.

"Walk with me," she said, and it was clearly a command.

She swept toward Myrka and took her by the arm. It was a firm hold, as one might take with a child set to bolt, and Myrka had the same instinct. Whatever Lady Ojardian held in her other hand, she did not want to talk about it within the manor walls. She steered Myrka out into the gardens, the high evergreen walls blocking out the worst of the winds but doing nothing against the cold. Lady Ojardian meant them to have privacy, but that also came without protection, even of cloaks from the stiff winter winds. They would not spot anyone sneaking up or listening in on the other side of a living wall.

Or perhaps it was a place the Lady could murder Myrka without witnesses.

Myrka stiffened and stopped, knees locked, nearly sending them both toppling over as Lady Ojardian tried to continue them on. She reached out to the browning-green wall and hissed as it pricked at her soft hands, but it kept her upright as she detached from Myrka. She used both hands to gather her skirts to protect them from tearing as she turned to face Myrka, her eyes snapping like flags in the wind that didn't exist within the hedge maze.

"That was unnecessary," the lady said, haughtily. "We are on the same side."

"*You* may have thought it unnecessary, but I was the one being manhandled. If the situation had been reversed, I doubt you would have suffered me to lay hands on you in the same manner."

The lady's head drew back as though she'd been slapped. Her eyes widened, her mouth opened, clearly about to retort, possibly that it wasn't the same thing at all, given their difference in station, but she swallowed that down. It seemed to taste sour.

"No, I don't suppose I would," she said evenly.

Now that she was free, Myrka loosened her knees again and stayed loose, ready to fight. She might not have any weapons, but she'd been in that situation before, and this was a Lady. Myrka had the advantage of years on the street and multiple fights with those bigger and more skilled than herself, as well as training with the Restoration and multiple weeks of trudging through horrible conditions to truly harden her. Even if the Lady had a hidden blade, Myrka was certain she could fight dirtier or, at least, outrun her considering those outrageous skirts. Myrka wouldn't be precious with herself or her skirts. She'd happily run straight through the vegetation, shouting bloody murder as she did so without fear for her reputation.

Apparently, she telegraphed all of that, because the lady held her hands out before her to show that she held no blades and had no intention of reaching for them, as Myrka asked, "What side do you think we're on together?"

"That of our people."

Myrka eyed her up and down. She doubted that. In her experience, people were usually in it for themselves. Particularly the nobility, who all wanted more power than they had, even though it seemed more than they deserved.

"How do you represent your people?" Myrka asked, trying to keep the sneer out of her voice but not terribly hard.

Lady Ojardian shrugged her shoulders, taking it all the way to her hands as though to ask whether she'd proven herself harmless and could drop them. Myrka inclined her head as though *she* was the great lady, aware that Lady Ojardian was showing her some deference and that perhaps she could at least hear her out. But no sooner had the thought occurred than she realized that both her hands had been open and that whatever note she'd taken from Myrka's room hadn't been in either one. It had been disappeared.

"Well, you see–"

"Wait. What was in the note?"

"I'm sorry?"

"The note. That you took from my writing desk. Don't tell me, show me."

Lady Ojardian looked sheepish and tucked the fingers of one hand into a sleeve to pull out the crumpled piece of paper. She presented it to Myrka and waited while she smoothed it out and read.

"I would have gotten there," she said. "If you'd let me."

"Of course, you would have," Myrka responded.

The writing was spidery, as though the pen could barely be kept to the paper, and when she read the message, she knew why. Ghost-writing.

R dead? U going to Nimistry. Bess on move.

"Who left this?" Lady Ojardian asked.

"You've no right to my secrets," Myrka said, "until I know they'll be safe."

"I could call you out. Your friend already languishes in our prison."

"Is this how we're to start, threats? It's not a very auspicious beginning. I've already been run out of my country and had a null burned into my flesh for fear of my own power. The threat of captivity or even death does not scare me. I was ready to die for my beliefs from the moment I joined the Restoration."

"The Restoration. Tell me more about that."

Myrka stared the Lady down. She didn't cross her arms, which would limit her options. She merely stood there, still as a statue, breathing and watching. Waiting.

She grew more and more chilled. If this was like to continue, she would just see herself back to the manor.

But before long, the lady huffed. "Very well. King Avize had one child with Queen Yaliss, but the boy was sickly and died young, even before the king's sister, Princess Inaya, left to marry your King Cyril. His queen died of an ague a few years later without producing another heir, and then King Avize came down with his injury in the siege. He hasn't remarried or named another heir and now, as you and Lady Cia overheard, he and some of his advisors have hatched this terrifying plan to put his soul into the body of this young boy, Hostill," Lady Ojardians said.

"It is against nature. Against the anima and the All. It is the darkest of magics and everything, to my understanding, that you're against. More than that, it is against the good of our people. Say it works, what happens then?" she continued. "Do we put this boy on your throne and let Jucar take us over so that 'King Avize' can hold dominion over Frizenze as well? It's a betrayal of our country, and the people will rise up. How will our king explain that he's now in the body of this boy? Who will accept it? And if the spell fails, if the king dies, then we have a civil war, a battle for control of our country in the midst of the Blood War. We'll be overrun."

"What do you propose?"

Lady Ojardian paused for a moment and closed her eyes as though she could see something play out behind them, perhaps the future. When she opened them again, there was a fervor there that Myrka had sometimes seen in the eyes of Vizzi, the Restoration's mouthpiece, when he spoke passionately on the street corners of Jucar.

"We stop it; kill the king now, before any of this madness. Otherwise, we end up fighting each other for ascendancy, which will only chew up our men and resources and leave us vulnerable to Jucar and the surrounding countries. We elevate the Council so that each Duchy is equally represented. We end the monarchy."

"Ah," Myrka said, turning to go.

"Do you not see it?" Lady Ojardian asked, amazed.

"My Lady," Myrka said, and it was a struggle to stay polite, "I see that what you want is to overthrow the man at the top so that you might climb higher. The desire is only couched in noble words. The powerful always want more. You will create a void at the helm of Frizenze. Uncertain that your Duke will be the one to fill it, you are willing to share your power. You may even believe some of what you've said. After all, what is the point of ruling a land with no resources whose armies have exhausted themselves battling for supremacy? If you've thought of your subjects at all, it is that you'd like to keep them around to lord over."

The lady's face iced over like a garden pond at the first freeze. "I have done nothing, and yet you call me a liar."

"You began with threats, my lady. That rarely bodes well for trust."

"Then let me begin again," Lady Ojardian said, and Myrka thought she saw a shift in the lady's face, the kind that might lead to an avalanche. Lady Ojardian's face was created more for haughty disdain than for humility. "My Lord's forte is statecraft, though clearly not mine. But women are so often disregarded and can move about much more freely, and it's you and your friend we must concern ourselves with here."

"Cia–"

"I can free her. I have a way. If you and she are willing to help us. The king and his men have already left. If you trust nothing else, trust that we want to get to them before there is nothing left of the boy you remember."

"And after?" Myrka asked.

"Perhaps you can help us forge new plans."

Myrka was starting to tremble in the cold and wondered whether she was too suspicious in thinking that another reason for Lady Ojardian bringing her to the gardens was so that she would have to make her mind up quickly or freeze to death. But she shook that off with the next tremors raking her body.

The king's march precipitated her decision. She missed her knives, the sharpness of their edges, and the illusion that they sharpened her mind. She missed the family she'd left behind in Jucar and the farm to which she could never return. Most of all, she missed Ludvin, the Restoration, and the clarity of their vision. Everything was so crystalline with the cause, when those at the top sorted these shades of gray and handed down orders as though everything was always black and white.

Now she had to decide. Was the enemy of her enemy her friend or was she being used? Did it matter if she was using the lady in turn to save Cia? Was she again going down a slippery slope, this time with morality rather than magic? Was that life, no matter what direction she turned? She didn't like it, but there was no avoiding it. She wasn't with the Restoration now. There was no one to tell her what to do.

It was her decision, and she chose the one that made her hate herself least. The one that would save Cia. Gave her the chance of saving Hostill and maybe Jucar instead of standing helplessly by.

"Yes," she said. "We will help."

"Good. I will release her when they march. No one will be worried about the prisoner or guarding the key. If they do not drag you along to ensure Hostill's good behavior, you will likely be locked in your room. I will send someone for you as well. I have it on good authority that you can pick the locks, but should there be any guards–"

"So, I just wait and hope that you come for me?" Myrka said, fists clenching and unclenching in the wish that she had her daggers and could do for herself.

"Yes," said Lady Ojardian. "You have my word."

Myrka tried not to scoff. So far, the word of the nobility had been nothing but dust in the mouths of the peasantry, enough for them to choke on.

Cia

Cia scrambled to her feet when she heard a key in the lock of her cell, afraid of what would come. Were they putting her to death for her supposed crimes?

She had no idea whether it was night or day. With nothing to do but get spun up in her own dark imaginings, time was just another enemy to combat. Anything could be happening to Hostill and the others while she wasted away here.

There was a grunt as the person on the other side of her door tried to push it open, and Cia called out, "Who's there?" to decide whether she should help or hinder.

There was a hissed, "Lady Ojardian, come quickly."

She leapt to the door, her heart pounding in her chest. She pulled as the lady pushed at the heavy wooden door, which was stuck in its frame, and it came free, scraping at the floor in a way that had the lady glancing back over her shoulder to make sure they'd not been heard.

Cia was out of the cell as soon as there was enough of a gap, and Lady Ojardian gasped at the sight of her in the horrible scold's bridle. She gestured at Cia to spin, and with some trepidation, she turned her back to the lady so that she could undo the leather straps. When the bridle dropped away, she caught it in her hand to keep it from clattering to the ground and swallowed the air as though it was water and she'd been dying of thirst.

She set the mask inside her cell, and together they closed the door again, hoping to delay anyone discovering her escape.

"Follow me," Lady Ojardian whispered. "Head down, in case anyone should look our way. But wait—"

The bridle had destroyed Cia's hair, and the lady pulled pins to let out more of it before twisting it up again and repining it more neatly, pulling whisps from it to hang around and cover her face, twisting them first around a finger so it would seem artful. Hopefully, they wouldn't look like they'd just come from a prison break. Best if no one paid them any mind at all.

The lady kept Cia between herself and the wall so she'd pass closest to anyone they encountered and could shield Cia with her body, but the halls were nearly deserted. Those they did pass ignored them but for offhand greetings, intent on their own missions.

They mounted an enclosed staircase Cia had never used, narrow with uneven steps, probably meant for the servants. Thankfully they met no one on their ascent. At the top, the lady peeked around the door in a way that would have seemed suspicious had anyone been present, but the hallway was apparently clear. Lady Ojardian stepped out, motioning for Cia to do the same and bringing her to the second door on the left. She knocked, three long and one short, and the door was opened from within. She entered, swishing her skirts aside for Cia to do the same and shutting the door immediately behind them.

She leaned against the door, hand rising to her heart as though to hold it inside her breast. She let out a deep exhale. "Thank the All."

Cia stared from her to Lord Ojardian, who had let them in. "What's going on? Why is the castle so empty?" she asked.

"The King's men have already left for the Sacrima with the boy, Hostill," the lady answered. "We have someone coming with your friend, Myrka, then we will meet our resistance on the way. With any luck, we'll catch up to the king's men. The palanquin may slow them down. If not, we'll meet them in battle at the Sacrima. We have to stop King Avize, and now, before he's out of our reach."

Before he takes over Hostill! came Cia's thought. *Before the boy is no more.*

She had to let Roha know that the king's men were on the march and that she was coming–*they* were coming. She could not let them fight the king's army on their own. It would be a slaughter.

She would reach out as soon as they were on their way, and she could find her inner place of peace and power.

CHAPTER THIRTY-TWO

Ulan

It seemed death was the only way out for Ulan and Haelin with extra guards and mageri on the ramparts and watching the gates. All were stopped, everything and everyone inspected, including the dead. But since the cemeteries became overfilled with bodies and those bodies began overflowing their borders, some of the royal city's dead were buried outside the walls. Once the Rot came, anyone even suspected of dying by it or by *anything* that could be transmitted from one person to another was taken even further away to an uninhabited island off Jucar's shore.

Some had called for a great cleansing pyre, as Bloody Bess was now doing with the plague houses and with All Souls. But the Church had cried sacrilege at burning what had been created by the energies of the All, and the scholars feared what might be released into the air with the ash and smoke. Bloody Bess had set herself above all of it.

Ulan only hoped that Bloody Bess's legacy would die a truer death than she and Haelin faced. She could remember no greater fear than swallowing the draught the rebels provided, meant to slow their heart rates and breathing to mimic death. Unless it was laying there in the hazy moments before it took effect, being wrapped in sacking with dried lavender and other herbs pressed between the layers over her face to protect her from the dangerous vapors associated with death, wondering whether the rebels would shroud her so securely she would suffocate before she could 'live' again. Grayness lapped at her like waves, wanting to carry her away with it, and she kept fighting, fearing that if she gave in, it would be her true end. But the draught was too strong.

She woke as she was being hoisted and swung, only the swaddling of the sacking material keeping her from jerking awake and giving herself away. Were they...just tossing her onto other bodies piled upon the shore? She landed on something that gave and shifted, so that she rolled down what felt like a small hill of bodies, crying out in her horror and instantly biting it off by sinking her teeth into her lip.

"What was that?" a man asked, fear quivering in his voice.

"Sometimes they release gases in death. It is nothing, you goose. Hurry it along. I'll not stay a moment beyond the necessary."

"This place–"

"For all they know, we bury their dead most respectfully, yes?"

The other man must have nodded, or Ulan lost his response in her own horror. Something sharp had cut straight through her sackcloth and was poking into her arm, denting the skin. One shift and she'd slice herself and let in whatever diseases it carried. There were no knives or daggers. The bodies would have been stripped of anything before being sent away, which meant it was likely the sharp end of a shattered bone. This place was no hallowed ground. A boneyard rather than a churchyard. A desecration. A–

She started to shake so badly she was sure she would cut herself or roll herself down another hill and into something even more foul. She closed eyes that weren't doing her any good and prayed all of her spiritus that the horrible men would leave. That Haelin was okay. That they'd both survive this. She tried to let the repetition of the prayers calm her, but each moment her concentration became worse and her panic rose to greater heights until she thought she'd scream.

One more breath, she thought. *One more breath. And another. Another beyond that.* She listened for the men. Were they gone or did she just need them to be?

She fought her way to sitting, lashing out against her bindings, falling a little further, feeling something squish beneath her. Was moisture beginning to seep through the bottom of her sackcloth? Was she being steeped with contagion?

She swung left and right, flapping her arms to loosen the swaddling until she had enough slack to rip the strips of sacking away from her body, then her eyes. She spit away hair that had fallen into her face. She blinked against the sudden light, saw that the men had indeed left, and jumped as the first thing to become clear was a mostly meatless skull, darkened by the elements. Flaxen hair still stuck to it in clumps, eyes gone from the sockets, possibly eaten by–she didn't want to imagine. There were white grubs in their place, horrible, burrowing. The color of dead flesh. And flies. So many flies. The sound and the smell…

She retched, but there was nothing in her stomach. The Restoration had been very careful about that. Even so, something thick and burning came up her throat and then ate its way back down when it didn't have the wherewithal to burst forth.

"Haelin?" she wheezed.

She looked around for movement but saw none but the flies. Bodies shifting. Gases passing, as the terrible man had said.

Then another figure fought to be free. Haelin slid nearly to Ulan by the time she was loose of her bindings, and then they were blinking at each other. Haelin, however, did have the power to bend over and unleash a stream of foul-smelling bile. Hardly enough to compete with the rank scents of death and decay.

"We have to make our way to the other side of the island," Haelin said, voice barely a gasp.

"Will it help?" Ulan asked.

Haelin met her gaze with a startled look. "For our ride, by darkest night."

Yes, Ulan knew that. She just…this place of death. She worried what they would be carrying with them. She'd like to cleanse herself in the waters, but it was far too cold. One dip might be the true death of her, even if she had anything with which to dry herself or clean clothing to change into so that she might leave these behind. And anyway, the effluvia… Maybe the Nim would have a way to cleanse them of any diseases…but no, if they had that, they might have stopped the Rot at its inception.

She and Haelin had taken a huge chance to get here. It occurred to her for the first time that Haelin must be very important to the Nimistry for all of this. More important than she'd let on.

"You worry that we will be catching," Haelin said. "The Rot is over."

"But is it? Or is it like an animal that hibernates only to return when things are more auspicious?"

Haelin chewed her lip at this, clearly disturbed. But she rose and led their way to the other side of the island, looking to the constellations above as their guide. It was a surpassingly clear night, but still a breeze swept the island as though a storm was brewing elsewhere. Or maybe it only seemed that way because they were so underdressed for the weather. They could only risk so much beneath their shrouds without drawing suspicion. The dead needed no protection against the elements. Ulan drew her arm through Haelin's and clung to her, hoping their shared body heat might help, but the closeness made for awkward walking on such unsteady ground.

Partly to distract herself and partly because the question needed to be asked, should have been asked prior, "Haelin?"

"Mhm?"

"In the royal city, what made you go by 'she,' when it is men who hold the greatest power?"

Haelin cocked her head to one side, as though considering Ulan's intent in deciding how much response she would give.

"It felt the most natural. I am Haelin, regardless. I went to the heart of Jucar and chose the role I did because it was the truest to me, and also because sometimes it helps to be underestimated. I am Nim, assuredly. I will always be Nim. But the most important thing we're given in this world is the power of choice. Birth doesn't decide me, you don't decide me. Even words don't decide me; they only help people with how to see me. And minds can be made up and then changed, as the Restoration is rethinking some of their positions. Nothing is final but death, and as we've seen with Ludvin, maybe not even that."

Ulan was quiet for a while, thinking, chewing. "So for now 'she'?"

Haelin laughed, and it seemed so odd on this charnel island. "Yes, spirit speaker, 'she.' A glorious speech, and that's all it comes to?"

"It was a glorious speech."

"Hmff."

"Too bad it was only me and the dead around to hear it."

Haelin squeezed her arm. "I suppose you will have to become a bard and tell the tales of my poeticism far and wide after we save the world."

Ulan tried to smile, "You might think otherwise once you've heard my voice."

"There will be time enough while we wait and only the dead to frighten. I have a tin ear."

⎯⎯⎯⎯⎯

To Ulan's relief, the dead did not rise up to talk with her. If any spirits lingered, they stayed behind with those they'd loved during life and so couldn't be horrified by what had happened to their remains.

As for herself and Haelin, their route headed them into the wind, which carried with it the scent of brine and rotting seaweed, but it was far better than the scent of the other things rotting on the charnel isle and brought them to a low bluff overlooking the water. Birds sailed overhead and called to each other as they approached, apparently not frightened off by the invasion of their island. Some even had objects in their beaks that Ulan preferred not to identify.

It wasn't a long hike to the water, though the bluff jutted out over it in such a way that Ulan despaired of an easy path down. Haelin scouted in one direction while she went the other...until she heard a rustling in the trees behind her. And a grunting.

The island was uninhabited. She'd assumed it was because it was so small and rocky. But what if it was something more?

Fear gripped her as she divided attention between the forest she'd come through and the cliff she was up against. Then her ankle twisted on a rock that she realized wasn't a rock at all, but a human skull carried all this way.

It could have been dropped by the birds from above.

Or by the trio of razorback boars rushing at her from the treeline with tusks the size of tent stakes.

She cried out instinctively, realizing only as she did that it was more likely to bring Haelin running toward danger than away from it. She was frozen for an instant, almost more afraid of the cliff than the boars, but only one promised a bloody and painful death. The other gave her at least a chance for survival.

Ulan stared down at the drop off, chose the most likely place, and took a deep breath. She dropped to her backside, legs bent before her so that she could scrabble her way to the first ledge that she saw. As she began to slide, she heard a grunt and the onrushing of the massive animals. Heart pounding, she pushed off. A tusk came down hard across her back, a massive blow that threw her out of control. Suddenly, she wasn't sliding on her backside, but pitching forward, hands tearing as she tried to catch and stop herself. Small, scraggly trees grew out of nowhere cracks in the face of the cliff and she reached desperately for their handholds, but the branches she caught came with her, shredded her palms. A bloody, brutal tumble down the side of a cliff.

She didn't know how far up or down she was when she stopped. Her stomach seemed to stay above, only reentering a moment later with a jolt that hurt as much as the fall.

For a moment, she lay in stunned paralysis. Then she convulsed, rolling onto her side in a fetal position, throwing up the thin bile and acid she'd swallowed back down previously. It burned everything in its path until her throat might be as perforated as Mervollian lace. It was no wonder no one lived on the isle or that there was always room for more bodies.

When Haelin called to her, she couldn't answer. Her throat was still on fire, but Haelin found her anyway, just as she found her own, less eventful way down the cliff. She asked what had happened when she saw Ulan's ashen face, the blood covering her. Ulan could only shake her head and wave Haelin on with whatever she had to say.

Haelin pointed out the cove where they were to await their ride, which was still a little ways down. Ulan slid more than walked, amazed she could do that much. Agony gripped her. One knee and ankle almost too painful to hold her upright, especially with scree and hidden ice trying to wick her feet out from under her, numerous cuts and blows calling out for her attention, but she wouldn't complain. She was alive. She could move, and anything that took her *away* from this All-forsaken place was just fine.

When they reached the shoreline, the wind added its wickedness, blowing them back against the cliffs, as though the island was determined to keep them because nothing was ever meant to leave it alive.

Haelin and Ulan huddled against the cliffs, taking turns sitting with one's back against the cold rock hugging the other to her chest.

They were nearly frozen when the boat arrived in the darkest night and had to be helped to their feet. Thankfully, the boatman came with cloaks and a skin of some strong spirit, which Ulan half spilled getting it to her lips, as she could no longer feel them or her fingers.

<hr>

The boatman was only the first part of the network that helped them escape. Everyone had been called back to the Nimistry. Haelin was one of the last of the stragglers. After that, anyone they hadn't heard from was missing and presumed dead.

Ulan was treated like one of them, though called *Sister.* Haelin was *Nimister,* but only once before returning to what she would be called out in the world. She was welcomed as though she were the heart and soul of their organization. Maybe all Nimisters were treated like much-loved relations. Ulan refused to acknowledge the longing in her heart or the tears in her eyes over such belonging.

Her own family had turned their backs on her when she'd returned from the Blood War pregnant with Dazia. Refused to take her back home. Ruggerio wouldn't have given a fig for what they considered morality, but he'd been living at the palace, and anyway, she'd never have gone to him for help or for approval. She'd made her own way in the world before, as a laundress and seamstress, bodies and garments, for the troops. She could use what she'd learned from the medics of herbs and stitching to eke out a living while calling herself a war widow, as she certainly was since she'd seen Reynal go down with her own eyes.

Haelin's network reacted to the tears in her eyes by enfolding her in their arms, which only made them flow in force. For Reynal. For Dazia. Now for Ludvin and Ruggerio.

She vowed they were the last for whom she would cry.

Then they reached the cave city. There was no other way to describe it. They'd been traveling for so long, the only indication that they were any closer to the journey's end was that her companions had more of a gleam in their eyes and had picked up their pace. Then suddenly they rounded a treacherous bend, and behind a twisted tree that had no business growing straight out of the fissure in the rock-face, the natural caves appeared, further shaped by human hands into dwellings flush with the mountainside. They were like something out of a fairy story. Like *The Sky People*. She half expected to see a woman with wings fly straight out of one of the caves, swooping down and casting a long shadow over the earth.

Haelin caught sight of her face. "They are amazing, aren't they? The first of our people to arrive came to hide out. Alone. But ni was seen by someone exploring the cliffs and sparked a legend. Many came to search for the Skybird, as ni was called, and some claimed to have caught glimpses, but none ever caught the being nimself…which is not entirely true. Later in life, ni allowed some to find nim. And ni shared nes caves. Thus began our history."

"And the wings?"

Haelin shrugged. "Lost to the ages. Maybe ni had a bird-friend as I have Bandy. Maybe nes powers allowed nim to fly. If only we could ask."

Ulan smiled at the wistful look on Haelin's face and thought she'd just ventured across one of Haelin's heroes. And why not? It was rare to know the origin of a legend.

The caves, so peaceful and perfect from the outside, were chaotic within. Too many people in too little space. Fires that must be creatively vented to avoid giving them away warmed the rock walls. Entrances were protected from the elements by layers of skins, but that meant it was stuffy inside, almost overheated, especially with the press of people and all the expelled breaths. Or maybe that was only how it seemed to Ulan after so many days and nights outside, as though she was breathing other people's air, as though it was unhealthful and too thick to swallow down.

But Haelin didn't let her pause, even as others dropped packs or stopped to embrace those they loved or even just recognized, familiar faces they might never have expected to see again, she pulled Ulan on. At the back of the cave they were in, there was a narrow section, only partially cut away, so that they had to slide through sideways to get to another chamber, where the air was not nearly as thick. It was also not very large, but had two possible passages leading off of it.

Haelin pulled her toward the one on the left, dropping her hand before she was all the way through. When Ulan emerged, Haelin was in the arms of someone roughly the size and shape of a doorframe, who was cupping her face in one hand and had the other arm wrapped around her waist. They were kissing as though they drew sustenance from each other and had been near to death.

When Haelin pulled back, the other said, "Let's never do that again," and she breathed, "No, never," and it seemed all had been decided.

Then Haelin remembered Ulan, and Ulan in turn noticed there were others in the room. "Grey, this is Ulan, who I told you about. Ulan, please meet Grey. Ni's one of the heads of the Nimistry."

Ulan put a hand out, not sure how it would be received. Mageri, she knew, were particular about touch. So used to taking power, they assumed everyone did the same. The Nim were probably the same, in fear of being exploited.

Grey took her hand. The other heads of the Nimistry to whom she was introduced, Bracha and Worlow, merely inclined their heads.

Then a chill plunged into her chest like a dagger, and her heart wanted to seize. She grabbed at Haelin to keep from collapsing, but whatever attacked, some new spirit, it was as though it needed an anchor and would be ripped away otherwise. But in setting its chill spikes into her, she was likely to be the one torn apart.

She'd never experienced anything like it. The freeze creeping toward her heart, the terror that her own soul would be ripped away and she could do nothing to stop it. Was this some attack sent by Bloody Bess?

Even Haelin's hands weren't enough to hold her as she suddenly went boneless, her own legs noodling out from beneath her as she slid to the ground.

Ulan? The voice like an ice pick to the brain—Ruggerio's voice? Oh, spirits, he was dead then. She'd feared it, but while she hadn't been certain she could at least hope.

Was he trying to take her with him?

Bloody Bess is readying the march on Frizenze, he said, and she felt a sharp tug, as though he was trying to unhook himself but didn't know how. She cried out and there was a flurry around her, but no one knew what to do. How to help. *We have to stop her.*

Ulan drooled.

"Ulan! Ulan, are you okay? What happened? Can you speak?" It was Haelin.

"Let her head down and elevate her feet, get some blood flowing back toward her head and heart," Grey suggested.

Dead? Ulan asked. It was all the thought she could pull together.

Flickering...out. Oubliette.

Get back! She shouted it with her whole being, giving one great heave to try to throw off his anchors before remembering that they were ghostly, but also that they were his. Ruggerio was putting in all of his substantial will to get this message to her. But he couldn't stay. He had to go back, to *live.* But he had to want it. If he thought he could do more good alive than dead, even in the oubliette, that's what he would choose, but if he thought otherwise, he would continue to haunt Ulan into the grave.

Haelin was elevating her feet and chaffing her legs, trying to get her blood flowing, but there was nothing she could do to reassure her. Nothing until Ruggerio released.

Her breath started to catch. And then, in an instant, he was gone, and Ulan gasped in the stifling air as though it was the sweetest thing she'd ever smelled.

Ruggerio dead was even more terrifying than alive.

"What happened?" Haelin asked. "Were you possessed? Are you all right?"

Ulan blinked several times, worked her mouth to form words. Whatever moisture she'd had was wicked clean away.

"Ruggerio," she said hoarsely. "He said that Bess marches on Frizenze. Our time is running out."

"So it's true. He's dead then? But why attack you?"

Ulan rolled her eyes until she met Haelin's outraged gaze. "Midway between life and death. That's why he tethered to me as he did. Don't think he knew what it would do."

"Or didn't care." Haelin cast a glare around the cave, trying to catch Ruggerio's ghost. "It won't happen again," she commanded, "or I'll find some way to end you myself."

But he was already gone.

CHAPTER THIRTY-THREE

Roha

Roha heard a scream from out in the forest surrounding the Sacrima and knew that Reynal had picked off another Crownsman creeping through the trees, coming for them. As the Sacrima was situated, there was no way to send an army in formation straight to their door. That gave the silent but deadly snake-man the chance to whittle down the king's numbers. Not that it would be enough.

The fact that ni could hear the scream meant the king's men were already too close.

Then suddenly came the horrible, rising buzz. The Crown mageri were at work. Something was coming for them.

"Ward, now!" Tehardy shouted.

"But Reynal!" someone protested.

"Now!" Tehardy yelled, irritated that it had to be said again, but fear coming through too, making nes voice tight.

Roha reached into nimself and pulled on that stream that flowed within, and all the way back to Cia as well, whether either willed it or not. Ni drew from the power there, joining it with that of the other

Sacristers as though driving nes stream into one giant tributary. A place of immense power. Ni wondered how the others saw it. Tehardy, as before, grabbed up the power offered nim and wove it into a ward all around the Sacrima. The one to keep the bosewights in would not do. *This* was meant to keep all others out, including whatever was making that buzzing sound coming from the sky and cracking the trees and killing the earth surrounding the Sacrima.

Tehardy stumbled, and Roha staggered a step with nim as something threw itself against the weaving as it was being finalized, tangled itself in the web. Tehardy rallied and snapped it taut, but the thing, thrashing and buzzing, got caught up within the spell, the ward.

Then there were more, flinging themselves against the ward. Ni could see them now–flying beasts with long segmented necks and tails, the former ending in teeth and the latter in a stinger, the bladed wings centered between them making that buzzing sound.

Stingblades.

Purely a mageri construct. Meant to rain terror from the skies, stingers crafted to slip through vulnerabilities in armor. They were like arrows that could fly on to take out another target. Spells and nulls could protect soldiers from having their energies stolen to power constructs, but not from the constructs themselves.

"Hold fast!" Tehardy yelled.

There was a *thwap* nearby, and Roha turned to see that a townswoman stood beside nim holding a bow, grinning fiendishly as she nocked another arrow. Other townspeople ranged about as well—some who served at the Sacrima, some from families they had aided who were invested in having their bosewights stay contained. Most covered all but their eyes in deference to the cold or so they couldn't be identified in their treason against the king if things went badly.

A stingblade fell, and another, but there was an entire swarm behind them. Stinging and biting and slicing with their wings, incrementally eating away at the ward. All while the live stingblade that had flown into the ward as it was being worked battled to tear it apart from within before its own energy was incorporated. It twitched its last and died, a ripple spreading across the working, a moment of calm before the furor of its swarm rose in response. As one, the swarm flinched away and then arrowed in, not as multiple small attacks, but as one giant, directed attempt to breach their ward.

All the Sacristers began to buckle under the onslaught, bodies reacting as though it was a physical attack. A hole appeared, small at first, then tearing until the body of the trapped stingblade fell through. The swarm flung themselves into the breach, and the working began to unravel completely.

Screaming from within the courtyard pierced the air.

Arrows flew but not fast enough. There were too many stingblades coming on too fast. Roha tried to throw a shield over nimself and the nearest archer, but ni'd given so much to Tehardy to weave into the wards, ni had little strength left. Nes shield held for the first sting-blade to come at them, but at the second, it gave way. Ni felt a moment of pure terror.

The stingblade came teeth-on, and Roha had no idea how to fight something that was offense, defense, and death in so small a package. Ni didn't have even an instant to consider strategy before it was on nim, its bite going straight for the neck. The advantage was that it was so small, it couldn't reach anything vital. The disadvantage was that its bite was poisonous. On its own, it couldn't deliver enough venom to overcome its prey, but that was why the swarm...

Roha ripped it away, cutting up nes hands on its wings, crushing them in the process, and flung it aside. It wouldn't be able to fly again, but more were on nim at once. Ni reached for nes daggers but couldn't wield them fast enough; ni'd no sooner slice at one than another would be on nim, and ni would have to grab for it lest ni risk stabbing nimself and delivering a deeper dose of the venom that now coated nes blade. Each bite, each sting, made nim a little weaker until ni staggered against the rampart wall and felt it judder under nes hand.

Roha moved to where ni could see below, surprised when no new stingblades attacked. Surprised enough to look around nim and see the remaining monsters fading out, the magic worn down. They'd done their job, taken down the ward so the king's men could get into the Sacrima, delivered their damage so the people inside could be easily overcome. Around the ramparts and the courtyard, Sacristers and townspeople were leaning against the closest walls or already fallen. Bleeding. Spent before the battle was even joined. And it would be soon. Below, ni saw exactly what ni feared, the king's men gathered with troops trailing off into the woods beyond where ni could see.

The closest soldiers were lashing together half-constructed ladders to scale the Sacrima walls. Beyond, where the wall curved out of Roha's vision and the gate stood, ni was certain a battering ram accounted for the shaking. The Sacrima was strongly built, but how long would it hold against such an attack? Especially now that the mageri had drawn the anima out of the surrounding land and cracked and killed what they could? Had their foundations been part of that? No, surely they had been within the Sacrima's wards.

Roha closed nes eyes and searched for calm and strength to bolster nim. Found it in the promise of Cia's reinforcements. Ni just hoped they would come soon enough.

Ni opened nes eyes again and made nes way to Tehardy, who lay with nes back against the ramparts, legs splayed out in front of nim. Tehardy's eyes were closed when Roha reached nim, and ni was afraid to find nim dead, but as Roha squatted, Tehardy's lids raised.

Nes eyes didn't quite focus, not both at once, anyway, but nes voice worked just fine. "Tell Iogo to protect the stone, defend it at all costs. Deedri will take the offense. You–*do not let the wards fail.* If our bosewights get out…"

Nes eyes drifted in different directions, and nes lids shut. Roha checked the pulse at Tehardy's neck to be sure ni still breathed, but there was no awakening nim again.

Iogo came running and dropped to Tehardy's side, slapping nes face. Roha grabbed nes hand before ni could do it again. "It's no use. The venom got nim. Tehardy said to protect the stone. You know what ni's talking about?"

Iogo nodded and made to yank nes arm back, but Roha wouldn't let go. "What stone?" ni asked.

"When there's a need to know, you'll know it." Iogo pulled harder, and Roha held harder. Ni didn't want to break an arm, but ni would do it.

"And if you fall? If you're unable to tell me later? I'm not letting you go, letting *this* go. Your king is coming here to swallow my friend whole. If this stone has anything to do with it, I need to know. I'm here to help, not hinder you. I swear it."

Iogo stared straight into Roha's eyes, nes golden-brown gaze blazing. Then something shot out of the arm ni held, stinging Roha until ni released nim. Iogo still had power to spare. No wonder Tehardy had designated nim to guard whatever this stone was. Something like the Stone of Gelerte?

"Fine, but touch me again without my permission and you will regret it to the end of your days. Touch the stone with ill intent and you won't live to regret it. Are we understood?"

Iogo stood, towering over Roha, who still squatted beside Tehardy. Ni stood as well, and they faced each other down across Tehardy's prone body.

"We are," Roha said.

Iogo gave a terse nod. "The Nim who serve here can choose to be taken outside of the Sacrima to die so that they may join the All. Most do. But some choose instead to serve eternally, to have their energies preserved within the Sacrima Stone to help power our wards."

Roha had wondered how they'd kept the wards powered without ever depleting themselves. Ni'd assumed it was long practice and minimal upkeep after the initial casting. Ni'd never imagined…

"It may be King Avize knows nothing about this. Certainly, we have tried to keep our secret. But his people have captured some of ours, and if anyone has been tortured or otherwise convinced to tell what they know, then the stone might be used to feed this horrible spell that he's contemplating. If the king needs to be kept locked into Hostill's body, as he's done with his own, he may think to sacrifice us to the stone. So much more convenient to trap our energies than to drag along unwilling humans who must be fed and clothed and kept from escape."

Roha gasped in horror. "But–"

"No," Iogo said, "it won't work. The sacrifice has to be offered. Otherwise, we may become bosewights, like the others here, and work against him, haunt him. He can't even *compel* us to perform his spell, except on pain of torture or death. We have free will up until the end. But people of power are so used to wielding it like a hammer, they fail to consider that not everyone is a nail. We will disperse our energies rather than let him pound us into the ground."

"Go," Roha said.

Iogo sketched a mocking bow. "So pleased for your permission."

Then ni was off, and Roha put nes back to the trembling ramparts to support nim while ni closed nes eyes and focused on gathering the threads of power to patch the wards. Ni was so exhausted the threads wanted to slip through nes hands, but ni reached further than nes own power, found the place where nes energies merged with Cia's, and asked *may I?* Ni didn't even know how. It wasn't language, but still, it was understanding, and the answer returned *yes*. Ni drew only a trickle, only what was needed to make certain the longstanding ward held firm, the bosewights still trapped with them and not unleashed upon the countryside. Ni entertained momentary fantasies of the spirits harrying the king and his men into death, but they would never be satisfied with those targets alone. Roha wished ni'd been able to save the other ward and keep the king's men out entirely.

Tehardy's purple dome of energies swirled, encompassing the walls, ringing the tower like a mist that quivered with each blow of the battering ram. At least the bosewight wards were not dependent on the gates being opened or closed; they held whether or not people were permitted entrance.

"Ladders up!" Deedri's sharp voice cried, taken up all along the ramparts.

Roha's eyes snapped open, and ni whipped around as the ends of a ladder slapped the stone beside nes head. Ni leapt to them and put all nes weight into thrusting the ladder away, but it was no good. There was too much weight or leverage. The ladder jumped in nes hands as ni held it. A man gusting out great breaths like a bull about to charge, pounded his way up, determination in his gaze as it met Roha's.

First up the ladder, he had to know he was expendable, meant to wear out his opponents, to fail so that others could succeed. But Roha couldn't let the sadness of his plight affect nim. His fate had already been decided. Ni was simply the vehicle. Ni grabbed nes daggers and drove one straight into the spot between his neck and shoulders as soon as he was within reach. He actually looked surprised, even betrayed, by the dagger sticking out of him, as though he expected Roha to wait patiently for nes death. Then he was falling away, hopefully taking the next man down the ladder with him.

Roha barely yanked the dagger out in time to keep it from falling away with him and waited on the next man up. Ni could kill them as they came, but eventually one would overwhelm nim. Or the battering ram would make it through that front gate, and the king's men would flood the courtyard. Ni needed something more.

Ni glanced around and spotted a townswoman down the ramparts who had fallen to the stingblades. Her chest still rose and fell, but her eyes were closed, and there was blood everywhere. Roha didn't think she'd rejoin the fight, and nes heart ached for the woman, for her family, but ni couldn't afford to mourn. Not then. But ni could honor her by continuing her fight, using her weapons. Roha wasn't as good with a bow as with daggers, but ni had trained with it, and at this range, ni couldn't miss. The Church had always thought they'd fight the Crown again one day. Their mistake was believing it would be a fair fight.

But people in power never wanted fair. They didn't want balance or peace. They wanted domination, and everyone else to pay for their prosperity. Their only peace came in knowing that they'd left no one with the ability to disrupt their power.

Ni shook all that off. Now was not the time. Immediately, ni nocked an arrow to the bow and sighted over the rampart. The next soldier had made inhuman time, or ni had lost it grabbing the bow. He was far closer than he should have been. Roha had little chance to aim but let fly as best ni could for his center of mass. It struck the soldier's upper arm, flinging it away from the ladder, but he held tightly with the other.

Roha reached for the quiver ni'd hastily slung over nes back, but it swung away from nim, as ni hadn't secured it properly. Ni cursed, used momentum to swing it back toward nes grasping hand and pulled an arrow, nocked it, only to find it pressed right against the soldier's head.

He used his head like a mace, swinging against the arrow,

knocking it out of nes hand. The soldier came off that ladder like he'd flown up the last rung, tackling Roha over the rampart and bringing them both crashing to the stone battlement. The bow cracked to kindling between them.

Roha's head landed on part of the villager's body, so ni wasn't as dazed as ni might have been. The soldier only had the one good arm, but another Crownsman would be following on his heels. Roha kicked and grappled. The soldier grabbed one of the daggers out of Roha's belt. Ni wrestled it with nes left hand while fighting to free the other dagger with nes right. The dagger slid loose of nes belt, and ni stabbed it into the soldier's side, just below his ribs. He cried out as his grip on Roha slackened and fell away.

Roha recovered nes dagger from him and rose, but the next soldier was on nim before the first even bled out, coming at nim from behind and swinging a sword to nes throat as though to play executioner. Ni managed to get the dagger up between nes neck and the oncoming sword, catching it on nes guard, but the blow reverberated down Roha's entire arm, sending needles shooting through that left it numb. If it had been meant as a killing blow, it would have dropped Roha, but ni realized the soldier had aimed with the flat of the blade. Roha thought of what Iogo had said. They wanted the Sacristers alive, at least for now. But it seemed they also wanted them knocked out and unable to resist.

Ni thrust the soldier's sword back, whirling with a kick to his knee that had all nes rage behind it. The man leapt back and grabbed a handful of Roha's cloak as it fluttered within range. Cries all along the wall indicated Roha's position wasn't the only one breached. The soldier pulled hard, and Roha tripped over nes own feet as ni lunged toward him and his outstretched sword. Roha crossed nes daggers to catch the blade and save nimself, but there was no time to get them properly into place. The sword rang into them with a force that had pain shooting all the way up nes arms, as though they might shatter.

"Drop the blades," the soldier spat. The smell of rotten teeth and all he'd eaten for time immemorial crossed the divide between them.

Roha tried to raise nes daggers as though to ask *these blades?* but the soldier was bearing down with too much force. Instead, ni risked pulling one away to slash at the cloak where he held it in one hand, hoping to free nimself. The soldier didn't miss the opportunity to slip his sword free of the lone dagger and swing it toward nes throat. Neither did Roha miss the fabric, though ni didn't cut as cleanly as ni wanted, catching as well the soldier's hand, which had the same effect. He released nim with a shout.

Roha leapt away quickly before he could grab nim again, but it was only a matter of time before it was him or one of his brethren now flooding the ramparts. Ni had no footing to fight with bodies every-where, some still living and breathing, potential hostages. And so, ni did the only thing ni could think of—ni dove over the side of the ramparts straight for the inner bailey, tucking nes blades away so ni wouldn't land on them.

Ni reached for that place of calm, pulled on a tiny thread of power, drawing inspiration from the whipping wind as ni fell, and gathered that wind beneath nes robes. They belled out like a tent, filling like a luminary that might fly away, and that was tempting. There was a moment where Roha wondered whether ni might float over the walls, find Hostill, steal him from the king's clutches, and carry him away, like a huge bird of prey swooping in on a mouse in a field. But it was a crazy thought. The king would have archers, for one, and would keep Hostill well-guarded, for another. Roha would have no chance.

Amid cries from above, Roha landed in the courtyard, the air escaping again from under nes robes. Ni stood facing the gates, which were bowing inward with every blow from the battering ram.

One by one, others floated down to join Roha. Had Deedri called orders or was ni one of the fallen?

The result was the same. Roha fought past the stingblades's poison to keep standing as those remaining formed up in the center of the courtyard, less than a dozen Sacristers, twice as many townspeople, armed with bows and blades, one with a sharpened spade, another few with pikes. A village against an army. During their last communi-cation, Cia said people were coming to help the Sacrima, Frizenze's noble-led version of the Restoration. Possibly, as with most nobility, they were too unused to doing for themselves to be effective. Or too used to backstabbing to keep their own secrets. Whatever the cause, there was still no sign of them. If they didn't arrive soon, they would be too late.

There was another massive blow at the Sacrima gates, then a cry from Roha's left. Ni turned in time to see a man fall from the ramparts into the courtyard, an arrow protruding from his chest. Soldiers were streaming from the ramparts now, some falling as quickly as the village archers could nock their arrows but not nearly enough.

Old Joe, the Sacrima's cook, armed with his largest knife, tried to step between Roha and the oncoming soldiers. *All* of the villagers tried to form a wall between the Sacristers and the king's men, even as the Sacristers tried to surround them, to take the place of the failed ward. Doing their best to protect those who knew of them in return, who were only in this danger *because* of them. But everyone exposed, villagers and Sacristers alike, were soon engaged, as the soldiers descended upon them, swords swinging.

Cracks from the weakening gates went straight through Roha's body as ni fell shoulder to shoulder with Old Joe. He could slice his knife through the air with a deftness the soldier on him could barely follow, allowing Roha to slide one of nes daggers into his side as he watched the wrong opponent for his opening, knowing he was meant not to kill the Sacristers.

But then ni missed the king's man flashing in with the hilt of his own sword, ringing nes head like it was a mallet and ni was meat he wanted to tenderize. But he had little experience with how hard to hit not to kill and so underestimated how much force to use to send Roha to nes knees. Old Joe finished him off for Roha, and they tipped their chins to each other in acknowledgment before two more foes were upon them. But Roha's vision was already blurred, and ni was dizzy and slow catching nes enemy's thrust.

From the gate came louder cracks. Wood splintering. It wouldn't be long before even more foes were upon them. Before that happened, Roha had to get to the gates. Had to search out an opportunity to snatch Hostill out of the king's grasp. The battle was horrendous, but it would be over if ni could draw the army off the boy. Best if they vanished, and the king never caught him again. Never caught *them*. Ni could save all of nes friends at once.

Heedless of getting stabbed nimself, Roha whirled, putting one dagger into nes opponent, another into Old Joe's foe, hoping it would give him enough of an advantage that ni wasn't leaving him to die. Ni only caught the soldier ni was fighting on the shoulder as he swept the flat of his blade at nes head, managing to take the blow on nes shoulder blade, sending a brilliant numbness through nim, as though stung by a swarm of bees. Muttering an apology to Old Joe, ni forced that dagger back into nes belt, hoping the hand would regain feeling as it had before, trusting in the other as ni lashed out with nes remaining dagger at any who might stop nim from rushing the gates, dodging arrows as if ni had some innate sense of them.

Roha reached the gates as they exploded inward and whirled quickly away to protect nimself from the splinters. Before ni could turn back to search for Hostill in the chaos of onrushing king's men, someone grabbed Roha painfully by nes hair and pulled nes neck taut. Ni drove a dagger backward, but the soldier thrust his blade into Roha's neck, drawing enough blood to let nim know he would certainly cut nim rather than suffer at nes hands. Roha debated anyway, better to lose nes head than be drained at the king's dark behest. But ni couldn't kill the spark of hope that ni'd come up with something. Or that rescue would arrive.

Fearing to so much as breathe lest the sword cut nim more deeply, Roha dropped the daggers. The soldier let up enough to whip Roha around like a ragdoll before putting the sword back to nes throat, making certain that Roha could see the demolished gates and the size and breadth of the king's army as they rounded up the other Sacristers and few remaining villagers. Then, as though a signal had gone out, each was brought to their knees by sheer force, so that they knelt to the army streaming into their sanctuary. They were bowed forward as the palanquin bearing their wasted king was set on the ground before them.

"Go!" a gruff guardsman ordered one of his men, pointing toward their tower.

No, not a guardsman. Roha glared up despite the death-grip trying to force nim down into a subservient posture. The man wore Frizenze's purple and black, his tabard decorated with more than its share of silver. An officer then, someone to be obeyed. A contingent of the soldiers broke off from the others and instantly rushed the Sacrima.

Roha flinched forward, thinking of Iogo and the Sacrima Stone, but the soldier holding nim yanked nim back by the hair, nearly pulling it out by the roots. His sword cut more deeply into nes throat, and ni had to stop for fear of severing something vital. The pain was as sharp as the sword. Nes blood seeped down nes front, freezing there, like the blood in Roha's heart at the chattering of bones in the beard of the mageri stepping forward. There were half a dozen moving to form a semi-circle on either side of the king's palanquin.

Roha had to remind nimself that the grounds were warded, that the mageri couldn't work their magic. Not here. That thought quelled nes fear until an exceedingly tall man ushered Hostill into the center of their circle, right beside the palanquin.

Roha gasped. Hostill was tied at the throat and hands in such a way that one pull would both choke and neutralize him. The other end of that rope was held like a leash in the hands of the tall man, who towered over the boy. Hostill's gaze was on the ground, dejected, until he raised it to search the courtyard. Roha's neck strained with the fight to keep nes gaze up against the push from the soldier determined to break nim, but ni met his gaze, and it was pure misery. *I'm sorry*, he mouthed, as though he'd failed Roha and not the other way around.

He was a boy.

Just a boy.

Roha could not let this happen.

There had to be something they could do. This was a sanctuary. What good was their power if it couldn't prevent something like *this*.

No, on fear of death, ni and the other Sacristers could not be made to do this thing.

"Pull back the curtains," the tall man said, giving a short sharp tug to Hostill's rope.

Hostill ripped his gaze away from Roha's and awkwardly pulled the curtains back from the palanquin to reveal King Avize, his body so small despite the pillows and finery that had been used to prop his body for comfort as he was carried along. He had wasted away. He wasn't conscious; his breathing was erratic. The trip had cost him, and he didn't look likely to survive much longer.

Roha was certain that praying to the All for someone's death would darken nes spirit, and so ni didn't. As for harboring it in nes heart...

Another man came along the other side of the palanquin, this one wearing an ornamented skull cap and a chain of office outside his cloak to mark his importance. "Your king requires your allegiance," he began, his voice well-suited to carrying across a courtyard. "This is your moment. If you choose to aid your liege, he will assume that your closed gates were intended to fend off invaders, as Jucar draws ever closer, and that you did not understand that it was your king coming to call. Your Sacrima will survive. If you choose to resist, he will understand that you've committed treason here today. As such, all your lives are forfeit, and we will begin putting people to death one by one until we have your cooperation."

Roha had so many thoughts, ni couldn't grab onto them all–the knowledge that they'd all be put to death anyway, the only possible difference being a slow, painful death versus a swift one. The question was whether the *king* was commanding anything at this stage or whether it was the people around him all trying to hold to the power their proximity granted them and what ni could do to stop all of this.

"What cooperation?" It was Deedri.

Roha fought to bring nes head around to see the condition Deedri was in, but the soldier holding nes hair twisted up in his fist yanked again, brooking no further resistance. Deedri sounded strong but also pained, as though struggling with broken or bruised ribs.

"Our doors would have been opened if you'd come with emissaries to query rather than conquer," Deedri continued. "But when an army marches on us, we defend. You would do the same. You *have* done the same. And the fact that you sent stingblades as your messengers and a battering ram to knock on our doors counters every argument you could offer."

"Your Sovereign need offer no argument, just as he should have encountered no resistance." The man's face was growing alarmingly red. He seemed to grow in size as he puffed up with his righteous anger.

"And yet, you came prepared for war," Deedri continued, crying out as the soldier guarding nim must have retaliated for nes disrespect.

"I never said the resistance was unexpected. Not from the *Nim*." He said it like it was a filthy word, and Roha could feel the others bristle. Everything they'd been through, and then to be blamed for it… Ni reached out to the Sacristers through the interconnected spell of the wards and felt them reach back. Tehardy too. They'd missed nim up on the ramparts, barely half-alive, but Roha was thankful to discover there was still a chance for nim. "You who have broken with the Church, broken with the Crown. You subvert all that is holy by cutting souls off from the anima here at this unhallowed place."

"Vidaris," a thready voice wheezed from the pallet, "on with it."

So the king was conscious. Or had become so.

A face suddenly appeared out of the emissary's puffed breaths like a dragon breathing smoke that presaged fire, a bosewight, face twisted horribly, showing them all how unhallowed the Sacrima was indeed. Soldiers holding the prisoners gasped, and the tall man, Vidaris, howled as the bosewight flew right for his face, then shot up his nose.

He grabbed for his nose as though to rip it right off his face and fell flailing to the ground. Another man, also in robes, stepped forward to kick him.

"Pull yourself together, man, get on with it!"

But he must see that Vidaris's hair was being ripped upward and all around as though caught in a sudden storm, his ears yanked and twisted in opposite directions as though the bosewights wanted to tear his face in half. Haunting figures appeared in the crowd. Faces rotted away, so there were only hollows for eyes and noses, mouths reduced to gums of tar and teeth stained with grave dirt. Tongues like eels pushed dirt and maggots onto the feet of the soldiers. One female bosewight tore her shroud and the flesh away from her chest along with it, bloody, ropey bits barely hiding the white of her ribcage revealed. Her squishy parts inside slopped out.

Howls arose. There were more pinches, punches, pain. The

bosewights were feeding off the blood of battle, the powerful emotions, gleeful for the newer, softer targets that had arrived, unused to ignoring their torments.

The unrestful spirits had gathered their strength, poised for the moment the king would end the Sacrima and the spell that held them prisoner. Ready to make their escape.

Vidaris got to his feet, cursing, holding his nose as blood dripped from it.

"Ignore them," he called. "They're just a distraction."

He snapped with his free hand, and as one, soldiers moved on the captured townspeople. They forced their heads to the earth, prostrating them, their heads all pointed toward the center of the circle. The mageri, the king, and Hostill were on one side and the Nim on the other. A sick feeling began in the pit of Roha's stomach. It only got worse as the king's palanquin was brought into the middle of the circle and set down. Hostill was led by his leash and followed into the circle by the closest mageri, a man whose wiry silver and black hair blew in the wind unfettered, but whose beard fell nearly to his knees and was weighed by so many beads of bone that it didn't blow but clicked with the sound of bones being rattled in a game of dice. Ni had thought it was solely a Jucari convention to weave the bones of the fallen into their hair and beards so that the sound would disconcert the enemy, but perhaps the Frizenzians had adopted it as well.

Or maybe ni had learned wrong.

The mageri cast his gaze over the gathered Nim, "Our spies tell us that there is one among you who is able to pluck out souls, who has surrendered those stolen by Bloody Bess of Jucar back to the collective spirit." His attention fell on Roha, who would like to have bored into him with nes hatred. "You?" he asked, as though he already knew.

"I will not touch this boy's soul," Roha said, loudly enough to ring throughout the courtyard.

He snapped, and soldiers yanked back the heads of two townspeople, a man and a woman right across the circle from Roha. Terror sparked on their faces as they struggled uselessly. Roha tried to surge forward, but the hand clenched in nes hair wouldn't allow it, and the sword at nes throat bit in. The soldiers yanked the man's and woman's heads back and slashed their throats, cutting so deeply they spurted blood geysers, spattering the soldiers' faces to mark their guilt.

The bosewights bathed in it, flying in and out, tormenting the soldiers. But there was not enough they could do, and ni felt someone steal the anima from the dying villagers before they could join the other spirits. It could only be the king's mageri taking it in to power their spell since they could rip no anima from the Sacrima land. Not with that centuries-old ward still intact.

The villagers would not become restless spirits trapped with the others who were too wicked to invade the anima. But now they could never become part of the All. Their sparks could never return to another form, renewing life. They were obliterated as though they'd never been, and the entire All weakened.

Somehow, Roha had to stop this insanity, but ni was held too tightly, and unlike the mageri, Roha would not draw more than ni had to give.

"We will do this with or without you," the mageri said, voice hard and completely unmoved by the deaths he'd caused. "You remove the boy's soul or we will rip it out of him. We'd rather not leave any vestiges, but it's a chance we're willing to take."

Roha had no doubt that they would. The mageri had always stolen their power, thus had access to so much they'd never bothered to learn precision. If they removed Hostill's soul, they might leave some of him behind to suffer, locked in there with the king, unable to control his own body, like Cia had when Garif had taken her over. The only thing Roha could do for Hostill was spare him. Make sure ni waited until the wards came down so that he could at least go on to the anima, be at peace.

Or…was there a way?

There had to be.

Roha could not let the king win. His plan was a perversion of nature. If it worked and King Avize realized he could use people this way, where would it end? When Hostill's body grew old and frail, perhaps he would transfer to another. Maybe even that of his own son to hold onto power. Ni wished it was unimaginable, and yet if Roha's mind had gone there, it was likely the king's more devious mind would as well. King Avize was in his way as horrible as Bloody Bess. He had to be stopped. If ni and Cia, Ruggerio and Ulan didn't win, didn't find a way to stop this war from destroying everything, both lands and beyond were doomed.

But first Hostill.

What Roha so desperately wanted to do was rip the king's soul out of his body and tip off Hostill to playact that things had gone differently. But ni dismissed it almost as quickly as it came. It could only be a fantasy. Hostill hadn't been raised to nobility. Certainly not to prince or kingship, and he'd only ever seen the king in bed. He'd never witnessed him walk or swagger, didn't know how to fight, knew no details of his life. One question would confirm that the transformation hadn't taken place and everyone in the courtyard would be slaughtered.

If Roha couldn't save the day, at least ni could prevent a massacre while still thwarting the king's will. If Lehren Gelerte's spirit could be saved to the Stone of Gelerte and the ministers of the Sacrima could choose to sacrifice themselves to the Sacrima Stone, perhaps Roha could transfer Hostill's consciousness to some sort of talisman. His body would still be alive. If it survived the transfer of the king's consciousness, and if Roha survived as well, there was hope that someday ni could undo the terrible wrong. They could still make things right.

"What do you need me to do?" Roha asked.

Ni pretended not to sense the heads twisting in nes direction. Sacristers and villagers who'd been willing to die for the cause must be certain that Roha was betraying them. Ni didn't dare risk anything that might reassure them for fear of giving nimself away to the king. As angry as they were certain to be, would part of them be the least bit relieved that they didn't have to die today? Ni hoped so; it was the only comfort Roha had to offer.

"Step forward," the mageri said.

Slowly, the blade moved away from Roha's throat and the fingers unclenched in nes hair. Almost instantly, nes scalp ached with spikes of heated pain as sensation returned. But ni could still hardly feel the cut at nes throat, the cold possibly working to slow the blood. When it was safe enough, ni stood, legs not wanting to work after all the time on nes knees, but ni refused to let it show. When Roha had them under control, ni walked into the center of the circle, sensed the soldiers close behind nim, evening things out as though all had to be equidistant around the spell circle. Nes whole body began to prick like nes head. Nothing about this felt right or good.

Hostill's eyes met Roha's. His were panicked, his body shaking, though he tried to still the reaction. Roha couldn't be sure what ni conveyed. Ni wanted it to be reassurance, but was afraid it was a plea for forgiveness.

"And now?" Roha asked the mageri in charge.

Ni swayed as there was a pull to nes power. Not the mageri—someone else. Iogo? Fighting a losing battle over the Sacrima Stone and desperately drawing from any source within reach, tied to Roha through their working of the wards?

The mageri stepped between Roha and Hostill, his beads clacking as he moved. But ni barely heard them over the pounding of nes heart. Keep the flow to Iogo and ni wouldn't have the power left to save the others. Shut it down and ni doomed Iogo and handed the Sacrima Stone to the king's men, possibly dooming them all anyway.

The mageri pulled a dagger from his belt, and Roha's head made the decision nes heart could not. It shut nim off from Iogo, from the wards. From everything and everyone. It was difficult, because Roha had always envisioned nes power like a stream. Even damming it up, there were holes where trickles might get through, but ni plugged up the leaks with reeds and plants and flowers that had fallen into nes stream. Locked nimself down, preserving the tiny ember of power ni had left, hoping it would be enough.

The wards jumped, faltering in the face of Roha's desertion.

The mageri held the dagger aloft as he muttered a spell, then struck as fast as a viper, slashing a wound across Hostill's palm. He thrust the boy's bleeding hand at Roha.

"Now," he ordered. "Draw the soul."

Hostill mouthed a plea for Roha not to do this thing.

"Do it or we kill them all!" the mageri shouted. Had to, because the bosewights were howling now, understanding that the wards were about to fail. "The Nim, the townspeople, the boy. His soul dies with or without you. You can at least make it merciful."

I'm sorry, Roha mouthed back.

Ni dove deeply into nimself, finding the shallow burbling of water remaining and pulling from nimself to turn that trickle into a stream that might reach into the tributary of Hostill's own anima. Ni felt Hostill's sense of betrayal like a dagger through the heart, tearing it into shreds that would never reknit as ni followed the force of Hostill's emotions to his bright, sharp, cacophonous center. So big and broad, as though he'd refused to be boiled down in the crucible of life. If Roha was a stream and Cia was the pendulum of fire to ice, then Hostill was defense so strong it became offense. He shone too bright to look on, was too prickly to hug, and too loud for listening.

Come with me, ni said. Roha didn't use nes power. Not yet, but it was coming. Just nes voice. Just their friendship. *Trust me. There's a way. I have to guide you, take you with me, but I can preserve you. We can get you back, later.*

How could you? Hostill lashed out.

One of his sharp, shiny, beautiful bits blasted into Roha, and ni recoiled as though lightning had flashed down and dried up that part of nes stream. Ni didn't have much left. He might kill Roha before ni could convince him otherwise. It would be the death of them both, but it would be his choice.

But ni had to make that choice clear to him. Right now, he was acting on emotion. He didn't know what ni meant to do. In the interest of time, ni hadn't been clear. Ni'd expected him to run on blind trust. Ni gathered the last of nimself, and flowed again along a new pathway.

I can't save your body, not right now. The king's men have us outnumbered and at their mercy. You can see that for yourself. The only hope is for me to preserve you in something and restore you when we defeat him. Cia has help coming but not soon enough. I can't promise that it will work, but I will give it everything I have.

The wards flickered again.

I'm sorry! Ni thought at him.

If Roha waited until the wards failed, the mageri wouldn't need

Roha's power. The Sacrima would be unprotected, and the mageri would steal the anima right from the land or the Sacristers, and rip out Hostill's soul themselves. There would be no saving him.

It was now or never.

Ni grabbed Hostill's sharp spirit and *pulled*. There was only a moment of resistance, and then he was traveling with Roha, out of his body and into the first thing ni could think of to hold his spirit. One of nes daggers. Roha knew where they'd fallen and had an attachment to them. *Ni would find them. Find him.* And ni would preserve him until ni could return him to his form.

Hostill's body began to crumple, and the mageri pushed Roha away, into the waiting arms of a soldier. "Take nim back with the others. See how we're coming with that stone–"

The blastwave knocked them all off their feet.

CHAPTER THIRTY-FOUR

Roha

Chaos erupted.

Roha was dazed, on the ground. That blast–it hadn't just been the wards failing and the remnants of the power blowing back on the Nim. It hadn't been that way when the defensive ward had fallen against the stingblades.

Iogo must have blown the stone rather than let it fall into King Avize's hands. Ni didn't know what that meant for Iogo or the others fighting with nim.

"Now. Do it now!" the mageri yelled, recovering, though from the sound of him, he was still on the ground.

Roha's sight hadn't yet realigned with reality. That or the world was spinning, juttering, dipping. Ni tried to stand, but it was like ni'd had too much to drink.

A soldier grabbed for Roha, caught nim by the clothing, but ni spun, vomited all over the man and nimself, and the hand withdrew. Another hand reached for nim and this time Roha gripped it between two of nes and bent it sharply backward. Roha could barely hear the cry over the howling and shouting in the courtyard.

A blow struck the back of nes head, broad across it like a beam, and ni went down again, was dragged by the hair back into the circle with the other villagers, the other Sacristers.

Nes vision was bruised. Trying to focus was going to make nim ill again, but Roha couldn't close nes eyes to what was to come.

"You, Nim," the king said, his voice a whisper of wind through dried leaves, "your king requires your service." He stopped to breathe; the rattle in his chest would have been painful to hear if not for what he was doing to hold onto power rather than join the All. "My mageri will transfer my soul." Breathe, rattle. "You will–"

He began coughing so severely that his entire body shook, and he gasped for air like a landed fish. He waved feebly for someone to continue his words, and his tall mageri picked up where he left off.

"You will create the ward to keep the soul locked into the new body, as you have with the spirits here. If you do so successfully and without the need for more forceable reminders from the king's men, your Sacrima will be allowed to remain."

"What about the townspeople?" Deedri asked. "They will live? You will let them go?"

"We will let them be a lesson to you."

With no further warning, the soldiers stepped forward and cut the throats of every one of the townspeople. The Sacristers gasped and struggled, losing more hair and blood to their captors as the mageri pulled the anima draining from the dying to power their spell. The forbidden chant filled the air as the mageri transferred their king, every bit as poisoned in spirit as the bosewights, into Hostill's body.

While the Sacristers stared on in horror, the mageri wearing the chain of office approached them and tossed an amulet at Roha's knees, a bloodstone wrapped in gold–red and gold, the colors of Jucar. "You will use this for the ward, and you will do it now. We can't leave the body any longer without a soul to animate it, and it must be locked in before it can escape."

"You need to let us rise. We need to touch the stone, to connect with each other," Roha spat at him.

He nodded and issued a sign to the soldiers, who let Roha and the others up, but held them tightly at sword point.

Some of the other Sacristers glared at Roha, as though ni had brought this upon them, but others only looked fearful or sympathetic, understanding that they had fought and lost. That Roha had been given no good options.

Roha held the bloodstone. It felt wrong in nes hands. Cold. Ni glanced around the circle of faces and ended with Deedri, who said, "We don't have any strength left unless we draw it away from our ward. It will fall. The bosewights…"

"If they kill us, the ward falls anyway," someone else pointed out.

"But then the king doesn't get what he wants," said another, who was then struck so hard from behind that ni fell into the arms of the Sacrister across the circle, bleeding where the blade had turned.

"But neither will my friend's body live on," Roha said quietly. It was dangerous, but there was no way to convey nes meaning without the soldiers overhearing. Ni could only hope they were too caught up watching when Hostill's body slowly lifted his head, then his hands, testing them as the mageri's spell took effect. The king learned the operation of Hostill's body as though it were a mechanical suit, operated by levers and pullies barely within reach. The king wore Hostill like a puppet. It was the stuff of nightmares.

And now they had to lock him in, if only so that the body survived until Roha could undo what had been done. Ni would make it nes life's work. That and to destroy both monarchs. Return them to the All or keep them from it, from ever returning to pollute their world again.

"We don't have a choice," Roha added, desperate for them to pick up on the urgency. Willing them to *trust* nim, even after so little time.

Deedri and the other Sacristers looked to each other, entire conversations in their glances, then Deedri nodded. "Hands," ni said.

They all joined together, Roha and the Sacrister on nes left both holding the amulet in their hands. Ni felt not just the energy from the anima-warding spell begin unraveling, pulling toward their circle, but the deep, soul-baring sadness of the other Nim at the undoing of their life's work. Their very purpose. The bosewights would be free now, loose on the land. Roha couldn't even try to catch them, return them to the All as ni had done on the battlefield. The very point was to keep them from seeping their venom into the purity of the collective spirit. But perhaps that was wrong too?

Ni was no religious scholar. Ni could take no stand on what was right or wrong here. Would the bosewights' bits of evil be torn apart, diluted by the everything of the All and so do no true harm, regardless of what the Church and the Sacristers believed? Did the All require the balance of good and evil, as it needed the masculine and feminine and everything along the spectrum?

Ni was not equipped to decide what the world needed, but here, there must be no room for doubt. Roha's course had already been decided. The wards were so thin now that the bosewights howled at them like storm winds. Hurled themselves against them like stones from a trebuchet.

Ni felt every blow as though it was against nes very body.

There was a huge commotion from outside the gates. Howling, cries, metal striking metal, but they couldn't stop now. They had come too far. If others had arrived, they'd done so too late.

The bosewights whipped into a dervish and took one more concerted run at the ever-thinning ward. It gave out as though blown apart, raw purple energies lashing free. But Deedri, who had been unraveling and reweaving, expertly drew them into the new working before they could harm the Sacristers with their backlash. They were chanting, chanting, so caught up, they couldn't defend. One with each other, with the amulet, with the working.

One with themselves and the All. At that moment, they were power and energy. And then, Deedri was done. The amulet sizzled and popped with energy, glowing in nes mind's eye.

"Go," Deedri said, and Roha knew the command was directed to nim.

The Sacristers dropped hands, and Roha opened nes eyes, looking with wonder at nes fellows. The amulet felt weighted, though ni knew it was not. A prod with the tip of a soldier's sword sent Roha forward on unsteady legs toward the king wearing nes friend's face.

Soldiers watched from all sides, ready with a killing blow should anything untoward happen. Roha moved to fasten the amulet around Hostill's neck, seeing only the boy for an instant through the tears that had sprung up in nes eyes. But then, King Avize held out his hand and proclaimed, "I'll take that."

There was no mistaking his deeper voice issuing from Hostill's lips like sacrilege. It reminded nim instantly of who ni truly faced.

Roha began to drop the amulet into his palm but couldn't make nimself let go of the last bit.

"Guards!" he cried.

They would cut off nes hands. Right there. The mageri would drink nim down.

Ni surrendered it and the king waved his men off. Stared Roha down even from his inferior height.

Then there was a huge bang, as the doors that had been ruined by the king's battering ram and reclosed against a rear attack were blasted through again, and the battle reengaged. Finally, it seemed the rebel army Cia promised had arrived. All within the courtyard looked toward the noise, and Roha realized ni could use the distraction to grab back the warding amulet and disappear into the crowd. If ni could find nes daggers in the melee, ni could return Hostill to his body and steal him away.

Roha turned, already reaching, but the king's bodyguards were faster, spiriting him away and out of nes reach, somewhere safe from the fighting, or at least behind a wall of their own flesh.

Ni cursed and spun instead to search for nes daggers. One of the soldiers guarding the Sacristers tried to grab nim, and ni dodged him by diving and somersaulting to nes feet. Roha spotted the daggers to the left and dove for them, coming up with one, landing painfully on the other, miscalculating in nes weakened state. But ni rolled for it and came up with the dagger just in time to sink it into the lower gut of the guard ready to impale Roha on his sword.

The sword still struck down, but ni was ready to deflect it with nes dagger. It was no small feat of strength, though, and it took all ni had to heave nes legs up, wrap the guard from behind and roll him to the ground so that ni could come out on top and finish the job, both daggers tasting his blood. Ni could not leave him alive to come up behind nim.

The other soldiers were prodding the Sacristers forward into the fight rather than toward the Sacristy for safety. They were depleted, no threat to the king, who had promised they could keep their Sacristy if they complied.

The king had lied, that was the only answer. He couldn't let them live as witnesses to what he had done, but he *could* order them to the front of his guard and let them stand as human shields for his men. He could claim that insurrectionists had killed them, smooth over the deaths of the villagers and Sacristers both now that he had what he wanted.

Roha didn't give the war cry that rose up from the depths of nes being, but as quietly as possible, ran to the closest king's man and buried nes dagger right at the base of his neck. He stumbled in his step, momentum still carrying him, and then went down silently, falling into the Sacrister before him.

His compatriot fell to another rebel blade that seemed to come out of nowhere. The other king's men passed glances back and forth and all around, watching for the next blow and uncertain of what to do as they spread out to keep control of the Sacristers. One decided that it was best to cut the Sacristers down so they had only themselves to look after. Maybe he felt as the Restoration did about those with any sort of power, although he clearly justified working alongside mageri.

His reasoning hardly mattered. He broke with the others, coming at Roha hard, his sword flashing. His swing was too wild. Perhaps flamboyant for the others, meaning them to follow his great moment. He certainly aimed to bisect Roha shoulder to hip, but ni had time to cut to the side. The point of his sword sliced nim a new scar, but didn't cut nim through and through.

The king's man raised his sword in preparation to swing again, but Roha rammed him. He compensated, catching nes daggers on his crossguard, and for a moment they were locked, glaring at each other. So close Roha could taste his fetid breath.

As he pulled his head back for momentum, ni could see he intended to slam it forward into nes forehead, so Roha thrust back hard to disengage. As ni did, ni drew a knee up into his groin. If he was going to play dirty, so was Roha. After all, this was war, and they'd already broken the rules.

The soldier started to fall, trying to use his sword to keep him from toppling entirely, but Roha used nes daggers to finish him off, then belted one and stole his sword for its greater reach.

Ni turned for the next opponent to see that the Sacristers were fully engaged with the other king's men, completely without weapons. And it wasn't going well. One was down. Others were blooded, and Roha couldn't tell whether the wounds were old or new.

Nes heart kicked. Ni pivoted, slashing the closest guard with nes new sword, handing it to Deedri as the guard fell beneath the onslaught. *Well, it was nice while it lasted.*

Ni whirled on the next, knifing him under the arm as he raised it to bring his sword down on one of the other Sacristers. His sword dropped to the ground, and the Sacrister picked it up to use it on him instead.

And so it went until the last of their guards was down.

But there was also one Sacrister, Coquin, who wouldn't rise, and two more with grievous wounds.

The fighting before and around them was intense. Swords ringing, shouts raised. The new influx was pushing the king's men into them. One of the rebels who had freed them, distinguishable by the flashes of their brown armbands beneath their cloaks, grabbed Deedri, as ni was the closest. "Find the boy, get to the Sacristy!"

Deedri nodded, and the rebel spun to guard their backs.

Roha craned to get a better view by which to see Hostill—or King Avize, as ni must think of him now—but the fighting was so close, ni could see naught else. His men had quickly spirited him away.

A soldier got past their vanguard, staggering into Roha, too intent on the attack flying at him. He caught a sword blow aimed at separating his head from his shoulders and was locked with the rebel. They stared each other down, neither about to win their battle, and so Roha ended it with one of nes daggers.

It was horrid stabbing a man who couldn't defend himself, but he would have had no compunction if the situation were reversed. Perhaps he would recover or perhaps he would go to the All, but ni couldn't worry about it now. A Crownsman had realized that the Sacristers were now unguarded and came at Roha with a great war cry, only to be grabbed up by Reynal, the snake-man, who suddenly loomed before nim, and flung the man halfway across the courtyard.

He must have joined up with the rebels at some point, perhaps led the way, and Roha was thrilled for it.

"Hurry. You have the boy?" he asked, echoing the rebel.

That quickly, nes heart fell. "They've taken him. We lost. He is King Avize now."

Ni hoped there would be time later to report that all might not be entirely lost. Once ni was certain who could be trusted that far.

His face twisted. "Go," he said, body bucking as a sword battered at his snake-like scales from behind. "The Sacristers know a secret route out. I'll cover your retreat and then follow. Others will lead the king's army on a merry chase through the forest."

He turned and dispatched the soldier hacking at him, and another, and was swallowed again by the fighting. A soldier got past him, and Roha cried as he would have cleaved Deedri's back. Ni spun and slashed straight through the soldier's stomach. Roha turned away from the sausage-casing insides spilling out.

"This way!" Deedri yelled.

Ni raced for the Sacristy, others surging along in nes wake.

It felt wrong to leave the fighting to others while Roha could still wield a weapon. So many had already died for nim. No, not for nim. Ni couldn't think of it that way. For their beliefs. For the evil happening in their very own kingdom. But it *felt* as though Roha and the others had carried the means to bring about King Avize's power-mad scheme right to him.

For now, Roha supposed the most important thing was to get away with the dagger holding Hostill's soul. If ni could only restore him, Hostill could save Frizenze and Jucar and end the Blood War all at once.

So, Roha was not running for nimself, but for Hostill and for the sake of the land and all the people who might be saved. Ni and the others had come to Frizenze for sanctuary and instead found an evil to equal that of Bloody Bess. And now it was living in Hostill's body.

Roha would never have known this lower section of the Sacristy existed if Deedri hadn't pulled aside a lever that opened a doorway leading to a set of stone stairs. They angled steeply and unevenly down into a room twice the size of an ascetic's cell. Roha would have assumed this section of the Sacristy to have been sheer bedrock. If pushed, ni might have believed a cavern could have been carved out for cold storage, but this staggered the imagination. Once at the base of the stairs, it was clear that something horrible had happened here. They had to step over bodies, Sacrister and soldier alike.

If Roha had a sense of wonder remaining in the midst of this, it was quickly overridden by the stench of death and voided bowels. There had been an explosion here of some sort. Magic gone wrong pricked at nim, the pedestal in the center of it was broken and charred, and at the far end of the room, the wall had half collapsed, a foot sticking out from the rockfall.

"Iogo!" one of the Sacristers cried, falling to nes knees beside one of the robed figures on the floor. Ni had tears in nes eyes and was trying desperately to revive the other Sacrister, though it must be clear it would do no good.

Another Sacrister ran to the back wall and began tearing away stones. Two more quickly joined nim.

Iogo must have decided at the end that the only way to save the Sacrima, or at least the others, was to destroy the Stone, even at the cost of nes life. But also, apparently, their retreat. The secret exit must have been intended as a way to spirit away the Sacrima Stone if it ever became necessary, but since that was impossible with the king's men already inside the secret room....

But it was no use. The landslide was too much for them, especially after all the abuse to which they'd been subjected.

There was a bellowing from outside the door, and Roha realized that it hadn't opened enough for Reynal to enter.

Immediately, the closest Sacristers to the door began to pull from their side as Reynal pushed from his. It was no use at first. It moved a fraction, but still scraped along the stone, the explosion having knocked it askew.

"Thump it," Deedri told him.

Reynal gave it a whack, presumably with his tail, and another in a different place, and they all tried again. The door started to give way. Slow, and then faster. All the Sacristers had to push themselves against the walls, but Reynal was able to enter, covered in dust and blood from his battles, dirt and dead leaves from his campaign in the forest.

He looked exhausted…until he saw Iogo's body, the foot beneath the rubble, the destruction all about. Sadness passed like a cloud before the sun and quickly became anger, and in that moment, his chest expanded with a huge indrawn breath, and he rushed the rockfall, pounding it with his fists as though he could reduce the boulders to powder. And while that didn't happen, rocks began to give way beneath his pounding. The whole room shook under his barrage, but when he was through, there was a hole again, an exit.

An escape.

"Run!" Reynal ordered, nearly collapsing. "I'll cover."

"Not this time," Roha said. "You'll be vulnerable in the tunnel, and anyway, you may need me to help push you out on the other end. I'll take rearguard. You go."

Reynal didn't argue, only nodded and dove into the tunnel, his scales brushing Roha on the way by, his strength mesmerizing and terrifying in equal measure.

The escape route angled down and down, not sharply, but not gently either. At a point it turned, and ni was not ready, even with the glow someone had created. Roha's weariness was such that momentum was the only thing keeping nim moving. But the wall diverted nim in the right direction, adding another bruise to the mass ni'd collected.

When ni spilled out at the bottom of it, the fresh air was chilling in its intensity. Dusk had given way to darkness. Someone grabbed at Roha's shoulder before nes eyes could adjust and said, "That way," with a push.

Roha went and went. Into the night, branches whipping at nes face and tree limbs tripping nes feet.

Until a hand finally landed on nes arm, and then a body appeared to block nim, and said, "You're safe now. You can stop," as though knowing Roha would continue on until ni fell face down in the forest and became one with it.

Roha blinked up into a face ni didn't know, wearing leather beneath cloak and hood. And then the man/soldier/stranger was thrust aside and Roha was attacked from the side, suddenly wrapped bodily, arms trapped to nes sides. Nes first instinct was to tense, ready to fight off the attacker until ni realized who it was.

Cia.

Thank the spirits.

"Roha," Cia said, almost reverently, white plumes of breath carrying nes name into the sky. "I thought never to see you again. Thank the spirits!"

"I've just said the same prayer. If you'll release me–"

Cia pulled away, her face closing off, and it sent an ache along Roha's spirit. Roha had never intended Cia to go far, and immediately reached out to enfold her so that it was clear the joy of being reunited was returned. Cia went as stiff as a board, and Roha feared ni'd made a mistake, that after all Cia had been through, the only kind of contact she could endure was that she'd initiated, but then she melted against Roha, her face pressing into nes breast, and Roha felt...

Ni didn't know what ni felt. Something stirred between them. Deep between them where the passage of their souls lay open...but now was not the moment to explore it. Hostill was lost. The Sacrima invaded, Sacristers and villagers killed. And hands were pulling at them both, calling them to something greater, though at the moment Roha could not imagine it.

They drew back, and their eyes met. Roha searched Cia's for fear, horror, a shrinking away, and perhaps there was a bit of fear lurking at the edges of the same wonder that must shine from nes own eyes, but there was a promise there as well. A promise of *later*.

They went together to where others were gathered, the surviving Nim, Reynal, the rebel soldiers with their brown armbands. Myrka, Roha was glad to see, though she only inclined her head to acknowledge Roha rather than truly welcome nim. There was a fury of discussion going on, but it all stopped when ni and Cia entered the fray.

One of the other Nim stumbled to Roha, arm bundled beneath nes cloak but bleeding through. "You were the last out. Tehardy?" ni asked.

Roha glanced around. Ni'd been hoping someone else had carried Tehardy away, but there was no sign of their leader, and Roha could only hang nes head and shake it sadly. The Sacrister hung nes head as well and stepped back where ni'd been, but Deedri quickly took nes place.

Deedri positioned nimself directly in front of Roha, eye to eye, as though to give the impression that it was just the two of them, a private conversation in the midst of a small army. "I understand that you returned the lost souls to the anima on the battlefield in the Dobrens Valley?"

Roha looked at all those gathered. The news would have traveled, and it was no secret–certainly not now. "I did."

"I must ask you to do it again. Those souls–the bosewights we kept contained–we can't let them ravage the countryside. We may have been forced to let down our wards, and Iogo to destroy the Sacrima Stone, but we can't let it all be in vain. We have to create a new stone and contain the bosewights again. Maybe we can even harness their energy to fight this new evil."

Roha gasped in a breath. It made strategic sense, but ni'd been thinking about the All–the positive and the negative, like the masculine and feminine. Returning spirits to the land was one thing. Even imprisoning them at the Sacrima wasn't so bad if it meant they didn't siphon strength from those left behind, but to draw on their energies without their consent... How did that make them better than the mageri who sucked away the power of the anima and left the land with nothing? Did it matter the magnitude, the mageri hurting so many while they would hurt so few, only the bosewights while leaving the living in peace? Or was that just what they would tell themselves to sleep at night?

"I–"

"Roha," Deedri snapped, "with Tehardy gone, I am your new leader. The longer we pause, the further away these bosewights get, possibly out of our reach. The more time they have to harry and harm those they love. If you have qualms, perhaps we can answer for them after the danger has passed."

Roha's spine stiffened, and ni glared down at Deedri, who was only a few inches shorter, but the high ground was a moral one. "I never swore to your Sacrima. I don't know these people you are with or what they will do with this power," Roha snapped back. "I will call the bosewights to the new stone on the condition that *I* will be the one controlling it. If you think to lead us, then you will need a new guardian for the Sacrima Stone. That is my condition, and it is not up for negotiation."

Deedri seethed but no less than Roha. Their breath seemed to battle in the chill air, clashing in great stormclouds. But finally Deedri nodded and reached deeply into nes cloak for a thumb-sized fire-opal, smooth and oval, which ni placed into Roha's hand and stepped back. Did they just have such gems lying around?

Roha took another breath, one where ni wasn't breathing in Deedri's exhales, and held it before breathing out again. Then ni looked for Cia. Ni had run through nes own reserves and knew the other Nim had as well. If Roha was to do this, ni would need Cia's strength, but even to ask seemed a violation, as though Cia had been right all along, and that tether, that connection, had been planted only so that it might be pulled on in a moment of necessity.

Yet Cia met Roha's searching glance, and nodded, acknowledging whatever it was that lay between them.

A moment private and unspoken into which Deedri intruded. "Well?" ni said impatiently.

Cia pushed nim out of the way. "Do you want to sit?" she asked, gazing into Roha's eyes.

Ni answered by collapsing as gracefully as possible onto the ground, and Cia laughed, a bark of surprise that sent a plume of white up into the air like anima escaping.

"Now is no time–"

For levity. Roha could almost hear the rest of the words out of Deedri's mouth, though someone quieted nim and pulled nim away before ni could finish.

Someone else muttered, "Don't you feel it," though Roha had no idea what *it* was, unless one of the Sacristers was like Ulan and could actually see the anima, and the bond that connected Roha and Cia was actually visible, which it shouldn't be while it lay fallow, inactive.

Then Roha was closing nes eyes, sending up nes own plumes of steaming breath called up from deep within nes core. Cia sat across from nim on the cold earth and reached out to take nes hands, and Roha allowed it, even making the stone vulnerable, unclenching nes fist enough so that it rested in their mutually cupped hands.

"How do I do this?" Cia whispered.

"Close your eyes, breathe deeply, relax and trust," Roha whispered back.

Cia squeezed nes hands in answer, and Roha heard her breathing change. Ni opened nimself as ni had nes hands, dowsing deep for the center of Cia's power, and felt such a rush of answering strength, ni was nearly swept away. Ni fought against the wave, overwhelmed, wishing ni weren't so exhausted. Ni'd only done this one time before, and that had been in extremis.

Roha allowed the same instincts to take over. If ni thought, fought, doubted, it would fall apart. Ni could not leave room for the possibility of anything but success. Do or die, as it had been on the battlefield, because these bosewights could not go on to cause the sort of destruction ni had seen at the Sacrima.

Roha took the power that Cia offered, and it was *strong.* Stronger than it had been. Something had changed, and Roha had no time to ask, because if ni didn't get a proper grasp of the power flooding in, ni would drown in it. Roha struggled to divert the power to the working as it roared over nim. Ni prayed, weaving the words to the spell and casting out the strands of the net that would draw in the bosewights. Like lures, like siren song. Irresistible and inevitable as fate. Ni felt it as the energies were grabbed up and reeled in, nimself and Cia at the other end of the line like fishers of souls.

One by one, the bosewights came screaming. Some tried to possess or overwhelm or terrify, but the pull was too strong, and their resistance over too soon.

When they'd drawn in as many as they could, when their energies flagged as the stone flared, they collapsed over it in a heap. The others covered them, straightening their limbs and leaving them to sleep in a huddle, cradling the new Sacrima Stone between them.

CHAPTER THIRTY-FIVE

Bess

What do you mean *all dead*?" she asked, glaring daggers into the back of the messenger who brought the news, since he refused to unbow and meet her gaze.

"The Desperata at the Druarian Sanctuary…they're all dead. Poison, it appears. I was ordered to ride with all haste to give you the news. It seems they were forewarned," he said.

Bess clenched her hands into fists until her filed nail drew blood. The pain sharpened her mind. Kept her anchored to the moment when she wanted to fly off into a rage, kick over the messenger, and drink him down for the power he would supply her. She'd used up most of what the Animist and others had brought her and was left with only their outright rebellion. Which she would somehow squash. And soon.

But first, she had to take down the traitor in her midst. "I want reports from all of the campaigns," she ordered him. "Immediately."

"Yes, my Queen."

"And send for Grygof. Right away. I don't care where he is or what he's doing."

"Immediately, my Queen," said the messenger, rising to go.

It would have been gratifying if it weren't clear how easily someone might say one thing and do another.

She paced, her thoughts racing. Only her Council, Strego, Erdain, Bowstan…only her inner circle had known they were going after the Church mageri. Even those on the campaign didn't know what they were doing until they arrived. That meant she couldn't trust even her closest advisors.

She'd known for as long as she contemplated the throne that she was on her own, that she had to be wary and keep her own counsel, but to outright undermine her and the good of Jucar… Why? What would come of that? What would it gain them but discovery and death? Because she would absolutely see to the latter and make certain that it was a particularly painful sort of ending. Public as well, lest anyone else contemplate thwarting her will.

Her guards announced Grygof, and she gave him entrance. He took a deep bow and stood, as forgettable as ever one would want in a spymaster.

"Yes, my Queen."

"You heard about the Druarian Sanctuary?" she asked.

"I did," he said evenly. He looked, as always, like someone's not particularly noteworthy uncle.

"You know it means that someone alerted them. I don't know why they would. Or why the mageri would poison themselves rather than abandon the Sanctuary, but I want you to find out who and why. Quietly, and as quickly as possible. I want them punished."

"Yes, my Queen. Though as to the why, if the Desperata thought they might be forced to use their powers, they might find drinking poison preferable, just as they abuse their bodies rather than reach for the anima."

"I want answers, not speculation. They may also have secrets they don't want us to discover. And the *who*, Grygof. Get me the who or I get myself a new spymaster. Is that understood?" Bess asked.

He glanced down at her bloodied hand but didn't comment upon it.

"Understood."

He bowed his leave, and Bess called for her maid. When the girl arrived, banking her terror, as always, Bess told her, "I will take your clothes, thank you."

"But what shall I do?" her eyes were wild now, and Bess almost laughed. She was as safe as swords in her presence. She'd disappeared enough maids already. One more was certain to be remarked.

"I will have one of the guards escort you back to your chambers and return your clothes when I've no more need of them, I assure you."

"I…yes, my Queen."

"Right here will do nicely," she said as the maid started for the modesty screen at the back of her chambers. She was too impatient to wait.

As soon as the overdress and apron dropped to the ground, she insisted that the maid help her change into them and tie her hair up under her mop cap.

Her maid clearly wanted to ask what she planned to do but didn't dare. It occurred to her that even dressed as she was, she likely couldn't go into a tavern by herself, unattended. But neither could she go guarded by her men. What then?

"Here," Bess said, going to her wardrobe and choosing her least ornate gown, one meant for traveling. Luckily, her maid was young and slim and they were much of a size. "You will wear this and take me to an inn, where I will give you coin for a drink. No one will notice your maid stepping out."

"For what?" she asked, unable to help herself.

"Never you mind," Bess answered, knowing she'd be hunting her next victim. Someone docile this time but full of power. She expected she'd have some time to watch and wait for the right prey.

When she returned, she hoped Grygof would have rooted out the traitor.

And she'd have good reports of the other campaigns against the Desperata. Against the Churches.

She'd be head of all the attendant power and resources and ready for a final march against Frizenze.

Soon, she'd be not just Queen but Empress.

The End

ACKNOWLEDGMENTS

This book would never be written without the support of my amazing husband, Peter Wheeler, who is in every hero I write. It also wouldn't exist without Debra Fleming and Kathy Hennessy, who heard all my trials and tribulations on our morning walks. To Debra, I want to say that your question about "What would be hardest?" was dead on, curse you!

I want to thank John Hartness for believing in me and my beloved characters, Erin Penn for her sharp eye, and everyone at Falstaff Books. Our merry band of misfits!

Especially, I want to thank my readers, because without you, Cia, Ulan, Roha, Hostill, Ruggerio...even Bloody Bess...would still just be words on a page rather than people who live and breathe in your imaginations. Yes, they'd still exist in my mind, but so would all the doubt demons. Reviews, retweets, any word from fans help keep them in check, and they're an unruly bunch! My own personal Shadow Girls.

By the way, if you want to find out the fates of all the above, tune in for the third and final book in the series, THE ILLUMINATED LANDS!

ABOUT THE AUTHOR

Lucienne Diver is the author of the **Vamped** and **Latter-Day Olympians** series, which Long and Short Reviews calls "a clever mix of Janet Evanovich and Rick Riordan". She also writes young adult suspense, including **FAULTLINES**, **THE COUNTDOWN CLUB**, and **DISAPPEARED**, where two teens investigate the disappearance of their mother and the story their father tells about the night she went missing.

On a personal note, Lucienne lives in the Hudson Valley of New York with her husband, the two cutest dogs in the world, and enough books to some day collapse the second floor of her home into the first. She likes living dangerously.

More information can be found on her website www.luciennediver.com.

ALSO BY LUCIENNE DIVER

Vamped series

Vamped

Revamped

Fangtastic

Fangabulous

Fangdemonium

Latter-Day Olympians series

Bad Blood

Crazy in the Blood

Rise of the Blood

Battle for the Blood

Blood Hunt

Stand-alones

Faultlines

The Countdown Club

Disappeared

The Shadow Girls series

The Shadow Girls

FRIENDS OF FALSTAFF

Thank You to All our Falstaff Books Patrons, who get extra digital content each month! To be featured here and see what other great rewards we offer, go to www.patreon.com/falstaffbooks.

PATRONS

Dino Hicks
John Hooks
John Kilgallon
Larissa Lichty
Travis & Casey Schilling
Staci-Leigh Santore
Sheryl R. Hayes
Scott Norris
Samuel Montgomery-Blinn
Junkle

Thank You for Supporting Independent Publishing!

We believe that you should be able
to read your books, your way.
That's why this Falstaff Books
print edition includes a digital copy
at no additional cost!

Just scan the QR code with your device,
follow the directions on Prolific Works,
and enjoy!
You can also join our newsletter when prompted,
and never miss an awesome Falstaff Release!

www.ingramcontent.com/pod-product-compliance
Lightning Source LLC
Chambersburg PA
CBHW051602100726
47898CB00001B/201